Navy SEAL turned Secret Service agent
Scot Harvath faces down America's enemies
in these acclaimed bestsellers from

BRAD THOR

TAKEDOWN

New York Times bestseller

"If you're the type who enjoys the TV show *24* and other high-octane thrillers, *Takedown* is the summer book for you. . . . Crisp and cinematic, with the focus on gun-blazing, gut-busting action."

—*The Tennessean*

"Brad Thor is the master of thrillers. . . . [His] descriptions are gritty, realistic, and true-to-life. . . . Enthralling. . . . *Takedown* should head the syllabus for anyone taking a class in Thrillers 101. A smart, explosive work that details events about to happen outside your front door. Highly recommended."

—*Bookreporter.com*

"An exciting yet frightening thriller. . . . Fans of Dan Brown and Thomas Harris will want to read Brad Thor's latest masterpiece."

—*Midwest Book Review*

"The action is relentless, the pacing sublime."

—*Ottawa Citizen*

"An explosive novel."

—Newt Gingrich

THE LIONS OF LUCERNE

"Fast-paced, scarily authentic—I just couldn't put it down."

—Vince Flynn

"A hot read for a winter night. . . . Bottom line: *Lions* roars."

—*People*

"For cliff-hanging escapism, this is it."

—*The Sunday Oklahoman*

"The action is nonstop, and Thor has a real gift for bringing exotic settings alive. A roller-coaster of a debut."

—Kyle Mills

"Thor's debut thriller rockets along. . . . A fast-paced and exciting novel."

—*Minneapolis Star-Tribune*

"[Harvath] definitely will take a place beside Cussler's Dirk Pitt® and Clancy's Jack Ryan."

—*Tacoma Reporter* (WA)

BOOKS BY BRAD THOR

Takedown
Blowback
State of the Union
Path of the Assassin
The Lions of Lucerne

BRAD THOR

STATE
OF THE
UNION

POCKET BOOKS
New York London Toronto Sydney

POCKET BOOKS, a division of Simon & Schuster, Inc.
1230 Avenue of the Americas, New York, NY 10020

This book is a work of fiction. Names, characters, places
and incidents are products of the author's imagination or
are used fictitiously. Any resemblance to actual events or
locales or persons living or dead is entirely coincidental.

ISBN-13: 978-1-4165-4369-5
ISBN-10:   1-4165-4369-4

This Pocket Books paperback edition March 2007

10 9 8 7 6 5 4 3 2 1

POCKET and colophon are registered trademarks of
Simon & Schuster, Inc.

Cover design by Jae Song

Manufactured in the United States of America

For information regarding special discounts for bulk
purchases, please contact Simon & Schuster Special Sales
at 1-800-456-6798 or business@simonandschuster.com.

For Sloane—
Welcome to the world, little one.

Cunctando Regitur Mundis

Waiting, one rules the world.

PROLOGUE

What I want, Chuck, is ten minutes of peace and quiet so I can think," snapped the president to his chief of staff.

Charles Anderson had never seen his boss like this. Then again, America had never faced a situation of this magnitude before. With less than three hours until he was expected to deliver his State of the Union address, President Jack Rutledge had already made the tough decision of evacuating Congress and settling on a videotaped address from the White House. The hardest call, though, still lay before him.

"Okay, people," voiced Anderson. "You heard the president. Let's give him the room. Everybody out. We'll reconvene in the Situation Room."

Once the Oval Office had cleared out, the president leaned back in his chair, closed his eyes, and massaged his forehead with the heels of his hands. His oath of office called for him to preserve, protect, and defend the Constitution—a body of laws, which obliged him, "to give to Congress information of

the State of the Union and recommend to their consideration such measures as he shall judge necessary and expedient." Never in a million years could
he have imagined that the execution of his duties
would lead to the unraveling of everything America
had fought to become.

He was reminded of the first State of the Union
address given by George Washington over two hundred years ago at New York's Federal Hall. With the
country in the fledgling stages of its great democratic experiment, Washington had focused on the very
concept of union itself and the challenges not only
of establishing, but of maintaining it.

How in the hell had things come to this? Rutledge
wondered as he opened his eyes and studied the
two folders on the desk in front of him. Each contained a different version of his State of the Union
address, and each had the potential to be equally
devastating. The fate of millions of Americans
would be decided by what he said and did in the
next three hours.

Though not a particularly religious man, President Jack Rutledge closed his eyes once again and
this time prayed to God for guidance.

CHAPTER 1

ZVENIGOROD, RUSSIA

THREE WEEKS PRIOR

Winter has come too early this year," Sergei Stavropol complained as he threw his long overcoat onto a chair near the door. He was the last of the four men to arrive. "I think this will be one of the coldest we have seen in a long time." Crossing over to the bar, he withdrew a decanter of brandy and filled a delicate crystal snifter. He was an enormous man with dark hair and a large nose that bore evidence of having been broken many times. At six-foot-three inches tall and two hundred seventy-five pounds, he was bigger than any of the other men in the room, but it was his dark, penetrating eyes that drew all of the attention and that had long ago earned him his nickname. Though he hated the "Rasputin" moniker, he found that it instilled in his enemies and those who would oppose him a certain degree of fear, and therefore he had allowed it to stick. His salt-and-pepper-colored hair was trimmed in a military-style crew cut. His skin was severely pockmarked and his left eye drooped slightly due to

a grenade that had exploded in his face as he was
pushing one of his men out of danger's way. While
he was twice as brave as his assembled colleagues,
he was easily less than half as refined, and as if to
demonstrate that very fact, he downed his brandy
in one long swallow.

The men around the table smiled at their
friend's behavior. Stavropol was as constant as the
northern star. In over forty years, nothing had
changed him—not money, not power, not even the
knowledge that he would go down in history as one
of the greatest soldiers Mother Russia had ever produced. In combat, he had saved the life of each man
in the room, some more than once, but they had
not gathered in this remote wooded area forty miles
west of Moscow to relive the past. On the contrary,
the four men seated around the worn oak table
were there to shape the future.

Outside, a breath of icy wind blew across the
gravel driveway of the centuries-old hunting lodge.
From its stone chimney, tendrils of gray smoke
could be seen only for an instant before being
sucked upward into an ever-darkening sky. As the
cold wind pressed itself against the formidable
structure, it moaned deeply.

Stavropol, the group's leader, walked over to the
fireplace and spent several moments prodding the
glowing embers with an iron poker as he pretended
to search for the appropriate words to say. It was an
empty gesture. He knew exactly what he was going
to say. Spontaneity was not one of his attributes. It

led to mistakes and mistakes were the harbingers of failure. Stavropol had rehearsed this moment in his mind for years. His raw determination was equaled only by his capacity for cold, detached calculation.

After a sufficient show of introspection, he raised himself to his full height, turned to his colleagues, and said, "It pleases me to see you all here. We have waited many long years for this. Today we embark upon a new and glorious chapter in the history of not only our beloved Russia, but of the world. Fifteen years ago we—"

"Were much younger," interrupted one of the men.

It was Valentin Primovich, the plodder, the worrier. He had always been the weakest link. Stavropol fixed him with a steady look. He had anticipated the possibility of dissension in the ranks, but not straightaway. Subconsciously, his hand tightened into a fist. He reminded himself to relax. *Wait*, he told himself. *Just wait*.

Stavropol attempted to soften the features of his face before responding. "Valentin, we are still young men. And what we may have lost in years, we have more than gained in experience."

"We have good lives now," said Uri Varensky, coming to the defense of Primovich. "The world is a different place. *Russia* is a different place."

"As we knew it would be," said Stavropol as his eyes turned on Varensky. He had grown soft and lazy. Had Stavropol been told fifteen years ago that the thick narcosis of complacency would one day overtake such a great man, such a great soldier, Stavropol never would have believed it. "You forget that the change came because of us. It was *our* idea."

"It was *your* idea," replied Anatoly Karganov. "We supported you, as we always have, but Uri and Valentin are correct. Times have changed."

Stavropol couldn't believe his ears. *Was Karganov, one of the greatest military minds the country had ever seen, siding with Primovich and Varensky? The Anatoly Karganov?*

Despite all of his careful planning, the meeting was not going the way Stavropol had envisioned. He stopped and took a deep breath, once again trying to calm himself, before responding. "I have seen these changes. Driving here from Moscow I saw them up and down the roadsides—old women sweeping gutters with homemade brooms, or selling potatoes and firewood just to make enough to eat, while the new rich drive by in their BMW and Mercedes SUVs listening to American rap music.

"In crumbling houses beyond the roadways, young Russian children smoke crack cocaine, shoot up with heroin, and spread tuberculosis and the AIDS virus, which are decimating our population. Where once we celebrated the deep pride we held in our country, now our posters and billboards only promote all-inclusive vacations to Greece, new health clubs, or the latest designer fashions from Italy."

"But Russia has made gains," insisted Karganov.

"*Gains*, Anatoly? And what sort of *gains* have we made?" asked Stavropol, the contempt unmistakable in his voice. "The Soviet Union was once a great empire covering eleven time zones, but look at us now. Most of our sister republics are gone and we are locked in pitiable struggles to hold on to those few that remain. Our economy, the *free-market* economy so widely embraced by our greedy countrymen, teeters daily on the verge of collapse. The rich have raped our country, hidden their money in safe havens outside of Russia, and sent their children to European boarding schools. Our currency has been devalued, our life expectancy is laughable, and our population is shrinking. What's more, not only does the world not need anything we have to sell, it also does not care to listen to anything we have to say. Where once we were a great world power—a superpower—now we are nothing. This is not the legacy I plan to leave behind."

"Sergei," began Karganov, the ameliorator, "we have all devoted our lives to our country. Our love for Russia is above reproach."

"Is it?" asked Stavropol as he slowly took in each man seated around the table. "I sense that your love for Russia is not what it once was. This is not a matter for the weak or the fainthearted. There is much work yet to be done and it will not be easy. But in the end, Russia will thank us."

An uncomfortable silence fell upon the room. After several minutes, it was Varensky who broke it. "So, the day we had all wondered about has finally arrived." It was not so much a statement of fact, as one of apprehension, tinged with regret.

"You do not sound pleased," replied Stavropol. "Maybe I was wrong. Maybe you no longer are young men. Maybe you *have* grown old—old and scared."

"This is ridiculous," interjected Primovich, normally the most cautious of the group. "Most of what you predicted would happen to the Soviet Union did happen, but it has not all been for the worse. You choose to see only what you want to see."

Stavropol was beginning to lose his temper. "*What I see* are three lazy pigs who have fed too long at the trough of capitalism; three senile old men who forgot a promise made to their comrades, a promise made to their country."

"You do yourself no favors by insulting us," replied Karganov.

"Really?" asked Stavropol with mock surprise. "The moment we have waited for, the moment we have worked so hard for, is finally here. We are finally ready to awaken the giant and on the eve of our greatest accomplishment, after so much sacrifice, so much waiting, so much planning, my most trusted friends are having second thoughts. What would you suggest I do?"

"Why don't we put it to a vote?" offered Varensky.

"A *vote*?" replied Stavropol, "How very democratic."

"It was fifteen years ago when we agreed to your plan, Sergei. We are not the same people now that we were then," said Karganov.

"Obviously," snapped Stavropol, "as oaths no longer mean anything to you." He held up his hand to silence Karganov before the man could respond. "I have to admit, I am disappointed, but I am not surprised. Time can dampen the fire in a man's soul. As some men grow older, it is no longer ideals but blankets that they rely on to keep them warm at night. I blame myself for this. We'll put this to a vote, as comrade Varensky has suggested. But first, let's attend to one other piece of business."

"Anything," responded Primovich. "Let's just get this over with."

Stavropol smiled. "I'm glad you agree, Valentin. What I want is a full list of the assets we have in place and how to contact them."

"Why is that necessary?" demanded Karganov.

"Since I am the one who started this, I will be the one to finish it. There must be no loose ends."

"Surely you don't intend to do away with them?" queried Varensky. "These are not mere foot soldiers."

"Of course not, Uri," said Stavropol. "The assets will simply be recalled to Mother Russia. That's all. That would make all of you happy, wouldn't it?"

A dead silence blanketed the table.

"And what if they don't wish to be recalled?" asked Primovich.

"I'm sure they can be persuaded. Come, we are

wasting time. I know there are warm beds waiting for all of you at home. Tell me what I need to know so we can move to a vote," said Stavropol.

The men reluctantly provided the information while Stavropol took meticulous notes. He was loath to commit sensitive information to paper, but trusting so many important details to his aging memory was an even greater risk.

While he wrote, he walked slowly around the table, his boots echoing on the wooden floorboards. The rhythm was much like the man himself—meticulous and patient.

When the necessary details had been collected, Stavropol allowed the men to vote. To a man, they all agreed to abandon the operation. It was just as he had feared. Primovich, Varensky, and even Karganov had gone soft. There was only one option available now.

"So, it has been decided," he admitted, stopping before the fireplace.

"Trust me, it is for the best," replied Karganov.

Primovich and Varensky voiced their agreement as they stood up and retrieved their coats.

"You can still do great things for Russia," continued Karganov. "I am certain the Defense Ministry would be glad to have your talents at their disposal. Maybe even a military academy position teaching the soldiers of tomorrow what it means to be a fearsome Russian warrior."

"You should take up a hobby," offered General Primovich, coming over to shake his old colleague's hand.

"A hobby?" asked Stavropol. "That's quite a suggestion. Maybe golf?"

"Certainly," said Primovich, a smile forming on his lips as Stavropol picked up the iron poker and pretended to hit a golf ball with it. Stavropol seemed to be taking things better than he expected. "I hear it can be very relaxing."

Primovich's smile quickly disappeared as Stavropol swung the poker full force against the side of his head and cracked open his skull.

For a moment, the man just stood there, then his lifeless body collapsed to the floor.

"Very relaxing indeed," sneered Stavropol as he let the bloody poker fall from his hands.

"What have you done?" screamed Karganov.

"You didn't actually think this would be as easy as taking a vote and simply walking away, did you? We have been working on this for over fifteen years. I have planned everything, *everything*—right down to the very last detail. I expected some resistance from Primovich and maybe a little from Varensky, but not you, Anatoly. Never you," said Stavropol.

"You have lost your mind," Varensky shouted as he made an end run around the table for Stavropol.

Stavropol drew a beautifully engraved, black chrome-plated Tokarev pistol from the small of his back and shot him before he had even made it three feet.

Karganov couldn't believe what he was seeing. Stavropol was insane, he was sure of it.

"So, what will it be, Anatoly?" asked Stavropol.

"Will you join us? Or will you go the way of Valentin and Uri?"

The look on Karganov's face was answer enough.

"As you wish," responded Stavropol, who then fired a single round into Karganov's head.

Upon hearing the gunshots, a second man, bundled in heavy winter clothing exited Stavropol's car and calmly strode inside to assist his employer. "With these men dead, we will have much more work now," he said as he helped Stavropol drag the three bodies out the back door.

Stavropol smiled. "Our list of assets in America is quite long. Over the years, we have lost an Aldrich Ames here, a Robert Hanssen there, but there are many more still in place. Everything will continue as planned and you, my friend, will have to clear space on your old uniform. I am sure Russia will create a brand-new medal for what we are about to accomplish."

The two men then worked in silence, digging shallow graves and burying the bodies behind the secluded lodge. They were not alone. Perched high above, on one of the area's heavily wooded trails, someone was watching.

CHAPTER 2

Frank Leighton was scared. In fact if the truth were told, the man was absolutely terrified.

The call had come in the middle of the night, the voice more machine than human. It sounded tinny, canned somehow, as if it was coming from far away. But it wasn't the sound of the voice that had shaken him. It was the message.

It took Leighton several moments to clear the cobwebs from his head—his sleep had been that deep. And why not? He was retired after all. Sleeping with one eye open while guarding against the cold knife blade that could be slipped between his ribs by a supposed ally, or listening for the telltale whisper of an anonymous assassin's bullet fired from a silenced weapon, were all part of his past. Or so he had thought.

Twenty-five pounds overweight and fifteen years out of the game, Frank Leighton took a quick shower, shaved, and then combed his head of thick, gray hair. The years hadn't been kind to him. When he looked in the mirror and said to himself, "I am way too old for this," he was telling the God's honest truth.

The initial spurt of adrenaline that had come with the phone call had long since passed, so Leighton decided to brew a pot of coffee while he considered his options. It was a short period of reflection, as he had no options. That was exactly the way the protocol had been designed.

When the coffee was ready, Leighton filled his mug to within two-and-a-half inches of the rim, then grabbed a bottle of Wild Turkey from the cabinet above the refrigerator and filled the mug the rest of the way. *The breakfast of champions,* he thought to himself as he took the mug and headed past a butler's pantry into the laundry and storage room that doubled as his home office.

While he waited for his computer to boot up, he gazed at a picture of his sister, Barbara, and her two kids. Maybe he should call her. Warn her. She still had the cabin in Wyoming. They would be safe there. He wouldn't have to tell her why. She would trust him. She would do what he asked. It was important for them to be safe, at least until he could complete his assignment. *How in the world,* he wondered, *had things come to this?* And after all these years.

The opening of his web browser interrupted Leighton's pondering. He went to the American Airlines website and ran through all of the international flights leaving from Washington that morning. When he found the flight he wanted, he began the process of booking the ticket. He had no idea if the old Capstone Corporation credit card still worked. It was the only way to reserve and pay for the flight, as he no longer kept large stores of cash in the house. That was something he had left behind in his old career, his old life.

If the card was still active, the little-known bank in Manassas, Virginia, would accept any expiration date he entered into the computer. Leighton had no need to fish the card, or the false passport that matched the name on the card, from its hiding place within the old lobsterman's buoy stored in a corner of the boathouse behind his home. When one's life has hung by a delicate thread for years upon end, certain things are never forgotten. He entered the credit card number by heart and waited while the American Airlines site processed his request. Moments later, a confirmation number and seat assignment appeared on the screen.

Leighton knew that a same-day ticket purchase was going to raise a lot of red flags, so transporting a weapon was out of the question. He would have to wait until he got there. Once he arrived, he would have access to more than enough firepower, and money—if everything had been left in place.

It had to have been. The fact that the Capstone credit card still worked, hell, the fact that he had even been called after all this time was reason enough to believe that he would find things just as he had left them fifteen years ago.

But what the hell was going on? Could it be a test? If so, why test him? Surely, they had younger, more capable operatives—operatives who were actually *active.* None of this made any sense. If you were going to run the world's most important horse race, why drag in old warhorses from the pasture for it?

Frank Leighton's mind was overflowing with questions and as they began to get the better of him, he slammed an iron door on his misgivings and second-guessing. He reminded himself of what they all had been taught, the one thing that had been drilled into them over and over again—*The protocol will never be wrong. The protocol is infallible.*

As he pulled himself together and shut down his computer, Leighton thought again about calling his sister. If his mission didn't succeed, at least she and the kids would have a chance. Then he thought again. No, he couldn't call her. Despite how much he wanted to, the protocol was explicit. There had been no indication that this was coming. Nothing. But at the same time, it was one of the eventualities they had been told to be prepared for—something coming out of the clear blue sky.

After Leighton had thought about it some more, he rationalized that there was one person he could call; someone like him—someone who would have been contacted as well. They wouldn't have to discuss details; the tone of their voices would say everything.

He retrieved his cache from the old lobsterman's buoy in the boathouse and brought it back inside to his bedroom where he quickly packed a small suit-case full of clothes. After throwing in what looked like an oversized PDA, he opened the manila envelope from the buoy and spread its contents across the top of his dresser.

The passport was going to need some tweaking. He would need to update some of the stamps and, of course, change its expiration date. He'd need to do the same thing for the driver's license. The credit card and false business cards were slid into various pockets of the sport coat he had hung on the knob of the closet door.

Other items, like the pre–European Union currency, which was no longer of any use, were dropped into a metal wastebasket. An old coded list of names, addresses, and phone numbers was recommitted to memory and then dropped into the wastebasket as well.

Now was the time to place the phone call. Leighton walked back into his kitchen, picked up the phone, and dialed. He felt like he was in one of those nightmares where everything moved in slow motion. The ringing of the telephone on the other end seemed to take forever. Finally, on the fifth ring, there was what sounded like someone picking up. Relief flooded through him. If the man he was calling was still at home, maybe he hadn't been activated. Maybe this was all some sort of mistake. The feeling, though, was short-lived as Leighton realized he had reached the man's voice mail. He didn't bother leaving a message.

Nothing but the assignment mattered now. He could trust no one. Everyone and everything at this point was suspect. He retrieved a bottle of starter fluid from beneath the kitchen sink and doused the contents of the metal wastebasket. There could be no trace left behind. Leighton set the wastebasket outside on his stone patio, struck a match, and watched as the assortment of papers went up in flames. When he was positive they were burned beyond recognition, he used the lid of his kettle grill to choke out the fire and, after emptying it, returned the wastebasket inside.

Two hours later, having expertly altered his false passport and driver's license with the drafting supplies he had held on to for just such a purpose, the house locked up and the suitcase in the trunk of his car, Frank Leighton pulled out of his driveway and headed toward the airport, committed to his assignment and the havoc he was about to let loose upon the world.

CHAPTER 3

Scot Harvath sat in the Hotel Del Coronado's Babcock & Story bar sipping one of their signature margaritas, but his mind was a million miles away. Coming home had not been easy for him, at least not like this, but his mother had insisted, and if nothing else, Harvath was a good son.

It had been ten years since they had laid his father to rest and on this anniversary his mother thought it appropriate that they do something to remember him. Scot didn't have the heart to tell his mother that he remembered his father almost every day, because he knew she did too. Michael Harvath had been a good man—a good husband, a good father, a good soldier, and the reason Scot Harvath had become a Navy SEAL.

It was during a training mission that Harvath's father, a SEAL instructor at the Naval Special Warfare Center, was killed in a demolitions accident. At the time of the accident, Scot was training with the U.S. Freestyle ski team in Park City, Utah. He had been with the team for several years at that point, much to the chagrin of his father. Michael Harvath had not worked as hard as he had to watch his son forgo college for a career in professional sports. The two had fought bitterly, as only two proud, head-strong men with passionate convictions can.

The fighting had been a strain on their relation-ship; one that Scot's mother had worked tirelessly to try to mend. It was as if she had somehow sensed that her husband's life was going to be cut short. It was only through his mother's Herculean efforts that the family stayed together at all. The stronger Michael pushed, the more Scot pulled away and pursued his own path. Father and son were more alike than either of them realized. By the time Scot figured this out for himself, his father was already gone.

The loss was devastating. Scot's mother had lost her husband, but it could be argued that the greater grief was Scot's, who had not only lost his father, but had lost him with so many things between them left unsaid and unfinished.

Up until his father's death, Scot had done ex-tremely well on the World Cup circuit and had been favored to medal in the upcoming Olympics, but try as he might, after his father's death he just couldn't get his head back into competitive skiing. It sud-denly wasn't important anymore.

Instead, he chose to immediately follow in his father's footsteps. After graduating from college cum laude in less than three years, he joined the

Navy where he passed the rigorous Basic Underwater Demolition/SEAL selection program, also
known as BUD/S, and was made a SEAL. With his
expertise in skiing, he was tasked to Team Two,
known as the cold-weather specialists, or Polar
SEALs. With an exceptional aptitude for languages
and a desire for even more action, Harvath applied,
and was eventually accepted, to Team Six, the
Navy's elite counterterrorism detachment, also
known as Dev Group. It was while he was with Dev
Group that Scot Harvath came to the attention of
the United States Secret Service.

Whenever a president made an appearance on or
near water, the SEALs were called upon to provide
support. Harvath was part of a contingent that assisted several such protective details for a former
president who loved to race his Cigarette boats off
the coast of Maine. Scot had proven himself to be
extremely talented on many occasions, but when he
discovered and defused an explosive device meant
to disrupt one of the president's outings, the Secret
Service stood up and took notice. They had been
looking for someone just like him to help improve
the ways in which they protected the president.

It took some doing, but the Secret Service eventually succeeded in wooing Scot to join their team.
After Harvath completed his courses at the Secret
Service advanced-training facility in Beltsville,
Maryland, he joined the presidential protective detail based at the White House. A lot had happened
since then. Harvath had not only rescued the presi-

dent from kidnappers and helped to prevent a major war in the Middle East, but also realized along the way that the life of a Secret Service agent was not for him. Surprisingly, the president had agreed and tasked Harvath to a new assignment.

President Jack Rutledge had added a new weapon in his war on terrorism. As part of his reorganization of the American Intelligence community and renewed dedication to countering terrorism, the president had created a special international branch of the Homeland Security Department, dubbed the Office of International Investigative Assistance, or OIIA. The group represented the collective intelligence capability and full muscle of the United States government to help neutralize and prevent terrorist actions against America and American interests on a global level.

Though Harvath's title at the OIIA was listed as a "special agent," very few people knew what his job actually entailed. The benign title led most to believe that he worked in the field, assisting foreign governments and law enforcement agencies in their counterterrorism efforts. That, after all, was the express mission statement of the OIIA. Had Congress known Harvath's true marching orders, the Office of International Investigative Assistance would never have gotten their budget approved.

Thinking about his deceased father often led Scot to think about the man who had become like a second father to him. It was this same person whom the president had tapped to head the new

OIIA—former deputy director of the FBI, Gary Lawlor. Having been the number two man in the world's premier law enforcement organization, Lawlor was a perfect choice. The president also appreciated the special relationship that existed between Lawlor and Harvath. It was precisely that relationship Harvath was considering when his girlfriend, Meg Cassidy, walked into the bar.

"Have you heard from him?" she asked as she sat down on the empty stool next to Scot.

"Nothing," he answered, spinning his cell phone on the bar in front of him. "What about in the room? Any messages?"

"None at all. What did the airline say?"

"It took my contact a while to get to the bottom of it, but he said that apparently Gary had gotten on the plane and that just as they were preparing to close the doors and push back, he jumped up and demanded to be let off. Flashed his credentials and everything. It freaked the hell out of the passengers."

Meg looked at Scot as he absorbed this piece of information. It would all probably turn out to be nothing, but for now it seemed worrisome, especially in light of his new job. Though Scot didn't go into a lot of detail, the fact that they had met when he had rescued her from a hijacked airliner in Cairo, and that in his mid-thirties he was in better shape than most men even ten years younger, told Meg that the new position the president had assigned him to probably didn't involve pushing a lot of paper. He was a soldier on America's front line in the war against terrorism, and Meg was smart enough to know what that meant. It meant not asking a lot of questions and being prepared for anything, even the worst. She was willing to do that for him. In the little over six months they had been together, she had come to care for Scot Harvath very deeply. So much so, that she was even considering relocating her entire business from Chicago to Washington, DC, moving away from all of her friends and contacts, and building a new life with this man.

With his ruggedly handsome face, sandy brown hair, blue eyes, and muscular five-foot-ten frame, Scot Harvath was quite a catch by any woman's standards, but it was the man inside that had most attracted her from the beginning. In addition to his wit and intelligence, there was something else. He was driven by one simple objective—doing the right thing no matter what the cost. In a world so often governed by self-interest, being in the company of a man like Scot Harvath made Meg realize what a noble life worth living was really about, but she also realized that the quality she most admired in him might also turn out to one day be his downfall.

Scot's desire to always do the right thing had made him unwilling to compromise or bend even a fraction of an inch when it came to his principles. He had been called arrogant at times, and Meg could understand why, but people who saw arrogance in him were missing the point. Scot Harvath believed. He believed in himself. He believed in his abilities, and what's more, he believed in his country and the jobs it sent him to do. No matter what the risk or how great the danger he always willingly stepped up when his country needed him.

Right now though, *he* needed something and it was more information. "What would make Gary jump up and demand to be let off the plane like that?"

"All I can think is that maybe he received a call or got paged at the last minute or something. He wouldn't go through all of that just because he forgot to turn the iron off at home."

"Have you tried the office again?" asked Meg, who was equally concerned and growing more worried by the moment.

"I've left messages everywhere and have been ringing his pager and his cell every half hour. Not only is he not answering, but nobody seems to know where he is—*nobody*. And that's not typical Gary. The guy sets up lunch dates months in advance. You should see his Day-Timer. I think people back in DC are beginning to get nervous about it."

"Do you think something happened to him?"

"At this point, I don't know what to think. Gary was a friend of my father's since before I was born. Half the reason he chose to head up the Bureau's San Diego field office instead of Miami was so that they could be closer together. They were like brothers and I know how much my mom means to him.

It's not like him to miss something like this and not call."

Meg had known the memorial was going to be tough, and the absence of Gary Lawlor had only made things more stressful. Though Scot hadn't said anything, she knew he appreciated having her along.

"Okay," she replied, after the bartender had poured her a glass of wine and then walked to the other end of the bar, "what about calling hospitals? I hate to go that route, but it seems to be one of the only rocks we haven't looked under."

As Harvath was reaching for his margarita, his cell phone rang again. On the other end was Alan Driehaus, the director of Homeland Security. "Where the hell are you?" he demanded.

"Coronado," answered Harvath.

"Where's Lawlor?"

"I've got no idea. He was supposed to be out here."

"Has he tried to contact you at all?" asked Driehaus.

"No, and that's what I'm worried about," responded Harvath.

There was a pause as the Homeland Security director cupped his hand over the mouthpiece of his telephone. Harvath could make out several voices in the background as Driehaus came back on the line and said, "I want you on the next plane back to DC."

"What for?"

"You'll be briefed when you get here. This is an urgent matter of national security, so don't waste any time getting back. And if Lawlor does make contact with you, I want you to find out where he is and let us know right away. Is that clear?"

"Crystal," said Harvath.

"Good," replied Driehaus, who then terminated the connection.

Harvath punched the *end* button on his cell phone, set it onto the bar, and reached for his wallet.

"What is going on?" asked Meg.

Scot finished downing his margarita and said to her, "I need to call my mother and let her know that we won't be making the memorial service."

CHAPTER 4

Gary Lawlor had taken his time getting to the apartment. Though more than twenty years had passed, he had not forgotten his tradecraft. After arriving at the airport in Frankfurt, he had taken a short commuter flight to Nürnberg and then a train to the outskirts of Berlin. Two taxis and a short subway ride later, he was back in the heart of a city that he had once known all too well. He dropped his suitcase off at an intermediate location and wandered the streets for a bit, getting his bearings before making his way over to check out the safe house.

The apartment had been selected because of its proximity to the Tiergarten, not far from the heart of what was then the commercial district of West Berlin. Lawlor noted that the reunification had only added to the area's hustle and bustle. The Bahnhof Zoo, the bombed-out Kaiser-Wilhelm-Gedächtniskirche, and the towering Europa Center all drew large crowds, which made it easy to blend in. With his neutral-colored overcoat and dull gray suit, Gary

Lawlor looked like any other German or Western European businessman making his way to an important luncheon meeting.

He took a circuitous route southward from the Nollendorfplatz, doubling back three times to make sure he wasn't followed. With the situation as it was, it was utterly impossible to be *too* careful.

The nondescript Schöneberg district was filled with smoky cafés and a wide variety of ethnic restaurants. Though some of the businesses had turned over in the last two decades, most of the neighborhood was still exactly the same as he remembered. As Lawlor reached the top of the Goltzstrasse, where the apartment was located, he was ready to breathe a sigh of relief when something caught his eye. Three doors before the apartment, two men were sitting in a black BMW. One was smoking a cigarette while the other appeared to be reading the paper. Ordinarily, this might not seem like odd behavior, except that the car was parked right in front of a half-empty café. Europe was all about café society and for these two men to be waiting for whatever it was they were waiting for in their car, instead of inside the café, gave Lawlor more than enough reason to pause. But, he couldn't pause, not now. It would create too much suspicion. In the world Lawlor had been thrust back into, there had to be two reasons for every move you made, every word you said, and every thing you did—the real reason and the completely plausible lie.

There were no stores or businesses to casually pop into where Lawlor was now walking. He had no choice but to keep moving and to hope that these men were just waiting for a friend.

It had been a long time since Lawlor had done actual fieldwork. His heart was pumping faster than it should have been and he fought to get it under control. All of his senses were on fire as adrenaline slammed through his bloodstream with each rapid thump of his heart. This was more than just an overactive imagination or the jitters. No, Lawlor knew the feeling all too well, just as he knew Berlin all too well. It was a feeling he had had many a night walking down the deadly backstreets on the other side of the wall. Something wasn't right.

As he came up behind the BMW, he could see the cigarette smoker watching him approach in the side mirror. A quick glance toward the driver showed that though he still appeared to be engrossed in his newspaper, his eyes were actually riveted on the rearview mirror. Lawlor's body stiffened. These men were not idly passing time, waiting for a friend to leave the café. They were conducting surveillance and Lawlor was willing to bet a year's pay on what they were surveilling. The decision to abandon the apartment came so quickly, it was more of a reflex than a conscious choice, but that was how they had all been trained.

If the apartment had been compromised that could only mean one thing—someone knew about them. But who? How could that be possible? The operation had been one of their most closely guarded secrets.

There was no time to figure it all out now. Lawlor needed to get the hell away from the area and find a way to warn the others. At least he had picked up on the surveillance before entering the apartment building. God only knew what was waiting inside.

As he passed the BMW, Lawlor stole a quick glance at the passenger out of the corner of his eye. What he saw stopped his heart cold. It couldn't be. The man he was looking at was dead. Lawlor knew this because he had killed him himself fifteen years ago. What the hell was going on? Was he paranoid? Was he seeing things? No, he had no reason to doubt his eyes, or his memory.

Even though nothing was making sense, Lawlor had to trust his instincts and his training. Raising his left shoulder and subtly turning his face away, he continued on. Despite what he had seen, he never once broke his stride.

Now two car lengths past, Lawlor began to entertain the thought that he might be home free until he heard what he knew were the sounds of the men getting out of the BMW and closing the doors behind them.

"*Entschuldigung, mein Herr?*" said the man who had been reading the paper in the car. Lawlor pretended not to hear and kept walking.

"*Herr,*" said the man again, "*bitte Halt!*"

In the reflection of a black panel truck, Lawlor

could see the men quickening their pace behind him. If it hadn't been obvious that he was the one they were speaking to, all doubts were erased when the man Lawlor thought he had killed said in English, "This is the last time we will ask you to stop."

Lawlor knew that the men would be armed. Outrunning them, at least at this point, was not even a consideration. That being said, he was prepared in case something like this might happen and quite literally had something *up his sleeve*.

As he wouldn't risk coming into the country with any weapons on his person or in his luggage, he had made a quick stop at a small shop near the train station in Nürnberg.

Lawlor stopped walking, his back to the two approaching men. He could still see them in the reflection of the black truck. Carefully bending his left wrist, he gently maneuvered the polished blade of the knife, which was hidden inside his sleeve, until he could feel the point in the palm of his hand. He then slowly shifted his weight to his right foot and drew his left arm across his chest. In one swift move he would drop his arm, delivering the handle of the blade into his palm, and lash out with the knife, hopefully killing the first attacker while he hit the other with the empty titanium briefcase he carried as a prop in his right hand. Unfortunately, Lawlor never got the chance.

The laser sight of the TASER X26 Shape Pulse Weapon painted a perfect red dot right in the center of his back. The men following him were more than six feet away when they saw his left arm disappear and his weight subtly shift to the right side. They didn't plan on letting Lawlor get the better of them. There was a quick pop as the nitrogen propellant sent the barbed ballistic probes ripping through the air at more than 180 feet per second and straight through his trench coat. The probes were attached to thin insulated wires that delivered a series of high-voltage energy bursts, overwhelming Lawlor's central nervous system. The result was an instant loss of neuromuscular control. In less than a second, he had slumped helplessly to the pavement and curled up into the fetal position, unable to think, speak, and—more importantly for his attackers—cry for help.

Stunned onlookers saw the knife drop from Lawlor's hand. When they saw the two men expertly cuff and place their victim into the backseat of the BMW, they were convinced that they had just witnessed a very legitimate undercover police action.

As the car sped away in a cloud of burning rubber, no one had any idea how dangerously far off the mark they were.

CHAPTER 5

hroughout the entire flight back, Scot tried to figure out what in the world could be going on. *Where the hell was Gary and what was the urgent matter of National Security that Driehaus was talking about?*

Upon their arrival at Reagan National Airport, there were two cars waiting. One was there to take Meg Cassidy back to Scot's apartment in Alexandria, while the other brought Harvath directly to Homeland Security headquarters.

When Harvath entered the director's secure conference room, Driehaus gestured to a chair about halfway down the smooth oak table. Sitting to his right were CIA Director Vaile and FBI Director Sorce. Harvath nodded at Vaile and Sorce as Driehaus said, "We appreciate your coming back so quickly, especially considering the circumstances that had taken you out to California in the first place."

Harvath was feeling guilty as hell for backing out of his father's memorial service and wanted to put those feelings behind him for the time being. "You said this was a matter of urgent national security?"

"It is," replied Driehaus as he extracted a thick blue folder from the accordion file sitting on the table in front of him, removed a series of glossy eight-by-ten photographs, and handed them across the table to Harvath. "Do you recognize any of these men?" he asked.

Harvath was taken aback to see that the pictures were a mix of crime-scene and autopsy photos of ten men who looked to range in age from their late forties to mid-sixties. Most looked to have been shot in the head while a couple had had their throats cut. After going through them a second time, he slid them back over to Driehaus and said, "I've never seen any of them before. Do their deaths have something to do with Gary's disappearance?"

"Maybe," responded FBI Director Sorce. "The bodies were found over the last several days and from the limited amount of information we've been able to uncover, all of these men were part of an Army Intelligence unit based in Berlin at the same time Gary was. What they were doing was highly classified and there is no record of it."

"So what? Gary was already out of the Army by the time he moved overseas. The fact that these guys were also with Army Intelligence is nothing more than coincidence."

The minute the words were out of his mouth, Harvath wished he could have taken them back. He knew how lame he sounded. He also knew that even he didn't really believe what he was saying. Of all people, Harvath was usually the first to say that there was no such thing as coincidence. That simple belief had saved his life more times than he cared to remember and he knew it was one of the primary tenets of the intelligence community.

"Agent Harvath, let's back things up a bit here. I can appreciate your loyalty to Gary," said Driehaus. "Why don't we begin by having you tell us what you know about him."

Harvath reached for the carafe of water on the table in front of him and poured a glass. He took a long sip as he collected his thoughts before speaking. "Gary Lawlor was a friend of my parents before I was even born. He'd been involved with Army Intelligence and met my father, who was a SEAL, when they were both in Vietnam. Through their work, they became pretty good friends and undertook several missions together. During one mission in particular, my father told me Gary had even saved his life. So, I guess you could say that if it wasn't for Gary Lawlor, I wouldn't be here today."

Harvath paused and studied the faces across the table from him before continuing. "After leaving the Army, Gary and his wife lived in Europe for a while before he returned to pursue a career with the FBI, where he specialized in areas ranging from counterterrorism to white-collar crime. He was eventually promoted to Special Agent in Charge of the San Diego field office and that's when I really got to know him.

"When my father died in the accident at the Naval Special Warfare Center in Coronado, Gary took a leave of absence from work to be with us and help us begin to put our lives back together."

Remembering his father's death and its aftermath caused Harvath to pause, and seizing the opportunity, FBI Director Sorce asked, "Agent Harvath, did anyone ever talk to you about the death of Gary's wife?"

"My mother did."

"What did she tell you?"

"Heide had been accidentally hit by a car in Europe."

"Did your mother tell you where in Europe they were when it happened?"

"It was in Germany, I think. What difference does it make?"

Now it was Director Vaile's turn to speak. "Agent Harvath, do you know what they were doing in Germany?"

"Heide's family was from there, and she owned an art gallery while Gary worked in investment banking."

FBI Director Sorce looked first at Vaile then at Driehaus who both nodded. "Scot, Heide did own a gallery in West Berlin and Gary was on the rolls of an American investment banking firm there too, but that was just a front for what they were really doing."

"What are you talking about?" asked Harvath, who leaned closer into the table as if it would force Sorce's words to make more sense.

"Did you know that Gary speaks fluent Russian?"

"Gary? Russian? Are you serious?"

"Extremely."

"No, I didn't know he spoke Russian, but there are lots of people who—"

"His grandmother was from Minsk," continued Sorce as he removed a file of his own and began reading from it. "She emigrated to the U.S. after her husband died during the First World War. She remarried and had three children, one of whom was the daughter who married Gary's father. Gary's parents worked long hours, and the Russian grandmother practically raised him herself.

"He was somewhat of a prodigy. By the time he was six years old, he not only could speak Russian fluently, he was reading and writing it as well. It was a cradle language for him and he took to it as well as he did English."

"So he's of Russian descent. Big deal. So are a lot of people in America. If being from a country that embraced communism at one point is a crime, you'd better get ready to lock up more than half of the people in Miami and a good majority of downtown San Francisco," said Harvath.

"Let me finish," replied Sorce. "It was precisely his Russian skills that made him so sought after in the Army and later with the FBI. Do you have any idea what Heide was really doing for a living before she was killed?"

"You said so yourself. She was an art dealer. My mother still has a lot of paintings from her gallery hanging in the house back in California." A bad feeling was beginning to build in Harvath's stomach. He didn't like the way things were going and he assumed that they were only going to get worse. When CIA Director Vaile chimed back in, he knew his premonition had been correct.

"Gary and Heide Lawlor," said Vaile, "were two of the United States' top recruiters of foreign intelligence agents during the Cold War."

There was a chuckle in Harvath's voice as he spoke. "Heide Lawlor worked for U.S. Intelligence turning spies for us?"

Nobody else at the table was smiling. The three faces staring back at Harvath appeared to be carved of granite.

"Their focus was on Eastern Europe," continued Vaile. "Heide Lawlor spoke German, Polish, and Czech. Gary handled the Russian transactions."

"You're not kidding, are you?" asked Harvath.

"He's not kidding," said Sorce. "In fact, Gary and Heide were so successful, they even received medals from the president in eighty-one at a top-secret ceremony at the White House."

Harvath had never heard any of this. And though it was difficult to believe, it did fit Gary Lawlor's character perfectly. The thing that scared Scot the most, though, was the realization of how little he might really know about Gary's past.

"I had no idea."

"What you also probably didn't know was that Heide's death was no accident."

Though Scot tried to maintain an impassive countenance, today would not have been a good day to play poker. Heide Lawlor had always been his "Aunt Heide." As she and Gary didn't have any children of their own, she chose to spoil him every chance she got. Christmases, birthdays, it didn't matter. Heide never needed a reason to show how much she cared for him. Now, the realization that Heide had been murdered sent a sharp pain rocketing through his heart.

Harvath asked, "Did Gary know?"

"Yes," said Vaile, "Gary knew."

"Who did it? And don't just tell me it was the Russians. I want to know who specifically killed her."

"His name was Helmut Draegar."

"*Was?*"

"Yes, *was*. He was undoubtedly the best operative the infamous East German Stasi had ever produced. His reputation was larger than life itself. It was said that he was the only man Carlos the Jackal ever feared. He was an extremely proficient linguist, an assuredly deadly assassin, and an operative's operative."

"Meaning?" asked Harvath.

"It means that his tradecraft was above reproach. He was a master of disguise and human nature. In the blink of an eye he could disappear, or have you eating out of his hand. Though the Russians had not given birth to Draegar, he was given honorary Russian citizenship—that's how highly they thought of him. In short, he was the ultimate spy."

"As you're talking about him in past tense, I assume he's dead. Am I correct?"

"Very," replied Vaile. "Lawlor killed him."

"Why was Heide targeted for termination?" asked Harvath.

"When you were as good at your job as she was, it causes the enemy to want to reward you with something other than a medal."

"But you said Gary was just as good. Why not target him as well?"

"Exactly our question," replied Vaile. "For a long time, we thought it was because the agents Heide had turned amounted to such major intelligence coups. Don't get me wrong, Gary had his successes as well, but Heide's were far and away of greater value. In short, while Gary might have been worth spending a bullet on, the prime target for the Russians was Heide."

"But they were always together, weren't they? I would have thought you could have gotten the two for the price of one very easily."

"It would make sense, wouldn't it?" asked Vaile. "Gary Lawlor had been credited with being extremely adept at keeping himself and his wife alive."

"Until Heide was hit by the car."

"Exactly."

Harvath placed his right elbow upon the conference room table and pinched the bridge of his nose between his thumb and forefinger. He wished they would get to the point.

Sensing his frustration, Vaile offered, "Maybe I can be a little more clear. Toward the end of the time Gary and Heide were operating in Europe, Berlin in particular, we suffered some major intelligence losses. Somebody provided the Russians with highly sensitive information."

"And you never caught the person," said Harvath.

"Correct. We looked at everybody, including the Lawlors—"

"Who obviously were cleared."

"At the time yes, but in light of recent events, Heide's death has been drawn into question."

Harvath was incredulous now. "Are you trying to say you think Gary had something to do with it?"

Vaile put up his hand to silence Harvath. "The Lawlors were working on agents from different parts of Russia and the Eastern Bloc and as such, reported to different supervisors. Shortly before Heide's death, she mentioned to her supervisor that she was concerned about Gary."

"How do you know this?"

"It took some digging, but I was able to track down a copy of her report in our files at Langley. She said Gary had changed somehow. She suspected he was working on some sort of project outside of his normal duties. He would disappear in the evenings and sometimes even for days at a time. He claimed it was work-related and he couldn't discuss it, but when Heide's supervisor looked into it, he informed her that there was nothing he could find to support Gary's story. Shortly thereafter, Heide was killed."

"This is ridiculous," said Harvath. "Gary must have been questioned up and down afterward."

"He was and he appeared very distraught over her death. It seemed genuine. It wasn't until he saw a copy of the report from Heide's supervisor that he started talking. At first, he said that he didn't want to sully his wife's good name. A couple of days later, Gary claimed that Heide had been growing paranoid before her death, that she had even been taking medication for it. She didn't know whom she could trust and she had even started disbelieving him. It was a difficult scenario for us. It was *he said, she said*, but she was dead and couldn't corroborate or deny anything Gary was telling us. We debriefed him extensively, but everything held up. A private doctor even confirmed that he had been treating Heide for paranoia and depression and that he had also been prescribing pills for her. Case closed."

"So what's the problem?" prodded Harvath. "You don't actually think he was up to something he shouldn't have been?"

CIA Director Vaile took a deep breath before responding, "At this point we have no idea what to think."

"All of this because there's been a string of murders of Army Intelligence operatives who were in Berlin at the same time Gary was? While I'll grant you that the murders are obviously connected to each other, you've failed to make the biggest connection of all—Gary to the victims."

"Actually," replied Driehaus, "we have made the connection."

Harvath was stunned. "What is it?"

"Several of the victims placed calls to Gary right before they were killed."

CHAPTER 6

Impossible!" growled Sergei Stavropol into his satellite phone, careful not to draw the attention of the various technicians and scientists working around him. "I don't care if that body is inside a wolf, a bear, or some farmer's hungry pig, I want you to find it, cut it open, and bring me the bones. Do you understand me?"

Milesch Popov, the twenty-two-year-old, knife-scarred entrepreneur on the other end of the line, was pissed off. Who the fuck did this man think he was talking to? "You paid me to retrieve the cars from the lodge in Zvenigorod. I could have sold those cars for a lot of money, but our deal was for them to disappear, permanently, and that's what I made happen. Then, you call me and ask me to go *back* to Zvenigorod to see what the police were up to. They were everywhere, but I went anyway and I took a look like you asked me to. That I did for free, out of good customer service, but what you're asking me now is out of the question because I—"

Stavropol cut to the chase and interrupted the young Moscow Mafioso, "How much?"

"This isn't about money."

"Don't be ridiculous. This is the new Russia. Everything is about money."

"Stolen cars are not exactly in the same category as dead bodies," said Popov, lowering his voice and readying himself for a tough negotiation.

"You are trying my patience, Milesch. I am a busy man. Name your price," demanded Stavropol.

Popov thought about it for a moment. In his line of work, he did not get to deal with many highly placed people like Sergei Stavropol. Whatever this was about, it was obviously serious. The papers had been full of the news of the disappearance of three generals and the discovery of two of the bodies behind the old hunting lodge in Zvenigorod. Popov knew his client had had something to do with it and that made the negotiation all the more dangerous. Then again, Popov had learned that men like Stavropol respect only men who respect themselves and set limits. "If I locate your missing package," said Popov, "I want five hundred thousand dollars U.S. plus expenses."

"You ungrateful, greedy little fuck," roared Stavropol. "I should cut your balls off!"

"Watch it, old man," responded Popov. "You don't want to give yourself a heart attack."

"Such insolence! Who do you think you are?"

"I think I'm the guy who's going to help you sleep at night. My guess is that until you figure out what happened to the unaccounted-for Karganov, a good night's rest is going to be a little elusive. Am I correct?"

Stavropol said nothing.

"That's what I thought," said Popov. "I want half of my money up front and the other—"

"No. I will give you ten thousand dollars in advance, the rest upon successful delivery of the package."

"Now who's being greedy?"

"Twenty thousand in advance, then, and you cover your own expenses," answered Stavropol.

"Seventy-five thousand, plus expenses, or I take the police to the lake where the dead generals' cars were mysteriously submerged."

There was a very long pause before Stavropol responded, "Fine, you have a deal. But, Milesch?"

"Yes?"

"When this is all over, you'd better disappear somewhere far, far away."

And with that, the line went dead.

CHAPTER 7

AIDATA ISLAND, GULF OF FINLAND

From Stockholm, Frank Leighton had taken the overnight ferry to Helsinki. Though he could well afford a first-class cabin with his credit card, he elected to take a lower-profile cabin in second class instead. This was no pleasure cruise and the less conspicuous, the better.

The city of Kotka, Finland, had the largest shipping port in the entire country. It was located approximately one hundred kilometers east of Helsinki along the coast of the Gulf of Finland, facing the Baltic Sea. Kotkansaari Island formed the heart of the city and Leighton knew it well. He knew its bars, its brothels, and every place that down-on-their-luck men would congregate.

The rusted trawler and battered dinghy were owned by a struggling fisherman from the nearby coastal village of Björnvik, and was named the *Rebecca*. With the sizable amount of American money Leighton had unearthed outside of Helsinki the day before, he was able to convince the weathered sea captain to part with his aging vessel and sail into early retirement.

The old man wasn't stupid. This was the chance of a lifetime, the answer to all of his prayers. The fishing had been getting steadily worse in the Baltic, forcing the fishermen to engage in dangerous and illegal forays into neighboring territorial waters, not only to poach fish, but for smuggling as well. Though the old man had never engaged in any illegal activity before in his life, he was definitely not getting any younger. The *Rebecca* wasn't getting any younger either.

With the transaction complete, the captain handed over the keys to the *Rebecca* and cut his crew loose. When Leighton mentioned that Spain was very nice this time of year, the old man was smart enough to respond that he had always wanted to see the place and would be booking a flight right away.

It had taken Leighton the better part of the morning and into the afternoon to purchase the supplies he needed. When the small island came into view, the sun was already beginning to set.

The Gulf of Finland was dotted with numerous small, uninhabited islands. Aidata Island, Finnish for *barrier*, was aptly named as it was surrounded by jagged rocks and unforgiving sandbars, making it virtually impossible to get to by boat. Leighton coaxed the trawler through a narrow channel on the far side of the island. The passage gave way into a tiny inlet, invisible from the open sea, which was just large enough to moor the *Rebecca*.

The rocky, windswept island was completely deserted. Even the sea birds seemed to avoid it. Its stark terrain was punctuated only by small scrub trees and sickly patches of grass.

After drawing the dinghy alongside the trawler, he loaded his supplies and once again checked the *Rebecca*'s winch. The last thing he needed was for it to snap or become damaged when he returned with his precious cargo. Satisfied that all was in order, he climbed down the rope ladder into the tiny rowboat and rowed himself to shore.

CHAPTER 8

Are you sure this is a good idea?" asked Meg as she watched Scot getting ready. "If they told you to stay out of it, maybe that's what you should do. Besides, won't the FBI be watching his house just in case he comes back?"

"Probably," answered Harvath. "Where's that container Rick Morrell dropped off for me?"

Though Harvath had originally had his differences with the CIA paramilitary operative, he and Morrell had grown to respect each other and had even developed a tentative friendship. As Scot removed the odd-looking suit from the black Storm case, he reflected on how it was good to have friends who could get their hands on the latest and greatest equipment.

A note was pinned to the outfit and read "I expect this back within two days and don't get any blood on it." *Morrell was all heart.*

"What is that thing?" asked Meg as she reached out to touch the alien fabric.

"It's a next-generation infrared camouflage suit. Not only is the visible pattern extremely effective against detection by the naked eye, but the material itself can reduce a person's thermal signature by over ninety-five percent."

"Making you virtually invisible to any Forward Looking Infrared or Thermal Imaging devices."

"You got it," said Harvath who had to remind himself from time to time of the comprehensive training Meg had received during their hunt for the terrorist brother-and-sister team of Hashim and Adara Nidal.

"Gary lives in a nice, well-to-do part of Fairfax. You think the FBI is sitting in front of his house with night vision devices?"

"It's not the guys in front that I am worried about. It's the guys in the back where Gary's property borders the woods. Those are the guys I want to be prepared for," said Scot as he slid a fresh magazine into his .40-caliber SIG Sauer P229.

Meg's eyes widened in surprise. "You're taking a weapon with you?"

Harvath glanced at the pistol for a moment and then placed it in the black duffel bag with the rest of his gear for the evening. "Ten men have already been killed," he said as he threw in two more clips of ammo.

"What do you expect to find there?"

Scot stopped his packing and looked up to meet Meg's gaze. "To be honest, I have no idea. I don't even know what it is I'm looking for. All I know is

that none of this makes any sense. Somebody has a
very deadly list and I need to make sure Gary's
name is not on it."

"But you said yourself that neither the FBI nor
the CIA know if Gary's a target."

"Meg, I know what you think, but I owe this to
Gary."

"Why?"

"What do you mean *why?*"

"He's a grown man. I love him too, but he can
take care of himself."

"What if he can't?" asked Harvath as he slid the
remaining items he thought he might need into the
duffel and pulled the zipper shut.

"You don't even know for sure that he needs
saving."

"Meg, I don't want this to—" began Harvath,
but he was interrupted.

"And even if he is in trouble, why should it be
you who saves him?"

"How about the fact that he's my friend?"

"Are you going to tell me this is something
friends do for each other?" she asked as she pulled
out a chair on the other side of the table from Harvath and sat down.

"In my world, yes," answered Scot.

"But Gary didn't do that for you."

Harvath knew what she was talking about.
When President Rutledge had been kidnapped and
Harvath implicated as the only surviving Secret Ser-
vice agent, Gary had seemed more concerned with

getting him to turn himself in, than in helping him figure things out. "That's not fair," he responded. "He came through for me. Maybe not right away in the beginning—"

"No, Scot, not at all. It wasn't until the bitter end. Not until you had provided him with enough evidence did he finally feel safe enough to help you. He didn't do it just because you two were friends. He did it because he was finally convinced that you *weren't* guilty. There's a big, big difference."

"I don't agree," said Harvath as he began walking toward his bedroom to get something.

Meg's next words stopped him dead in his tracks. "Well, maybe we can agree on this. Gary Lawlor isn't your father."

"What the hell is that supposed to mean?" said Scot as he came back into the dining area of his small apartment.

"It means exactly that."

"Meg, if you're trying to somehow evaluate my psyche, you're wasting your time and my time. I don't care what you think you learned from Oprah or *Redbook*, or wherever you're getting this stuff, but there are some people out there that are perfectly fine and don't have any *issues* whatsoever."

The statement was so patently defensive that Meg had to take a moment to remind herself of what it was she was trying to achieve before responding. She cared enough for Scot Harvath—no, scratch that. She loved Scot Harvath enough to want him to see it for himself. Shoving it in his face wouldn't get her anywhere, but leading him to it might.

"When was the last time you went skiing?" she asked.

"What does that have to do with anything?"

"A lot. At one point in your past, you were a damn good competitive skier. Now, you don't even ski recreationally."

"This has gone beyond ridiculous, I've got someplace I have to be," said Harvath as he went into his bedroom, retrieved the last things he needed, and walked past Meg toward the door.

"All I'm saying, Scot," offered Meg, "is that it's not your fault that you and your father weren't speaking when he died."

Once again, Harvath stopped in his tracks. Without turning he said, "It was at least fifty percent my fault."

"And the other fifty was his," said Meg as she walked over to him. She put her arms around him as she turned him around to look into his eyes. "I want you to know that if he was here right now, he would be proud of you."

"You didn't know him."

"No, but I know you and I know what your mother has told me about how much you two were alike. You carry around a tremendous amount of guilt about what things were like between the two of you when he died. Even if you had continued skiing, he would have been proud of you."

"I'm saying goodbye now."

"And I'm saying that Gary Lawlor's approval is not going to make you feel any better about what happened between you and your father. Let the government find him. You deal with enough danger in your life without having to go and look for it. You don't need to do this."

"Yes I do. Ten men have died. I won't just sit here and cross my fingers and hope that Gary isn't marked for the number eleven slot," said Scot, as he turned and walked out the door.

CHAPTER 9

I t was a blustery night with heavy snow predicted in the forecast. Though Harvath didn't relish having to cover footprints made in freshly fallen snow, he welcomed the cloud cover as it helped to block out the moonlight.

On his initial drive down Lawlor's street, he had missed the surveillance. It wasn't until an hour later that he dared to make another pass and noticed them cleverly hidden in a house across the street.

A white Lincoln Navigator sat cleanly off to one side of the driveway up against one of the garage doors, but why not tuck it away in the oversized three-car garage and protect it from the impending storm? When Harvath drove by for the second time, he got his answer.

As one of the garage doors opened, a casually dressed man whom Harvath assumed was the owner of the house, stepped outside to take his recyclables to the curb. Sitting alongside a silver Mer-

cedes coupe and a red Volvo station wagon was a
car that screamed FBI—a slightly worse for wear
dark blue Ford four-door. Either these people were
concerned about the ability of their maid's vehicle
to weather the approaching storm, or they were trying to help keep the Ford out of sight from people
who would recognize it exactly for what it was.
Harvath was willing to bet it was the latter.

The most commanding view would have been
from one of the upper-floor windows facing the
street, and a quick glance up was all Scot needed to
confirm that he had located one of the surveillance
teams. The only question remaining was who was
covering the back?

Meg's words were still ringing in Scot's ears as
he pulled his black Chevy TrailBlazer onto a deserted side road about a mile-and-a-half behind
Gary Lawlor's home. Though he didn't want to, he
had been thinking about what she had said. Unzip-
ping the duffel bag in the cargo area, he tried to put
it out of his mind and concentrate on what lay in
front of him.

After suiting up and placing the rest of his gear
into a small, camouflaged backpack, Harvath set off.

He moved quietly, using a small GPS device to
lead him through the forest to the rear of Gary's
property. When he reached the edge of the tree line,
he found a spot with a good view of the back of the
two-story Colonial-style house and removed a set
of night vision goggles. The wind was blowing in
fierce gusts, and a light snow had begun to fall.

Harvath took his time scanning the perimeter and didn't see anything—no intrusion-detection measures and no FBI agents. Either the Bureau wasn't holding out much hope that Lawlor would return to his house or, more likely than not, they had already been inside and the team across the street had been left in place to "sit" on the residence while they applied, ipso facto, for a full-blown FISA warrant to search the premises and catalogue anything they had previously found as evidence. Either scenario was fine by Harvath. The absence of a surveillance team in back wouldn't make his job a complete walk in the park, but it would make things easier.

He took off the night vision goggles and reached into his backpack for his modified Beretta Neos. With its modular design, it looked like a weapon straight out of a *Star Wars* movie. Its magazine held ten rounds of .22 LR–caliber ammunition and the full length of the weapon, before the modified stock and silencer were attached, was only twelve inches, making it very easy to conceal. It was also an extremely accurate weapon, especially when coupled with the advanced, next-generation Starlight scope Harvath had brought along for the job.

Having attended many barbecues in Gary Lawlor's backyard, Scot was familiar with the motion-activated security floodlights installed around the outside of the house. This was probably another part of the reason the FBI had felt the need to only post one team to watch his residence.

As Scot pulled the trigger for the first shot, he said a silent prayer of thanks that the neighbors' houses were set far enough apart not to be able to hear the *crack* of the silenced rounds as they slammed into and disabled the floodlight sensors.

He disassembled the Neos, put it back in his backpack, and put his night vision goggles back on. After slowly scanning the perimeter for any signs that someone might be watching, he made a run for the rear of the house. Fifteen feet before the back door, he already had his lock pick gun in his hand. A few moments' work on the dead bolt and he was inside.

He hoped Gary hadn't changed his alarm code. He found the panel in the mudroom, next to the door leading in from the garage, and entered the four-digit code Lawlor had given to him the last time he was out of town. It worked. Like most people, Gary was a creature of habit.

Five or six coats, including the Holland and Holland hunting jacket he had received as a gift from the president, hung from an orderly row of pegs above a wooden storage bench where Harvath stowed his backpack and night vision goggles. He attached a red filter to his compact M3 Millennium SureFire flashlight, making the beam virtually invisible to anyone outside the house, and continued on.

The kitchen was neat and orderly, just like Gary himself. There wasn't a dish in the sink, or a spot of grease on the stovetop. Harvath hadn't thought about it before, but the degree to which Lawlor kept his house in order was almost sad. Who did he do it for? He lived alone and besides the occasional summer barbecue, no one ever saw the house except for him. It didn't seem healthy.

Placed above the cabinets were mementos Gary had collected during his travels throughout Europe. There were German beer steins, a drinking bowl from Sweden, a ram's horn cup from Hungary, a hand-painted Irish jar—the assortment covered almost every country and every type of drinking vessel. Each one, Gary had once explained, had its own special story and special meaning. At the far end of the cabinets was the collector's edition bottle of Maker's Mark Harvath had given Lawlor as a Christmas present. It made Scot glad to see that his gift occupied such a place of prominence in his home.

There were fresh vegetables in the fridge along with a new carton of milk. Whatever had caused Gary's disappearance, it certainly hadn't been something he had seen coming.

Harvath decided to focus on where he knew Lawlor spent most of his time. He sat at the desk in Gary's study going through his bills and personal papers trying to find some sort of clue as to what had happened. Numerous commendations and meritorious service awards lined the walls, along with pictures of Gary and Harvath's father in Vietnam and later with his mother as the three of them enjoyed parties at the house in Coronado and took fishing trips to Mexico. The centerpiece of the room was an enormous oil painting of General George S. Patton and his bull terrier, Willie, short for William the Conqueror.

Gary had modeled himself in many ways after the hard-charging general and was a compendium of Patton information. He was always citing one or another of the general's famous quotes: *Do not fear failure. Do more than is required of you. Make your plans fit the circumstances. There is only one type of discipline— perfect discipline.*

Harvath felt guilty for being here alone and going through Gary's bank and retirement account statements, but he knew he had to do it. It was only after he had computed Lawlor's healthy, yet not by any means legally unachievable net worth, that he realized how ridiculous the exercise was. If Gary had been selling out his country, he wouldn't have been stupid enough to hide his ill-gotten gains in plain sight. Then what was it? Harvath had come to believe that everyone, no matter how careful they were, always left behind some sort of clue, but there didn't seem to be anything here at all.

Frustrated, and wondering if the FBI had already bagged any promising items, he left Lawlor's study and climbed the stairs to the second floor. The guest bedrooms and baths were clean—both literally and figuratively. He approached the master bedroom with a sense of déjà vu. Prowling around Gary's empty house like this reminded him of what it felt like to return to his parents' house after his father's burial ten years ago. His mother had been too distraught to do anything. Closing out his father's affairs had been left to Scot and Gary. Going through his personal effects, his papers, his clothes—it all felt just like this. It was as if Gary had died. He hoped to God he was wrong.

As he entered the master bedroom, the first thing he noticed was the neatly made bed. The sheets and blankets looked so perfectly tight that Harvath knew he could bounce a quarter off of them military style, just like his father had always done to him.

He ran his finger along the top of the dresser where there was only the slightest trace of dust. Socks, underwear, and handkerchiefs had been neatly pressed and folded and placed in separate drawers. A small brown leather box contained two watches, several pairs of cuff links, several tie clips, and a discarded wedding band.

In the closet, stacks of crisply starched shirts sat in a perfect row along the shelf, while a line of suits hung in gradation of color above a phalanx of perfectly polished wingtip shoes. As Scot marveled at the man's penchant for organization, he noticed that something was slightly out of place.

All of the suits were enshrouded in clear plastic dry cleaner's bags. One in particular, though, seemed to have been hastily hung. The bag was not covering the entire suit and it was bunched up where it had been slid between its two neighbors. Harvath noted that the suit was black and wondered if maybe Gary had thought about packing that one for the memorial service and at the last minute had changed his mind and shoved it back in his closet. Possible, but not likely. Not unless Gary was running behind and had been in a tremendous hurry. For all he knew, some careless FBI agent had pulled it out and shoved it back in place, but somehow he doubted it. They would have left things exactly as they had found them so on their return they could videotape everything the way Gary had left it.

Scot searched the bathroom. There was no deodorant, toothpaste, toothbrush, or razor evident, which made sense as Gary had been about to take a trip when this entire thing, whatever it was, went down. The toilet and sink were spotless, but the chrome wastebasket was filled with discarded tissues. Harvath pulled several of them out, only to discover that none had been used. *That was strange.* He kept digging only to find that the entire garbage can was filled with unused tissues. *What was Gary hiding?*

After emptying the can of tissues, Harvath could clearly make out the remnants of a small fire. There was a trace amount of ash and some melted plastic around the seam in the bottom of the can. A quick check of the shower confirmed Harvath's suspicions. The ceiling above had been slightly browned as if by smoke. Some ash was still visible around the drain. Apparently, Gary had burned something in the shower and had tried to rinse the can out afterward. When he couldn't get rid of all of the evidence, he decided to fill the can with tissues. But why? What did he need to hide so badly that he had to burn it? For the first time, Scot's confidence in the man was shaken.

As Harvath continued to search the bathroom, he flipped open the lid of the laundry hamper and was stunned by what he discovered. Inside were three days' worth of clean, warm-weather clothes—most still perfectly folded. The forecast in Southern California had called for temperatures in the mid-eighties. It was as if Gary had just dumped the clothes right out of his suitcase instead of taking the time to put them away back in the bedroom. A poorly hung suit was something Harvath could chalk up to a thoughtless Bureau investigator or packing in a hurry, but now signs were starting to point more toward a hurried *unpacking*.

Even though Gary hadn't bothered to call him, he might have phoned someone else. That someone might know what had happened to him. At the same time, Harvath knew that even while the Bureau waited for a FISA warrant, they would have already established a trap and trace on Gary's phone and would have been going through all of his incoming and outgoing phone logs.

Harvath also knew that if the Bureau had been in the house, which was almost a slam dunk considering the well-being of its former deputy director was currently in question, they would have most likely relied solely on the phone company to provide them with Gary's phone activity. That meant that the phones themselves might at least catch Harvath up on the most recent activity.

Leaving the master bedroom, Scot walked downstairs to the study where he picked up the phone and hit the *redial* button. There was a long pause and clicking noises before a series of ear splitting tones, which sounded like a fax machine at full volume, blasted on the other end. *Must have been a wrong number*, thought Harvath as he hung up. But why wouldn't Gary have found the right number and tried again? None of this was making any sense.

Harvath hit *69 to see who Lawlor's last call had been from. The automated voice gave a Maryland area code followed by a seven-digit number, which Scot wrote with a pen onto the palm of his hand. At least it was something. Whether that something would actually be worthwhile was another question entirely, but he didn't have any time to toss that possibility around now. If there was a trap and trace, the FBI would now know that someone was in the house and that the phone had been used. He had to get out.

As Harvath took one last look at the pictures on the walls of Gary's study, he whispered into the darkness, "Where the hell are you?"

CHAPTER 10

Gary Lawlor spat the blood from his mouth, looked into the eyes of Helmut Draegar, and said for the third time, "Fuck you."

The large, stone room, with its out-of-date furniture, empty filing cabinets, and antiquated communications consoles, was cold and damp. From the little Lawlor could remember of being transported here, it was someplace deep underground. Estimating the probable amount of time he had been incapacitated by the Taser, Lawlor figured they must still be somewhere in Berlin, or just on its outskirts. Often, he could hear a faint, but distinct rumbling, like jackhammers, and thought that they must be near some sort of construction, which wasn't any help because in Berlin, that could be anywhere.

"Though this gives me great pleasure, it is not working, is it?" asked Draegar as he set down the oblong strip of leather-clad iron he had been using to beat his prisoner and removed his black leather gloves. "We should try something else."

He motioned to his assistant and, for the first time, Gary noticed the flesh of Draegar's right hand. There was something uneven about it. No, not uneven, but *wrong*. The color was off. Then he realized. *It was a prosthetic.*

Draegar's assistant, addressed as Karl, was a sinewy man in his late forties with opaque eyes and a sickly, jaundiced complexion. He wheeled over a large surgical lamp and plugged it into a nearby outlet as Draegar said, "I see you looking at my hand."

"How?" said Lawlor.

"Wolves caught in snares have been known to gnaw off their own leg in order to escape. Do you think when presented with the same obstacles human beings would be any different?"

Lawlor wanted to vomit.

At that moment, Karl flipped the switch and the murky room was suddenly awash in bright fluorescent light. As he adjusted the lamp, it flashed briefly in Lawlor's eyes and caused him to see spots before it was lowered to focus on his mouth. *What the hell were they doing?*

The answer came quickly enough as his captor wheeled over a small stainless steel surgical tray and unrolled a worn leather case containing a series of long, chrome-plated picks, probes, mirrors, and dental pliers. "I actually first saw this in a movie," said Draegar as he carefully selected the tools he would need and began placing them off to one side of the tray. "It takes a very precise hand, if you will,

but can yield great results. The key is in prolonging
the life of the exposed nerve for as long as possible,
but if the one you are working on dies, which with
this method inevitably happens, not to worry. We
just expose a new one."

With his hands and feet flexi-cuffed to the old
wooden chair he was sitting upon, Lawlor could
only stare in disbelief as Karl plugged a portable
electric dental drill into another wall outlet, unrav-
eled its long cord, and then brought it over and set
it down on the tray next to the other instruments.
Instinctively, Gary clamped his teeth together as
tight as he could.

Draegar noticed the ripple roll across Lawlor's
jaw and said, "Resistance. Excellent. It will help
keep things interesting." As Karl maneuvered himself behind Lawlor, Draegar continued speaking,
"One way or another, I will extract the information
I need from you."

Though Lawlor's body was tense in anticipation
of the sheer agony Draegar had in store for him, in
a small, removed corner of his mind there was clar-
ity. Draegar had used the word *need*. Though the
former Stasi operative obviously took pleasure in
torturing him, he would not kill him, at least not
right away.

But the primary question that dominated Gary
Lawlor's mind was how in the world Helmut Draegar had survived Gary's attempt on his life. Night
after night he had lain awake devising the method
by which he would kill the man who had murdered

his wife. When the time came, he had carried out his plan in perfect detail, even allowing himself time to watch the explosion as it shook the ancient building and spat a thundering cloud of smoke and fiery debris into the night sky. But somehow, here Draegar was. How was it possible? How could he have escaped?

As Karl's hands gripped the side of Gary's head and his fingers tried to pry their way into his mouth, his mind was jolted back to the present. The man was strong and Lawlor did his best to resist him, thrashing in his chair as much as his restraints would allow.

"Pitiful," said Draegar as he delivered an agonizing blow with a truncheon to Lawlor's groin area, "but to be expected."

As Lawlor opened his mouth, a whoosh of air burst forth along with a deep groan of pain. Karl was ready for the reflex and shoved two rubber blocks between his teeth as far back as they would go. The blocks caused Lawlor to gag, but nothing he could do would dislodge them. They were wedged in tight, forcing his jaw wide open and fully exposing his teeth.

The blocks set in place, Karl stretched a tight metal band across Lawlor's forehead, bending his neck backward, until the band locked into a restraining device on the back of the chair.

Draegar positioned his lamp so he could get a good look into Gary's mouth and began slowly probing his teeth with one of the sharp dental picks.

"Americans take oral hygiene very seriously, don't they? You have lovely teeth. Absolutely lovely for the most part," said Draegar as he continued his exam. "But, I am a little concerned with this one here." He emphasized his point by adding pressure to the pick.

Lawlor's body involuntarily convulsed.

"Just as I suspected. Do you know much about teeth?" asked Draegar, who waited for some sign from Lawlor. When he didn't get it, he pressed down with the pick again and watched Lawlor's body tense against the restraints as if it had been jolted with an electric shock. "You see, inside each tooth is what we call pulp that provides the nutrients and nerves to the tooth. It runs like a little thread right down into the root. When it is diseased or damaged, as yours appears to be, the pulp can die, exposing the nerve. That is the pain you are feeling now." Once again he pressed down with the pick and watched Lawlor's body thrash like a man in the electric chair, before continuing. "The obvious course here would be to dig out the pulp, clean out the area, and seal it. The procedure is commonly known as a root canal."

Draegar removed the pick from Lawlor's mouth and set it on the tray beside him. "You are actually quite lucky that I discovered your tooth problem. Had it gone on much longer, it could have been quite a mess, but I think we may have gotten to it just in time. It is quite painful, isn't it? In fact, I would imagine that the anticipation of my further prodding has to be just as dreadful as the act itself."

Lawlor fixed Draegar with a cold, hard stare.

"If you answer my questions, we can be done with all of this. No more pain. No more fear of pain. Tell me what I need to know and it all stops," said Draegar as he swabbed Lawlor's damaged tooth with a short-acting topical anesthetic. "Are the same men still involved? Has the team been updated? What is your contingency plan if they fail?"

Lawlor closed his eyes and let his body go limp, as if resigning himself to surrender.

"That's it," said Draegar. "Cooperate and all of the pain goes away."

After several moments had passed, Lawlor opened his eyes.

Draegar smiled. "You are ready to answer me now?"

Though the rubber blocks had his jaws stretched to what felt like the breaking point, Gary steeled himself, opened his mouth even wider, and retracted his tongue, providing Helmut Draegar with unfettered access to his tooth.

Through the bright glare of the surgical lamp, Lawlor was able to enjoy a brief moment of victory as he saw the surprised reaction on Draegar's face. The look was soon replaced by one of sadistic determination as Draegar lifted the old dental drill and pumped life into it via its foot pedal on the floor.

The nauseating smoke from the drill bit burning through his tooth bothered him only for a second. Soon, there was nothing other than a roiling tidal wave of pain.

CHAPTER 11

Being an agent of the OIIA had several advantages, not the least of which was access to the vast resources and databases of the Department of Homeland Security. Ten minutes was all it had taken for Harvath to track down the name and address attached to the phone number he had pulled from Gary Lawlor's house. He was fairly confident that he had never heard Gary mention anyone named Frank Leighton before, but that didn't mean they weren't somehow connected. When it came to Gary, Scot was no longer taking anything for granted.

The Leighton residence was one of only a handful of houses along a quiet country lane known as Waverly Island Road, just outside downtown Easton, Maryland. The Cape Cod–style dwelling faced a farmer's field across the road while its backyard sloped gently down toward the Tred Avon River, one of the Chesapeake Bay's many tributaries. Though the snow had been falling for most of Harvath's drive, it began to let up around Annapolis and by the time he had crossed the Chesapeake and had arrived in Easton, it had stopped altogether.

Making more than one pass down the practically deserted road at three in the morning was out of the question, as it would only draw undue attention, especially if the FBI was sitting on Leighton's house. Though many people often got lost on the country lanes that dead-ended at water up and down the Eastern Shore, the last thing Harvath needed was to attract notice.

He found a secluded spot at the end of the road and after parking the TrailBlazer, grabbed his gear and walked back along the shoreline toward his target.

He had tried calling Leighton's house three times from his encrypted cell phone on the drive down, but no one had answered. If there was a trap and trace on Leighton's line, the FBI were going to have a very difficult time deciphering where Harvath's calls were coming from.

After surveying the rear of the property with his night vision goggles and not seeing anything, Harvath tried calling the house again. No one answered, so he decided to make his move.

Using a thick line of trees for cover, he made his way along the southern edge of the property until he was parallel with the rear of the house. He waited for several minutes crouched among the trees and scanned the area once more before darting across the snow-covered lawn toward the back door. With his lock pick gun in hand, he had the

door open in a matter of seconds and was creeping
quietly down a short hallway.

The house was cold and it was not just "somebody had turned down the heat for the night cold,"
but rather "somebody had not been in the house for
a while and had not needed the heat" kind of cold.

Harvath passed a small bathroom and an empty
guestroom. As he neared the end of the hallway, he
noticed a digital thermostat mounted on the wall.
Flipping up the cover and using the filtered beam
from his flashlight, Harvath cycled through the
daily settings. The system had been set to maintain
a constant, bare minimum temperature for every
day of the week. Harvath was getting the feeling
that whoever Frank Leighton was, he didn't plan on
being home for a while.

The house was tidy, but not overly so. After
checking the rest of the bedrooms and finding them
empty, Harvath entered the kitchen and did a quick
scan. Upon opening the refrigerator, he saw that
though it contained at least six different kinds of
salad dressings, both of the vegetable crisper drawers were empty and there were no salad fixings.
When he looked underneath the sink, he found a
metal garbage can with a clean liner. Somebody had
not only set the temperature down before leaving,
but had also removed all of the perishables from the
fridge and taken out the trash. Out of curiosity, Harvath removed the garbage-pail liner and was surprised at what he found beneath. The can was
blackened from having something burned in it and

showed trace remnants of ash—just like the garbage
can at Gary Lawlor's.

Had Leighton and Lawlor burned the same
thing? If so, what was it? What connected these
two besides ownership of metal wastebaskets and a
penchant for burning things in them? Was Leighton
somehow part of the mystery surrounding Gary's
disappearance? What the hell was this all about?

Quietly, Harvath moved past a butler's pantry
into the laundry-and-storage room that doubled as
Frank Leighton's home office. He looked at the pictures pinned to the corkboard near the desk while
he pushed the power button on the computer and
waited for it to boot up. There was a photo of a
woman with two children and he wondered if
maybe she was Leighton's ex. There had been no
women's clothes in the closets, nor had there been
any woman's touch in the house to suggest that he
was currently married or living with someone.

A quick perusal of the contents in the sole desk
drawer produced the usual bank and mortgage
statements, all in Leighton's name, as well as a recent *to do* list. While several of the items had been
checked off, other items such as *pick up dry cleaning*
and *haircut* were devoid of check marks. Several un-
paid bills also lay in the drawer, their due dates
drawing nigh. It all contributed to the picture of yet
another very hasty departure.

As Harvath sat down to examine the computer,
which had finally completed its start-up, something
on a shelf across from the desk caught his eye. An

ornately painted beer stein held a handful of pens
and colored pencils. He rolled the chair over to the
bookshelf and removed the mug. The front featured
a detailed relief of "Checkpoint Charlie"—the former border-control checkpoint between East and
West Berlin with the phrase, "You are now leaving
the American sector," in English, Russian, French,
and German. Oddly enough, at the very bottom of
the mug where it flared out was wrapped a piece of
barbed wire. Even more interesting, was that as odd
a drinking vessel as it was, Harvath had seen one
just like it before in Gary's kitchen.

He remembered Lawlor getting on the subject of
beer steins one night and telling Harvath that because of the bubonic plague and subsequent health
ordinances of the sixteenth century, all food and
beverage containers in Germany were required by
law at that time to be covered to protect their contents. To make them easy to open and close with
one hand, the Germans had devised a hinged lid
with a thumb-lift.

As Harvath now turned the mug around, he saw
the same inscription on the back as on Gary's. It
was a passage written in German entitled, "*Für die
Sicherheit.*" Translating into English, he read it aloud
and said, "For the Security. If one of us is getting
tired, somebody else is watching over. If one of us
starts doubting, somebody else is believing with a
smile. If one of us should fall, somebody else will
stand for two. God will give a companion to every
fighter."

Though it was the second time in his life he had read the inscription, Harvath still had no idea what its significance was. The one and only time he had asked about it, Gary had shrugged it off as a simple memento of his time spent overseas.

As he took a closer look, Harvath noticed that the stein appeared to have been commissioned by a pub called the *Leydicke,* because its name was not only engraved upon the lid, but was also painted on the bottom, along with a serial number. Leighton's was number seven of only twelve. Harvath wasn't about to risk another trip back to Lawlor's house, but he was sure that if he did, he would find that the same barbed-wire-wrapped stein resting above Gary's kitchen cabinets was a perfect match for Frank Leighton's. It probably also had a serial number from the same batch. *Had Leighton and Gary known each other in Berlin?*

Scot set the stein back in its place and rolled himself back over to the computer when he heard it chime. Leighton's web browser had opened to an Internet weather site that had been established as his home page. Clicking on the tab next to the address field, Harvath dropped down a list of the most recently visited websites. At the top of the list was American Airlines. Scot clicked on the link and moments later was transported to their home page. The site recognized that it was being accessed by Leighton's computer and asked him to enter his password. Harvath took a couple of incorrect stabs before the site finally shut him down.

He scrolled through Leighton's Outlook Express and found nothing out of the ordinary. Like everyone else with a computer, Leighton was plagued with electronic junk mail. Harvath was about to give up when he noticed that Leighton had received an auto-confirmation email from American Airlines for a round-trip ticket purchase to Stockholm, Sweden. The ticket had been issued in the name of Johan Saritsa for same-day travel three days ago. The return was set for a month later, but Harvath figured the date was probably bogus and the return flight would go unused.

Leighton obviously had not anticipated an automatic email confirmation of his flight purchase. Now, Harvath had the alias he was traveling under and with a couple of well-placed phone calls, would be able to get the full credit card number Leighton had used to pay for his flight. The haystack had not necessarily gotten any smaller, but the needle had just gotten a little bit bigger.

Harvath was about to turn on the printer and print out a copy of the flight confirmation, when he heard something from the kitchen. With barely a sound, he was out of the chair with his SIG Sauer drawn. Someone was in the house.

He pulled the night vision goggles from his backpack, powered them up, and put them on. Leighton could have returned, but he doubted it. His gut told him somebody else was inside and he had learned long ago that his gut was seldom wrong.

Hugging the wall of the laundry room, he focused on slowing his breathing. He counted to three and then button-hooked around the laundry room door into the short hall leading to the kitchen. With his pistol out in front of him, he swept it along with his eyes from left to right and back again. *Nothing. Could he have imagined it?* he wondered as he moved cautiously forward. Maybe it was just the heater kicking on. It had been getting progressively colder in the house and part of him had been willing the old Cape Cod to warm up.

As he neared the kitchen, he stopped for a moment and listened. He could hear what sounded like air blowing through the heating vents. Maybe it was the heater after all.

Just at that moment, the door to the butler's pantry exploded open, and before Harvath could react, someone knocked him onto the floor. The figure clutched furiously at Harvath's right hand, trying to tear away his weapon.

Harvath fought back hard, delivering several sharp punches to the man's kidneys. The intense pain caused the man to let up on his assault, and that was the edge Harvath needed.

He pushed himself away from his attacker and struggled to regain his feet. His mysterious assailant, though, was faster. The man lashed out with a sweeping kick that took Harvath's legs right out from under him. He hit the floor hard, with his head crashing into the wall, which sent his night vision goggles flying. The pistol, though, was still grasped tightly in his hand.

The only thing he was seeing were stars and all he could do was point his sidearm in the direction he believed his attacker to be. As he did, there was the quick *schlink* of what sounded like two pipes being fitted together, followed immediately by the sound of something slicing through the air. It was only as his assailant's telescoping baton hit Harvath's pistol and knocked it from his hand, that he fully realized what the noises had been.

Harvath pulled his new Benchmade Auto AXIS knife from his pocket and depressed the button, which swung the blade up and locked it into place, but it was knocked from his hand as well. As an added measure, his attacker delivered a searing blow to the upper thigh of his right leg with the tactical baton.

The man was good—too good, especially to be part of an FBI surveillance team, and as Harvath's vision cleared he could see that his opponent was already regaining his feet. He didn't want to risk another spinning kick and having his legs taken out from underneath him again, so he used his feet to propel him backward as fast as he could go along the floor into the kitchen. The minute he took off, his attacker was almost right on top of him. Harvath made it as far as the kitchen sink before the man took another swing with the baton and connected with his ribs.

As the man raised the baton for another strike, Harvath rolled hard to his left out of the way and ripped open the nearest cabinet door. The baton missed its mark, and Harvath thrust his hand under the sink. The first thing he touched was Frank Leighton's canister of starter fluid. Pulling the canister from the cabinet, he flicked off the lid and sprayed the fluid in his attacker's face as the baton came down again and caught him in the shoulder.

With a yelp of surprise, the man dropped his weapon and his hands flew to his poisoned eyes. The fumes from the fluid caused him to gasp for air.

Harvath leapt to his feet and threw a blistering kick into the man's abdomen. As his attacker fell to the floor, Harvath swept the countertop with his arm until he found what he was looking for.

He ripped the cord from the coffee maker and positioned himself behind his attacker, wrapping the cord around the man's neck. "Who the fuck are you?" he commanded as he applied pressure. The man could only gasp for breath and Harvath realized he would never get anything from him like this.

He withdrew the cord from around the man's neck and shoved him face forward onto the floor. Harvath used the cord to bind the man's hands behind him and then searched him for additional weapons. He found a semiautomatic Smith & Wesson, which he tucked into his waistband, and a small Motorola radio. Apparently, this guy wasn't working alone. He unplugged the man's earpiece and microphone from the unit and then hoisted him up and leaned him over the edge of the sink, where he turned on the water so his captive could rinse his face under the faucet.

While the mystery man was flushing out his eyes, nose, and mouth, Harvath kept one hand firmly on the cord binding his wrists and used his free hand to turn up the volume on the Motorola. Before Harvath could make any assessments of how dangerous it was to leave the house and who might be waiting for him outside, he had to find out who he was dealing with.

"Bath time's over," said Harvath as he yanked the man's head from beneath the faucet and spun him around to face him. "I'll ask you again. Who are you? FBI?"

"Fuck you," he replied.

"Fuck me? Fine," answered Harvath as he slammed his fist into the man's solar plexus. He waited several moments for him to catch his breath, then withdrew the Smith & Wesson and pointed it at him. "I'm done playing around. I want to know who you are and what you're doing here."

The man appeared unsteady and wobbled as if he was going to pass out. Harvath tried to steady him as his head lolled backward. Then right out of the blue, it came snapping forward and connected with Harvath's, accompanied by a loud crack. Harvath should have seen it coming. And because he didn't, he was once again seeing stars.

By the time he was able to shake it off, the man had already run out of the kitchen down the other hallway toward the back door. He chased after him, but came to a dead stop when he reached the hallway, as four heavily armed men were blocking his way. As the laser sights from their submachine guns lit up his chest like a Christmas tree, Harvath realized he was not only outmanned, but outgunned.

When the man who had attacked him had been untied, he walked back up to Harvath and hit him harder than he had ever been hit before in his life. The blow to his stomach made him double over in pain. The man retrieved his Smith & Wesson, placed it against Harvath's chest as a bag was pulled over his head, and said, "All my life I've been waiting to kill one of you."

CHAPTER 12

Milesch Popov drove back into the town of Zvenigorod, singing along to the Snoop Doggy Dog tune "Gin and Juice" that was pumping out of the stereo system of his new Jeep Grand Cherokee. The lyrics, " . . . with my mind on my money and my money on my mind," were profoundly appropriate. Though Popov had no idea what he was doing, with a seventy-five-thousand-dollar advance, he knew he could figure it out pretty quick. And lest anyone should forget, the deal he had so artfully negotiated with Sergei Stavropol was for seventy-five thousand *plus* expenses, against an eventual five hundred thousand U.S. upon delivery of the package—General Anatoly Karganov's body, or what was left of it.

Popov had all but convinced himself that the new Cherokee could rightly be categorized as an expense. He needed it and was sure that Stavropol would appreciate his rationale. Zvenigorod was no Russian backwater, at least not anymore. Because of its wooded hills and crystal-clear rivers, it had often been called the Russian Switzerland, but now with the influx of rich New Russians building their weekend dachas along the river, it was truly beginning to feel like it. In fact, prices for everything had gotten so ridiculously out of control around Zvenigorod that the running joke among the locals was that the only difference between Zvenigorod and Switzerland was that Switzerland was cheaper.

With the right car and the right clothes—a Giorgio Armani suit, another legitimate business expense, Popov had no doubt he would be looked upon as just another rich Muscovite fleeing his harried city life for the peace and tranquility of the Russian countryside. Popov, though, hated the countryside. It reminded him of the orphanage in Nizhnevartovsk, in northeastern Russia on the western edge of Siberia, where he had lived until he ran away when he was ten. It had taken him nine weeks to travel the almost fifteen hundred miles to Moscow, stowing away in the occasional truck, but more often than not traveling by foot, and once he had finally arrived, he never looked back. Over the next twelve years, he suckled at the underbelly of Russia's largest city, building a modest, albeit successful empire of his own, specializing in extortion, racketeering, and stolen automobiles. To those unfamiliar with him, Popov might have appeared to be out of his league on this job, but in truth, he was blessed with the gift of being a lot smarter than he looked.

The old hunting lodge was still surrounded by

crime scene tape when he brought the Grand Cherokee to a stop in the driveway. There didn't appear to be any cops around and he breathed a quiet sigh of relief. He didn't welcome the thought of having to put his fake state inspector credentials to the test. But in all fairness, there wasn't much he wasn't prepared to do for a five-hundred-thousand-dollar windfall.

He grabbed the brown file folder off the passenger seat and climbed out of the car. "I fuckin' hate winter," he mumbled to himself as he turned the collar of his expensive overcoat up against the wind. Images of sunshine, scantily clad women, and a nice vacation villa somewhere in the Greek Islands crowded his mind and he pushed them aside so he could get on with the job at hand. The sooner he got some answers, the sooner he would get paid.

The file he was holding, just like the Cherokee and the Armani suit, was another justifiable business expense. He had gone very far out on a limb to get it, and he would charge Stavropol dearly for it, but it represented a huge savings in time for him. In his hands he held all that not only the local police knew about the case, but also information from Russia's prestigious FSB. He had read it several times over and though it represented the efforts of some of the country's top criminologists, Popov was not one to let others do his thinking for him. Besides, he had a piece of the puzzle that the cops didn't; he knew that Stavropol was somehow involved with the murders.

Popov removed a stiletto knife from his pocket and cut the crime scene tape sealing the front door. After a few moments of working on the antiquated lock with his picks, he was inside. The great hall, with its enormous fireplace, was where the police believed the murders had taken place. As he walked around, Popov could see where blood had stained the floor and walls. He wondered what Stavropol's beef had been with the three men. They had been respected military leaders, just like him—great warriors. He was about to ask himself how Stavropol could kill his comrades and then realized how stupid he was being. He saw it on the streets of Moscow every day. That was simply how the world worked. Anyway, it had nothing to do with him and what he was being paid so handsomely to figure out.

Out of the three missing generals, the police had retrieved only two bodies. One had been bludgeoned to death and the other shot. The third was anyone's guess, though they did find traces of blood in the empty grave that matched Karganov's blood type.

If the two men had been murdered in the great hall, the quickest way to dispose of the bodies would have been to drag them through the kitchen and out back. He followed the trail of blood through the kitchen and briefly referred to the file, which positively identified the blood trails as belonging to both Varensky and Primovich, but noted that there was no trace of blood there that could be attributed to Karganov.

Outside he found the three graves were still cordoned off, but had been steadily filling with snow. As he examined the crime scene photographs in his file, he positioned himself in the different places that the cameraperson must have stood to take the shots. He focused his attention on the pictures of the empty grave, which was believed to have held Karganov's body, and read the report again. When the police found it, it appeared to have been disturbed, though by what, they couldn't say. Besides the traces of blood in the grave, there was nothing specific to indicate that a body had been there.

Popov had done his homework. He knew that Zvenigorod was not known for its wolves and that if any animal had actually gotten to the body, it would most likely have been a wild boar. But boars and wolves would eat their catch on the spot; they wouldn't have dragged it away. And when wolves and boars feed, they leave evidence behind, yet there was none. Finally, it seemed that Primovich and Varensky had bled more heavily than Karganov—a sure attractor for a carnivorous animal. All that blood, and yet their graves were untouched.

No, it wasn't a wild animal at work here. Popov was sure of it. Karganov had somehow gotten out of that grave and had left under his own power, or someone had helped him.

Though he had ruled out one possibility, Popov appeared no closer to answering the big question: Where the hell was General Anatoly Karganov? A chill wind and a blast of icy snow froze the back of his neck and the sharp jolt caused him to ponder for the first time what might be at stake if he didn't succeed. Men like Sergei Stavropol might respect those who set limits and drove hard bargains, but there was one thing that they certainly didn't respect and that was failure. He had heard about Stavropol and what had happened to men who had disappointed him—even his own soldiers.

Popov tucked the file under his arm and hurried back to the Cherokee, possessed suddenly by a motivation even greater than a mountain made of money—the desire to stay alive.

CHAPTER 13

SOMEWHERE OUTSIDE ZVENIGOROD, RUSSIA

Anatoly Karganov awoke with a start. Being buried alive had a way of doing that to people. Once you thought you were over the horror, you began to let your guard down. You no longer consciously replayed the terrible events over and over again in your mind. You stopped thinking how lucky you were to be alive. Your energies then turned toward making sure it never happened again. But the terror still lurked behind the curtain of consciousness, lingering in your psyche, waiting until you were most vulnerable to pop out and force you to relive the horror all over again.

But as he awoke, the slender, yet firm hands of a woman were there once again to calm him. Where she had come from, he had no idea, but in his delirium, he was convinced that she must be some sort of angel who had snatched him from the jaws of death. He had heard his soldiers tell of extraordinary visions they had witnessed on the battlefield as they teetered on the threshold of death, and now he was certain that this was what was happening to him.

The woman placed a cool compress on his forehead in an attempt not only to calm him, but also to help assuage the fever that had racked his body for the last week. Bullet wounds were extremely prone to infection and try as she might, most of her efforts appeared to be in vain. Karganov was hanging on to life, but just barely. She changed the dressings, administered the antibiotics, and kept him nourished. That was all she could do. The fight was Karganov's at this point, not hers, at least not entirely.

The man had cost her precious time. He had information she needed, but he was in no condition to give it. It was extremely difficult to play nursemaid to one of the men responsible for her father's greatest embarrassment and eventual downfall, but she had been lucky to find him alive at all. The bullet wound had been serious, but not fatal, though the subsequent infection could prove to be the man's ultimate undoing. When they had rolled him into his grave, he landed on his side, with his arm above his head. It had been just enough to create a small pocket of air. With the grazing wound the bullet had caused to his head, it was a wonder he had regained consciousness at all, but he had. The man's primal instinct for survival and self-preservation had eventually kicked in and he had managed to claw his way out of the grave and collapse beside it.

The woman who now tended him had been

watching the meeting from the woods. The distance had been less than optimal for the operation of her parabolic microphone. All she had been able to pick up were scattered words and phrases. There had been names—maybe first names, maybe last, as well as a few names of American cities. She also had made out the words *airspace* and *guidance systems*. They were pieces of a maddening puzzle that, without the overall picture from one of the players, was near impossible to comprehend, much less begin to put together.

She knew only what her father had known. In his last days, as the cancer ate away at what was left of his body, he chose to die at home. Though the doctors told him they could make him more comfortable if he remained in the hospital, he chose to return to the things that had provided so much comfort during the darkest days of his life—his books and his only daughter. After all, he was Russian, and thereby no stranger to discomfort.

His daughter followed the doctors' orders to the letter, administering the morphine in the appropriate doses at the appropriate times. When he shared with her the secret of his undoing, the reason why their previously comfortable life had been reduced to one of shame and hardship, she thought that it was the medication speaking and not her father. It was too fantastic to be believed. There were so many things that didn't make sense. She just smiled at him and pretended to listen as her mind wandered. It had been in-

credibly painful to watch her father die such an ig-
noble death.

When the time came, she paid for his funeral
out of her own pocket. That was expected, as was
the fact that no one from her father's professional
career and years of service to his country had attended his memorial. The state had all but turned
its back on her father many years ago, though it
could never prove any of the allegations against
him. In Russia, allegations were enough to break a
man, and indeed they had. She comforted herself
with the fact that at least her father had not died
alone. Broken, yes, but not alone.

And so had been the measure of her defiance.
She had stood by as her father's most formidable
defender right until the end. This was one of the
greatest reasons his ranting had hurt her so deeply.
After years of her defending him, he died admitting
that the state had been right all along. He drew a
large measure of satisfaction from the fact that
though they had known what he was up to, they
could never prove it. He had outsmarted them. He
had outplayed them at their own game.

The daughter had followed in his footsteps,
choosing the same career, and by all accounts had
exceeded her father. She had been one of the best
Russia had ever seen, and the state never bore her
any overt ill will for her father's failings. They did,
however, whisper and talk behind her back, but this
made her want to succeed all the more. She wasn't
only doing it for herself and the advancement of her

career, she was also doing it for him. And through it all, her father had reminded her never to confuse the state with the country. Governments, as well as political ideologies, would come and go like the tides. What mattered most was her country and the people who dwelled within it and relied upon it. "Never forget that you are a Russian first," he always told her. And she never did.

It took her several emotional days to sort through her father's belongings and close up his small house. She saved the photos, some of his favorite books and classical records, and the few mementos he had retained of her mother. The items she didn't want, but which she thought might be useful to the old woman next door who had been so kind to her father over the years, especially as his illness progressed, she placed in a box and left in the center of the room.

The last thing she had to do she almost relegated to a phone call, but her emotions got the better of her. She drove her aging Lada hatchback the three miles to the small garden plot her father rented. Here he proudly grew crops of beets, onions, radishes, potatoes, cabbage, and watermelon and even nourished a prodigious apple tree.

She unlocked the toolshed and opened its double doors, the musty, earthen smell reminding her of the long days in summer she used to spend here with her father, toiling in his beloved garden. After losing her mother at such a young age, she had made her father the center of her universe, the sun around which everything else revolved. As she selected the few clay pots that the windowsills of her tiny apartment would accommodate, she suddenly felt very much alone in the world.

In the corner of the shed was the bright yellow bucket and gardening tools she had used as a little girl. She had often asked her father why he never threw them away and he always responded that they reminded him of a simpler time—a time before she had begun to question his every decision. But such, he would sigh, was the natural progression of life.

She placed the yellow bucket and its tools along with the clay pots in the back of her Lada. The remaining gardening equipment would go to the renters of the neighboring plots who in the summertime had relaxed with her father after a long day's work in their gardens and drank kvass, the beerlike beverage made from fermented black bread. She smiled as she remembered how her father would constantly tease her for turning her nose up at it. Thankfully, there were always wives present at these gatherings of the men, which meant delicious cups of cold Russian tea. She never lost her appreciation of the time she had spent in that garden. Even after she grew up and moved into the city, she still came back on weekends just to be there with her father. Often they went for long stretches not saying a thing, just working in the soil, the simple act of being close to each other saying all that needed to be said.

It being winter, and the middle of the week,

none of the neighboring plot renters were anywhere to be seen. From the bag on the front seat of her car, she removed a tattered rag doll. It had been a gift from her father when she was four years old. The doll was dressed in the typical clothes of a peasant farm girl. It had been her constant companion for years and she had always brought it on their trips to the garden plot. She looked down at the doll and smiled. It had been many things for her throughout its life—a playmate, confidant, even the embodiment of her departed mother, and for it now to aid her in deceit was something she never would have imagined. Such, though, was the nature of her training. A believable falsehood must always be in place before conducting a clandestine operation.

The ground was frozen, so she chose the pointed shovel from the shed and walked to the rear of the plot. She felt somewhat embarrassed, like a naïve child searching for pirate treasure as she counted off the prescribed paces from the apple tree. She remembered her father telling her how he had planted it the year she was born. He loved to say that it had grown tall and beautiful, just like his daughter.

She set the doll down and began to dig. Had anyone come along and asked what she was doing, she could present the doll and explain that she was laying it to rest at the base of her father's favorite tree. If any of the neighboring plot renters had happened by, they would not only have known the significance the tree held for her father, but they would also recognize the little peasant doll. It would have made sense for her to close a chapter of her life by burying part of her past.

The work was slow going and the raw winter wind bit at her cheeks. She was beginning again to consider her father's words as nothing more than the ravings of a sick and dying man when the shovel hit something that gave forth a resounding *thud*. She brought the point of the shovel down again and felt something splinter beneath it. Quickly, she shoveled more dirt from the hole until she could trace around the edges of a small wooden crate about two feet square.

She dusted the earth from the top of the box and saw that the wood had begun to rot. Using the point of the shovel, she pried the top loose. Sealed in a clear plastic bag inside was her father's old battered leather briefcase—the same one she had watched him leave for work with every day and return home again with at night. It had looked like any briefcase any ordinary father would carry to his office. Staring at it now and realizing that her father and his job had been anything but ordinary, the briefcase now seemed ominous. The fact that he had chosen to bury it in the relative anonymity of his garden plot perhaps meant that his almost unbelievable story might have been more than the mere ranting of a drugged man on his deathbed.

As she held the old leather case in her hands, she began to think that maybe the reason the story had seemed so unbelievable was because it was so frightening. She hoped that the contents of the case could tell her more, but she couldn't examine it, not there. For a brief moment, she held the doll close against her cheek and stroked its hair. With a final kiss goodbye, she laid it within the rotting wooden box, replaced the lid, refilled the hole, and then returned with a heavy heart to her tiny Moscow apartment.

What she read that night filled her with swells of emotion. There was awe at the extreme ambition her father had uncovered and fear of what that ambition might still unleash. She also felt pride as she realized why her father had done what he had done. There was no shame in his failure. His motives were above all else those of a true patriot. He had put Russia first, and in its future he had seen his daughter and a chance still to unmask a terrible evil before it had the opportunity to strike.

It was the dossier her father had compiled that had put her on the generals' trail. The contents of that briefcase had led her to be in the woods beyond the hunting lodge in Zvenigorod, risking not only her career, but also her life. What her father had started, she would see finished, but she needed her patient to break through the haze of his fever and give her some sort of clue as to how to proceed.

As she wrung out another damp cloth, the man moaned yet again and she reached for his arm to check his pulse. It had weakened significantly. Karganov was getting worse, and Alexandra Ivanova had hit the absolute bottom of her limited well of medical knowledge.

CHAPTER 14

I'm going to ask you again," said the man Harvath had struggled with inside Frank Leighton's house. "Who are you and what were you doing there?"

"Actually, I work for Martha Stewart, but times have been tough, so I pick up the occasional decorating job on the side," replied Harvath as he glanced around the rural farmhouse where his captors had taken him. He had absolutely no idea where he was. All he knew was that after three hours in the trunk of a car with a hood over his head, he was happy to finally be sitting in an upright position.

"Very funny, wiseass. I suppose all of these are just tools of the trade?" said the man as he did a quick inventory of the gear that had been spread across the large kitchen table. "Looks like you were planning on doing one hell of a redecorating job on somebody—SIG Sauer semiautomatic in forty caliber with a fully loaded clip and two spares. Modified Beretta Neos, complete with silencer. IR camouflage suit. Night vision goggles. Lock pick gun . . . I'm not screwing around with you anymore. I want some answers."

"Okay," said Harvath, "you got me. I don't work for Martha Stewart."

"No shit."

"Actually, I work for *Ladies' Home Journal*, and I'm doing an investigative piece on how to make your neighborhood a safer place to live. I'm hoping it'll be a three-parter with photographs and the whole shebang. You'd be great for it. Could I get you to agree to sit for an interview?"

"Shut the fuck up."

"Now you're sending mixed messages. You want me to talk, but you're also telling me to shut up. *Ladies' Home Journal* did a great article on this very same thing. It's an age-old problem. Now, what I suggest—"

"That's it, asshole," said the man as he tipped the chair Harvath was handcuffed to over backward. It landed with a loud crack and Harvath's head thudded against the tiled floor. "From this point on, things only get worse for you. Do you understand me? I have no time and even less patience. You're going to start answering my questions, or I swear to God I *will* kill you. Something tells me your government probably wouldn't raise much trouble over losing you."

"My government?" snapped Harvath as he tried to shake the stars from his head and focus on the man towering above him. *Who the hell was this guy?*

And who was he working for? He certainly wasn't with the FBI. If he was, Harvath would have been dragged down to the Washington field office or FBI headquarters and all of this would have been cleared up by now. Whoever this guy was, he was operating way out on the edge. There was no way they could be working for the same team. That left Harvath with only one possible conclusion—somehow, the Russians were on the same trail he was. "If you know anything about my government," Scot continued, "then you know I won't be forgotten that easily."

"Losing you will be painful for them," said the man, "but I'm sure you're not irreplaceable."

Harvath could tell the man was trying to lead the interrogation somewhere and he decided to follow, at least for the time being, to see where it was going. He had to figure out what was going on and who he was dealing with. Somehow, this man seemed to know who he was, or at least that he worked for the United States government. "No one wants to believe they are replaceable," said Harvath, "but it is a fact of life. That being the case, there are plenty more out there who will eagerly take my place."

"And that is precisely what we want to know," said the man. "How many are there? Who are they? Where are they? How do we contact them? We want all of it. If you cooperate, maybe we can work something out."

Harvath's head hurt and lying flat on his back

with his hands cuffed to the sides of a kitchen chair was not helping his thought process any. "You want to know who and how many would replace me?" he asked.

"Yes."

"There's thousands. Tens of thousands. Hundreds of thousands even. All it takes is time and the right amount of training."

"That's the problem with you and your countrymen," said the man. "You believe all of your own propaganda."

"It's not propaganda, my friend. We have the best-trained people in the world," responded Harvath.

"Is that how you found Frank Leighton?"

"Who says I found him?"

"You found his house."

"I told you—"

"*Ladies' Home Journal*, I know," replied the man who, standing to Harvath's left, kicked him hard in the ribs. "And I told you to stop fucking around."

Harvath struggled for several moments to regain his breath before responding. "Actually, you told me to shut the fuck up."

The man kicked Harvath again.

"We know your people were aware that Frank Leighton was one of ours."

Jesus, thought Harvath through the pain, *who the hell is this guy?*

"We know you were there to terminate him. Who did the others? Was it you?"

"What others?" coughed Harvath, "I don't know what you're talking about."

"So it wasn't you who killed our other operatives? Bullshit," said the man as a he delivered a third and even more severe kick to Harvath's side.

It took several moments for Harvath to get his breath back and while he gasped for air the man continued, "So, it's our mistake? This is just a simple case of being in the wrong place at the wrong time? I think we both have to agree that judging from the array of goodies on the table over there, you were not simply skipping through the woods to Grandmother's house to deliver a basket full of pies. Remember what I said about things getting worse? My boot to your ribs is going to pale in comparison to what I have planned for you. I hope you haven't grown too attached to your testicles, because I'm going to hang them from my rearview mirror next."

Harvath's cold stare spoke volumes.

"You think I'm kidding? Take a look at these," said the man as he held a rusty pair of pruning shears above Harvath's face and worked the dirty blades back and forth. "I think they'll do the trick just fine. We'll go slow so you can appreciate the entire show. I hear in parts of the world eunuchs are still hired to watch over harems. What a shitty job that would be, huh? Water, water everywhere and no mouth to drink it with. It's up to you. Tell us what we need to know and once we have it confirmed, we'll talk about making a deal. We're holding all the cards."

"Oh, yeah? Well you can shove the whole deck right up your ass."

"I was hoping you'd say that," said the man, with a twisted smile, as he righted Harvath's chair and affected a perfunctory cleaning of the shears by wiping them on the sleeve of his shirt.

He had just begun cutting up Harvath's left trouser leg, when another man walked into the kitchen and said, "Hold up on the prisoner."

"And the good cop appears just in time," quipped Harvath.

"Shut your fucking mouth," said the man as he stopped clipping halfway up Harvath's lower leg.

"There you go again. *Let's talk, no, shut up. Let's talk, no, shut up.* If you'll let me call my editor, I'm sure she'd be happy to fax over a copy of that whole communications skills article."

"You're trying my patience," said the man as he turned, "Why are we stopping?"

"Orders."

"We don't have time for this. Orders from whom?"

"Goaltender."

"What does Goaltender care about this piece of shit?"

"A black Chevy TrailBlazer was found abandoned not far from Leighton's house."

"So?"

"They ran the plates. We're supposed to uncuff the prisoner and make him comfortable until Goaltender gets here."

"Goaltender is coming here? You've got to be kidding me. What for?"

"Apparently he wants to talk to the prisoner himself."

"But that car could have easily been stolen. How do we know this is the guy it's registered to?"

"I described the prisoner to him myself and we also got a DMV photo match. Goaltender says to take the cuffs off, but not to let him out of your sight until he gets here."

As his colleague left the kitchen, the man removed a key and unlocked Harvath's cuffs. "It looks like I'm done asking the questions for the time being."

"Then I've got more than a few of my own," replied Harvath. "Why don't we start out by you telling me who the hell you are and who you work for?"

"I'd take it easy if I were you," said the man as he finished uncuffing Harvath. "Goaltender will be here soon enough and believe me, when he asks you a question, you'd better answer it."

"Who the hell is this Goaltender? What is he some kind of a hockey buff?"

"Oh, don't worry. You'll recognize him the minute you see him. And keep in mind," said the man, "that while he's talking to you, I'm going to be on the other side of the room sharpening my pruning shears. All it will take is one nod from him and I'm going to finish what I started."

"What's to stop me from taking out your precious Goaltender? It seems to me it would have been smarter to leave my handcuffs on."

The man smiled and said, "Part of me would like to see you try, but then again there's part of me that wants at least a little piece of you left for myself. You'd never make it. They'd tear you to shreds. Goaltender has the best bodyguards in the world."

Harvath had to laugh.

"What's so funny?" said the man.

"That's one area that I can guarantee my people do better than anyone else."

"We'll see," said the man.

"You bet we will," replied Harvath.

CHAPTER 15

After removing his handcuffs, Harvath's interrogators gathered all of the equipment from the long table and left him alone in the kitchen. It only took a few minutes to confirm his suspicions that though nobody was in the room, he was still being watched. The entire kitchen was covered by several strategically placed miniature cameras. A further visual exploration of the room revealed sophisticated intrusion detection systems and a discretely mounted air quality monitor, the kind used to check for airborne particles a lot more dangerous than pollen and ragweed. Whoever owned this place had certainly put a lot of money into it and took its security very seriously.

Harvath found a clean mug and poured himself a cup of coffee from the pot brewing next to the stove. Peering out of the window above the sink, he learned several things. The first was that the window was made from thick synthetic glass, most likely bulletproof. The next was more of a confirmation of an earlier gut feeling—he was indeed in the middle of nowhere.

Finally, after much persistent squinting against the light from behind him in the kitchen, he was able to discern several men in winter camouflage on patrol outside. Whoever this Goaltender was, he took his security seriously and money seemed to be no object. Though it was good, there was still no way it could be anywhere near as thorough as what the United States Secret Service provided the president.

That thought was still swirling around Harvath's head along with what possible clandestine purpose the fortified farmhouse could possibly serve and what these people wanted with him, when he heard the telltale sounds of an approaching helicopter. It came in quickly and landed even faster. Whoever the pilots were, they were very good. Harvath had no idea the helicopter was even there until seconds before it landed.

Through the swirl of snow kicked up by the unmarked, blacked-out craft, Harvath could see a group of people hop out and quickly make their way toward the house. As soon as the party cleared the rotors, the helicopter lifted off and disappeared. It was done with military precision and Harvath had to admit he was more than a little impressed.

He assumed that the mysterious Goaltender was a member of the party who had just been dropped off outside and he readied himself for the encounter.

Two of the men who had taken him prisoner at Frank Leighton's house entered the kitchen and instructed Harvath to set his coffee cup down. They quickly searched him to make sure he hadn't secreted anything outside the view of the cameras that could be used as a weapon and then pointed him to a lone chair on the far wall of the kitchen. These people were obviously extremely careful and took nothing for granted. Harvath had to hand it to them. It was exactly the way he would have done things.

He took his seat as instructed and waited. From beyond the kitchen, there was a chorus of indistinguishable voices as the party from the helicopter entered the house. Several minutes passed and then the voices grew louder as the party approached the kitchen. When the first member of Goaltender's security detail entered, Harvath's jaw nearly hit the floor.

"Palmer?" he said, the confusion clearly resonating in his voice.

"Harvath?" replied Secret Service agent Kate Palmer. "What the hell are you doing here?"

"Apparently, the local 4-H club has an interesting way of soliciting new members," said Harvath as he began to stand up.

"Don't stand, Scot. I need you to remain seated until I say otherwise," replied Palmer as three other agents entered behind her and swept the kitchen.

Harvath recognized two of the other three Secret Service agents as former colleagues of his from the president's protective detail. Though he nodded to them, they ignored him until they had determined that the room was completely secure.

"What the hell is going on here?" asked Harvath.

Kate Palmer spoke to the agents, who then left the room, before turning her attention back to Harvath. "We've got a very big problem that I am not at liberty to go into. You're free to stand up now if you want."

"Thanks," said Harvath as he rose from his chair. "What do you mean, you can't go into it?"

"I'm not authorized to discuss it."

"Well who is?"

"I am," said a voice from the entryway to the kitchen, which Harvath immediately recognized.

"Mr. President," he replied even before he had fully turned around.

Kate Palmer spoke into her sleeve microphone, "Goaltender will be ready to travel shortly. All teams be prepared to move."

Harvath looked back at Agent Palmer and then turned to the president and said, "You're Goaltender? Your call sign has always been Hat Trick. Why the change? What's going on here?"

"You and I have a lot to talk about, Scot," responded President Rutledge. "Agent Palmer, if you would be kind enough to show the defense secretary in and give us the room, please."

"Right away, Mr. President," said Agent Palmer as she exited the kitchen.

Once Defense Secretary Robert Hilliman had entered the room and the rest of the Secret Service agents had left, the president said, "Scot, I'd like you to meet Secretary Hilliman."

"Mr. Secretary," replied Harvath as he shook hands with the man.

"I have heard a lot about you, Agent Harvath. I'm sorry that we should have to meet under these circumstances."

"I'm the one that's sorry, Mr. Secretary," replied Harvath. "I have no idea what this is all about."

"That's why we're here," said the president as he motioned the two men toward the long kitchen table. "We don't have much time, so let's get started."

When the trio was seated at the table, the president said, "Scot, I need to know what you were doing at Frank Leighton's house."

Harvath shot an uneasy glance at the defense secretary.

"Don't worry about Bob. He's one of the few people in Washington I know I can trust. That's why I appointed him," said the president.

"No offense, Mr. Secretary," responded Harvath. "It's just that someone very close to me has disappeared under some very strange circumstances."

"No offense taken, Agent Harvath. I assume we're talking about Gary Lawlor?" asked the secretary.

"Yes."

"How were you able to connect him with Frank Leighton?" asked the president.

"When I was in Gary's house earlier tonight—"

"Wait a second," interrupted Hilliman. "That was you? You were the one who got inside and used his phone?"

"Yeah. I needed to find out what happened to him," answered Harvath.

"And what did you find?"

"Probably not much more than you already know. He had apparently gotten off his flight to San Diego, come home, repacked for another destination, and hastily burned something in a trashcan in his bathroom.

"He had erased his caller ID log, so I picked up his phone and punched star sixty-nine to see who his last call had been from. That's how I got Frank Leighton's number. I traced it and then got the address in Easton."

"I'm not going to ask," said Hilliman, "how you got into Agent Lawlor's house. You must have gotten into Leighton's house the same way. I saw the impressive array of gadgetry that my people picked you up with."

"*Your* people?" said Harvath. "Those guys work for the Department of Defense? What does the DOD have to do with Gary's disappearance?"

"In a moment. Do you know where the term *Cold War* comes from, Agent Harvath?"

"If I remember correctly, there was an American journalist named Lippmann who wrote a book in the late forties called, *Cold War*. The title was meant to reflect the relations between the USSR and its World War Two allies—the United States, Britain, and France—which had deteriorated to the point of war without actual military engagement.

"Foreign policy on both sides seemed singularly focused on winning the Cold War. After we created NATO, the Soviets created the Warsaw Pact. There didn't seem to be a local conflict anywhere in the world where the U.S. didn't choose one side and the Soviets another. This maneuvering eventually gave way to the arms race, where both sides competed to have the most advanced military weapons possible."

"And what brought about the end of the Cold War?"

"That was actually a year before I was graduating and it was all we talked about," replied Harvath. "There were a lot of theories floating around, but the one that made the most sense to me was that we simply outspent the Soviets. That's how we won the Cold War."

"Are you aware, Agent Harvath, of how that affected defense planning by the United States?" asked the secretary.

"Sure," answered Harvath. "The Berlin Wall came down in November of 1989. Germany then united less than a year later and joined NATO. The Warsaw Pact disbanded and we signed a conventional arms control treaty that provided for major cuts in both American and Soviet forces. Basically, all of the intense debating over nuclear policy came to a sudden and screeching halt.

"Our greatest enemy was defeated, so we began slashing our military spending starting with our presence on the European continent and then what we had invested here at home. The once formidable Red Army was suffering from not only a lack of supplies, but also from a lack of morale. If they couldn't even put down revolts in their own country, how could we expect them to pose any threat to us? They were finished."

"Or so we thought," replied the defense secretary.

"What are you talking about?" asked Harvath.

"What if the Cold War hadn't ended?" said the president.

"Are we talking about a hypothetical here? Like what if there had been a different outcome?" asked Harvath.

"No," replied President Rutledge. "What if the Cold War didn't end? What if we thought it had ended, but the Soviets were just playing possum?"

"That would be the greatest Trojan horse in history. But it would be virtually impossible. I mean, look at the condition their country has been in since the end of the Cold War—life expectancy falling, rampant corruption, fifty percent annual inflation. A lot of people could argue that it is worse now than it has ever been."

"And many opinion polls out of Russia would agree with you," offered the defense secretary. "An overwhelming percentage of middle-aged and older Russians believe that their lives were significantly better under Communism."

"But why are we even talking about this?" asked Harvath.

"Agent Harvath, do you have any idea how much the international community, both private and public, has funneled into Russia since the early nineties?"

"I don't have an exact figure, but it has to be in the billions of dollars."

"Try tens of billions. Of which, several billion have gone astray."

"I've read about that," said Harvath. "The Russian mafia has slithered its tentacles very thoroughly into the Russian banking system, right?"

"You're half right. As far as we're concerned, there is no Russian mafia."

"No Russian mafia? What are you talking about?"

"After the collapse of the Soviet Union, the KGB underwent several face-lifts. When it emerged, it had a new name, had placed one of its own colonels in the president's seat in the Kremlin, and was making megabucks by taking even greater control of its country's illegal activities," said the secretary.

"Are you telling me the Russian mob is actually run by the Russian Federal Security Bureau, formerly known as the KGB?"

"You catch on quick, kid," said Defense Secretary Hilliman.

Harvath ignored the remark and studied the graying, sixty-something defense secretary with his neatly pressed Brooks Brothers suit, wire rim glasses, and blue silk tie. "I guess not," said Harvath. "With all due respect, does this have something to do with Gary and the deaths of the Army Intelligence operatives from Berlin? Because this isn't making any sense."

"That's enough of the questions, Bob," interjected the president. "Let's focus on the answers."

"Yes, Mr. President," responded Hilliman, as he placed his briefcase on the table and extracted a large manila envelope. He fished out an eight-by-ten color photograph, handed it across the table to Harvath, and said, "Three days ago, security staff at the Mall of America in Bloomington, Minnesota, received a tip and discovered a Russian suitcase nuke hidden within the NASCAR Silicon Motor Speedway exhibit."

Harvath was at a loss for words. "I can't believe this. The *Russians*? That's insane. Why would they do something like that? Are you positive the device was one of theirs?"

"There's no question. Both the Cyrillic markings and laboratory tests on the fissile material have come up positive for Russia."

"How could they have gotten a suitcase nuke into the United States?"

"During the Cold War, our borders were a lot more porous than they are now," said the secretary.

"You think that's when this thing came in?"

"According to interviews we've conducted with Russian defectors over the years, the Soviets were actively trying to smuggle these things in. We even had a former Russian nuclear scientist testify before Congress about it."

"So why haven't we conducted an all-out search for them?"

"We did. In fact we conducted several searches and spent a lot of money but always came up empty. Either the stories were bogus or the devices were too well hidden."

"Wait a second," said Harvath. "Even if the Soviets had been able to pull it off, we're talking at least twenty years ago."

"At least."

"Then in this case, time, to a certain degree, is on our side. Russian suitcase nukes, just like our backpack nukes, needed to be refreshed at least every seven years to assure maximum potency."

"Unfortunately," responded the defense secretary, "your information is incorrect. Both the United States and the Russians had been experimenting with a hybrid fissile material with a seriously expanded potency and shelf life."

"How potent?" asked Harvath, studying the photograph of the device.

"Somewhere between forty-five and fifty kilotons. And although we live in a megaton world today, I don't have to remind you that the device the U.S. dropped on Hiroshima nicknamed 'Little Boy' was only a twelve-point-five-kiloton device and 'Fat Man' dropped on Nagasaki was just twenty-two.

"With the amount of people who visit the Mall of America on a daily basis, the death toll would have been astronomical. Factor in the right weather patterns to disperse the radiation and the fact that the mall is only fifteen minutes from the downtown areas of Minneapolis and St. Paul, and the death toll would've skyrocketed even higher. The entire country would have been put into an immediate panic, with everyone wondering if it was an isolated incident or if their town would be next."

"Was the device active?"

"Thankfully, no."

"How was it smuggled into the mall in the first place?"

"We don't know," said Hilliman. "The FBI has been poring over security footage, but they haven't come up with any leads. For all we know, it could have been broken into several pieces and then reassembled inside."

"Why do I get the feeling this isn't the end of the story?" said Harvath.

"Because it isn't," replied the president. "Bob, show him the rest of the photos." As the defense secretary slid a stack of Polaroid photos across the table the president continued, "We found these pictures in an envelope taped to the top of the Mall of America device. Apparently, we were led to the first nuke so there'd be no doubt in our minds that we are dealing with very serious players."

Harvath studied the photos, which showed similar devices placed in the trunks of cars and inside nondescript vans parked in front of recognizable landmarks in major cities like Chicago, Dallas, San Francisco, Seattle, Miami, Denver, New York, and Washington, DC. After he was finished looking at them he asked, "Are we positive that this isn't just one device that has been on a grand tour of the United States?"

"We're sure," answered the president. "Several years ago, we began helping the Russians implement a real-time computerized monitoring system to keep track of their nuclear weapons. Before that, every Russian nuclear device had a paper passport recording where and when it had been made, where it had been transported and stored, when it had undergone maintenance, and so on.

"It was in our best interest to help the Russians put into action an accounting system for their weapons, which would hopefully prevent them from falling into the hands of any third parties. It was also an opportunity to try and peek behind the curtain and see what was in their arsenal. Suffice it to say that they did everything they could to limit our access to sensitive information. One of our operatives, though, did come across a list of weapons from the early eighties that had been exported to undisclosed locations outside of the USSR."

"And were those weapons suitcase nukes?" asked Harvath.

"Correct," responded the president. "By enhancing the photos we could clearly make out the serial numbers. They're a match for the ones on our Russian manifest."

"How many devices were listed as exported on that manifest?"

"Twenty-five."

"How many pictures were in the envelope?" asked Harvath as he reexamined the photos in front of him.

"Nineteen."

"So with the Mall of America device, that makes twenty. What about the other five from the Russian manifest? Do we believe those devices are also in the United States?"

"They could be," said the president. "Or they could be in major cities of our international allies."

"Why? Concurrent strikes?"

"Or, more likely, to be used as a means of dissuading our allies from coming to our aid."

"Coming to our aid for what?" asked Harvath.

The president removed a folded piece of paper from inside his suit coat and handed it to him. "It was slid in between briefing papers I received from the National Security Council. And before you say anything, it is being vigorously investigated, but no, we don't have a single lead at this point."

Harvath didn't allow his face to reflect the utter shock he was feeling as he read the letter.

President Rutledge:

By now you have authenticated the device we strategically placed within your Mall of America and you have seen a representative sampling of the other weapons we have at our disposal. These weapons have been repositioned throughout your country where they will be guaranteed to wreak the most physical and psychological damage to the

United States. Neither small town, nor large city will be spared the horror of nuclear destruction. Americans will be forced to live in fear, never knowing where the next device will be detonated. The realization that no place in your country is safe will soon impact every American.

The era of arrogance and America's misguided international policies has come to an end. In your State of the Union address on January 28, you will announce to the world that the United States has seen the error of its ways and is removing itself from global politics to focus upon pressing domestic issues. In addition to removing all of your forward-deployed troops on the Korean Peninsula, Iraq, Afghanistan, and elsewhere, you will close down all of your International Development Missions, will surrender all of your seats at the United Nations, and will immediately divest the United States of any involvement with any of the organizations listed at the end of this letter.

If you have not made this announcement in full within the first three minutes of your State of the Union address next week, a device will be detonated promptly at 9:05 eastern time, and every hour thereafter, until you come to your senses or America lies in smoldering ruins.

So has the world and the balance of power changed. Pitiable is the leader who does not know when he is beaten and arrogantly leads his people into the mouth of the abyss itself.

Sincerely,
The New Union of Soviet Socialist Republics

As Harvath finished reading the list of international organizations at the end of the letter, which included, among many others, the International Monetary Fund, the World Bank, the World Trade Organization, and the G-8, he said, "This is insane. What they're talking about is tantamount to economic suicide."

"And that's what the Russians want," replied the defense secretary. "The business of America *is* business. It's not our military that makes us strong, it's our economy. Take that away and we'd have no military. We'd have nothing."

"But if the U.S. even hinted at such an isolationist policy, we'd be done for. Confidence in everything we stood for would evaporate. Faith in our currency, our economy, even our way of life would fail. Our markets would collapse and we'd be plunged into an economic winter that would never thaw."

"Exactly," said Hilliman.

Harvath couldn't believe he was having this discussion. "Not only is this whole thing insane, but there is no way they could ever get away with it. You've spoken with the Russian president about this already I assume."

"I was on the phone to him the minute we verified the device was one of theirs," answered President Rutledge. "We spoke again when I received the letter."

"And?" said Harvath expectantly.

"And he said very much what we thought he would say. After we gave him the serial number from the device at the Mall of America, he looked into it and called us back. He claims the suitcase nuke was a regrettable loss from a storage facility raided three years ago by Chechen rebels, the fashionable Russian scapegoats. He claimed the Chechens must have sold the nuke to a terrorist enemy of the United States. The thing is, because of the Russian manifest we have, we know the device was never anywhere near that storage facility and that it couldn't have been stolen three years ago because it hasn't been in Russia in at least twenty."

"So he's lying," said Harvath.

"But, why is he lying?" responded the president. "Is he lying because he's embarrassed that Russia lost a nuclear device, which has turned up in a plot against the United States or is it something else?"

"What did he say about the letter?"

"He denied any knowledge of it and said that it was regrettable that a terrorist organization was claiming to be operating under the mandate of reestablishing the Soviet Union. He, of course, pledged any assistance the United States might need from Russia and asked to be kept abreast of all events as the situation developed."

"How nice of him," replied Harvath. "Do you believe him?"

"Absolutely not," said the president as he took the note back from Scot.

"Mr. President, if I may?" said Defense Secretary Hilliman.

"Please," responded the president, who folded the note and put it back inside his breast pocket.

"Agent Harvath, American intelligence, in particular the FBI, has long suspected the Russians might have smuggled man-portable nuclear weapons into the United States, but until now, we had never had any concrete evidence. We have dispatched Nuclear Emergency Support Teams to cities across the country where those photos were taken, but we're holding out little hope of uncovering any of the devices."

"Why not?" asked Harvath.

"For the same reason we haven't uncovered any over the last twenty years—they've been too well hidden, and even when they come out of hiding, the fissile material is incredibly well insulated. We've alerted law enforcement agencies to be on the lookout for suspicious activity involving the kinds of cars and trucks pictured in those Polaroids, but for all we know showing us the devices inside of cars and trucks was just a way to further throw us off the scent. Besides, every car and truck in those pictures was different and there has been nothing that the FBI can use to track even one of them down.

"As far as the Mall of America device is concerned, we've got it at a secure facility now and we're taking it apart, trying to discover if it has any sort of unique signature that could aid us in our search for the other nukes, but it's not looking good."

"Could this get any worse?" asked Harvath.

"Yes," replied the secretary. "And it has. Now comes the Gary Lawlor connection."

"If you are going to try and tell me that he is somehow aiding the Russians—"

"No, that's not why he left the country."

"He left the country? Then why is his house being watched, and why was I taken down at Frank Leighton's?"

"Agent Harvath, what I am about to tell you goes beyond top secret. You are not to discuss this with anyone other than the president or myself. Am I understood?"

"Yes, sir."

"Good. Are you familiar with the code names *Last Dance* and *Dead Hand*?"

"Of course. Last Dance was our code name for the procedure that would automatically launch our nuclear missiles at Russia if they ever struck us first. They had the same setup in case we ever preemptively struck them, which was called Dead Hand. The guarantee that either side would always retaliate with overwhelming force is what gave birth to the acronym MAD—mutually assured destruction—but we haven't threatened the Russians, so what's the point of all this?"

"The point could be one of two things," said the secretary. "Either we really are dealing with a terrorist organization that wants to strike fear into the heart of every American while simultaneously turning us against an old enemy who, at best, has been a very shaky ally, or this is a bona fide move by the Russians to try to finally win the Cold War."

"If it was the latter, that would explain their be-

havior over the last couple of years. They did everything they could to keep us out of Iraq. They've
gone to insane lengths to help the Iranians with
their nuclear program. I can't think of much of anything the Russians have done in recent memory
that wasn't directly opposed to our international
policies. In fact, their behavior has actually been
pretty arrogant, especially in light of the deplorable
state of their own country."

"Agreed," responded Hilliman.

"But even so," continued Harvath, "we still have
a ton of ICBMs with some damn sharp tips, and
though we don't talk about it much anymore, mutually assured destruction is just as real now as it
was twenty years ago. Nothing has changed."

"What if it has?" asked the secretary. "We know
the Russians still have sleeper agents here in the
United States. For every Aldrich Ames and Robert
Hanssen, there could be God only knows how many
others we have never gotten wise to. If Russia
wanted to hold us hostage, all they would have to
do is strategically place their man-portable nukes
around the country and let us know that we had the
proverbial gun to our heads. We'd go looking for
the devices, but if they were well hidden enough
and we couldn't find them in time, tens if not hundreds of thousands, even millions of Americans
could be killed."

"But we would retaliate," responded Harvath
with even more conviction. "And our allies would
retaliate, even if devices were detonated in their

cities. The Russians would be signing their own death warrant. We'd wipe their country off the face of the earth."

The president looked at Harvath and said, "What if we'd lost the ability to respond with conventional nuclear weapons?"

"Mr. President," replied Harvath, "I don't understand. Are you saying that somehow the Russians have gained control over our launch capabilities?"

"We have no idea, only suspicions at this point."

"Based on what?"

"As far as we're concerned," said the secretary, "the integrity of our nuclear weapons has not been compromised. Every one of them, whether they're in a silo, on board a submarine, in a secure Air Force depot, or someplace else, all check out as fully operational."

"So where do your suspicions come from?" asked Harvath.

"Over the last eight months, the Defense Intelligence Agency has been investigating what the Air Force believed to be random guidance system control problems in some of its patrol flights over the Bering Strait between Alaska and Russia."

"What kind of problems?"

"It only happened a few times, but pilots reported hitting what they referred to as an invisible wall when they were a specific number of nautical miles out into the strait. Their otherwise perfectly functioning electronic systems all began to fail and they lost control of their aircraft. The only thing that saved those planes was turning around and coming back. Since the problem could never be duplicated, we began looking into all sorts of natural phenomenon from sunspots to magnetic interference from the North Pole. Then, quite by accident we heard that the Finnish Air Force had experienced a similar problem. In fact they even lost one of their F-18 Hornets to it."

"Where did they experience their problem?" asked Harvath.

"At different spots along their border with Russia. We asked the Signal Intelligence division of the NSA to get involved and they began monitoring electromagnetic radiation, in particular radar emissions, around Russia. At the same time, we began to quietly look around for any other similar invisible walls around the former Soviet Union that either military or civilian aircraft may have come up against."

"And?"

"Apparently the Chinese, the Poles, and the Ukrainians have all encountered similar problems. When we compared the pilot accounts to the intelligence the NSA had gathered, we discovered that at the same time the pilots reported losing significant control of their aircraft, certain portions of the Russian air defense system were operating unusually."

"*Unusually?*" asked Harvath. "How?"

"The electromagnetic signature emitted by all of the radar installations within range of the incident was somehow different. The NSA people couldn't explain it. All they could say was that the anomaly was present in all confirmed cases of pilots who reported losing control of their aircraft near Russian airspace."

"My God," breathed Harvath, "if this is some sort of new technology and it could be applied to missiles as well, the Russians would be virtually—"

"Impervious to attack," said the president, finishing his sentence for him.

"What if it doesn't guard against missiles?"

"Based on the sophistication that we've seen," replied Hilliman, "we're assuming that it does. The only way to be completely sure would be to launch a strike of our own and at this point we can't justify that."

"But they're holding a nuclear knife to our throats."

"That's where this gets tricky," said Hilliman. "Everything points to Russia, but it's all circumstantial. The Russian government claims they know nothing about a plot to plant enhanced suitcase nukes in different locations around the United States. Yet, when asked about one of the devices specifically, the Russian president gave us a bullshit response. The letter President Rutledge received calling for America to step off the world stage was slipped in between his briefing papers, which suggests that whoever is behind this has the ability to control someone in a not-so-insignificant position within our government. Then we add another ingredient—a number of pilots who claim to have lost control of their aircraft near Russian airspace. It's still not enough to make a case for striking first."

"Are you telling me that you're not convinced?" asked Harvath.

"No, the president and I are very much convinced."

"But if we can't launch our missiles, then we're dead in the water."

"Maybe not completely," replied the secretary. "Twenty years ago it was decided that we needed a backup for our backup. If the Russians were ever able to somehow take away our ability to launch missiles, we needed a way to rebalance the chessboard; if not entirely in our favor, then at least enough to help put us back on equal footing and reestablish the reality of mutually assured destruction. We did that by creating an operation code-named *Dark Night*—a team of twelve Army Intelligence operatives who could sneak man-portable nukes into Russia underneath their radar so to speak, and hold them hostage from within. Much in the same way we are being held hostage now."

The pictures of the men Harvath had seen in Secretary Driehaus's conference room suddenly reappeared before his eyes and though he was afraid of the answer, he asked the question anyway, "Have you activated them?"

"We have."

"And?"

"They're all dead. All except for two of them."

CHAPTER 16

Y ou've heard of the tip of the spear? Well, these guys were the bolt on the door—our absolute final line of defense," said Secretary Hilliman.

Harvath listened intently, taking in every piece of information.

"During the eighties, we had a lot of assets forward deployed in Europe. There was no point in having teams stateside that could lift off in under two hours if it was going to take at least six more to cross the Atlantic. The Dark Night operation evolved from a group of Army Intelligence operatives based in Berlin. They could not only quickly respond to terrorist incidents on the continent, but they had also been trained to blend in with the locals and organize resistance if the Soviets ever overran the wall and they found themselves behind enemy lines. They were expert marksmen, possessed exceptional language abilities, and were highly skilled in their tradecraft. In fact, the CIA used them to help train many of their own people. In short, they were not only highly trained counterterrorism operatives, but also some of the best intelligence agents the United States has ever produced. And the man in charge of them all was Gary Lawlor."

Harvath raised his eyebrows and looked as if he was about to speak, when Hilliman held up his hand and continued. "After Vietnam, Gary remained attached to Army Intelligence. He retained his rank and received four promotions as he worked his way through the FBI. As far as they're concerned it was because of his Russian skills that the government borrowed him to recruit foreign intelligence agents in Eastern Europe during the Cold War. In reality, he had been called upon by the Defense Department to assemble and coordinate the Dark Night team."

"What about Heide, his wife?" asked Harvath. "I heard a lot of things in my debriefing with Secretary Driehaus."

"She was a bona fide recruiter of foreign intelligence agents."

"So that's why she was sanctioned and not Gary?"

"Correct. But the reason she was sanctioned in the first place was because she was so good at what she did," replied the secretary.

"What about what Driehaus said about her suspicions of Gary toward the end?"

"Like I said, she was good at what she did. That also made her a good student of human behavior. In the weeks before her death, there had been a lot of suspicious activity in some of the Soviet satellites in Eastern Europe. The Russians were moving nuclear missiles into places like Prague and Budapest. Gary

STATE OF THE UNION   133

and his team were sent in to investigate. Something he did had obviously made Heide suspicious and she looked into it. She spoke with her handler, and he came back and told her he couldn't support any of what Gary had been telling her. Shortly thereafter, she was killed in the hit and run. We needed to develop a cover for Gary's actions because other U.S. agencies that had no idea what he was really up to started looking into his life. The Dark Night operation had to remain out of their reach and totally classified."

"Hence the alternate codename the president is using right now?"

"Yes."

"And this facility?"

"Was created several administrations ago in case any of our established command centers were ever compromised. It was all part of the overall plan. The need for secrecy overrode all else. Though he fought it in the beginning, Gary eventually relented and agreed to let us put together the story about Heide being on medication and fighting severe paranoia and depression to throw off the pending CIA investigation. We used one of our doctors, backdated some files, records of office visits, prescriptions, and that was that. Heide's people bought it and though Gary wasn't too happy about sullying his wife's reputation, he could see the bigger picture and went along with it."

"He has always put his country first," said Harvath.

"As did Heide, which I think was his one consolation. Somehow he knew she would understand why he had to do what he did. There was no choice. After the wall came down and Russia began to fold in on itself, we put the whole Dark Night operation out to pasture. In fact, all of the guys, except for Gary, eventually retired from the military."

"You never replaced them?" asked Harvath. "You didn't update the team with active operatives?"

"As far as the Defense Department was concerned, we had won the Cold War and the need for the team had passed."

"But you left the nukes in place."

"They were hidden well enough and it was easier to leave them there than to try and smuggle them back out. We looked at it as sort of an insurance policy. If the need ever arose, we'd have them on the continent ready to move."

"But not the men to move them."

"That," said the secretary, "was a possibility we hadn't fully considered."

"You'll have to find replacements for the Dark Night team."

"We have to tread very carefully," said Hilliman. "If this is the greatest Trojan horse in history, the Russians will be throwing everything they have into it. We know the Soviets probably have planted long-term sleepers in the U.S., but obviously we don't know where. They may be in the government, the military, or possibly even in the administration. There are very few people we can trust. Even as the FBI and CIA are looking for Gary and trying to get to the bottom of who killed those ten Army Intelligence operatives, they still don't have the full picture. We have to assume that the Russians essentially have eyes and ears everywhere."

"There's got to be some people you can trust."

"There are—to greater or lesser degrees. I have a core contingent of operatives from the Defense Intelligence Agency and if need be, I can pull from a handful of Diplomatic Security Service personnel in the countries where the nukes are and let them carry out the assignments, but we've got two pretty big problems."

"What are they?" replied Harvath.

"With the State of the Union address only a week away, we don't have very much time to train a replacement team and get them in place. And, probably the biggest problem, though we know where the nukes were hidden, we have no idea how Gary's guys planned to get them in place."

Harvath was dumfounded. "What do you mean you have no idea?"

"Operation Dark Night was established as an independent covert-action team. Everything was highly compartmentalized. In fact, the word *team* is somewhat of a misnomer. Once activated, the operatives were to go their own separate ways and the only thing they would have in common was a shared point of contact—Gary Lawlor.

"The men had access to money, safe houses, and weapons caches secreted in both Western and Eastern Europe. We have general knowledge of how the men were going to go about achieving their objectives and what their targets in Russia were, but not the nuts and bolts of their plans. Gary encouraged all of them to be highly creative in their assignments."

"So you have to coordinate with Gary."

"And he's disappeared," responded the president.

Harvath wanted to hope for the best. "Just like he was supposed to do when you activated him, correct?"

"I wish it was that simple," said the president. "A strict protocol was developed for the Dark Night operation that would allow us to maintain some semblance of control back here in Washington. Part of that protocol involved communication, and Gary has failed to check in since leaving the U.S."

"Do you think they may have gotten to him?"

"Anything's possible. No matter how you look at it, he's gone far too long without contacting us. Until we get a better handle on things, we're playing this very carefully. Especially until we figure out why they would take out everyone on the Dark Night team except for Lawlor and Leighton."

There was only one answer that seemed to make any sense to Harvath and he offered it. "Obviously the two of them must be more useful to the Russians alive than dead. But why did you place an intercept team at Leighton's house?"

"Gary was the lead member of the Dark Night team. He knows more than anybody, so we can understand why the Russians would want to take him alive, but ignoring Leighton doesn't make any sense. We were toying with the idea that maybe they just hadn't gotten around to him yet, and with the FBI sitting only a two-man team on his house until they compiled enough evidence for a warrant, we decided to deploy some of our own, more sophisticated assets there as well on the off chance we might get lucky. That's how they found you."

"Great," replied Harvath as he rubbed his ribs and tried to change the subject. "If this was classified above top secret, how did the Russians get a hold of the names and whereabouts of the Dark Night operatives in the first place? In fact, considering that the entire operation had been deactivated, why did they even bother going to all that trouble to take those men out?"

"Our best guess is that they were covering their bases. The Russian assassins were given their targets, and they carried out the sanctions," replied Hilliman.

"But how did they get the names?"

"We don't know, and at this point we don't have the resources to investigate. Our goal is to protect the American people from an impending attack and maintain the sovereignty of the United States."

"As it should be," replied Harvath. "So let's try another tack. How were the Dark Night operatives to be activated?"

"The Army maintains a database of personnel it believes possess useful skills and abilities, long after said personnel leave the Army. For example, after the terrorist attacks of September 11th, all

Special Operations personnel, especially those with Arabic language skills were contacted just to make sure the Army knew where they were in case it needed to reach them. Taking into account the considerable amount of time and money used to train these personnel, you can appreciate why we keep tabs on them even after they leave the service.

"We scrubbed the records of all the Dark Night team members clean. There was not only no mention of Dark Night involvement in their files, but there was no valid current contact information in the Army's general management system. Besides their participation in the Dark Night program, they had been involved in many other international interdictions, which made them a lot of enemies. Suffice it to say, that the United States government thought it better to conceal their whereabouts than to allow them to become public through some freedom of information error."

"So how could someone have found them?" asked Harvath.

"The president and I were made aware of the Dark Night team by our predecessors. We were told that no one else knew and that it was to remain that way."

"Well, somebody obviously found out."

"Right, which means either someone on the team talked—"

"Which is highly unlikely," interjected Harvath.

"Or, there was some other sort of breach."

"How were the men contacted?"

"To facilitate some of its more clandestine operations, the Defense Department maintains a front company out of a townhouse in Foggy Bottom called the Capstone Corporation. Capstone owns several safe houses and apartments throughout Europe, including Gary's in Berlin, which different teams have used over the years. In the basement of the townhouse is a secure computer network.

"The computer was programmed so that upon being given the command by the president, it could simultaneously contact each of the twelve Dark Night operatives via telephone. They'd be prompted to enter an authentication code, and once their identities were verified they would be activated.

"Could anyone have eavesdropped on these calls?" asked Harvath.

"No. The computer was able to detect any taps, and even if someone had found a way around it, most of the process sounded like a personal computer conducting a handshake with a server," replied Hilliman.

"Or a high-pitched fax machine on full volume?"

"Yes, but how'd you know?"

"I'm guessing Gary Lawlor placed a call to your computer in Georgetown. When I hit the redial button on his phone, I received those same tones. But you said the computer would have called him, not vice versa."

"No, our records show that Gary did call back into the system to check on the status of the other team members. As the team leader, that would have been his responsibility—to know who had been contacted and activated."

"Now I understand why Leighton called Gary's house," said Harvath. "If I had been activated after all these years, I would probably call my old team leader too before flying halfway around the world to nuke an old enemy we all thought was dead. But what about the other operatives? Does Gary know they're dead?"

"No. They were all killed before they were activated. We put out the call to activate the team, but only Leighton and Gary were alive to receive it. Based on when Gary called back into the system, all he would have known was that the rest of the team hadn't been reached yet."

"And yet whoever killed them missed Gary and Frank Leighton," mused Harvath.

Hilliman nodded his head. "Taking out ten highly trained American operatives, all of whom were scattered around the country, is no small feat. I don't care if those men were retired. They were not easy marks. Whoever did this spent a lot of time planning."

"But it still doesn't explain why they didn't take out Gary and Frank Leighton."

"There's a lot of this that doesn't make sense, Agent Harvath, and at this point we can only focus on what we know. For the sake of the United States, this mission has to succeed."

"I agree, but with ten out of twelve guys dead and Gary now missing, how can it?" asked Scot.

"That," replied the president, "is where you come in."

CHAPTER 17

At six hundred miles per hour, the luxuriously appointed Cessna Citation X, secured for Harvath by an affiliate of the Capstone Corporation, lived up to its reputation of being the fastest business jet in the world. It quickly rose to an altitude of 51,000 feet where its fuel economy could be maximized and commercial airline traffic was nonexistent. With a top speed of Mach .92, they were flying at nearly the speed of sound, screaming across each mile of the 4,100 that they needed to travel in less than six seconds apiece.

While the twin Rolls-Royce AE-3007C engines hastened the plane across the Atlantic, Harvath tried to quiet the thoughts in his mind. He had been given only a few moments to call Meg. To each of her questions he could only answer, "I can't talk about it." That hadn't sat well with her at all. When asked when he would be home, his answer followed right in the same vein, "I have no idea." Her silence on the other end was deafening. This was the real

test of their relationship. He could be called anywhere at any time to do anything, and Meg Cassidy
would just have to deal with it. Right now, though,
she wasn't dealing well with it at all. Discretion dic-
tated that he be careful how much he told her over
the phone. He wished he could share with her the
incredible importance of what he was embarking
upon, but that would have served nothing more
than to make her fear not only for his safety, but for
hers as well.

She had remained quiet, and when Scot failed to
add anything further, she said good-bye and hung
up the phone. Halfway through the flight, he realized that when she had asked him when he would
be home and he replied that he had no idea, what
he should have said was simply, "Soon. Real soon."
But of course at this point, half an hour into his
flight and over nine-and-a-half miles above the Atlantic, it was a little too late to be coming up with
the right answer. He began to wonder if Meg Cassidy would be able to weather the storms that the
demands of his career would undoubtedly visit
upon their relationship.

Harvath took a deep breath and tried to focus on
the matter at hand. The Citation X would make the
journey in less than seven hours, and he needed to
get his head in the game. As his breathing slowed,
he slipped into a Zen-like state somewhere between
sleep and wakefulness. His colleagues in the SEALs
had always remarked at his uncanny ability to slip
into this state of deep relaxation, especially before

some of their most dangerous missions. For Harvath, it was relaxing after a mission that had always been the hardest part for him. His adrenaline seemed to continue to flow for several days as his mind replayed the events his body had undergone. Relaxing and even sleeping before a mission had never been a problem for him because he realized that a sharp, focused mind was the best weapon he could bring to bear in any situation. He took full advantage of the flight to rest both his mind and his body, as he had no idea what he was in for when he landed.

After clearing customs for General Aviation, Harvath passed two rather menacing-looking, machine gun–toting border guards and made his way outside to find his cab.

Leaning against a somewhat worse-for-wear Mercedes sedan with a taxi light atop and deeply tinted windows was Harvath's old friend Herman Toffle, or "Herman the German" as he was more affectionately known. He stood at least six foot four and weighed somewhere in the neighborhood of two hundred and fifty pounds. He had dark hair, deep green eyes, and a closely cropped beard that had begun to show smudges of gray. Scot had become friends with Herman during his SEAL days when they had conducted cross-training exercises together. Herman had been a member of Germany's famed GSG9 counterterrorism unit and until a bullet injury to his leg forced him out had been legendary not only for his on-the-job bravado, but also for his sense of humor.

"Taxi, mister?" smiled Herman as he took Harvath's bag and chucked it into the trunk. Harvath slid into the back as Herman got into the driver's seat and with no ceremony whatsoever started the vehicle, lurched out of the parking space, and pointed the Mercedes toward central Berlin.

Three blocks after leaving the airport and confident they weren't being followed, Herman pulled the Mercedes into a parking garage, parked next to a large bakery van, and came around to the rear passenger-side door.

"Get out here where I can see you."

Harvath obliged and Herman immediately wrapped him in an enormous bear hug. "You've gotten smaller."

"No I haven't," said Harvath, patting his friend's stomach. "You've just gotten bigger. Your wife must be feeding you very well. How is she?"

"She's doing very well, but you didn't come to Berlin to talk about Diana."

"Not this time, my friend," said Harvath. "I'm here on a very serious operation."

"And so you said on the phone. But you're not working with the German government, at least not officially."

"Correct."

"Well, in that case," said Herman as he banged his ham-sized fist against the large bakery van they had parked next to, "I'd like you to meet a few of my distant cousins."

Harvath heard the van's door slide open and then boots hitting the ground as, one by one, a group of eight men in plainclothes rounded the van and lined up in front of him. Herman informed his friend that he had used his contacts to round up an off-duty Berlin SWAT unit specializing in hostage situations and counterterrorism operations. It was known as the *Mobiles Einsatzkommando*, or MEK for short.

"Funny, there doesn't seem to be much of a family resemblance between you and your cousins," said Harvath.

"Of course there is," replied Herman who, with a smile, opened his jacket to reveal the butts of two large semiautomatic pistols. "You just have to look closer."

In unison, the men then all drew back their winter coats as well to reveal a startling array of weaponry. Harvath had always thought that the Secret Service was good at hiding their gear, but these MEK guys were in a class all by themselves. He saw everything from Heckler & Koch MP5s and MP7s to G36-Cs, modified tactical shotguns, and even street sweepers. One thing was for certain; not only did these boys come to play, they came to win.

Scot shook hands with the men as Herman introduced them. Once the introductions were complete, the men climbed back into the van and Herman led Harvath to the trunk of his Mercedes where he popped the lid to reveal a mini-arsenal.

"I am assuming that as you are not here with the full knowledge and blessing of the German government, you didn't come armed. Would that be a reasonable assumption?"

"Very," replied Harvath.

"I figured as much. Take your pick," said Herman with a wide sweep of his hand. "We can't have you running around the streets of Berlin naked."

"You're all heart, Herman," said Harvath as he removed a .45-caliber H&K USP Tactical pistol from the trunk and pulled back the slide. "Does this model come with any upgrades?"

"Nothing but the best," answered Herman as he opened a black plastic Storm case and stood back so Harvath could choose. Scot had brought his filtered SureFire flashlight with him from home, along with his Benchmade Auto AXIS folding knife, and so bypassed Herman's selection of tactical lights, choosing instead a LaserLyte sighting system that could be mounted on the rail system beneath the USP's threaded barrel. He selected a silencer, grabbed a handful of empty clips, a box of ammunition, a brand-new BlackHawk Industries tactical holster, and a couple of flashbang grenades, and stuffed the whole lot into his pockets.

As he began walking back around the car, Herman said, "I've got body armor too."

"I don't plan on getting shot," answered Harvath.

"No one ever does. I didn't, and now everywhere I go, I'm followed by one leg that just can't keep up with the rest of me."

Scot knew his friend was right and returned to the trunk where Herman handed him a bulletproof vest from an American company called First Choice, the best body armor manufacturers in the world. The vest was made of an ultra–high molecular weight polyethylene fiber material known as Spectra. It was considered to be far superior to Kevlar because it was much lighter and with its nicely tapered edges, was much more comfortable to wear. When properly fitted, Spectra was virtually invisible under clothing. Harvath had had a lot of experience with First Choice, as it was what both the Secret Service and the president always wore.

He fastened the Velcro straps firmly around his body, and then put his three-quarter-length black leather jacket back on.

Herman took the taxi light off the top of his Mercedes and after securing everything in his trunk, pulled out of the garage with the bakery van trailing four car lengths behind.

Even though Harvath had left DC at six in the morning, with the time difference, he hadn't arrived in Berlin until just before seven p.m. local time. The weather was very much the same as in DC—overcast and cold. The temperature gauge on Herman's dash read minus nine degrees Celsius. Harvath did the math and even though he had begun his SEAL career with their cold weather detachment known as the Polar SEALs, the thought of sixteen degrees

Fahrenheit still made him shiver. He found the button for his seat warmer and set it on high.

Herman laughed, "I don't like the weather here either, that's why I live in the south. The winters in Berlin are terrible. Too damp. It's less than two hundred kilometers to the Baltic. You're lucky there was no fog. Your flight could have been delayed indefinitely. That's the problem with Berlin. You never know what the weather is going to do."

As they drove into Berlin, Scot loaded his empty magazines with .45-caliber rounds while Herman explained that he and his men had been watching Harvath from the moment he had entered the General Aviation terminal at Tempelhof Airport and had not seen anyone following him. Harvath knew that if he had had a tail, his exchange with Herman at the snack bar, establishing what was referred to in tradecraft as their respective bona fides, would have revolved around a different subject and Harvath would have left his friend there and taken a bus into the city center where they would have met at an alternate location. Such was the way fieldwork was conducted. When it came to the location of clandestine meetings, all operatives held to the acronym PACE. It stood for: primary, alternate, contingency, and emergency. There was always a backup to the backup.

Herman spoke over the radio to the MEK operatives behind them in the van as they neared the Schöneberg neighborhood where the Capstone safe house was located. One of their men had been sitting in the café up the street from the apartment building entrance and was giving the word that no one had been in or out so far this evening.

Harvath and Herman drove slowly up Goltz- strasse, while the MEK van dropped men off on ad- jacent streets to make their way to their respective entry points. They found a parking space on Pal- lasstrasse, checked their weapons, and then got out and locked the car.

The temperature had dropped at least another five degrees, and Harvath turned up the collar of his coat and tucked his head down.

As he and Herman made their way toward the safe house, Harvath's warm breath rose into the night air, moisture clinging to his eyebrows and coating them with ice.

Harvath's pulse began to quicken as they neared the front of the building. He slid his hand inside his coat and touched the butt of the H&K USP. He had no idea if they would find Gary Lawlor inside or not, but at least it was a place to start. He took one last look across the street where the bloodred color of a neon bank logo above two ATMs caught his eye. He hoped it wasn't a harbinger of things to come.

Refocusing his mind on the task at hand, Har- vath walked up to the front door of the building with Herman, who appeared to be coughing, but was discretely radioing commands over the throat mike hidden by his heavy scarf. Harvath found the nondescript keypad in the entryway and entered the five digit code that the defense secretary had given him back in DC. The heavy door clicked open and Harvath and Herman entered.

The lobby was prewar Berlin with a vintage, cage-style elevator surrounded by a twisting staircase with wrought iron railings. The yellow plaster walls were cracked and peeling, and the black-and-white tiled floor was badly in need of polishing. The marble stairs were worn from generations of use. Battered bicycles with old, shabby locks leaned against each other in a haphazard array along an alcove at the far end of the lobby. A row of tarnished mailboxes was punctuated by what appeared to be a secondhand baby carriage that its owner most likely couldn't fit into the small European elevator and had no desire to lug up God only knew how many flights of stairs.

An overpowering scent of cheap disinfectant hung in the air, and the smell reminded Harvath of some sort of third-world hospital. It was not a good thing to be reminded of before going into a potentially hostile situation.

Every move they made threatened to echo off of the lobby walls, so they took pains to move as quietly as possible. While Herman crept off to the service entrance to let in the other team members, Harvath remained in the lobby watching the front door and the stairs. He removed the sound suppressor from his coat pocket and screwed it onto the threaded barrel at the front of his pistol. He activated the LaserLyte sighting system and pointed the gun toward the floor, sweeping the beam in a wide arc across the tiles.

Herman soon returned with several of the MEK members.

"We left one man at the service entrance and we have two more on the roof, ready to rappel down," said Herman. "If anyone approaches the front door, our operative, Max, who's in the café, will let us know. Are you ready?"

"For what, I don't know, but I'm ready," replied Harvath.

"If they're holding him in there, we'll get him."

Harvath nodded his assent and Herman gave a series of rapid orders over his throat mike. One of the men disabled the elevator, and then the team made their way up to the third floor.

By the time he reached the final landing, Herman was breathing heavily, but it was obvious from the look in his eyes that he was thrilled to be back in the game. Harvath wished he could share the same level of enthusiasm. He hadn't told his old friend the full story of why he had come to Berlin. He couldn't. All he was able to tell Herman Toffle, former GSG9 counterterrorism operative, was that he needed his help and that he would have to trust him, which he did. A combination of Herman's word and the reputation of Scot Harvath in the international Special Operations community was all that was needed to get the MEK men on board. If the truth be told, German Spec Ops operatives were

no different from their American counterparts—if
there was an opportunity for a little excitement,
they were all over it.

The lead MEK agent, a very muscular man of
medium height named Sebastian, waved over one of
his operatives and instructed him to feed their
snake—a long fiber optic camera—underneath the
door and into the apartment to give them an idea of
what might be waiting for them on the other side.
The operative slid the snake slowly into the apartment and spent several moments looking into the
monocle viewfinder before raising his head and giving Sebastian the all clear.

Sebastian tested the doorknob to see if it was
locked and then motioned to Herman, who radioed
the men on the roof to get ready. The plan was that
they would rappel down and smash through two
windows in the rear of the apartment at precisely
the same moment as the rest of the team came
through the front door. After a final check with
their man, Max in the café, Herman began counting
backward from five in German, "*Fünf, vier, drei, zwei,
eins, null!*"

At the zero mark, the team sprang. One of Sebastian's men had a mini–battering ram and with one
blow, shattered the lock and flung the door wide
open. With their weapons drawn, the men charged
into the apartment, right as their teammates from the
roof came crashing through the rear windows. Everything had been orchestrated with absolute perfection.
The team fanned out, clearing the rooms in a matter

STATE OF THE UNION   153

of seconds, but there was no sign of Gary Lawlor.

Harvath began moving from room to room, looking for any clue that Gary had been there or might have left some indication as to where he was going or where he might be, but there was nothing.

Several of the men sat down in the small living room and began disassembling their weapons. As Harvath entered, he noticed Sebastian, the team leader, standing next to a bookcase near the front windows. As Sebastian removed one of the books from the shelf, Harvath noticed a red-dot trace along the wall.

"Get down!" he roared as he leapt across the room.

The pinpoint-targeting device came to rest square in the center of Sebastian's chest and the chance that it had come from the laser site of one of his team members was all but impossible. They were professionals through and through, and would not have played games like that.

As he knocked into Sebastian, Harvath's highly attuned senses heard the crack of glass, followed by the sensation of being pounded in the chest three times in quick succession by a sledgehammer.

Before he and Sebastian had completely rolled to the safety and cover of a nearby sofa, the room was awash in a sea of splintering wood and crumbling plaster.

"Where is the shooter?" Harvath heard one of the MEK operatives yell in German as he quickly re-assembled his weapon.

"Across the street," responded another who had powered up his night vision goggles and was sneaking a peek out the window. "On top of the roof."

As the rest of the men crawled over beneath the windowsill and readied to take up firing positions, Harvath's pain receptors kicked in and he began clawing at his bulletproof vest. His left side was completely on fire. It felt as if a pair of branding irons were searing into his skin.

He reached underneath his coat and unfastened the Velcro straps, which secured the vest in place. He pulled the chest portion away from his body, but the burning continued. His fingers shot frantically inside, trying to assess his injuries, but touching his left side only made things worse.

Sebastian's men were already at the window, showering the roof of the building across the street with hot sheets of silenced lead as Harvath struggled to get out of his leather jacket. He was able to slide his right arm out with little difficulty, but when he moved to free his left arm, his ribs erupted in even more pain. It was the same area that had been repeatedly kicked by his interrogator before the president had called off Defense Secretary Hilliman's DOD attack dogs.

With the jacket hanging off his left shoulder, Harvath gave up on trying to take it the rest of the way off and reached as far as he could around his left side to see if he was bleeding. He drew his hand back and looked at it. *No blood.*

A hail of brass shell casings fell all around him

and the air was thick with the smell of cordite as the MEK operatives continued firing at the roof across the street. Harvath wrestled with the vest until he was finally able to slide out from underneath it and then laid there panting, only able to gulp in short, painful gasps of air. Turning the body armor inside out, he noticed that two of the three rounds had actually penetrated the Spectra, but had been stopped short of entering his body. He offered up a silent thanks to Herman Toffle for insisting he wear it.

Taking the sniper fire full force to his side had knocked the wind out of him, and so Harvath focused on his breathing until he slowly got it back under control. He then did a more thorough triaging of his injuries and decided that he had probably received a severe bruising, or worse, several cracked ribs. From his combat medical training, Harvath knew the biggest risk from broken ribs was puncturing a lung. He drew in another painful breath of air and was confident that though it hurt like hell to breathe, neither of his lungs had been punctured. As far as a course of action for his ribs was concerned, there was nothing that could be done. While some people might tape or wrap damaged ribs, all it served to do was remind you of your injury. Harvath didn't need any extra reminders, he was sure the pain would be reminder enough.

Several of the MEK operatives had already left the apartment in pursuit of the shooter across the street when Sebastian made his way over to Harvath and helped him to his feet. Sebastian was a man of few words. He offered a simple *thank you* and Harvath shook his hand in return. Herman Toffle, on the other hand, was anything but a man of few words.

"What the hell is going on? It looks like your friend is in more than just a little bit of trouble," said Herman as he limped over to Harvath on his bad leg. "I know you agreed to pay for the beer tonight, but that's not going to be enough for Sebastian and his people now. Look at this place."

Harvath ignored Herman as he worked one of the bullets out of his Spectra vest.

"Are you listening to me?" continued Herman. "Why would a sniper have been staking out this apartment?"

"Whoever it was, that was no ordinary sniper," replied Harvath, holding up the bullet he had retrieved from his body armor. "Nine millimeter. Full-metal jacket."

"*Nine millimeter?*" said Herman as he accepted the round from Harvath and held it up to get a better look at it. "Why not use a high-velocity rifle round like a 308 or 223?"

"Because the shooter wasn't using a rifle."

"Why not? Why take the time to stake out the apartment, but not bring the right equipment?" asked Herman as he handed the round back to Harvath.

"Who said he didn't bring the right equipment? Nine millimeter is a very fast round. With a ported silencer and a bipod, even a small weapon can be very effective at this range. This is a narrow street. The shot wouldn't have been that hard. And the best thing about a small weapon is that it's extremely easy to conceal."

"Even with body armor on, that was a very brave thing you did," said Herman.

"I reacted, that's all."

"Well, call it what you will, but I'm sure Sebastian appreciates it."

"He would have done the same thing for me."

"I'd like to think so. He's a good man. That's why I asked for his help. Now, tell me, did you have any idea the apartment was being watched?" asked Herman, his eyes searching Harvath's for any indication that he might not be telling the truth.

"Of course not. I told you everything I knew," Scot replied.

"About the apartment, but not about your friend. All you said was that he had gone missing and you had reason to believe he might be being held against his will in here."

"That's true."

"What about the rest of it? Who is this friend of yours and what was he up to?"

Harvath had hoped things wouldn't come to this. Herman had agreed to help him, no questions asked, but being ambushed by the sniper had now altered the arrangement and Harvath knew it.

"All I can tell you is that he is one of the good guys and we need to find him very soon," said Scot.

"Or else what?" asked Herman, not happy that his friend was keeping him in the dark.

"Suffice it to say that there is a very serious time element at work here and an incredible amount of lives hang in the balance."

"Yet you're not working with the German government."

"I told you, the assignment is too sensitive. I brought you in because I knew I could trust you."

"But not with the full picture," responded Herman as he massaged his forehead with the broad palm of his hand.

Harvath remained quiet.

"I understand that in this business secrets must be kept, sometimes even between good friends, but Sebastian and his people don't know you; not like I do," said Herman. "They are doing this as a favor to me and they are going to want answers—answers that I'm not equipped to give them. What am I supposed to say?"

"I don't know," answered Harvath, just as frustrated as Herman. "There's got to be something here. Something that someone didn't want us to find."

"That, or they knew people were going to come looking for your friend and they wanted to stop them."

"Either way, we've got to search the apartment again."

"Well, we'd better search fast. According to Sebastian, the Polizei are already on their way."

CHAPTER 18

After another quick search of the apartment proved fruitless, Harvath, Toffle, and the rest of the MEK operatives had quietly stolen out of the building and fanned out in separate directions just as the first police cars began arriving on the scene to secure both ends of the Goltzstrasse.

Two hours later, they had met back up at their prearranged rallying point—a half-empty Bierstube on the eastern side of the city.

Sitting with the men at a quiet table in back, Harvath stared blankly at the old German movie posters covering the walls, stained a deep yellow from years of nicotine accumulation. He couldn't help but feel that he had let Lawlor down by not finding anything of use in the apartment.

The men made small talk as they unwound and kept the waitress busy going back and forth for beers and shots of Jägermeister. The cold, caramel-colored liquor warmed Harvath's stomach and, mixed with the strong German beer, was beginning to deaden the throbbing pain coursing up and down his left side. It felt like he had been hit by a tank.

His mind drifted to what Meg had said back in his apartment in Alexandria. The idea that Harvath might have devoted most of his adult life chasing the elusive respect of his father was something he didn't feel comfortable wrestling with. That in turn made him wonder about Meg. Things had moved quickly between them, and he began to wonder if maybe they had moved along too quickly. A feeling of hopelessness was beginning to well up inside him. Suddenly, he caught himself. *What the hell was he doing?* This wasn't like him. He needed to get his head back in the game. *Concentrate on the assignment,* he told himself. People always leave clues—it's just a matter of looking hard enough until you find them. He needed to uncover a lead, something that would help them find Gary.

Sebastian was talking on his cell phone as Herman raised his empty glass to get the waitress's attention and said, "What do you want to do next?"

"What can we do?" replied Harvath. "The way I see it, the only option we have now is to canvass the neighborhood and see if anyone remembers seeing Gary."

"That's a lot of work," said Herman, "and it could draw a lot of attention."

"It might not be necessary," said Sebastian, folding up his phone and placing it back in his pocket.

"Why not?" said Harvath.

"You'll see. Follow me."

As Harvath stood in the parking lot behind the Bierstube, he tried to find some way of keeping warm other than stomping his feet, which sent shudders of pain through his left side. Sebastian explained that he had been on his cell phone with his operative from the café across from the Capstone apartment building. Apparently, the man had something he wanted them to see. When Harvath asked what it was, Sebastian smiled and held up his index finger in a gesture that said, "Be patient."

Moments later, a pair of bright halogen headlights came slicing into the lot and headed right toward them. They belonged to a brown BMW, which skidded to a stop directly in front of where they were standing. The driver climbed out of the car, walked over and shook hands with Sebastian and Herman. They spoke in rapid-fire German that was too fast for Harvath to understand. Finally, the driver motioned for Harvath to follow him.

"Sorry to have missed all the fun," said the man, with only a trace of a German accent, as they walked around to the trunk of his car. "My name is Max."

"Nice to meet you," said Harvath as they shook hands.

When they reached the trunk, Max pressed a button on his keyless-entry device and the trunk popped open.

Harvath leaned forward to peer inside only to have Max say, "Be careful, he bites. Although we are working on that, aren't we, Heinrich?"

The man lying on the floor of the trunk was dressed like a waiter, and as he began to sit up he let loose with a string of colorful German expletives, most of which, from what Harvath could gather, were directed at Max's mother.

Max responded by slamming the lid of the trunk down on Heinrich's head.

"What's this all about?" asked Scot, as Max raised the lid again, revealing a somewhat stunned Heinrich who looked like he was ready to shoot his mouth off again, yet might be thinking better of it.

Max leaned in and grabbed Heinrich's face between his thumb and forefinger, squeezing the man's lips into a tight pucker that made him look like a fish. "Heinrich has a little present for you."

"Let me guess. Did he see something?"

"Oh, he certainly did. You see, Heinrich is a waiter at a certain café on Goltzstrasse, and it turns out we used to know each other from the days when I investigated narcotics. He told me he was clean, but based on what I found in his pockets, I think he may be telling an untruth."

Harvath looked hard at Heinrich and then shifted his gaze to Max. "And?"

"And, well, Heinrich came on duty right when I was preparing to leave. Everyone in the café was watching the policemen outside and talking about what had happened. When Heinrich saw me, he tried to sneak back into the kitchen, but seeing as how we are old friends, how could I pass up such a wonderful opportunity to get reacquainted? For some reason, Heinrich was acting very nervous, so I helped him into the men's room where I went through his pockets and found that he was not as clean as he claimed to be. Isn't that right, Heinrich?" said Max as he used his free hand to pat the man firmly on the head where even Harvath could see a very nasty lump was already rising.

"In the course of our conversation," continued Max, "he asked me why the police had been spending so much time hassling people on the Goltzstrasse. When I asked him to be more specific he told me that yesterday he saw two policemen staking out the apartment building up the street and that they had eventually busted some businessman by zapping him with a Taser. They then cuffed him, threw him into the back of their car, and sped away."

Harvath couldn't believe what he was hearing. "What did the man look like?"

Heinrich, happy to spit out what he knew and hopefully get away from Max, said, "He looked like a businessman in a suit with a long overcoat. Okay?"

"More," said Harvath. "Height, age, weight, hair color . . ."

"Gray hair. He was an older man. Maybe he was in his late fifties or early sixties. I am not sure. He was medium height and not thin, but not fat either. That's all I know."

Harvath pumped him with further questions

and listened as Heinrich the junkie waiter repeated the same story he had told Max.

"Is it common for German police to subdue suspects with stun guns?" asked Harvath.

"I don't know," said Heinrich scared of what might happen if he didn't answer every question the American was asking.

"He wasn't talking to you, *Dummkopf*," said Max, slapping him in the head. "He was talking to me." Turning toward Harvath, he said, "No. Using a stun gun to subdue a suspect is very unusual. That's why I thought you might want to hear Heinrich's story for yourself and have a chance to ask him questions. Do you have anything else?"

Harvath asked Heinrich to describe the "policemen" and their car. The waiter gave the best description he could, stating that he did not really get a good look at anything. The car might have been a Volkswagen, or it could have been a Mercedes. He couldn't tell. As far as the license plate was concerned, he hadn't bothered taking a very good look at it. What was the point? Besides, the car pulled out and took off so fast, he wouldn't have been able to see anything if he wanted to. The cops had been in such a hurry, he was surprised they hadn't broadsided anyone when they tore through the intersection at the end of the block.

When Harvath had heard enough, he nodded to Max that he was finished. Heinrich knew what was coming and flattened himself down in the trunk just as Max slammed the lid shut.

Just in case Heinrich might be listening, Herman drew the men several yards away from the car so they could talk. "Now we know at least part of what happened to your friend."

"Those guys obviously weren't cops and to go to that great a risk in broad daylight," said Max, shaking his head, "someone must have wanted your friend very badly."

"I agree. So, what do you want to do?" asked Sebastian.

"If Heinrich saw something, chances are somebody else did as well," replied Harvath.

"Like what?" said Herman "Something that looked like a police arrest? Even if we could find witnesses, they will have their own version of what happened. You know how these things go. People subconsciously color events with their own details—things they thought they saw. At best, we might get a partial description of the men who jumped your friend."

"Or maybe a partial license plate," responded Harvath.

Herman rubbed his forehead again with the butt of his hand before responding. "I think the odds are not in our favor."

Harvath was getting progressively more frustrated. "*Not in our favor?* I don't know how you conduct investigations in Germany, but—"

"The police conduct investigations," answered Sebastian, "and they are already crawling all over that neighborhood questioning everyone about the shooting. Herman is right. The odds of finding someone with something of value are not in our favor. Witnesses are too unreliable."

Harvath told himself to calm down. He knew that often his temper could get the better of him. These men were on his side. They had stuck their necks out to help him and he needed to bear that in mind. There had to be something they could do. Seeing red was not going to help. Then it hit him! *Seeing red.*

"What about video?"

"*Video?* What video?"

"There was a bank across the street from the apartment. They had two ATM machines outside with a red logo above them. What about their security footage?"

"You mean footage from cameras positioned to monitor people going in and out of the bank and using the ATMs?"

"Yes."

"I would imagine the footage would only show people going in and out of the bank and using the ATMs."

"But it might show something else."

Herman shook his head. "It's a long shot."

"At this point, a long shot is all we have," said Harvath.

"He may be right," said Max. "Many of the security cameras now incorporate improved wide-angle lenses with increased depth of field. In case of a robbery, there's a lot more information available on what was happening outside the bank, such as where the escape vehicle was parked, which direction it took, and so on."

"Speaking of which," said Harvath, glad that his theory was gaining ground, "what about the traffic cameras at both intersections on Goltzstrasse?"

"Those I am not so sure of," responded Max. "They only activate when a traffic violation has taken place and they are limited to photographing the vehicle while it is in the intersection."

"But it sounds like the car we're looking for may have committed a traffic violation leaving the scene," said Harvath.

"It's possible," replied Max.

"Of course it's possible, especially if they were in a hurry. With a snatch and grab, the key is to get away as fast as possible. You don't wait around for anything. You want to get the hell out of there."

"But even if we did agree with you about the footage," said Herman. "How are we going to get access to it?"

"That's simple," said Max with a smile, anticipating the challenge. "We'll go in and take it."

"Absolutely not," replied Sebastian, who turned his attention to Harvath. "I appreciate what you did for me in the apartment and I don't want you to doubt that, but this has become very dangerous. What we did for you, we did as a favor to Herman and that favor is now over. Without some clear and evident threat to German national security, there is nothing else we can do for you."

Harvath had known that this moment would come. He had been trying to figure out exactly what, and how much, he could tell Herman and the rest of the MEK operatives to extend their cooperation, but not jeopardize his assignment. As he stood facing Herman, Sebastian, and Max, he made a decision. It was the moment of truth, or half-truth at least. He carefully reviewed in his mind what he was going to say and offered, "The United States is being faced with a very serious and imminent terrorist action that is to take place in less than seven days. The man I came looking for has information that could help prevent that attack. The terrorists know this and we believe that is why he was kidnapped."

"What kind of attack are we talking about?" asked Sebastian.

"Something very big that will happen in several different U.S. cities on the same day."

"And what is the threat to Germany?"

"There is a remote chance the terrorists may have plans to target the major cities of our allies as well."

"Do you know who the terrorists are?" asked Herman.

Though he hated to do it, he had to. Harvath looked his friend right in the eye and kept on lying. "No, we have no idea."

"So," continued Sebastian, "you are saying that there may or may not be plans to launch a major terrorist action within the Federal Republic of Germany by a group of unknown persons sometime within the next seven days?"

"Yes."

"Why hasn't your government shared this information with us?"

"Because it's highly speculative as to the risk Germany faces."

"How speculative the risk should be up to us to ascertain."

"I agree, which is why I am telling you this."

"In all fairness, you haven't told us much," replied Herman.

"You now know what we know. Listen, this whole thing can be derailed if we locate the man I am looking for."

"Who is he?"

"I can't say."

"Can't say, or won't say," queried Sebastian, "because I have to have more than you've given me if I am going to authorize any more cooperation."

Harvath met Sebastian's gaze and realized he was going to have to give the man something substantial. "His name is Gary Lawlor."

The three men standing in front of him were stunned.

"The deputy director of the FBI?" asked Herman.

"Former deputy director," replied Harvath, "He now heads a new division of our Department of Homeland Security called the Office of International Investigative Assistance."

"What does this office do exactly?"

"Their mission is to help solve and prevent terrorist acts against Americans and American interests both at home and abroad."

"And your connection here is?"

"Gary Lawlor is my new boss," said Harvath, hoping that the bone he had thrown them had enough meat on it to make them happy.

"So no more Secret Service?" asked Herman.

"No more Secret Service," responded Harvath.

"I guess that will have to do for now," said Sebastian.

"So you're in?" replied Harvath.

"Yeah, we're in. Here's what I am prepared to do. Since we are apparently going to continue without official sanction, I want this contained. If it blows up in our faces, I don't want to drag my entire team down. I will let the rest of the men go. Max and I will get a hold of the bank and traffic footage—"

"How do you plan on doing that?" asked Harvath.

"I think we'll let the police do it for us."

"Won't they be suspicious of the involvement of two MEK operatives?"

"Not if they think we're fellow investigators," said Max as he fished a set of authentic-looking credentials out of his pocket that identified him as a special federal investigator.

Sebastian walked over to Max's BMW and as he opened the door and climbed into the passenger seat, said over his shoulder, "We'll call you on Herman's cell phone as soon as we have everything and tell you where to meet us."

Max followed, slapping the side of the trunk to make sure Heinrich hadn't fallen asleep and said, "Time to get back to work, Liebling."

Moments later, all that was left in the parking lot was a pair of tire tracks in the light snow that had begun to accumulate.

"Back inside?" asked Herman.

"No. I've got someplace else in mind."

"Really? I didn't think you knew Berlin very well."

"Actually," responded Harvath, "I don't. This is a place a friend of mine used to frequent. Let's get going. I'll explain in the car."

CHAPTER 19

AIDATA ISLAND, GULF OF FINLAND

rank Leighton had called the number from his satellite phone two times more than he probably should have. Nothing was making sense. He was completely isolated. He had had no human confirmation of his assignment at all and that made him even less comfortable than he already was about what he was preparing to do. If his handler failed to make contact, he would have no choice but to assume the worst and put the final plan into action. He would get the device as close as he could to his target, set the timer, and run like hell. God, he hoped it wouldn't come to that.

Once again he heard the words as if they had just been spoken to him, "The protocol is infallible. The protocol will never be wrong." Frank Leighton had been trained to follow through on his orders and that was exactly what he was going to have to do. Still, if he could just get some sort of confirmation . . .

There was no choice but to slam the iron door

back down on his misgivings and focus his energy on the task at hand. According to his initial readings, the device was still stable even after all these years. Good, that only helped to make his job that much easier. He didn't want this to turn into a suicide mission.

Leighton used nothing more than the light from a filtered headlamp to illuminate the rocks he was clearing to create a makeshift path down to the beach. Once the slope was clear, he unpacked what could best be described as a child's wagon on steroids. The lightweight, brushed-aluminum cart boasted knobby rubber tires attached to a sophisticated air shock suspension system. Frank Leighton wasn't leaving anything to chance.

He loaded the wagon with stones, equivalent in weight to the deadly payload he knew he would soon have to transport, and maneuvered it down to the beach where his dinghy was moored. He went back and forth several times, memorizing the terrain, paying close attention to every potential pitfall until he knew it well enough to make the trip with his eyes closed..

His task complete, he disassembled the wagon, covered over its tracks, and rowed the dilapidated dinghy back out to the rusting fishing trawler. On board, he brewed a small pot of strong Finnish coffee and prepared a meal of pea soup, rye bread, herring, and pickled cucumbers. His training had taught him that food was a cover just as important as being able to speak the local language. While it might seem strange to the uninitiated, a good operative knew that mankind still relied on its sense of smell, though not nearly as much as other senses. Many Special Forces soldiers in Vietnam were convinced that their ability to elude detection came in part only after they began eating, and thereby smelling, like their enemy. The additional benefit of eating like a local was that should the galley of the trawler ever be searched, it would yield nothing out of the ordinary.

He took his meal to the wheelhouse and listened to the marine radio chatter of lonely Finnish and Russian fishermen plying the cold Baltic Sea. Several men spoke of an approaching storm, and Leighton felt a chill as a gust of wind found its way through a poorly insulated gap between two of the windows. He was glad he didn't have to be out there tonight, but at the same time, he dreaded how soon he would have to move. He decided to try to make contact one more time.

CHAPTER 20

SOMEWHERE OUTSIDE ZVENIGOROD, RUSSIA

It had taken Milesch Popov two years to find the weapon he now held in his hand. He had been watching an American documentary on modern-day gangsters when he first saw it—the Thompson ZG-51 Pit Bull. The .45-caliber pistol was the rage with all the high-level crime kingpins in East L.A. While lesser wannabe gangsters were running around with their nine millimeters, classy, more self-confident original gangsters were fully strapped with Pit Bulls, complete with a depiction of the notorious dog.

Popov had an engraver give the pit bull on the pistol's slide a huge set of balls. Then, carved right in front of the animal, was the outline of a naked woman on her hands and knees with a huge set of tits covered by the letters O.G., for original gangster. What Popov lacked in class, he definitely made up for in creativity.

As he pulled back the slide of his Pit Bull to chamber a round, Popov made a mental note to invoice Stavropol for this recent purchase of custom ammunition. After all, it was a legitimate expense, one which Popov couldn't imagine conducting his business without. The armor-piercing rounds were made from hardened machined steel that had been hand-dipped in Teflon. With his enemies relying more and more on heavily armored cars and bullet-proof vests, complete with titanium trauma plates over their hearts, he needed every advantage he could get.

The armor-piercing rounds had become his signature and though they did seem a bit of an overkill for what he was about to do, he had modeled his career on the old Russian proverb *While fame travels slowly, at least notoriety travels fast*. The runaway orphan from Nizhnevartovsk had learned much during his short time in this world.

The missing general had been easier to find than Popov had expected—though he wouldn't inform his current benefactor of that fact. No, he would let the famous General Sergei Olegovich Stavropol believe that he had moved heaven and earth to track down his quarry. In reality, it had been as simple as driving to certain shops in and around Zvenigorod, making inquiries.

After having examined the empty grave at the hunting lodge, Popov had decided to operate under the assumption that General Anatoly Karganov was indeed wounded, but not dead. Either he had escaped under his own power, or someone had helped him. Under the circumstances, Karganov would not have been able to return home. It would have been too dangerous. In fact, if his injuries were serious enough, he might not have been able to travel very far at all.

At the very least, Karganov probably would have needed some sort of medical attention. With this in mind, Popov had visited not only every physician, but also every veterinarian within a fifty-kilometer radius. Popov had a way of making most people, especially hardworking law-abiding citizens, feel uncomfortable around him. Maybe it was his slightly repugnant, street-savvy demeanor or the way his eyes held you in their gaze and never let go that made most people automatically assume he was a special investigator or some other State law enforcement officer. Not one soul bothered to ask him for identification. His suit alone, hell, even his shoes, cost more than what most of the people in the Odinstovo area saw in an entire year. Whoever he was, Milesch Popov was important and conveyed the distinct impression that failing to cooperate with him brought with it a slew of undesirable consequences.

When the physician and veterinarian trail went cold, Popov moved to the next item on his checklist—stores that sold any type of medical supplies. He left no stone unturned. If a shop carried anything that even remotely resembled what he was looking for, he paid them a visit.

It was at the end of a very long day, when most of the shops were preparing to close, that his efforts appeared to be finally paying off. *"Dobri vyecher,"* he said in an officious tone to the aging shopkeeper, as he scanned the provincial pharmacy's scantily stocked shelves. "Do you sell bandages?"

"*Da*," replied the old man, pointing to where the bandages were.

"And antibiotics?"

"*Da*," repeated the old man as he came around the counter to help direct his wealthy young customer.

"How about antiseptic?"

"We're all out," said the man as he shook his head.

When Popov asked him why he didn't have any antiseptic on hand, the shopkeeper explained that a young woman had come in and bought all that he had. She had also bought several boxes of bandages and a healthy amount of antibiotics.

Immediately, Popov's interest was piqued and his questions began flowing. *Did the shopkeeper recognize her?* No, he didn't. *Was she local?* No, she was definitely not local. *What did she need the medical supplies for?* She didn't say. *Do you know where she is staying?* No, but he did direct her to the market around the corner where she could buy food and order firewood.

And, without so much as a "*spaseeba*," Popov was out the door and headed toward the local *rynok*.

The woman who ran the market prided herself on being well informed on everything that happened in their small village. In other words, she was an insufferable gossip. It took very little for

Milesch Popov to coax out of her the location of the
dacha where the old woman's son had delivered the
order of firewood. It was only three kilometers
away.

Popov hid his car up the road and picked his
way by foot through scrawny trees with bare, claw-
like branches to the dilapidated house. Above the
poorly shingled roof, small tendrils of smoke rose
into the sky from a rusting stovepipe. In the driveway sat a lone Lada hatchback. As Popov approached it, he withdrew his stiletto and slashed
both of the Lada's front tires. Returning the knife
to his coat pocket, Popov maneuvered himself
closer to one of the dacha's rear windows to get a
good look inside.

In his thin, Italian calfskin loafers, his feet were
beyond freezing, but when he saw the man propped
upright in a small metal-framed bed with his head
wrapped turban style in a long white bandage,
Popov was suddenly infused with a surge of
warmth.

He crept a safe distance away from the house,
withdrew his cell phone, and dialed. Stavropol answered on the third ring.

"I have found your package," said Popov.

"Where?" asked Stavropol, the moan of a ship's
horn discernable in the near distance.

"Out in the countryside."

"I knew it," purred Stavropol. "Listen carefully.
I'm going to give you an address. I want you to put
the body into the trunk of your car and drive it—"

"There's a small problem."

"I paid you to find a body, not problems. Now I want you to put him in your—"

"He's alive," interrupted Popov.

"What do you mean, *he's alive?*"

"*Alive*—as in *not dead.*"

"That's impossible," snarled Stavropol.

"I was just looking at him. He's got a bandage around his head and he's sitting upright in a bed."

"Are you sure it's him?"

"Would I be calling you if I wasn't? He looks just like the picture you sent me, so either it's him, or he's got a double with a very bad head wound."

"Head wound," reflected Stavropol. "Damn it. Is he alone?"

"I don't know. I only took a quick look through the window. I think there might be a woman in there with him," replied Popov.

"I want you to find out for sure and then kill them both."

"*Kill them both?*"

"Don't act so unsettled, Milesch. I know you've killed before. That's why I chose you."

"Our deal was only that I find him," responded Popov.

"That's when we thought he was already dead."

"Well, killing him and anyone else who's with him is going to cost you more."

"How much more?" asked Stavropol, not surprised that Popov was asking for more money. Had Stavropol been closer, he would have done the job himself, but he couldn't risk losing Karganov in the time it would take him to get there. Stavropol waited longer than he should have for Popov to respond and when he didn't, he said, "Popov, are you there or not? What's going on?"

Alexandra Ivanova pressed the silencer of her nine-millimeter Walther P4 hard against the spot where Milesch Popov's left ear met his skull. The steel tube felt like ice to him, but that was only part of what made him freeze. He was absolutely amazed that anyone could have snuck up behind him. He had been so careful. Or so he had thought.

"You'll have to call them back," said Alexandra. "Drop your weapon and hang up now."

Stavropol's voice could be heard coming from the cell phone, "Milesch? Milesch? What's going on there?"

Popov didn't move. He just stood there in shock.

"No second chances," said Alexandra as she readjusted the angle of her silencer and then pulled the Walther's trigger.

There was the sound of a muffled cough and then Popov roared in pain as his earlobe was torn from his head in a spatter of blood and pink tissue. Both his weapon and the cell phone fell to the ground as his hands shot to the left side of his head, frantically searching for what was left of his ear.

Stavropol's voice could still be heard shouting through the cell phone, "Popov! Popov! What's happening?"

Alexandra shattered the phone with a bullet and then gave Popov a quick kick to the back of one of his knees, knocking him down. As he clutched desperately at his ear, the snow running red with his blood, Alexandra retrieved his Pit Bull and ordered him to get up.

"Over to the car," instructed Alexandra, waving her Walther in the direction of the Lada. "Hands on the hood. Let's go. Legs spread apart—wide."

Popov did as he was told, the blood running down his neck, staining the white collar of his expensive dress shirt. "I don't know who you are—" he said as Alexandra tucked the Pit Bull underneath her jacket at the small of her back.

"*Zatknis'!*" *Shut up!* she ordered as she used her free hand to pat Popov down for additional weapons. She found the stiletto and tucked it in one of her pockets. She also found his State Inspector credentials with the name Leuchin, as well as a wallet with a driver's license under the name Popov.

"As the man you were talking to was calling you Popov," said Alexandra as she removed his handkerchief from his front pocket, "I'm guessing this State Inspector identification is a fake, and looking closer at it, a rather bad one at that. Turn around."

"I'm going to fucking kill you, you bitch!" spat Popov.

"You had your chance and you blew it, remember? Now, take your coat off."

"*Yob tvoyu mat!*"

"Fuck *my* mother?" asked Alexandra as she pointed her weapon at Popov's kneecap and fired. "No, fuck yours."

Popov fell to the ground screaming. "You bitch! You fucking bitch!"

"*Khvatit' niyt' oozhe,*" *Quit your complaining,* she said. "I only grazed your knee. Now get up and take off your jacket."

Popov struggled upright and did as he was told.

"The suit coat as well. Good. Now, throw them both off to the side."

When Popov had done what Alexandra had asked, she balled up the handkerchief and threw it at him. After he had dabbed his ear and then tied the handkerchief around his wounded knee to stem the bleeding, Alexandra waved her pistol in the direction of the cottage. "Inside," she commanded. "Let's go."

Popov led the way while Alexandra followed several paces behind, her Walther pointed right at the base of the man's spine.

They entered the small ramshackle dwelling via the kitchen door. Alexandra waved her pistol at a lone chair against the wall and said, "I want you to sit down over there and don't move."

As Popov sat down in the chair, he watched Alexandra cross to a large, cast iron stove. She deftly flicked open the grate with the toe of her boot. The fire inside had burned down to almost nothing but glowing embers. She threw in another piece of wood and kicked the grate shut. With her pistol still trained on Popov, she put one hand on the door jamb and looked into the dacha's other room to check on her patient who had just started to come around.

Satisfied that he was okay for the moment, Alexandra returned her attention to Popov. "So," she began, "you must be my repentant husband."

Popov pretended that he didn't know what she was talking about, but the look in his eyes was confirmation enough.

"That's what you told the old lady who runs the *rynok*, isn't it? We had a fight, I left Moscow to think about things for a while, but you couldn't stand us being apart any longer and wanted to find me so you could make it up to me? She bought it at first, but after you left she began to worry. What if you were coming here to do me harm? Little did she know how right she was," said Alexandra as she removed the Pit Bull from underneath her jacket, released the magazine, and ejected the chambered round.

"Armor piercing," she remarked, as she picked up the lone bullet and rolled it between her fingers. "Who the hell are you, Mr. Milesch Popov?"

Popov just stared at her as she placed his pistol and its ammunition on the top of a faded hutch resting atop an old sideboard near the stove. *How could a woman so beautiful be so vicious?* he wondered.

Long slim legs, narrow waist, ample chest, full lips, green eyes, and shoulder-length blond hair indeed made Alexandra Ivanova beautiful, very beautiful, but that beauty had often times been as much a hindrance to her as it had been an asset. Because of those startling good looks, she had had to work harder than most to earn the respect of her peers, both in the Russian Military and then later at the FSB. Too often, she was seen as just a pretty face. Her male superiors had always coveted her and she was constantly fending off their advances. More times than she cared to remember had she given herself to a man only to be betrayed in the end. They had no desire to relate to her as an equal, they only wanted to possess her as a thing, an object. She eventually decided that if given the chance, people will let you down every single time. There really was no one she could trust.

Though this attitude made for a very lonely personal life, she much preferred being in control and keeping people at a distance than opening herself up to the hurt that would certainly follow from allowing someone to get too close.

"You are going to tell me everything I want to know," she said as she kept the gun trained on him while she filled a kettle of water and placed it on the stove to make tea for herself and her patient. She had been standing outside in the cold waiting for Popov to show for quite a long time. The fire in the stove had nearly gone out and her toes were frozen completely through. There wasn't much that she hated more than the bleary Russian winters. It was no wonder that the death toll from alcoholism soared during this time of year.

"Who are you and what are you doing here?

Who were you talking to on the phone? Who sent you here?" she demanded.

"If I tell you, they'll kill me."

"If you *don't* tell me, *I'll* kill you," replied Alexandra, squeezing off a shot from her silenced Walther that splintered one of the chair's wooden slats right between Popov's legs.

He flinched and his hands instinctively went right to his crotch. He hid one behind the other and began extricating the knife hidden behind his belt buckle.

"Hands!"

"You're crazy. You know that?" said Popov, trying to buy more time.

Alexandra fired two more rounds into the chair, shaving off one of the legs and causing Popov to topple over onto the floor.

"*Ebaniy v rot!*" *Fuck*, he yelled when his shoulder slammed into the floorboards.

Alexandra didn't notice that the man failed to reach out with both hands to break his fall.

"That's it," she said. "I'm going to kill you right there if you don't tell me something of value in the next thirty seconds."

"Who the hell are you?" said Popov as he stared up at her.

"Twenty-eight, twenty-seven," continued Alexandra.

"All right, all right," offered Popov. "I was hired to find out what happened to General Karganov."

"It sounded to me like you were hired to kill him and me for that matter."

"Originally, I was hired just to find his body."

"By the people who killed him, correct?" demanded Alexandra.

"I have no idea who killed him, or tried to kill him I should say."

"Bullshit. Who hired you?"

"Please. Can't I at least sit up?" pleaded Popov. It was a voice he had not heard himself use in a long, long time. It was the voice of the pitiful, defenseless orphan, but here he thought it might work. If she thought he was defeated, broken, she might let her guard down. It only had to happen for an instant. That was all he needed and she would be dead before her body hit the floor.

"I will tell you what you need to know," continued Popov. "I just want to sit up so I can stop the bleeding."

Alexandra nodded her head and stepped back, well aware that she had already fired six of her eight shots. She didn't want to waste any more ammunition.

Alexandra set two teacups and saucers on the edge of the sideboard. She placed a tea bag in each cup and then walked slowly backward to the stove for the kettle, never taking her eyes off Popov.

She poured the boiling water into the first cup and as she began pouring it into the second, she heard her patient stir in the other room. He let out a long, struggling moan as if he was having trouble breathing.

Alexandra was so intent on the noise emanating

from the other room that she failed to pay attention to the teakettle. As the lid fell off, the scalding spray of hot water caused her to drop it and with a startled cry, snatch her burning hand to her mouth as her gun fell to the floor. It was an opportunity Popov had to take advantage of.

No second chances, he thought to himself as he shot out of his chair and went straight for Alexandra's throat. Before she knew what was happening, he was on top of her. He swung his right arm like a hammer, crashing it down onto her forearm with a force that reverberated throughout her entire body. Popov then swung the back of his left hand in a wide arc toward her face.

Even in the dull light of the kitchen, she saw the glint of the blade coming at her. Without enough time to raise her arm in a defensive block, Alexandra simply turned her head down and offered her attacker her face, rather than her throat. As unthinkable as the bargain was, it was the only thing she could do to save her life.

The blade cut into her scalp just above her temple. Hot blood rolled down her cheek and she spun her body away from Popov. As she continued to move, Popov continued thrashing at her with his blade. She put up her arms to defend herself and in a matter of seconds he had slashed her leather jacket to ribbons. In the scuffle, her gun was kicked across the floor, and she had no idea where it had gone.

Popov was in control and he knew it. Like a cat

who had cornered a field mouse and was playing with it before the final coup de grâce, he drove his beautiful blond captive into a corner of the small kitchen and wondered if maybe killing, at least her, at this point was a little premature. Surely she could be good for something else before she died. If she was good enough, maybe he'd even give Stavropol a discount on her murder.

He decided that the old adage of an eye for an eye very much applied to this situation. He would need to start by cutting off one of her ears. She would scream her pretty head off and it would be messy, but in a very perverse way, Popov thought it would be fun. In fact, it would be like the snuff film one of his underworld colleagues had once shown him. Right at the height of the action, the moment of greatest passion, the greatest pleasure, that's when he would kill her, but not before then. The buildup would be a sensually excruciating game of foreplay. He was growing hard just thinking about it—pumping the seed of life into her as the spirit of life oozed out of her.

The gun, Alexandra thought. *Where the hell was that goddamn gun?* She had to find it.

Her eyes swept left and right across the floor and then finally spotted it, sticking out from underneath the kitchen table.

She needed to draw Popov's attention away from the table, and so she raised her hands in a classic martial arts fashion.

Confident in his advantage, Popov laughed and

said, "Do you mean to do me harm, little girl?"

Alexandra hoped to unbalance him by stirring the hornet's nest. Clenching and unclenching her fists as if she was limbering up to really go at it, she said, "I don't know if your face could be any more ugly, but I'd like to give it a try."

She had hit a very raw nerve. Though Popov might appear vain, he was incredibly insecure, especially about his face. "You don't like it?" he asked. "You'd better get used to it as it is the last face you are ever going to see. In fact, before you die, I think I would like to finish what I started. I've only given you a little kiss with my knife. Soon, you two will become much more intimate and then we'll find a mirror together and decide whose face is more ugly."

Alexandra swung at him and caught nothing but air as Popov easily stepped back from the punch and laughed. She swung with her other arm and missed again, encouraging more laughter from Popov. "You're actually not as fearsome as I thought you'd be. Especially not without your gun."

"*Poshol k chyortu*," *Go to hell*, she spat, as she put her hands back up in a traditional boxer's stance. She moved her head and shoulders from side to side, looking for an opening.

"Is this supposed to intimidate me?" asked Popov.

Alexandra didn't bother answering. She threw an obvious jab with her right hand that Popov easily parried away. He was about to say something else when seemingly out of nowhere Alexandra landed a left cross, followed by a right hook. Obviously, Popov knew nothing about boxing and one of the sport's most popular three-punch combinations.

As an added measure of security, Alexandra lined up and kicked the stunned Popov in the nuts with everything she had. His eyes rolled up into the back of his head and he doubled over in pain. The forward weight was more than his injured knee could bear and he fell hard onto his side. Alexandra moved around him and dove for the kitchen table and the gun lying just underneath.

She was less than a foot away from it when she felt Popov's hand grab her leg. He was clawing his way up her body, desperate to get to the gun before she did.

She was beginning to think that all was lost when the fingertips of her left hand touched the long metal tube of the weapon's silencer. Alexandra struggled beneath Popov, using her free hand to slap at his head and shoulders.

Millimeter by millimeter her fingers slid down the weapon, brailling its features until she could finally feel the trigger guard and knew the butt of the pistol was almost in her grasp. As she was about to close in on it, Popov grabbed the silenced Walther, struggled to his feet and aimed it at her head. "I'm beginning to think that you might be more fun dead," he said, wiping the blood away from where Alexandra's left cross had caught him in the mouth. "What do you think?"

"Zhree govno i sdokhnee!" she replied.

"Oh, I do plan on dying one day, but I don't plan on eating any shit before it happens."

"Guess again," said a man behind Popov, who then whacked him in the side of his head with an antique bedpan.

As Popov hit the floor, the Walther discharged, its silenced round ricocheting off the kitchen's iron stove before exiting through the leaded-glass window above the sink.

Though Karganov had succeeded in ringing Popov's bell, the young mafioso had been hit much harder many times before in his life. He quickly shook it off, and spun on his haunches to train his gun on the injured general. Karganov knew he was beaten. *"Govno,"* Russian for *Shit!* was the last thing that escaped his lips before Popov drilled a round right between the man's eyes.

Minutes later, the fog of gun smoke still hung thick in the air. Alexandra Ivanova had no idea if the ringing in her ears was from her own screaming over the loss of General Anatoly Karganov, or from the deafening roar of the Pit Bull as its .45-caliber armor-piercing rounds raced out of the barrel and tore through the flesh of the onetime orphan from Nizhnevartovsk, and now lifeless Moscow crime figure, Milesch Popov.

CHAPTER 21

What I'm asking for, Mr. President, is your guarantee, right now, as a member of NATO and the elected leader of the Republic of France, to stand by us on this one," replied President Rutledge, who then fell quiet as he listened to his counterpart's response.

Several moments passed, during which the American president couldn't help rolling his eyes. He couldn't believe what he was hearing. When it was his turn again to speak, Rutledge had to fight to keep his temper in check. "No, this isn't an *American* problem, it's an *international* problem and no, we are not interested in having you mediate it for us. There's nothing to mediate. The sovereignty of the United States is not negotiable.

"Benoit, all countries committed to freedom and peace must take a stand in the war on terror, no matter where that terror comes from. Like it or not, the bloodlines of our two nations are forever intertwined. French blood was spilled in helping to forge our nation and create our sovereignty, and American blood has been spilled in not one, but two great wars in helping your countrymen preserve yours. I can't state more strongly that we believe—"

Interrupted by a retort from the French president, Rutledge again fell silent for several moments before responding, "Benoit, I want you to listen to me and listen good. You've been waffling ever since we sent you the file on this from Langley. I know you have problems within your own political party right now and I've also got a good idea of what the current disposition is across the European Union toward the United States, but I want to make it completely clear that America resents the fact that you are even weighing what your position should be on—"

Rutledge gripped the phone so tightly he was sure he was going to crack the receiver as he was interrupted yet again. Finally, he lost it and the diplomacy with which he was trying to conduct their conversation evaporated. "I don't give a good goddamn what parallels you think you see between this situation and what happened with Iraq. I'm not going down that road. If your intelligence people want to see the bomb we have in our possession, they're welcome to it. In fact, they should, just in case you end up with one in your backyard. The reason the Brits got the first look was because MI6 already had operatives over here doing a cross-training exercise with some of our people.

"Benoit, I have a lot of phone calls yet to make,

so I'm going to save us both some time and cut right to the chase. We agree with you one hundred percent that by all acceptable standards, the intelligence we have thus far is not independently actionable. But when you connect the dots in that file we sent you, they form a very scary picture. You don't need to be a lifelong analyst to see that. Millions of people in America could die. Entire cities could be reduced to nothing more than piles of radioactive rubble. If the situation were reversed and we were talking about you potentially losing Paris, Marseilles, Lyon, and maybe even twenty more cities, what would you want to be hearing from your allies?"

Moments later, and for the first time since the situation had broken, president Jack Rutledge allowed himself to relax. "Thank you, Benoit. I'm glad we can count on you," he said as he hung up the phone.

The feeling of relaxation, though, quickly dissipated as Rutledge's chief of staff, Charles Anderson, who had been simultaneously reviewing the top-secret folder containing the nuclear evacuation plan for the president and his daughter, hung up the extension he'd been listening in on and said, "Well done. Only twenty-three more calls to go."

arvath and Herman drove through the Schöneberg district once again, though Herman made sure to steer well clear of all of the police activity near the Goltzstrasse. They passed the Rathaus Schöneberg, which Harvath recognized as the site of Kennedy's famous *Ich bin ein Berliner* speech, and when they finally reached Mansteinstrasse, they turned left and found a parking space. The minute Harvath laid his eyes on the Leydicke Pub at number 4 Manstein-strasse, he knew why Gary Lawlor had chosen it.

It was in a relatively quiet neighborhood with easy access to public transportation. Though it might attract some tourists, by and large its clientele was going to be regulars, which made picking out anyone who didn't belong there a lot easier. The pub was close enough to the safe house to be easy to get to, yet far enough away so that when coming or going, you had plenty of time to make sure you weren't being followed. Scot saw a sign outside pro-claiming that the bar had been operated by the Leydicke family for over one hundred years. If Gary Lawlor and Frank Leighton had patronized this bar often enough to get their own steins, chances were very good that somebody in the family was going to remember them. Harvath's real hope was that one of those memories would be a recent one.

The Leydicke was a traditional German drinking establishment, known as a *Kneipe*, with lots of carved wood and heavy oak tables. There was a distillery on the premises, and in addition to a wide variety of beers, the Leydicke offered a superb selection of sweet wines and liquors. They looked to be the only people in the place and easily found an empty table. As they sat down in the semidarkness of the dimly lit bar, it felt like they had stepped back in time. For ambience alone, Harvath would have given it five stars, but he wasn't writing a review, he was here for information.

When a waitress failed to arrive and take their order, Herman suggested they go up to the bar.

"*Ich möchte gerne zwei Bier, bitte,*" said Scot when they got there.

"Big or small?" responded the barman in English, picking up on Harvath's American accent and the fact that he asked so politely, unlike a local who would have simply said, "*zwei Bier, bitte.*" The man was short, about five foot four with a large stomach that hung over his white apron. His wire-rimmed glasses rested upon a rather bulbous nose, which stood guard over a thick and unkempt mustache. He was easily in his late sixties, if not older, and balding.

"Big, I guess," replied Harvath.

"We're closing, so you get small," said the barman.

"So much for German hospitality," responded Harvath under his breath. Herman just rolled his eyes.

When the bartender placed their small beers in front of them, Scot withdrew a picture taken of him along with Gary Lawlor at one of Gary's summer barbeques and handed it across the bar. "Look familiar?"

Before the man could say anything, Harvath caught the slightest hint of recognition on the man's face, which he quickly masked.

"*Nein,*" he said, handing the photo back.

"You've never seen the man standing next to me in that photo?" asked Harvath.

"*Nein.*"

There it was again. The tell. Most people would have missed it, but his Secret Service training to detect what scientists referred to as microexpressions, the subtle and almost imperceptible facial cues that subjects unknowingly give off when they are not telling the truth, made it clear to Harvath that the man was lying.

"Maybe we could talk to one of the managers?"

"There is no manager here."

"Well what about one of the family members? One of the owners?"

"I am Hellfried Leydicke, the head of the family and the owner of this bar."

"Maybe you should look at the photo again," said

Harvath as his eye was drawn to one of the shelves behind the bar, above the liquor bottles. "This man was a pretty good customer of yours a long time ago."

"I am sorry, but I do not know him. Please finish your beers, the bar is now closed."

Herman shook his head. "No large beers *and* no information."

"Herr Leydicke," interjected Harvath. "This man's name is Gary Lawlor. He's a very good friend of mine and he's in a lot of trouble. I came a long way to help him. Look at the photo once more."

"I don't need to see the photo again," commanded Leydicke, "You need to go."

Scot gestured to Herman and then pointed behind the bar. "See that beer stein up there? The one with the barbed wire?"

"Yeah."

"Do me a favor and get it down. I think it might help jog Herr Leydicke's memory."

Herman leaned over the bar, reached up, and grabbed the mug.

Having explained Gary's Berlin connection to Herman on the drive over, Harvath said, "Flip it over. Gary's team consisted of twelve guys. Each man was given a custom-made mug just like that one. On the bottom was a number out of twelve. What does Herr Leydicke's have?"

"Zero out of twelve."

"That seems fitting enough as he wasn't actually an official team member. But you were a member of the family, so to speak, weren't you? Those men spent a lot of time in here, didn't they?"

"I don't know what you're talking about. Those steins are simple tourist items," replied Leydicke.

"Really?" said Harvath remembering what Defense Secretary Hilliman had told him toward the end of their meeting when he remarked on how Gary and Frank Leighton had the same numbered beer steins in their houses. "Because the way I heard it, the team members had all taken turns sneaking up onto the wall at night to snip their own authentic piece of history. How'd you get the barbed wire on your mug? Did you slip on your night vision goggles one evening and scale the wall praying that the East German border guards wouldn't see you and open fire? Something tells me you didn't. Somebody else risked their life to get it for you. On the back of the mug where it talks about *Für die Sicherheit*, For the Security, that was their unit motto. What security did you help to protect?"

Leydicke was silent. Harvath knew he had hit the nail right on the head. "Listen," he continued, "we need to talk. Most of those men you knew are dead, and not from old age either. Someone has killed them. There are only two left and I don't want to see anything happen to them."

After several moments, Leydicke relented and said, "Let me lock up and we'll talk."

The bar closed for the evening, Hellfried Leydicke set a tray of food along with three *large* Bären Pils beers on the table in his office.

"I don't understand any of this," said Harvath as he reached for one of the beers. "Gary just arrived on your doorstep two days ago, dropped his bags, and said he'd be back in a little while? That was it?"

"More or less," responded Leydicke. "We hadn't seen each other in years, but I could tell that something was wrong."

"Why is that?"

"After all this time, he didn't ask any questions about the family, how business had been—you know, no chitchat."

"Did he say anything at all about what he was up to or where he was going?"

"No, he simply asked if he could leave his bag here and that he was going to be back later."

"But he never came back?" asked Harvath.

"No, he didn't."

Scot set his beer down and began to look through Gary Lawlor's suitcase. After several moments, he pulled a sleek black device that looked like the old Apple PDA known as Newton out of the bag.

"What's that?" asked Herman.

"It looks like an oversized handheld computer," replied Harvath, flipping open the cover and powering it up. "One of the early ones from the eighties."

"Your friend doesn't keep too up-to-date on his technology, does he?"

"No, he doesn't. In fact he hates computers. He always gives me shit for the Ipaq I carry. He says that if it ever goes on the fritz, I'll be screwed. He never would have owned something like this. He still carries around a paper Day-Timer scheduler. It's as thick as a phone book. This PDA doesn't fit his personality."

"Have you looked through the programs on it? Anything interesting?"

"Not really," said Harvath as he scrolled through. "He's got a contact database—"

"Any listings in Berlin?"

"None that I can see. The appointments, the To Do list—they're all pretty innocuous," he answered, convinced now more than ever that the PDA was something other than it appeared."

"It must have been part of his cover," said Herman.

Harvath powered down the unit and asked Leydicke, "Has Gary gotten any deliveries here, Hellfried? Maybe somebody stopped by looking for him?"

"Nobody has been here looking for him," replied Leydicke, "but there have been a few phone calls over the last two days."

"Phone calls?" said Harvath. "From whom?"

"I don't know."

"What did the person say?"

"It was a code, something the team used to use years ago," he answered. "For security reasons, there were never supposed to be more than four of them in the same public place at one time, but they always disregarded the rule and came here to drink together. If they wanted to know if any of their teammates were in the bar, they would call up and ask if Alice was here. Like in the song."

"You mean as in, 'Alice? Alice? Who the f—'" began Herman.

"Yes," said Leydicke, cutting him off. "The Smokie song from the seventies."

"I don't get it," replied Harvath. "What's this song?"

"It was originally a polka tune, but it got remade as a pop song," said Herman. "After the singer sings, ' 'cause for twenty-four years I've been living next door to Alice,' everybody in the bar, the nightclub, wherever, would respond, 'Alice? Alice? Who the fuck is Alice?' Even if you were alone in your car, you still shouted it out."

"It was a popular joke at the time," added Hellfried. "If none of the guys were here and someone called and asked for Alice, I'd say Alice doesn't live here anymore. And if any of the guys were here, I'd answer—"

"Alice? Alice? Who the fuck is Alice?" said Herman with a smile, obviously anxious to finish the phrase.

"Cute," said Harvath. "What does this have to do with these phone calls for Gary?"

"That's just it," said Leydicke. "After his team was sent back to the States, I never received anymore calls like that. It was their special code. Now all of a sudden, I'm getting several calls a day asking for Alice."

"Are the calls from different people?" asked Harvath.

"No, the same man," said Leydicke.

"What did you tell him?"

"At first, I told him Alice didn't live here anymore. Then when Gary dropped off his bags, the next time I got the call I said Alice had gone out and should be back soon."

"Can you tell if the calls were local or long distance?"

"With the German phone system, you never know, but I don't think they originated inside Berlin."

"Why not?"

"There was a pause on the line."

"You mean like a delay?"

"Yes, a delay."

"So, there's a delay and it's the same person calling you. Did you recognize the voice? Could it be one of the team guys?"

"According to you," answered Leydicke, "all but two of the team members are dead. So if Gary's alive, who would that leave?"

"Frank Leighton," said Harvath. "Is it his voice?"

Leydicke paused a moment as he tried to remember his old customer. "It could be, but it has been a very long time."

"When does he usually call?"

"It varies."

"There must be some pattern to it. He would know that somebody from his team would be here at a set time if he needed to call in."

Leydicke smoothed down the few loose strands

of hair on his bald pate and thought about it a moment. "It was strange to hear a call like that after all these years. At first, I thought it was one of the old guys making a joke, but when I tried to talk to him, he just hung up."

"Do you always answer the phone here?"

"Of course I do. It's my bar."

"Okay. Now I need you to think. Is there any pattern to when the calls come in?"

"No," said Leydicke. "Except—"

"*Except* what?" prompted Harvath.

"There seems to be one last one in the evening. He'll call right as we're about to close."

"And what time do you normally close?"

"In about half an hour."

"Good," said Harvath. "That gives us just enough time to get ready."

CHAPTER 23

Harvath knew it was Frank Leighton on the other end of the line when Leydicke responded to the caller's inquiry with, "Alice? Alice? Who the fuck is Alice?" and then handed the phone to him. The next several seconds were going to be very tricky and though he had spent the last half hour trying to figure out what to say, Harvath needed to tread very carefully. For all intents and purposes, Leighton was quite literally a walking time bomb. The last thing the United States needed was for that bomb to go off before they were ready.

"Mr. Saritsa," said Harvath, using Leighton's alias, "I want you to listen to me very carefully. I have a message from Goaltender. He needs you to hold. I repeat. He needs you to hold."

"Who is this?" said Frank Leighton after a brief pause.

"For the moment, you can call me Norseman," replied Harvath, using the call sign that he had acquired in the SEALs and that had followed him through the Secret Service. It had been given to him not so much because he looked like a Viking, though he was as ferocious a fighter, but rather because of a string of Scandinavian flight attendants he had dated during his SEAL days. "You need to listen to me. The person who should have taken this call has gone missing. Goaltender sent me to find him. Until I do, you need to remain in place."

"Why should I believe you?"

"Because there's been a death in Alice's family. In fact, most of the family has tragically passed on. Do you understand what I am saying? You're the only one left who can run the family business. In memory of Alice, we'd like to put some people in place at some of her other offices, but it is going to take a little time to do that."

"How much time do we have?"

"Not much."

"If you are who you say you are, you'll know how to execute the emergency contact plan. You've got twenty-four hours, or else I roll," said Leighton, who then promptly hung up.

Harvath handed the phone back to Leydicke. He knew Leighton wouldn't call back. As he sat back in his chair and massaged his temples, he wondered how the hell he was going to figure out what the emergency contact plan was between Gary and his operatives.

"So?" asked Herman. "How'd it go?"

"Just great. We've got a whole twenty-four hours."

"And after that?"

"After that, is after that. Let's focus on what's in front of us now," said Harvath, concerned that he may just have pushed Leighton beyond recall.

Herman was about to make a comment when his cell phone rang. "Ja?" he answered after flipping it open. He talked back and forth with someone for several moments. Looking at his watch he said, "*in eine halbe Stunde*," then closed the phone and put it back in his pocket.

"What's up?" asked Harvath.

"That was Sebastian."

"Did he and Max get the footage?"

"Yes, we're supposed to meet them in a half hour," said Herman, standing up from his chair.

After gathering up Gary Lawlor's suitcase and PDA, Scot and Herman followed Leydicke to the front of the bar where he unlocked the door, shook their hands, and watched the two men disappear into a steadily falling snow.

The oddly named Küss (Kiss) Film und Video Produktion company was located in an old derelict warehouse building in a rather seedy and run-down section of the former East Berlin. Herman found a parking spot a few spaces away from the entrance and he and Harvath walked up to a reinforced security door where Herman rang the intercom. A voice over the speaker responded, "*Wer ist da?*" Herman identified himself and a buzzer sounded as the door's automatic lock released.

Harvath followed Herman inside past numerous wooden pallets stacked high with large cardboard boxes emblazoned with the company's not so subtle logo—a glossy pair of red lips pursed in a kiss. He noticed conveyor belts with shrink-wrapping machines and off on the other side of the beat-up warehouse, transparent pneumatic doors leading into a pristine clean room with racks of video-duplicating equipment. He also had counted no less than seven security cameras since they had walked through the front door.

"Where the hell are we?" asked Harvath as he and Herman approached a large, padded door at the rear of the warehouse. It was covered in deep, red leather and studded with brilliant chrome rivets.

"I'll let Max explain. This is his friend's business," said Herman as they opened the door and stepped into an opulent lobby area that stood in stark contrast to the warehouse behind them. The floors were covered in black marble that was so highly polished it shone like a mirror. Hanging on the wall behind a granite receptionist's station was the company's logo done up in bright neon. A low-slung, brushed-aluminum table fronted an opulent white leather sectional, and when Harvath caught sight of a series of framed movie posters on the wall, his suspicions of what kind of films and videos the company produced were all but confirmed.

He was about to say something to Herman when Max appeared from the adjacent corridor and called them over.

"Max, what the hell is this place? Peter's Porn Emporium?" asked Harvath.

"Actually," said Max, "it's Marc's Porn Emporium. Better known as Küss Film und—"

"Video Produktion," interrupted Harvath. "I know. I saw the sign. The lips are a nice touch. What the hell are we doing here?"

"Looking at your videos. Marc has developed a very interesting niche in the Berlin postproduction market, but I think it will be more interesting if he tells you himself. He's in the back. "I'll show you."

Max turned and walked back down the corridor with Scot and Herman right behind him. They passed a fully equipped state-of-the-art soundstage, booths for audio recording, a master control room, and several high-end editing suites. It was in the very last suite that they found Marc Schroeder, the president and CEO of Küss Film und Video Produktion seated in front of a wide flat-panel computer monitor, hard at work. As his guests entered, he spun in his chair and stood to greet them. He was tall, about six feet, clean-cut with perfectly creased khakis and a neatly pressed oxford shirt—not at all the picture Harvath harbored in his mind of a porn producer.

"Marc, I'd like you to meet Scot Harvath and Herman Toffle," said Max.

Schroeder shook Herman's hand and upon shaking hands with Harvath joked, "I understand you're the reason we're all here. Do you know what I charge for coming in after hours like this?"

"I would have thought you do your best work at night," replied Harvath.

"A man with a sense of humor. I like that! Please, take a seat," laughed Marc, as he cleared away a stack of videocassette sleeves from the leather couch behind him.

"I'm not going to stick to this, am I?" asked Harvath.

Marc continued laughing and rolled his chair back over to his ergonomically designed edit station. "There's that sense of humor again. You Americans love to kid."

"Who's kidding?" said Harvath under his breath to Herman. "Marc," continued Scot, trying to move things along, "What about our footage? Were you able to get anything from it?"

"The first thing I looked at when Max arrived were the digital stills from the traffic cameras. All they show are individual cars in the midst of committing traffic infractions. Without knowing what specific car you are looking for, it is not very helpful. The cameras cover the intersection only and nothing parked up the street, so I decided to set that aside.

"The bank footage, on the other hand, was much more promising. The bank uses very-wide-angle lenses on its outdoor cameras."

Harvath watched while the image in front of them broke down into hundreds of little blocks and became a blur as Schroeder scrolled backward until he got to the point on the tape that he wanted.

"Here we are. Two days ago." He pushed play and sat back in his chair.

Harvath watched for a few moments and then said, "I don't see anything. It just looks like the outside of the bank to me."

"Watch the top of the screen," offered Schroeder. "It's coming in five seconds."

Harvath watched until he saw what appeared to be two or more men huddled close together move quickly across the screen. "Can you enhance that?" he asked, leaning forward on the couch, excited by what he might have just witnessed.

"No problem. Let's watch it again with full zoom," said Schroeder who punched a series of commands into his Avid.

They watched it again and this time it was obvious that there were three men, two of whom looked to be half-carrying a third as if he were drunk. *Or incapacitated by a Taser.*

"Marc," said Harvath, "show it to me again, but this time can you run it in slow motion?"

"Of course," answered Schroeder, who ran it back again.

"Shit," exclaimed Harvath after watching it a third time. "They enter from one side of the frame and in a matter of seconds exit out the other. You can't see any faces at all. It's almost as if they were purposely trying to avoid the video cameras."

"Either that, or they got lucky," said Herman.

"Is there anything else you can do to enhance the picture, Marc?" asked Harvath.

"We can run it again with the mathematical filter."

"Do it."

Harvath watched again and though the image was slightly better, it still wasn't good enough. The surveillance tape had caught three men moving together across the street, two seeming to half-carry another, but even with all the enhancements, the quality wasn't good enough to identify any of them, not even Gary. The disappointment in the room was palpable.

Harvath sat there staring at the screen as the video footage continued to unfold. He couldn't believe that they had come this far only to be turned away with nothing. He was getting ready to get up from the couch when, all of a sudden he yelled, "Stop!"

Both Max and Herman stared at him as Marc paused the feed.

"Run the tape backward five seconds and play it again," said Harvath.

Schroeder did as Harvath instructed and ran the footage again.

"I don't see anything," said Max.

"Neither do I," replied Herman. "What are you looking at?"

"Run it again," was Harvath's answer, "but this time take it back and start it from where the men walk out of the frame."

Schroeder rewound the tape to the appropriate point and let it play.

"Nothing," said Max, frustrated.

"Scot, it's an empty street scene," added Herman.

Suddenly, Marc Schroeder sat up straighter in his chair. He couldn't believe his eyes. He swiveled around, looked at Harvath, and said, "Lower screen right?"

Harvath nodded in reply.

"*Lower screen right?*" argued Herman. "There's nothing there."

"Yes there is," returned Schroeder. "Right on the very edge. I can't believe I didn't catch it. I'll put a spotlight on it for you."

Moments later, with the lower-right-hand portion of the screen highlighted, they all saw it. Just barely in frame, was the back of a late model BMW with part of its license plate visible. Then it was gone.

CHAPTER 24

Karl Überhof's apartment was located just off Unter den Linden, once one of the best-known boulevards in all of Europe and the preeminent thoroughfare of East Berlin. With the information they had gathered from the bank footage, Marc Schroeder was able to scan the digital stills from the traffic cams until they had found what they were looking for. A black BMW had in fact blown through a red light at the intersection of Grunewaldstrasse and Goltz-strasse. By comparing the time code stamped on the digital traffic cam photo with the time code on the bank footage, they knew they had a match. The picture gave them a complete license plate number, which jibed with the partial they already had. With one phone call, Sebastian was not only able to get the registration information on the car, but his contact was able to fax him the driver's license photo of the man it was registered to—Karl Überhof. Though the quality wasn't the best, it was still good enough for their purposes.

Harvath had been against storming Überhof's apartment, especially after what had happened at the Capstone safe house. Though he didn't believe Überhof had any idea they were on to him, at this point, he was their only lead. After weighing all of the potential outcomes, Harvath decided they would be better off shadowing him to see where he might go.

Sebastian didn't agree. He and his men had checked Überhof's parking garage and had verified that his black BMW was there, which likely meant that the man was upstairs asleep. Sebastian wanted to surprise Überhof in his bed, confront him with what they knew, and force him to talk.

"And if he's a professional?" Harvath had asked. How long might it take until they finally broke him? What if they couldn't break him? What if they screwed up and killed him? What then?

No, Harvath had reasoned, it was better to let Überhof take them right to Gary Lawlor. And though Sebastian had eventually agreed, he had also brought up a very good argument. What if Gary actually was in Überhof's apartment? Merely staking out his place wasn't going to tell them that. What's more, what if Überhof and whoever he was working with were torturing Gary? What if when they got to him it was too late? How long was Scot prepared to sit outside and do nothing?

It was one of those textbook *damned if you do, damned if you don't* scenarios that all too often presented themselves in hostage situations. The weight of the decision was not one Harvath enjoyed having on his shoulders, but he accepted responsibility for it nonetheless. In the end, he agreed with Sebastian that a time limit should be set. It was the decision that made the most strategic sense. If Überhof didn't show his face by the appointed time, they would kick the door in and take down the apartment.

Having not slept much over the last two days, Harvath appreciated being able to close his eyes for a while, even if it was stretched out in the back of the MEK's mock bakery truck. He'd slept in worse places and if there was one thing his training had taught him, it was that sleep was a weapon.

Because of the damage to Harvath's ribs, Sebastian had offered to take his shift and give him more time to rest, but Harvath had refused. He awoke at the appointed time and walked over to his position at an all-night café on the other side of the Bebelplatz. He passed an illuminated piece of art—a hollowed-out chamber with empty bookshelves that commemorated the Nazi's famous book burning on that spot in May of 1933. He stopped to read the inscription by Heinrich Heine, who saw his books burned along with other "subversive" authors such as Sigmund Freud. The plaque read, "Nur dort wo man Bücher verbrennt, verbrennt man am Ende auch Menschen." *Wherever books are burned, ultimately people are also burned.*

Harvath, per Herman's suggestion, kept his German speaking to a minimum. He took a table in the corner by the window and simply ordered, *"Ein Kaffee, bitte,"* and when the waitress returned with the small pot that contained about two cups known as a *Kännchen,* he paid her and then reached for the newspaper from the empty table next to him. He pretended to read as he watched the street outside.

The current shift of MEK operatives were similarly placed at strategic points around the block, the idea being that if Überhof made a move, he was likely going to engage in a maneuver known as an SDR—surveillance detection route. In other words, he was going to make darn sure that he wasn't being followed. By having men placed in different locations, they would be able to follow Überhof, hopefully without him knowing.

After sitting for two hours in the stiff wooden café chair, Harvath was glad that his shift was coming to an end. Outside, it had grown warmer, turning the snow to a cold drizzle, but the unusual change in temperature brought with it a very undesirable side effect—fog.

Where Harvath could see clear across the Bebelplatz when he had first entered the café, now he could barely see three feet outside its windows. As he set the newspaper in front of him and pushed back from the table, the voice of one of Sebastian's operatives crackled over his earpiece. Überhof had been spotted leaving his apartment and was making his way across the Bebelplatz. The operative was following, but having trouble keeping him in sight in the thick fog.

As Harvath made his way to the large, etched glass doors at the front of the café, he spoke into his sleeve mike and asked the operative to give him an idea of where he was. "*Staatsoper*," replied the man, referring to the opera house on the other side of the square, "coming toward you."

"Good," said Harvath. "When you get to the café, I'll take him."

"*Kein Problem*. I'll let you know as I approach."

Moments passed and Harvath waited impatiently in the café's vestibule, his face turned away from the entrance as he pretended to appear interested in a flyer for a meeting of some working people's consortium. It looked like communist propaganda to him, but then again he shouldn't be surprised, the Communist Party was still very much alive and well in Europe. *What people will waste their time on*, he thought to himself. Just then, his earpiece once again crackled to life.

"Crossing the street now. Arriving at your location in—" said the operative, but his transmission was suddenly cut off.

"I didn't hear you," said Harvath, pushing the earpiece further into his ear. "Say again."

Harvath waited but there was no response. He tried to hail the operative again, but still there was nothing.

A loud cracking sound drew his attention toward the entrance of the café. The etched doors shuddered on their hinges, and Harvath spun just in time to see the bloody body of the MEK operative who had been trailing Überhof slide down the glass. The small group of patrons inside began screaming and several of them rushed toward the windows in the front of the café to see what was happening.

Harvath bolted outside with his H&K drawn, but couldn't see Überhof anywhere. The fog was too thick. He could barely see his hand in front of his face. He pulled the fallen operative away from the door and turned him over. "Man down. Man down," he repeated over his radio, but it was too late. The man's throat had been sliced from ear to ear. How could Überhof have known he had a tail? For a moment, a tidal wave of images threatened to flood Harvath's mind—the faces of men that he had lost in previous operations, men whose safety he had been responsible for. All of a sudden, he felt a large hand grab his shoulder. Harvath spun, his H&K raised and ready to fire.

"Come on," said the voice of Herman Toffle. "Überhof's getting away."

"Wait," said Harvath, as he turned back to the dead operative. "There's something not right here."

"I know," replied Herman, "He's dead. Let's go. I'll radio Sebastian to come get him."

The radio! That was it. "No," said Harvath. "His radio's gone. Überhof took it. He'll know every move we make."

"Then we'll figure something else out, but we need to move."

"How are we going to follow him in this?"

Herman held up a long black tube about the size of a tennis ball can, which Harvath immediately recognized. It was a SpecterIR portable thermal infrared imaging weapon sight. Weighing only three pounds, the SpecterIR used next generation hybrid uncooled FPA heat imaging detector technology, which offered true "see in the dark" infrared capability. Darkness, smoke, dust, rain, and, most important, fog, were all rendered virtually transparent to the simple-to-operate scope.

"Where'd you get that?" asked Harvath.

"I borrowed it from one of the sniper rifles in the back of Sebastian's van," replied Herman, "but none of this is going to matter if we don't get behind this guy and see where he's going."

"Okay. Let's go. You lead."

"No, you lead. You'll be my eyes. I'll track him with the scope and you walk in front of me," said the much larger Toffle as he put his beefy paw on Harvath's shoulder and shoved him toward the edge of the square. "Move out."

As Harvath led the way up Unter den Linden, Herman kept one hand on Harvath's shoulder for balance while his attention was focused on their target, who was almost a full block ahead of them. Using the BlackHot thermal imaging option, every item seen through the Specter's lens with a high heat signature was rendered black. Herman preferred it to the White Hot option, as it was easier on his eye during such prolonged use.

Überhof knew what he was doing and was proving himself to be quite a pro. Though he moved at a good clip, he still stopped repeatedly to check and see if he was being followed. In the fog, though, the best he could do was listen. Without his own thermal imaging device, he could see only what was right in front of him. For all intents and purposes, the man was completely blind, but when one sense is taken away, others become heightened, and both Harvath and Herman knew they had to be careful.

They quickly developed their own unspoken language. A slight squeeze of his shoulder told Harvath to slow down. A harder squeeze called for an all-out stop as it indicated Überhof had halted somewhere up ahead and was trying to detect if anyone was behind him.

At Friedrichstrasse, Überhof made an abrupt turn and Harvath and Herman were forced to cautiously hightail it up to the corner out of fear of losing him. When they caught sight of him again, he was making his way toward the entrance of one of the stations for Berlin's subway system known as the U-Bahn. Herman pocketed the SpecterIR scope and suggested they approach the station from different directions. Harvath agreed and crossed the street.

Entering the station, Harvath did a quick look around without breaking stride toward the brightly colored automated ticket machines, but so far, there was no sign of Überhof. He peeled a note off of the thick wad of euros he had been given before leaving the United States and bought a three-zone, all-day ticket, not knowing where this little chase might lead them. He was just about to validate his ticket and make his way down the escalator to the platform, when Herman quietly whistled to get his attention.

"So much for us not being together," mumbled Harvath as he joined Herman in front of the station manager's glassed-in control booth.

Herman grabbed a system map and pretended to search for their destination as he said, "Look at the station master's closed-circuit cameras. What do you see?"

"I see our guy standing toward the end of the platform," replied Harvath.

"What else?"

"Nothing really."

"Exactly," responded Herman. "This early in the morning, there aren't many people using the U-Bahn. I'm concerned that if we go down to the platform too soon, he might spot us."

"What are we supposed to do then?"

"He's on the U6 platform waiting for the train going south—"

"That's the train that goes to Tempelhof Airport. What the hell is he up to?"

"I don't know, but here's what I want to do. We wait here until the train enters the station. It looks like he is going to get on board the last car. There are always people running into the U-Bahn at the last minute. We'll do the same. We'll run down to the platform, hop on one of the forward cars, and then make our way back so we can watch him."

Harvath didn't like it. He didn't like any of it. Tailing someone on a subway was one of the most difficult things to do. If the subject got off and you followed and then the subject jumped back on at the last minute, what could you do? *Nothing.* In plain English, you were fucked. Harvath had come too far to get fucked at this point. He was racked by the age-old surveillance dilemma—*Do you play him? Or do you pop him?* With one man already dead, his ribs killing him, and a surveillance scenario in the subway system of Berlin that was severely less than optimal, he was beginning to think that they were quickly closing in on the only sane alternative—to pop Überhof and lean on him like a C-17 Globemaster full of bricks until he told them what they needed to know.

Herman seemed to sense what he was thinking. "We have a few minutes before the next train arrives. I am going to call Sebastian on my cell phone and let him know what we're doing. He can space men along the line and have them get on at different stations. Don't worry. We're not going to lose him." And with that, Herman walked back toward the stairs to the street level and got on his phone.

Harvath had to admit, it sounded like a halfway decent plan. By switching the members of the surveillance team, maybe they could still follow Überhof without his knowing, and *maybe* he would lead them to Gary Lawlor. Then again, that's how they had started this whole thing and someone had already died. But maybe Überhof had just gotten lucky.

Maybe the operative had screwed up somehow.

Neither of those ideas sat well with Harvath. He reminded himself of how well trained Sebastian and his men were. Writing off the operative who had gotten killed as careless or unlucky, wasn't right. That being said, the fact that Überhof had picked up on a tail so fast and in such thick fog really unnerved Harvath. *Not only was Überhof good, he was dangerous*, Harvath decided. Underestimating him any further would be a big mistake.

Herman returned from making his phone call just as the rumble of an approaching train could be heard.

"Did you get a hold of Sebastian?" asked Harvath, his eyes glued to the black-and-white monitor inside the station manager's glass booth.

"Yes and he's going to do what we asked, but you need to know that he and his men are very upset and want Überhof dead."

"If he'd killed one of my teammates I'd want him dead too, but this is our only chance to get to Gary."

"And they understand that. They're professionals. They'll do what they're supposed to do," replied Herman.

"But when it's over," offered Harvath, "I don't care what they do with the guy."

"I thought you might feel that way. Let's make a move for the platform. That train's not going to sit there for long."

The buzzer, which signaled that the doors were

about to close, was already sounding when the pair
hit the bottom of the escalator and ran for the first
car. They passed a large mirror mounted at the end
of the platform that allowed the train's engineer to
look back down the entire length of his train and
make sure everyone was onboard before pulling out
of the station. As they jumped aboard the train,
something in the mirror caught Harvath's eye.

"He got off!" yelled Scot as he turned and
lunged for the closing doors.

Startled passengers watched as the two men
pried the doors open and squeezed out of the train.

"You'd better be sure about this," said Herman
as he looked up and down the platform as the train
began to pull away, "because I don't see him."

"Give me the scope," said Harvath.

Herman handed it to him and then casually
walked along the edge of the platform covertly
studying the faces in each of the bright yellow
U-Bahn cars as the train picked up speed and pulled
out of the station.

Harvath didn't bother examining the faces of the
U-Bahn passengers. He knew Überhof had gotten
off. It had just been a flash in the mirror, but Harvath was confident about what he had seen. He was
also pretty sure he knew where the man had gone.

It took the Specter scope less than ten seconds
to power all the way up. At the far end of the platform, Harvath held it up to his eye and peered into
the heavy blackness of the faintly illuminated train
tunnel.

"Unless he was lying down on the floor," said Herman as he rejoined Harvath, "he wasn't on that train."

"I know," replied Scot as he adjusted the Specter.

"So where is he?"

Harvath handed Herman the scope and said, "About fifty meters down along the wall on the right-hand side. Take a look for yourself."

After watching Überhof pick his way down the tunnel for several moments, Herman asked, "What the hell is that asshole up to?"

"I don't know," answered Harvath, pulling out his H&K and screwing on the silencer, "but I think we ought to go find out."

CHAPTER 25

They followed Überhof for more than fifteen minutes until he came to a short metal service door and disappeared through it. When they passed through the door, they found that it led to a long, low-ceilinged tunnel. Several minutes later, it opened up and they were amazed by what they saw.

"What is this place?" asked Harvath as he shined his SureFire flashlight around the abandoned, cobweb-covered U-Bahn station.

"*Geisterbahnhöfe*," replied Herman. "Ghost station. I didn't think any of these existed anymore."

"What the hell is a *ghost station*?" demanded Harvath as he painfully pulled himself up onto the filthy platform.

With its dreary green tiles, old-fashioned signs, and the Communist-era propaganda posters hanging above the benches, the station looked like it had been frozen in time—a true relic of the Cold War. Harvath could see an old newspaper kiosk that must have once sold cigarettes and magazines, but which had been retrofitted into a machine-gun nest.

"When the Soviets built the wall, they split off the subway system in East Berlin into its own network. Because of a quirk in geography, two of the West Berlin lines needed to pass briefly through East Berlin before circling back around to the West. It was very strange. You could ride through East Berlin and see stations like this completely abandoned except for the stern-faced soldiers standing on the platforms with machine guns."

"And those abandoned stations were what you called *Geisterbahnhöfe*?"

"Yes, but after the reunification, all of the stations were supposedly reopened."

"This one must not have gotten the memo," replied Harvath as he ran his finger along the dirty tile.

"You know, it's strange," said Herman. "I don't even know what line this is on. I am trying to figure out what might be above us."

"What about this?" said Harvath as he lifted an old metal directional sign from the floor, blew the dust off of it, and showed it to Herman. "*Russische Botschaft*? I know *Russische* is German for Russian, but what is *Botschaft*?"

"Embassy," replied Herman solemnly. "Russian Embassy. Jesus."

Harvath studied the serious look on Herman's face and said, "What is it?"

"Something very bad. The ground beneath Berlin is riddled with bunkers and networks of tunnels," he answered. "The Gestapo built them under a direct order from the Führer. Not only were they used as fallout shelters, but also as interrogation facilities where some of the most horrific torture you could ever imagine was carried out.

"After the war, many Gestapo agents were absorbed by the Russians and placed into the *Ministerium für Statessicherheit*—"

"You mean the Stasi?" asked Harvath. "The East German secret police?"

"Yes. The old Gestapo agents trained many of the Stasi. I heard terrible stories when I was with the GSG9 of what went on down in these tunnels and forgotten bunkers. Many people were brought down here never to be seen or heard from again," said Herman, who then realized the implication of his words and was quiet.

Harvath felt a chill run down his spine as he resigned himself to the only logical reason Überhof could have for keeping Gary Lawlor in this horrific sort of underworld. Pulling back the slide on his H&K, he verified that he had a round chambered and then activated the LaserLyte attached to the rail system beneath the barrel.

No words needed to be spoken between the two men. Harvath simply nodded his head and their search of the ghost station began in earnest.

Harvath held his pistol out in front with both hands while he and Herman cleared the station. So far, it was empty. Harvath was about ready to suggest that they go back down to the platform and search farther up the unknown line, when he saw something out of place across the lobby.

It was a vintage Soviet-era cigarette machine, complete with a picture of Comrade Lenin puffing away on his favorite brand. Harvath walked over and began examining it from all angles.

"What are you doing?" said Herman as he joined him, careful to keep his voice down. "I thought you didn't smoke."

"I don't, but doesn't it seem odd to you that there was a kiosk on the platform that would have sold cigarettes and there's also a cigarette machine here?"

"No, not really. Germans back then liked to smoke. In fact, we still like to."

"And the fact that there are no other vending machines, no ticket machines or anything else still in this station doesn't bother you?"

"Now that you mention it," replied Herman, "a cigarette machine, especially back then, would have been worth a lot of money. If nothing else, you'd think some soldiers would have taken it at some point and sold it on the black market."

"Exactly," responded Harvath, who threw his shoulder up against the machine. "The way it's wedged into this alcove, I can't get it to budge. I think it must be bolted to the wall."

"Move over," said Herman. "Let me give it a try."

Harvath got out of the way, and the enormous German planted his feet and then wrapped his huge arms around the thing. He tried three times to move it without success.

"Now I know why no one ever stole it," he said as he gave up and took in a deep breath. "Something *is* holding it to that wall. But you can't get to the bolts. How would you service it?"

"Good question. It doesn't make sense, unless—" said Harvath, trailing off as an idea struck him and he illuminated the pull knobs on the front of the machine with his flashlight.

"What are you thinking?" asked Herman.

"Do you have any idea what kind of cigarettes Lenin smoked?"

"No, why?"

"Because the Soviets used to infuse a lot of their clandestine operations with symbolism. How about *Sobranies*?"

"The black Russian cigarettes?" responded Herman, confused. "How should I know?"

"Let's give them a try," said Harvath who pulled the handle and waited for something to happen.

"Maybe you should try putting some money in first."

"I don't think so," replied Harvath, as he chose another handle. "How about *Sputnik* brand?"

Once again nothing happened.

"If you'd tell me what you're trying to do, maybe I could help you," offered Herman as he leaned his shoulder against the wall and tried to understand what Harvath was doing.

"Of course!" said Harvath, careful to remember to keep his voice down. "*Leningradskie* brand would have been his favorite. How stupid of me."

Harvath pulled on the handle for *Leningradskie* cigarettes and to his surprise, it came out significantly farther than the others. Nothing else happened.

"Maybe you should try an East German brand," joked Herman.

"I can't tell the difference," replied Harvath. "Which one is East German?"

"Pull the knob for the *F6* smokes. It used to be quite popular in the East."

Harvath did and just like the knob for *Leningradskie* cigarettes, this one also came out significantly farther than the others. He stood back from the machine and thought for a moment.

"I still say you need to put some money in," quipped Herman.

"And I think its much easier than that once you figure it out," said Harvath as he reapproached the machine with a new idea and pulled the knobs for the *Leningradskie* and *F6* cigarette brands at the same time.

All of a sudden, there was a series of noises from inside the cigarette machine that sounded like heavy metal bars bumping over the teeth of thick metal tumblers. There was a groan of metal on metal as the entire tiled alcove, cigarette machine and all, shuddered and then began to swing inward.

"Open sesame," said Harvath as he raised his H&K and pointed it straight ahead.

"*Fick mich*," joined Herman, drawing his second weapon.

With a Beretta .40-caliber 96 Stock pistol in each hand, he looked like some sort of modern day cowboy and Harvath told him as much.

"You'll be glad I brought the twins," answered Toffle, kissing both of the Berettas in turn. "Anyone who goes to this much trouble to conceal what they're doing is not going to be very happy to see us coming."

"Then let's make sure they don't, got it?"

"Do *I* have it? What am I, new? Maybe we should double-check with Helga and Kristina here," said Herman waving his pistols. "Do *you* have it, girls?"

"Very funny, Herman. Let's just not fuck this up."

Herman shook his head and the pair moved inside.

Following the dimly lit tunnel, they came upon two abandoned rooms that looked like they hadn't been touched in half a century. Dust and cobwebs covered everything. They moved farther down the hall and discovered a rusted door that looked like a ship's bulkhead. Though they were somewhat muffled, Harvath could distinctly make out voices coming from the other side. As the voices weren't speaking in English, he waved Herman over, and Herman pressed his ear up against the door as well.

"How many are in there?" Harvath asked.

"At least three, maybe more," whispered Herman after listening for several moments.

"Can you tell if Gary is in there?"

"I don't know. One of the men seems to be giving all of the orders, but his German is not very good. He says he's come a long way and is very pissed off that the men have not done their job. He's chewing one of them out for being late. I think the late man is Überhof. He says he was late because he was being followed, but he took care of the problem and no one followed him here."

"Good," replied Harvath, who then got up and signaled that he was going to take a look at the rest of the hallway.

Pipes of varying sizes were suspended from the ceiling and appeared to run the length of the tunnel. Like most of the bunkers and fallout shelters he had seen during his career, Harvath correctly assumed that the pipes were used to channel various utilities throughout the underground complex.

He came upon several more rooms, all more or less in varying states of neglect and disarray. It was hard to tell what sort of function they may have once served. All that mattered was that they were presently devoid of other human beings.

At the end of the hallway, Harvath was stopped dead in his tracks by another blast door with a red sign marked *Betriebsraum*, which was framed by two lightning bolts. Though Harvath had no idea what the word meant in German, he figured it was probably a mechanical room of some sort. Looking up, he saw that all of the utility pipes fed through the solid rock above the door and into whatever room lay on the other side. He tried spinning the large crank handle on the outside of the door, but it wouldn't budge. Even when he tucked his H&K under his arm and ignored the searing pain in his side as he tried with both hands, nothing happened.

Harvath decided to forget the door and quickly made his way back up the tunnel to where Herman was still listening against the bulkhead door.

"Anything new?" he asked, taking up a position next to Toffle.

"I think there's somebody else in the room with them."

"What makes you say that?"

"Because, they're speaking English now."

"Is it Gary?"

"I can only hear what sounds like questions. I thought I heard somebody responding, but now, there's nothing. What do you want to do?" asked Herman, as he backed away from the door.

"You know what I want to do," said Harvath, pulling two flashbang grenades from his coat pocket. "Are you ready?"

Herman Toffle patted his injured leg, the same leg that had forced him into early retirement from his beloved GSG9 position, and responded, "I've been ready for this for a long time."

CHAPTER 26

The powerful man circled Gary Lawlor's chair like a bull zeroing in on an injured matador. He hadn't introduced himself when he entered the bunker, and he didn't need to. Though very much the worse for wear, Lawlor was still with it enough to know who the man was. Someone from the Russian Military High Command, especially someone like General Sergei Stavropol, was a person whose reputation preceded him.

"You don't seem surprised to see me," said Stavropol.

"It was only a matter of time before someone from Mother Russia showed up," mumbled Lawlor, his cracked and swollen lips revealing a mouth full of broken and damaged teeth. "I'm just surprised at the poor level of help you are hiring to do your dirty work these days."

"Helmut took a personal interest in your case. He can be very persuasive, but he doesn't seem to be having that effect on you. Not to worry, though,

I'm here now and I'm sure the two of us are going to get along just fine."

Lawlor laughed. It was a dry, hacking cackle, the best he was capable of, but he choked it out nonetheless.

"You're laughing. You don't think I'm serious?" asked Stavropol.

"You may be serious, but you won't be successful," spat Lawlor between his laughs, which turned into a fit of coughing.

"You don't sound so good. You may have aspirated some of your own blood. Or maybe you have a punctured lung? Have they been a bit rough on you?"

The understatement caused Lawlor to begin laughing again, which in his condition invariably led to another coughing fit.

"You need to relax. You'll cough yourself to death, and that wouldn't be good. Not at least until we've had a chance to talk."

"I've got a manicure in a half hour, so let's get on with it," rasped Lawlor.

"Very funny. You like to joke, don't you?" asked Stavropol. "You like to have a good time?"

"Is that a rhetorical question?"

"Judging by some of the photographs I have, I guess it is."

Photographs, wondered Lawlor. *What the hell is he talking about?*

"I assume you'd like to see them?" said Stavropol.

"I already have naked pictures of your wife," replied Lawlor.

"Actually, these are pictures of your wife. Though she's not naked, I thought you would appreciate some of the final surveillance photos that were taken of you both before her tragic accident."

"*Accident*," repeated Lawlor, the bile rising in his throat. "Fuck you."

"So that means, *no*? You don't wish to see the photos? That's a shame. We were actually quite proud of that operation. But, it's all water under the bridge, I can understand that—"

"Not water under the bridge. Now that I know you were involved, I am going to kill you too."

"Me?" asked Stavropol, feigning surprise. "Considering your current situation, that would really be something to see."

"First Draegar and then you," hissed Lawlor.

"All in due time."

"I promise you it will come."

"Be that as it may, I have other photos you might like to see," said Stavropol as he produced another set.

"Paste yourself up a fucking scrapbook. I'm not interested."

"Don't be too sure. There's some people in here you might recognize."

Lawlor turned his face away and Stavropol nodded to Draegar and Überhof, who came over and grabbed hold of Lawlor's head and forced him to look at the pictures.

"You're quite an enigma, Mr. Lawlor. You and your wife never had children. You don't have any other family to speak of. You're not even particularly close with any of your coworkers, except," said the man presenting a new photo, "for this one."

The picture was of one of Gary Lawlor's barbecues. From the angle it was taken, Lawlor figured the photographer must have been using a long lens somewhere in the woods behind his house. Two things about the photo disturbed him deeply. One was that the picture had to have been taken sometime in the fall, which meant that they had been watching him for several months and he had never noticed it. Two, and this was probably the worst thing, was the person singled out on the photo with a red circle drawn around his head complete with mock crosshairs. That person was like family to him.

"Your silence speaks for itself," said Stavropol.

"I can guarantee you'll never get to him," replied Lawlor.

"Really? So he's that good? Is he as good as the men on your Dark Night team?"

There was no point in pretending. Lawlor knew that they were on to the Dark Night operation. How, he had no idea, but the key was not to give them anything that they didn't already have, anything that would aid them in shutting down the operation altogether.

"He's even better," said Gary.

"Well, that's good for him, because from what

my people tell me, your other operatives were some of the easiest kills they have ever made."

Lawlor couldn't believe his ears. *It wasn't true.* Stavropol was lying. This was his way of breaking him down, trying to get him to talk.

"Would you like to see pictures?" asked Stavropol, as he ran through a series of photos that all but confirmed for Lawlor that his team was dead. Except for one, it seemed.

"So what?" said Gary.

"So if you don't want to see what happened to them happen to this fellow," responded Stavropol as he brought back out the picture of Harvath with the crosshairs through his head, "I suggest you tell me about your contingencies. What was the next step if your team failed? Certainly your pathetic operation wasn't your country's last hope."

Stavropol was much cooler, more controlled in his interrogation than Draegar. He referred to what he *wanted* to know rather than *needed*. That made him all the more dangerous in Lawlor's book.

"I don't care how good you think you are," said Lawlor. "You'll never get him."

"Really?" asked Stavropol. "What about Helmut? I'm thinking about letting him do it. I think he'd have a very good chance of succeeding."

Gary knew that Stavropol was serious. He had no doubt that the man would fulfill his black promise to the very letter. He wished there was a way he could warn Scot, but that didn't look as if it was going to happen. The one thing that Lawlor could take solace in was that he knew Scot Harvath would avenge his death. No matter how much cajoling, favoring, swapping, and pressure he had to put on people, Harvath would discover Gary's real past and would eventually track down his killers. Gary only hoped that Harvath would do a better job avenging his death than he had Heide's. The mere fact that Helmut Draegar was still alive, much less had managed to get the better of Gary and take him prisoner was more than he could bear. No, Scot was a better operative than Gary had ever been. Scot would see to it that Gary's killers were brought to justice—the *right* kind of justice.

"So," said Stavropol, removing a magnificently engraved pistol from beneath his suit coat, which shone with an amazing brilliance in the murky, semidarkness, "are you going to make it easier on your friend, or harder?"

Lawlor's mind struggled under the weight of what he was being asked to do. It was one of the most painful decisions anyone could ever be faced with. Scot was like a son to him. At the same time, there wasn't room for choosing. He had an assignment and the freedom of his country hung in the balance. The only reason that Stavropol hadn't killed him yet was because he had something they not only wanted, but *needed* to know. He had no choice. He would take the information with him to the grave. Based on the photos of the slain Dark Night operatives he had seen, they hadn't gotten to

Frank Leighton. And if they hadn't gotten to Frank Leighton, then there still was hope.

Gary cleared his throat and repeated, "Like a ghost. By the time you realize he's in the room, it will be too late."

"We'll see about that," said Stavropol as he pointed the gun at Gary's chest and cocked the hammer. "I am not going to waste any time torturing you. Either you answer my questions or you die. Your decision is that simple."

"I couldn't agree more," replied Lawlor. "Fuck you."

At that moment, the rusted bulkhead door came flying open. It slammed against the inside wall where it cracked and fell off its hinges. Draegar yelled, "Grenade!" just as two flashbangs were pitched into the room.

Helmut and Überhof dove for cover, but not Stavropol. The roar of his Tokarev reverberated throughout the room as two blinding flashes of light accompanied by a pair of deafening concussion blasts erupted from the flashbangs.

The cacophony of sound bounced off the stone walls and came racing back with twice the amplitude. As Harvath and Herman entered the chamber, Überhof and Draegar, who had shielded their eyes with their arms and opened their mouths to counterbalance the overpressure effect of the grenades, began firing toward the entrance from different sides of the room.

The air had immediately filled with smoke and

dust. With the reduced visibility, it was hard to tell where anybody was, much less who anybody was. The only thing for sure was that the room was much larger than any of the others they had seen in the bunker. It looked like some sort of abandoned command and control center.

Herman let loose with a high barrage from his twin Berettas in an effort to pin down their opponents while Harvath tried to pinpoint exactly where the shooters were, so that he could take them out without accidentally hitting Gary.

The echoing gunfire that filled the chamber was extremely deceptive. Harvath knew that they were looking for at least three men, but the intensity of shooting quickly dropped so that it seemed to only be coming from one person. The shooter was firing as he moved along the other side of the room. *Where the hell were the other two?* wondered Harvath.

His question was momentarily forgotten as Überhof, who had stopped to reload, now opened up from a new position—crouched behind a long row of antiquated communications equipment. For a moment, Harvath could almost picture the ghosts of operators sitting there with bulky headsets straddling canvas military caps, but a bullet whizzing by his ear snapped him back to the seriousness of the moment.

The communications console was perched upon a raised platform against the far wall, putting Überhof on the high ground, which provided him with a considerable advantage.

As Harvath studied the man's position, he noticed that hanging behind the console was what appeared to be an enormous light-up map of Berlin, and it gave him an idea. After finally getting Herman's attention, he motioned to the map and indicated what he wanted to do. After loading two new clips, Herman nodded his head and once again created a blanket of cover fire.

Harvath rolled out from his position and started shooting at the two brackets holding the heavy illuminated map to the ceiling. When the first bracket shattered and began to give way, he turned his H&K on the second. In a shower of sparks and twisted metal, the enormous map came crashing down, filling the narrow space behind the communications console and the wall, sending more dust and debris into the air.

Harvath and Herman waited, but nothing happened. It was all quiet. *Too* quiet. They knew that there were at least two more bad guys in that room, *but where were they?* Harvath motioned to Herman to hand him the Specter scope. He pushed the power button and waited for what seemed like an eternity for the device to power up. As he scanned the room, he caught movement in the far corner. Was it the other two hostiles, or was one of them holding Gary at gunpoint while another remained in hiding somewhere in the chamber? That was the problem. With the Specter scope, there was no way to tell.

"Don't move," yelled Harvath raising his weapon. "Stop where you are."

The figures in the scope kept moving. Harvath was about to fire a warning shot, when all of a sudden they disappeared from view. It didn't make any sense until he heard the unmistakable slamming of a heavy metal door.

Without thinking twice, Harvath got up and ran for the back of the chamber. When he reached the door and tried to raise the heavy iron handle, he was too late. It had already been locked from the other side. Once again, he was stopped dead in his tracks by another blast door with a red sign marked *Betriebsraum*, framed by two lightning bolts.

"Damn it," he swore under his breath.

"Scot," yelled Herman. "Get over here. I think I've found Gary."

Harvath rushed to where Herman was trying to saw off the flexi-cuffs that bound Lawlor to his chair. Scot pushed him aside and knelt down. Taking the knife away from him he began working on the cuffs himself and said, "Check that guy behind the communications console, then get back over here. I'm going to need your help."

Gary had been shot. A large red stain covered his chest and his breathing was slow and shallow. He had been knocked over backward in his chair and once Harvath had the felxi-cuffs cut away, he sat him up, trying to make him as comfortable as possible.

Looking at his face, Harvath was amazed that Herman had recognized Gary at all. He had been beaten to a pulp. Both of his eyes were practically swollen shut and his lips looked like they had been pumped up to five times their normal size. His face was covered with various cuts and contusions and his hair was matted with dried blood.

"What the hell did they do to you?" asked Harvath, more to himself than to Gary.

Lawlor tried to speak, but Scot told him to be quiet. He was gurgling as if blood was in his lungs.

Harvath tore Gary's shirt open to the waist and tried to wipe away some of the blood from around the entry wound. This was what you always worried about in a hostage situation—that the hostage-takers might go down swinging, starting with a defenseless hostage. It was every counterterrorism operative's nightmare—not getting there in time.

As Harvath assessed Lawlor's injuries, the man tried to push his hands away. He was rasping again in his fluid-filled whisper, which Harvath couldn't understand. When Herman began to make his way back over to them, Gary became even more insistent.

"Gary," commanded Harvath, "calm down. You've been shot. I need to look at this wound. Now quit fighting me."

Lawlor's strength amazed Harvath as he continued to try to resist. It didn't make any sense. The closer Herman got, the harder Gary began to thrash.

Finally, Lawlor gave one last push that was strong enough to topple Harvath over and grabbed his gun. Before Harvath could stop him, Gary had pulled the trigger three times and fired at another figure that had been creeping toward them.

"Is he dead?" whispered Lawlor, as Harvath stared at the body.

When Harvath didn't respond, Lawlor repeated with more emphasis, "*Is he dead?*"

"Yes," said Scot.

"Make sure."

"Gary, he's dead."

"Make sure, goddamn it!"

Harvath went over and felt for Überhof's pulse. There was none. "He's definitely dead."

Lawlor said something that sounded like "good," before dropping the pistol and collapsing into unconsciousness.

CHAPTER 27

I thought for sure he was trying to kill me," said Herman as he and Harvath sat just outside the operating room where Gary Lawlor was still being worked on. He had been in surgery for more than nine hours. When they had finally climbed out of the U-Bahn system and bundled Lawlor into an ambulance, it was well past ten o'clock in the morning.

Lawlor had lost a lot of blood, and getting him out of the *Geisterbanhöfe* had been a nightmare. Herman had managed to find an old stretcher in the bunker, but between his bad leg and Harvath's bruised ribs, it had taken forever for them to retrace their steps back to the functioning Friedrichstrasse station where they could call for help.

A team of Sebastian's men came back to the *Geisterbanhöfe* and after securing the empty rooms used shape charges to blow open the locked doors marked *Betriebsraum*. Harvath had been right. The *Betriebsraum* was indeed a mechanical room, complete with generators and an air filtration system, but there was also something else—a concealed passageway with a circular metal staircase, leading all the way up to the Russian Embassy. Once Sebastian's men realized what they had discovered, they wisely backed off. They had enough explaining to do to their superiors already, especially with one of their team members dead. Besides, even if they had wanted to breach the Russian Embassy, which several of them were eager to do, it was considered sovereign territory and could have created a serious international incident.

Instead, Sebastian's men secured the body of Karl Überhof, who, beneath his jacket, had concealed a small-caliber sniper weapons system with full-metal-jacket nine-millimeter rounds. The mystery of who had been shooting at them from across the street of the Goltzstrasse safe house seemed at least partially solved. The remaining two questions were who the hell was Überhof and who had he been working for?

Sebastian had spent the rest of the day trying to keep his own ass, as well as those of his men, out of the proverbial fire. He had had no choice but to come clean with his superiors. Well, *relatively* clean at least. Out of respect, he had left Harvath's name out of it. He told his commander that they had been operating on a tip from an informant. Though the story wasn't going to hold forever, he hoped at least it would buy Harvath a little bit of time. It was the least he felt he could do for him. The phone call about Überhof's sniper rifle and the hidden stairwell leading to the Russian Embassy had come in just moments ago and was the last "favor" Sebastian had said he could do for Harvath. He and his men were being watched too closely now.

"I thought he was trying to kill you too," answered Scot, turning back to Herman and continuing their conversation, "until I saw Überhof coming up behind you."

"Thank God, Gary saw him or we'd both be dead now."

Harvath just nodded his head as he reflected on what the past couple of days must have been like for Gary. The doctors said it was a wonder he was still alive at all. No one could understand how he had survived. No one, except for Scot Harvath. Gary was a fighter, a survivor. It was something they shared in common.

"What about our other guys?" asked Herman, trying to respect Harvath's silence, but wanting to connect some of the dots. "The ones that got away. Who do you think they are?"

Herman brought Scot's attention back to the present. "Taking into consideration that the bullet pulled out of Gary was a 7.62 Soviet M30, along with the VIP access to the Russian Embassy these guys had, I think it's pretty safe to rule out the possibility that they are of Norwegian descent."

"You think the Russians are involved?" asked Herman. "What possible connection could there be between terrorists targeting the United States and the Russian Federation?"

"A bigger connection than you may think."

"You're joking, right? When you said you were dealing with terrorists, in this day and age I automatically assumed you were talking about Islamic terrorists. Now you're saying the Russian Federation is behind the threat against America?"

"Herman, we have very little to go on here."

"All of a sudden, I don't think so. We have Karl Überhof—a deceased German national obviously schooled in tradecraft who was able to take out a highly trained MEK operative, and our Soviet ammunition–firing tunnel rat who scampered away with a friend up into the Russian Embassy. I want you to look me in the face and tell me that you don't see any connection."

Harvath set his chair back down on the ground and looked directly at Herman. It was time he told him the whole truth. "Several days ago, we discovered an enhanced suitcase nuke just outside one of our major cities."

Herman was shocked and it took him several moments to compose himself. "What do you mean by *enhanced*?" he finally asked.

"Capable of a much larger yield than is normally associated with man-portable nuclear devices."

"My God," said Herman. "And this is what the terrorists have planned?"

"At this point we are confirming nineteen out of a possible twenty-five devices inside the United States."

"And the balance may be in cities of America's Western allies?"

"Yes."

"Where'd these devices come from?"

"Where do you think?" replied Harvath.

"Russia?"

"Bingo."

"But I don't understand," said Herman, leaning forward in his chair toward Harvath. "What about mutually assured destruction?"

"Suffice it to say, the Russians have found a way around that."

"How is that possible?"

"They have developed some sort of air defense system that is impregnable."

"And now what? They want to take over the United States?"

"Just about. They want us off the world stage so they can fill the void and be the world's predominant superpower."

Herman was floored. It was all too much. He had watched the Berlin Wall fall. In fact, he had even been there. He and several of his teammates had traveled to Berlin with sledgehammers and had spent hours cracking away at the enormous barrier, handing out pieces to anyone who wanted them. He had watched as people streamed across the no-man's-land known as the *death strip* to be reunited with friends and loved ones in the West. Then the Soviet Union itself came tumbling down. At the time, it had all seemed beyond belief, but everyone had eventually gotten used to it. But what Harvath was telling him now was absolutely beyond comprehension. "Is there more?" he asked, stunned.

"There's Gary's involvement and how he fits into hopefully stopping this from happening, but that has to remain classified," said Harvath.

Both of the men sat back in their chairs, staring off into separate directions.

After several minutes, it was Herman who broke the silence. "What's the timetable?"

"The deadline is the president's State of the Union address in six days."

"And you're sure the Russian government is behind this?"

Harvath broke off from what he was staring at and said, "If it weren't for the air defense system, we might have our doubts, but there's enough evidence pointing to the people at the top. They claim they know nothing about what's going on, but we believe otherwise."

"What are you going to do?" asked Herman.

Harvath was about to answer, when he noticed one of the admitting nurses walking in their direction.

"*Herr Harvath?*" she asked in German as she approached the two men who immediately stood up.

"*Ich bin Herr Harvath,*" replied Scot, wondering why it wasn't one of the operating room staff coming out to give him an update on Gary's condition. Suddenly, he had a bad feeling.

"*Es tut mir leid, Sie damit zu belästige—*" the nurse began.

"I'm sorry," said Harvath. "*Sprechen Sie Englisch bitte?*"

"Yes, I speak English."

"Good. What's going on?"

"You have visitors."

"*Visitors?* I'm not expecting any visitors. Who are they?"

"I don't know. Foreigners of some sort."

"They're not German?" said Harvath, thinking that it might be Sebastian or one of the guys from the MEK team.

"No, these men are definitely not German. Only one of them spoke, and his German is very bad."

A man who speaks very bad German? Harvath shot Herman a look before continuing. "What do they look like?"

"Big," replied the nurse, holding her hands way out.

"How many are there?"

"There are two of them. I explained that this area is off-limits and that they are not welcome here. I offered the waiting area in the ICU, but they declined. They asked me for something more private."

"Where are they now?"

"In the surgeons' conference suite down the hall," she said pointing. "Room 311. I can show you if you like."

"No, thank you," replied Harvath. "I can find it."

The nurse smiled and walked away. Once she

was out of sight, Harvath removed his H&K, made sure that a round was chambered, and then tucked it back beneath his jacket.

"Who do you think it is?" asked Herman.

"I don't know, but I don't like it."

"Do you want me to come with you?"

"No. You stay here and watch over Gary. No matter what happens, don't leave him. Agreed?"

"Agreed," said Herman, putting his hand on Scot's shoulder. "Be careful."

"Me? I'm always careful," replied Harvath.

Herman forced a smile as Scot walked off down the hall.

Arriving at room 311, Harvath found the door closed. He listened, but didn't hear anything coming from the other side. He pulled out his H&K and wrapped it in a towel he had taken from one of the hospital's linen closets.

"*Zimmermädchen*," he said, not knowing what the appropriate term for housekeeping was in a German hospital. At the same time, he didn't care because whoever was in this room wasn't a very good German speaker to begin with. His goal was to get whoever was inside to peek their head out so he could get the drop on them.

"*Danke, wir haben schon gegessen,*" replied a voice from the other side of the door. *Thank you, but we've already eaten.*

"*Ich komme morgen zurück,*" *I'll come back tomorrow morning,* replied Harvath, who pretended to be leaving, but instead stepped just beyond the door frame and began counting. When he got to ten, he grabbed the handle and threw the door open.

The men on the other side immediately reached for their guns, but then dropped their hands.

"Where the hell did you learn your German?"

"High school, *Hogan's Heroes*, and the occasional trip to Milwaukee to visit my uncle for Oktoberfest," replied a tall, muscular, blond-haired, blue-eyed man in his mid-twenties who looked as if he belonged on a beach in Southern California, or in a Chippendales review somewhere.

"You trusted this guy to do your talking for you?" asked Harvath to the other man.

"My mistake. He said he could speak German. If I had understood what he was saying, I never would have let him open his mouth," replied the second man who was just as tall, but slightly less muscular than the first. He looked to be in his mid-forties, with close-cropped, jet-black hair with a little bit of gray showing at the temples. His impassive, angular face could have been carved from a solid block of granite, and the deep cleft in his chin looked as if it had been chipped there with an ax.

Harvath lowered his weapon. The last thing he wanted to do was accidentally shoot two friends. Gordon Avigliano was a good kid and had a bright future ahead of him, and Rick Morrell was not only a skilled operative, but also someone Harvath had grown to respect. They were both members of the CIA's paramilitary division known as the Special Activities Staff. Scot had known Rick Morrell during his SEAL days when Morrell had left to join the CIA and they had become reacquainted during a top-secret operation to track down the extremely deadly Middle Eastern terrorist duo of Adara and Hashim Nidal. "What the hell are you guys doing here?"

"The boss sent us," replied Morrell.

"Vaile?" said Harvath, referring to the director of the CIA. "Why the hell would he have sent you guys here?" Then it hit him and he raised his H&K again. "If he thought because we're friends you two could just walk in here and take Gary into custody, he was sorely mistaken. He's still in surgery, for Christ's sake. He's not going anywhere with you guys. You have no idea how far off the mark your boss is on this one."

"Easy breezy, cover girl," said Avigliano. "We're not going to take Gary anywhere."

"Bullshit," said Harvath, backing away from the two men. "How'd you even know we were here? I only made one communication and I know you are not surveilling *him*."

Harvath was referring to the anonymous voice mailbox that only the president had access to where Harvath could leave coded updates. He had only left one, stating that he had recovered the package, but that the package was damaged. As best he could, he explained the situation and that he would leave another message once Gary was out of surgery.

"For fuck's sake, Harvath. Would you calm

down?" said Morrell. "Vaile didn't send us. In fact, he has no idea we're all here."

"Who's *we*?"

"Carlson and DeWolfe are back at the hotel."

"Then if Vaile didn't send you, who did?"

"*Our* boss," repeated Morrell, as he waved his index finger in a circle, taking them all in. "Goaltender."

Morrell had used the president's call sign assigned to him as part of the Dark Night operational plan.

"And what exactly is your assignment?" asked Harvath, even more concerned now that it was obvious that Morrell and his team were on the inside.

"There's been a change of plans."

"*Change of plans*?"

"Apparently something has happened. I was instructed to tell you that we don't have any pieces left to rebalance the chessboard. Somehow the other side has found where we were hiding our toys. Goaltender said that would make sense to you. Does it?"

Harvath's blood ran cold. "They've found our nukes?"

"I was just supposed to give you that message. Goaltender wants to talk to you," replied Morrell. "We brought a sat-radio with us, and Carlson and DeWolfe are busy setting up a secure link."

"Why you?" asked Harvath. "Why send your team?"

"Because he knows you trust us and therefore so

does he. He knows together we'll get the job done."

"And what job is that?"

"When we get back to the hotel, you can ask him yourself."

"What about security for Gary?" said Harvath. "The people we're after might not be done with him yet. They could come back. I've got a very old and trusted friend watching over him right now, but he won't be able to pull all the shifts. And if these guys came back in force, as good as this guy is, I can't guarantee what the outcome would be."

"Not to worry. We've arranged for a few visiting medical students to conduct a rotation here and keep an eye on Gary," said Morrell, who signaled to Avigliano to open the door to the conference suite's adjoining room.

Harvath couldn't believe his eyes. Standing there in surgical scrubs and white lab coats were two of his closest friends from the White House security detail, Secret Service agents Tom Hollenbeck and Chris Longo.

"I'll be damned," said Harvath. "If it isn't Doctors Moe and Larry. There's just the two of you? You couldn't get a third to play Curly?"

At that moment, the sound of a toilet flushing came from the suite's private bathroom and then the door opened revealing a third man in a white lab coat, tying the drawstring on the pants of his scrubs.

"That figures," said Harvath, as he recognized who it was.

"Surprise, surprise!" crowed Doctor Skip Trawick with a mock Scottish accent. The semiretired Special Forces medic had been instrumental in helping Harvath rescue the president from Gerhard Miner and his team of Swiss mercenaries two years ago.

"Because Longo and Hollenbeck know absolutely nothing about medicine," said Morrell, getting things back on track, "Goaltender thought it would be best to have at least one real doctor along for the ride."

Satisfied that Gary was now going to an appropriate level of security, Harvath marched the trio of "doctors" down to Herman Toffle, where he explained what was happening. While Longo, Trawick, and Hollenbeck worked out how they were going to handle shifts, Morrell and Avigliano followed Scot and Herman down to Herman's Mercedes, where Harvath transferred his and Gary's bags to the trunk of Morrell's rental car.

"Well, I guess this is it," said Herman, extending his hand, a slight edge of disappointment noticeable in his voice. It felt good getting back in the game, even if it was short-lived.

"Actually, Herman," began Harvath, "I was hoping you might stick around a little bit longer. Those are good guys back up in Gary's room, but they don't have near the experience that you do."

Herman brightened. "And, they speak lousy German."

"That's true," smiled Harvath. "Would you

mind hanging in with them for a little longer? I'd feel better knowing you were up there with Gary."

"How can I say no to a friend in need?"

"I was hoping you'd feel that way," said Harvath. "I want you to keep me up to speed on Gary's progress and call me the minute he's out of surgery. He's the only one that can help us make contact again with Frank Leighton." *If Leighton's even still alive*, thought Harvath.

"Don't worry," replied Herman. "I'll let you know as soon as I hear anything."

It was raining again as they pulled out of the parking structure and though the fog had dissipated, the evening still felt dense and impenetrable.

As the small sedan became ensnarled in evening Berlin traffic, Harvath leaned his head against the leather headrest and looked out the rain-streaked window. A heavy sense of foreboding weighed on his mind. The surgeons' lack of confidence in Gary Lawlor's prognosis was definitely troubling, but more than that, he was concerned about the message Rick Morrell had delivered on behalf of the president. *All of our pieces have been knocked off the chessboard.*

CHAPTER 28

Rick Morrell pulled their car into the underground parking structure of the distinctive semicircular building known as Berlin's Kempinski Hotel Bristol. After finding an empty stall, Morrell used his keycard to summon the elevator and the three men rode to the sixth floor.

When the elevator doors opened, Gordon Avigliano led the way down the lavishly carpeted hallway to a rich mahogany door where he rapped out a quick code.

"Housekeeping," said Avigliano in a high-pitched voice, shouldering his way into the room as DeWolfe opened the door for them. "Fluff your pillow? Chocolate mint?"

"Scot," said DeWolfe, shaking his hand and ignoring Avigliano. "Good to see you again."

"You too," said Scot, genuinely glad to see the operative who had helped rescue him from Adara Nidal's terrorist compound in the Libyan desert last year.

"Hey," shouted Carlson, who walked over and grabbed Scot Harvath by both shoulders so he could look at him, "why wasn't I surprised when they told me you were in trouble?"

"Nice to see you too, Steve," replied Harvath.

"Now that we're all reacquainted," interjected Morrell, who had locked the door behind them and was making his way to the center of the room. "Maybe we can get started."

Morrell turned to DeWolfe, "How are we doing?"

The communications expert was bent over a map of the world, complete with latitude and longitude lines, upon which he had placed a clear plastic slide. "I'm just working out our elevation and azimuth," he replied.

"What about the electronic countermeasures?"

"I swept the room three times and placed the ECMs in the appropriate positions, so don't worry. Not only is nobody listening to us, but even if they wanted to, they couldn't. All of the equipment is working perfectly, and everything is tip-top."

"Good. This is the first time I have been hand-picked by the president for an operation, and I don't intend to screw it up. In fact, this is our first scrambled communication with him and I expect it to go off without a hitch. Is that clear?"

"Yes, sir, boss," responded DeWolfe. He was aiming for one of the Defense Department's dedicated satellites and as he computed the best "takeoff" angle for their transmission, Carlson assembled a wire spiderweb satellite dish the size of a dinner plate, connected it to their fully digitized and fully encrypted Harris manpack SATCOM radio, and then placed the dish on top of the coffee table.

According to DeWolfe's calculations, they had twenty more minutes before they would pass into their optimal broadcast window, so Morrell allowed Avigliano to run out to pick up orders of the lamb and salad sandwiches packed in pita bread known as Döner Kebabs. Though Morrell would have preferred Cokes, when Avigliano returned with a beer for each of the men, he let it slide.

Harvath had grabbed a quick shower and shave and after dressing in a black sweater and a new pair of jeans, joined the rest of the team in the living room. He sat down on one of the leather couches, opened up Gary Lawlor's suitcase on the floor in front of him, and began to go through it again.

Carefully, he removed each piece of clothing and, after thoroughly examining it, folded it and set it on the couch next to him.

"Where'd you get that?" asked DeWolfe, as Harvath was emptying out the contents of Lawlor's shaving kit.

"What?" said Harvath, holding up a tube of toothpaste. "This?"

"Not the toothpaste. That other thing you've got sitting there next to those clothes."

"This organizer?" asked Harvath, reaching for the oversized PDA that had been vexing him since he had first found it in Gary's luggage.

"Yeah, let me look at it," said DeWolfe, who

crossed over to where Harvath was sitting and took the device from him. "Interesting."

"What's interesting?"

DeWolfe had powered the device up and was scrolling through its programs. "I haven't seen one of these in ages."

"I know. It's an antique," replied Harvath as he looked over DeWolfe's shoulder to see what he was doing. "Gary hates almost anything computerized, so I figured the organizer was part of his cover somehow."

"You mean to tell me you've never seen one of these things before?"

"Of course I have, but by the time I got my PDA, it was about a quarter of the size of that thing."

"When you were a SEAL, didn't you ever work with a burst transmitter?"

Harvath's eyes widened. "*A burst transmitter?* That's what that thing is supposed to be?"

"Yup. It uses one of the early modem cards with a pop-out phone jack. Did you find any telephone adaptor plugs in that bag?"

"As a matter of fact," said Harvath holding up a small clear plastic box, "I did, but how do you know about all of this?"

"When I was studying communications and electronic surveillance at the Agency we got to play with one of these. The device was set up to look like one of the early PDAs. It actually was a pretty simple and pretty clever way to camouflage what, in its day, was a cutting-edge burst transmitter."

"Speaking of camouflage," interrupted Morrell, who had walked over to see what DeWolfe was looking at. "Where's that Tabard IR suit I lent you back in DC?"

"It's in safe hands," replied Harvath, his attention still focused on the burst transmitter.

"Whose hands? I'm responsible for that and those Tabard suits aren't cheap."

"Kate Palmer is holding on to my stuff for me until I get back."

"Secret Service Agent Kate Palmer?" asked Carlson. "The one who works at the White House?"

"Yeah," said Harvath, motioning for DeWolfe to hand the device back to him. "Why? You know her."

"No, but she's hot. You don't suppose when we get home you could—"

"Not a chance."

"Why not?"

"Because," replied Harvath, "you're not her type."

"What's that supposed to mean?" asked Carlson.

"It means, I know what kind of guys she likes and you're not it."

"Oh yeah? Well maybe you're wrong. What kind of guys does she like?"

"Guys like Avigliano—tall, blond, and *good-looking.*"

"Oh, so in other words she's got no taste. Why didn't you say so?"

"Fuck you," said Avigliano from across the room.

Harvath ignored them and turned back to De-Wolfe. "The burst transmitters I've worked with were in conjunction with field radios, not telephone lines. Plus, they were much smaller. Why would he want to lug something like that around? Why not upgrade and go with something more compact?"

"From what I understand, the Dark Night operation was established in the eighties and after the Soviet Union fell, the team was retired, so there was no need for it. Don't get me wrong, though. This thing might be a little out of date, but it's still good technology."

"I've never seen one like this masked with all that PDA software. Do you know how it works?" asked Harvath.

"Sure," said DeWolfe, ejecting the PDA's stylus and reaching across Harvath to tap the screen. "Let's say you were a handler like Gary and had several different operatives you were going to need to communicate sensitive information with. The burst transmitter allows you to type out your message, encrypt it, and then send it in a quick burst over the telephone. To the uninitiated, it sounds just like a fax tone, but if you have one of these little beauties and the proper encryption key, you can unencrypt the information and read the message on the screen here."

A fax tone, thought Harvath, recalling the shrill tone he had heard over Gary Lawlor's home phone when he had redialed the last number Gary had called before disappearing. That must have been what he was hearing, *a burst transmission*.

"On any op," continued DeWolfe, "you would want to compartmentalize as much as possible, so Gary would have had a specific encryption code for each one of his operatives. All he would have to do is select that code program and make sure it was up and running before he spoke, or 'bursted' for lack of a better term, with that particular operative."

"And those code programs are in that device?" asked Harvath.

"They should be. The software is not only a type of camouflage, but it also acts as a gateway to the encryption programs."

"How so?"

"On these models, it was as simple as pulling up the calendar function and going to a specific date. The date is the actual gateway for your encryption programs. When you tried to enter an appointment on that date, you would be prompted to enter a security code. Normally, it's a four-digit numeric code derived from a specific mathematical equation; something that would have relevance for both the operative and his handler. To unlock the encryption program you would have to do a simple math problem and then use the answer as your code. You type it in and the encryption program would then engage and you'd be ready to go. The important thing to remember is that Gary had a lot of operatives."

"So?"

"So the more operatives he had, the more code information he would have had to keep straight. It has been my experience that the more numeric codes you have to assign and memorize, the more likely you are to start assigning them based upon things that are easier and easier for you to remember, but which would have no relevance for any unauthorized persons trying to hack into your system."

"That makes sense," said Scot, remembering one of Gary's favorite mottos. It was an acronym he was always referring to—KISS, Keep it simple, stupid.

"But remember, it's a two-step process. You'd need to know how to access the general domain for the operative, such as a birth date, and then you'd need the numeric code to open the encryption program so the two of you could communicate freely."

"I suspect you would also need to know," added Harvath, "when and where the two of you were supposed to connect."

"That goes without saying," replied DeWolfe. "You could have all the other information, and yet if you were sitting at a pay phone at the train station waiting for it to ring, when you should have been at a pay phone at the drugstore, you'd be shit out of luck."

No kidding, thought Harvath. Even though he now understood the true nature of the burst transmitter, it was of no use to him without knowing how to unlock Frank Leighton's encryption program or what the emergency contact plan was.

As the time for their encrypted communication with the president drew near, DeWolfe did a final check of his equipment and then outfitted Harvath with a headset. Morrell pulled one of the over-stuffed chairs up to the coffee table and donned a headset as well. Avigliano handed him a briefcase and then slid over three of the large hard-shell equipment cases from the other side of the room.

"I have Goaltender on the line," said DeWolfe. "We are ready to proceed."

"This is Norseman," said Harvath. "Go ahead, Goaltender."

"Is BenchPress on the line?"

"Yes he is," replied Harvath, who had never cared much for Morrell's ridiculous code name; a code name he knew Morrell hadn't received from his superiors or his peers, but rather had chosen for himself.

Even though Harvath had grown to like Morrell, that still didn't change the fact that the man could be an arrogant, insufferable prick a lot of the time and his code name seemed to perfectly reflect his inflated sense of self. Though on many occasions Harvath had been tempted to suggest an alternate two-syllable code name that might more suit the man such as *dipshit*, *dumbass*, *dumbfuck*, or *dickhead*, he had miraculously managed to keep his mouth shut and thereby had refrained from doing damage to a friendship that was still very much in its infancy.

"Norseman," continued President Rutledge,

"you received my message about the condition of the chessboard?"

"Yes, sir. But I don't understand. What happened?"

"Somehow, the other side knew where our devices were hidden. We sent in teams to prep them and get them ready for transport, but they were already gone."

"*Gone?*" said Harvath.

"Yes, all of them have been stolen."

"Do we have any leads?"

"We're going back over satellite imagery, but we're not holding out much hope of getting them back. The Russians would have been very careful in covering their tracks."

"So what are we going to do?"

"We've developed a plan, which I pray to God will work, called Operation Minotaur," replied the president.

"*Operation Minotaur?*" repeated Harvath.

"Yes. BenchPress has the file and he will explain everything to you."

"Sir, what about our remaining operative in the field? He still has one last device."

"Unfortunately, that man is of no use to us anymore. We need to pull him from the game before he becomes a greater liability. BenchPress will explain that as well." There was a pause on the line as the president took a deep breath and said, "Things are very tense back here. The time is drawing nigh for us gentlemen and we have no other options available. This is it. We either win or we lose. The fate of America is in your hands. Don't let us down." There was a click followed by a hiss of static as the president terminated the connection.

Morrell looked at DeWolfe and, referring to the status of the transmission, asked, "Are we clear?"

"We're clear," said DeWolfe.

"*Operation Minotaur?*" mouthed Harvath. "What is this all about?"

"The Minotaur is a mythical creature—"

"From ancient Greece who was half-man, half-bull, and was confined to a labyrinth on Crete. Yeah, I know that, but what is this new op all about?" said Harvath.

"This is a little something the president and his team came up with," responded Morrell. "The focus of this operation is going to be on the bull, and lots of it."

an we just back up here for a second?" asked Harvath. "Rick, start this thing from square one for me, would you?"

"Okay, from square one. The secretary of defense and the president briefed me on Operation Dark Night as well as the situation concerning the man-portable nukes we're facing at home. Being the tactician he is, the secretary kept making military references to chess. As you probably know, the president—"

"Doesn't play chess," replied Harvath, finishing Morrell's sentence for him. "He's a poker man. We played a lot when I was on his protective detail."

"And what's the one thing you can do in poker that you really can't do in chess?"

Harvath thought for a moment and then said, "Bluff."

"Right again. Though there are some feints and deceptive strategies you can pull in chess, all of your pieces are out in the open for your opponent to see."

"But all of our pieces have been knocked off the board, at least that's what the president has said."

"That's true. The president green-lit a series of tactical teams to go to the European locations where our man-portable nukes were hidden, only to discover that they had all been removed."

"By the Russians, of course."

"That's what we're assuming," replied Morrell.

"So, where's that leave us?"

"It leaves us with only one operational nuke."

"Frank Leighton's," said Harvath.

"Correct."

"But if the Russians knew the identities of all of the other Dark Night operatives and the location of their nukes, how'd they miss Leighton?"

"We don't think they missed him," said Morrell.

"Wait a second. You think they not only know who Leighton is, but where he and his nuke are?"

"Yes."

"But why would they purposely let him slip through the net?"

"He isn't all the way through yet."

Harvath wasn't following. "I can understand them wanting to get their hands on Gary. He was in charge of the operation. He had knowledge that could prove valuable to them. They might have even believed he knew about more than just his own op, but Leighton doesn't make any sense. If they let him get this far only to grab him, then . . ."

Morrell almost could see the lightbulb go on over Harvath's head as his voice trailed off.

"Then?" coaxed Morrell, leaning back in his chair.

"They would be catching Leighton, an American, in the act of actually trying to smuggle a nuclear device into their country," said Harvath, the pieces beginning to tumble into place.

"And they could claim it was a covert attempt at a first strike by the United States."

"But I'm sure we would disavow any knowledge of Leighton. It would be a tough sell, but *one* guy with *one* nuke *couldn't* bring down an entire country. It would be somewhat embarrassing for us, but—" Harvath let the sentence hang in the air as he thought about it for a moment and then realizing, said, "Shit."

"What?" asked Morrell.

"If the Russians' plan to blackmail us failed somehow, they'd have a huge ace up their sleeves. With ten other American-made man-portable nukes in their possession, they could lie and claim they had found them hidden all over their country. It would be no use for us to disavow Leighton. It would just look like he was the only American operative unlucky enough to get caught and that we were denying what everyone else would see as a fact. Add it all up and the Russians would have an overwhelming case against us as being the aggressors. Considering the state of international opinion against us these days, the rest of the world would probably buy the Russian story no matter what they had done to start everything. *That's* why they let Leighton live."

"That's what we believe."

"Then we've got to stop Leighton. The Russians probably have him under surveillance right now and are just waiting for him to sail into their territorial waters so they can pop him."

"Well, you've uncovered the *man* part of the Minotaur. Now let's get to the *bull*."

As Avigliano slid three hard-shell equipment cases out of the closet and opened the lids so Harvath could see what was contained inside, Morrell continued. "Exact working replicas of the American nukes the Russians already have in their possession."

"The beauty of it all is that they aren't even a quarter of the weight of the real deal," added Carlson. "One person can lift these without even breaking a sweat."

"But that's the thing. They aren't real," said Harvath. "You've got all the Preparation, but no H."

"Yeah, but the Russians don't know that," answered DeWolfe.

"What are we planning to do, plant fake nukes all across Russia?"

"Not only are we planning to do it, we're going to do it," answered Morrell. "Carlson and DeWolfe will be on one team, and Avigliano and I will be on the other. We're going to conduct a whirlwind photo tour of as much of the country and its critical infrastructure as possible."

"They look awesome," replied Harvath, "but there's still only two of them."

Morrell emptied the contents of a padded manila envelope onto the table. "That's why we have a little something I like to refer to as our force multiplier."

Harvath examined the square metal objects. "Interchangeable serial number plates. Good move."

"The Russians are going to enhance the photos we send them, just like we did theirs."

"Let's say they do buy it, where's that put us?"

"At best, they think America had another ace up her sleeve that they never caught and the board is rebalanced."

"And at worst?" asked Harvath.

"They don't buy it and you sure as hell better pull off your part of the assignment."

"Which is?"

"Taking down their air defense system."

"Well at least I get the easy job," said Harvath. "Russia's about how big a country, do you think?"

"Six million, five hundred fifty-two thousand, seven hundred square miles," offered Avigliano. "Please make sure you let Agent Kate Palmer know that in addition to being tall, blond, and *good*-looking, I also have quite a head for geography."

"As I was starting to say," replied Harvath. "Finding the command and control structure for that air defense system has got to be like looking for a needle in a six million, five hundred fifty-two thousand, seven hundred square mile haystack. Do we have any leads? Do I get any help on this at all?"

Morrell opened his briefcase and handed Harvath a folder. "When this whole thing broke, we conducted a search of our intelligence databases. The search came up with one hit. In the mid-eighties, a Russian KGB officer named Viktor Ivanov was engaged in trading information with the United States from time to time. He was deemed a somewhat reliable source, as far as double agents go, until he presented the CIA with a conspiracy theory so outlandish, they chose to write him off as no longer reliable."

"What was his theory?"

"Ivanov said that he had uncovered a plot by five of the Soviet Union's top generals to win the Cold War by convincing the USSR to roll over and play dead while they invested in a covert weapons program that would allow them to return stronger than the U.S. At this point, you've pretty much seen how the rest of their plan pans out."

Harvath was shocked. "No one checked into this guy's story?"

"Of course we did. The CIA took it seriously at first. Ivanov had never given them bad information before, but they worried that he might have been setting them up."

"Setting them up for what?"

"Who knows?" answered Morrell. "Back then, everyone was suspicious. They were always on the lookout for not only the double, but the triple cross. The long and the short of it is that the Agency dug real deep, pulled a lot of their Soviet contacts in and tried to corroborate Ivanov's story,

but they couldn't. So, in the end, they cut him loose
and refused to use him any more. They thought he
had gone around the bend and didn't want to waste
any more of their time or resources on him."

"So where do I find him?" asked Harvath.

"You can't. He's dead."

"Then what's in that file?"

"Not *what*, but who. Ivanov's daughter, Alexandra Ivanova."

Morrell opened the folder and handed it to him.
Harvath's eyes were immediately drawn to the picture stapled to the inside. Alexandra Ivanova was
gorgeous.

"Former Russian military, Ivanova was recruited
about eight years ago over to Russia's Foreign Intelligence Service, known as the—"

"SVR," added Harvath absentmindedly as he focused on the dossier in front of him. "Following in
the family footsteps."

"Indeed. She has been posted in several international cities, including Hong Kong, London, and Istanbul. She speaks English, Arabic, and Mandarin
in addition to her mother tongue and when her
back is against the wall, has shown herself to be an
extremely deadly assassin. Don't let her looks fool
you, this lady should be treated with the utmost
caution."

"She doesn't look that bad to me," replied Harvath.

"Be that as it may, you're to be extra careful
with her. Do not underestimate her at any time.

Now, her father used her from time to time for some of his more delicate assignments and she was known to be a confidant of sorts to him. He was obsessed with this plot by the generals, and it eventually cost him his job, though the Soviets could never prove that he was trying to tip us off. Apparently, Ivanov was very Hoover-esque in the files he kept on people and that fact alone was probably the only reason he was never bumped off. He probably scared too many people with what he had buttoned down. We believe he most likely passed along some, if not all, of his files to his daughter before he died. At least that's what our analysts think from the short amount of time they had to look at his dossier."

"And what makes you believe that if this woman does know something, that she'll share it with me?"

"The father was no Communist. He was more of a nationalist who put the good of his country, often to the detriment of his career, ahead of the self-serving desires of his government. From what we've seen, the daughter embodies a lot of that same ideology. If she has any information, the president has the utmost confidence that you will do whatever it takes to get it out of her."

"What does that mean?" asked Harvath, who after taking one last look at Alexandra Ivanova's photo, set the file down on the coffee table.

"Those are the president's words, not mine, so you take them to mean whatever you want."

"I bet I know what it means," said Carlson, who had picked up the folder and was looking at the photo. "God, this chick is hot. You know, when this is all over, Harvath, maybe you could—"

"Put that folder down," snapped Morrell. "You're not cleared to see what's in there."

"If that's what a 'hard' assignment looks like," said Carlson, setting down the folder, "I'll trade jobs with you right now, Harvath."

"Thanks, but no thanks," replied Harvath. "I think I can suffer through this one."

"What's that girlfriend of yours going to think about you cozying up to a nice Russian hottie like that?" asked Avigliano, who had picked up the folder and was now looking at the picture.

"As far as I'm concerned," answered Scot, "she's not going to know."

"Good for you," said Carlson peeking over Avigliano's shoulder to get another look at the photo. "What happens behind the Iron Curtain, stays behind the Iron Curtain."

"Goddamn it! Nobody touches this file again, am I understood? In fact," said Morrell, as he snatched the folder away from Avigliano and turned to Harvath, "have you seen everything you need to see in here?"

Harvath nodded his head.

"Good," replied Morrell. "DeWolfe, toss me a burn bag."

"Do I get to see the photo first?" asked the communications expert.

"What the fuck is this, *Let's Make a Deal*? No you don't get to see the photo first. You get to hand me a burn bag and you get to keep your fucking job. How about that for a deal?"

"Hey, everybody else got to see what this Russian chick looks like. I don't know why I—"

"All right, goddamn it. If it'll get you to shut the hell up, give me the burn bag and I'll let you see the fucking picture. Jesus, you guys are a pain in the ass."

DeWolfe winked at Harvath as he brought one of the special, heavy, lead-lined bags over to Morrell. True to his word, Morrell allowed DeWolfe a quick glimpse of the photo before dropping the entire file into the bag. Unlike diplomatic burn bags, into which shredded classified documents were placed and then taken to an incinerator room to be burned later, the modified field burn bag Morrell and his team were carrying provided one-stop shopping for destruction of sensitive materials. After sealing the top of the bag, Morrell set it on the floor and brought his foot down on top of it, breaking the vials of corrosive chemicals inside which quickly ate away at the file and left nothing behind in the bag but a soggy pulp.

"So how do I meet this Russian SVR agent?" asked Harvath, getting the conversation back on track.

"We're working on that right now, but first we need to focus on getting you into Russia," responded Morrell.

"And how do we plan on doing that? More bull?"

"Kind of. You're coming with us to pick up Frank Leighton."

"Where is he?"

"His op was a bit different than the others. We know his was maritime. He was to sail his nuke right into St. Petersburg harbor, so unless he's moved from where his nuke was hidden, which there's no reason to believe he has, right now he's on a small, uninhabited island off the coast of Finland. With the Russians knowing as much as they do about him, he's no good to us anymore. The plan is for us to get him and his device to safety on the mainland, while you sail his boat out into the Baltic toward St. Petersburg."

"Right into the arms of the Russian Navy. This doesn't feel so good."

"Don't worry," said Morrell, "You'll have help."

"Help from whom?"

"You'll be working with a SEAL team stationed aboard the USS *Connecticut*." Morrell saw the sudden shift in Harvath's expression. "Feeling a little bit better about it now?"

"Maybe, but how are you planning on getting to Leighton if the Russians have him under surveillance?"

"We'll be using the Navy's new Advanced SEAL Delivery System."

Having been part of the Navy's Special Warfare Development Group—a SEAL think tank in Little

Creek, Virginia, where new weapons, equipment, communication systems, and tactics are developed, Harvath was very familiar with the 65-foot long mini-submarine known as the ASDS, which could covertly deposit operatives practically within spitting distance of any shoreline anywhere in the world.

"That might get you in under the Russians' radar," said Harvath, "but what about Frank Leighton's? This guy is former Army Intelligence. You can't just walk right up to him and say, 'Surprise! We're the good guys and there's been a change of plans.' If he doesn't know you're coming, who knows what he'll do."

"We know," said Morrell. "He's on a do-or-die mission, and if taken by surprise, his options would be very limited. None of the potential scenarios are ones we're willing to accept. That's why you need to reestablish communication and prep him on our arrival."

"Why me?"

"Because you've already spoken with him once. If we throw anyone else in the mix at this point, it could blow everything out of the water."

In light of the fact that they were discussing a waterborne operation, Harvath didn't very much care for Morrell's choice of words.

"We've got one very serious problem," replied Harvath. "Leighton expects our next contact to be via the emergency contact plan established by Gary Lawlor, and I have no idea what that is."

There were less than four hours left and Harvath wondered what the hell his next move was going to be. Pulling out his cell phone, he dialed Herman Toffle at the hospital for an update on Gary.

"He's still in surgery," said Herman, "but it looks like the doctors are getting ready to close. I was going to wait until they had finished and wheeled him into recovery before calling you."

"How long?" asked Harvath.

"From what the nurse said, about forty-five minutes to an hour, but that's just for completion of surgery. He's under general anesthesia. There's no telling how long it will take until he comes around and when he'll be able to communicate."

"I'm on my way," said Harvath, hanging up the phone. Turning to Morrell he said, "I need your car keys and DeWolfe."

"What's up?" asked Morrell as he tossed Harvath the keys to his rental.

"I've got an idea of how we might be able to put some lipstick on this pig. If I'm right, maybe we can stop things from getting too ugly, too early."

As Harvath engaged the rental car's onboard navigation system and selected his destination—the Virchow-Klinikum campus of Berlin's Charité Hospital, located along the banks of Berlin's Spandau Canal, DeWolfe toyed with Gary's burst transmitter, trying to find a way into the encryption program.

"You talked about numeric codes," said Harvath, speeding through an intersection to avoid a changing light. "In the SEALs we'd normally have a four-digit code with a backup in case the first one was ever compromised. For our system to work, we would take whatever the current code was and subtract that day's date. That was it."

"That's essentially how this works. Your missions were probably like the ones we've been deployed on. We'd only need to do burst transmissions back to the command and control structure, not to other operatives in the field, so you didn't need lots of additional codes."

"Exactly."

"That's when it's easy. As the commo guy, I got to set our encryption codes myself. I wanted something significant that I could always remember, so whenever I could, I liked to use important dates from the Revolutionary War. My favorite was 418."

"April 18th?" asked Harvath.

"Yup. April 18th, 1775. We'd subtract the 418 from 1775 and then add the date of whatever day we were transmitting on. That was our code. As far as communications are concerned, April 18th, 1775, was one of the most historic."

"April 19th was when the battles of Lexington and Concord happened," said Harvath, quiet for several moments as he thought before responding. "Then the night before would have been when Paul Revere was charged with taking the message to Concord that the British were coming."

"Very good," replied DeWolfe. "You know your stuff."

"Yeah, I only wish I knew Gary's stuff."

"You seem to know him pretty well. Like I said, it is probably going to be something that was significant for him and easy for his operatives to remember. Do you have any idea what numbers would have been memorable or significant for Gary? They'd need to be numbers that his men could also relate to."

Harvath racked his head for strings of numbers that would have meant something to Gary, but which also would have held relevance for his operatives. That meant, though, that anything personal to Gary, like his anniversaries or addresses, wouldn't qualify and so Scot dismissed those right off the bat. The hard thing was that on top of not being a computer guy, Gary wasn't much of a numbers guy either. *In fact*, thought Harvath, *it would probably be a toss-up over which he hated more—computers or math.*

When it came to logistical and organizational competence, Gary had both of those qualities in spades, but like it or not, the old man would have had to have used some sort of math to organize his burst transmissions. Harvath wondered if maybe he was overthinking the problem before him. *Keep it simple, stupid*, he heard from somewhere in the back of his mind.

He spent the rest of the drive trying to free associate, but without very much luck.

When they arrived at the hospital, Herman was waiting for them at the nurses' station. Harvath quickly introduced DeWolfe and then followed Herman down the hall to the recovery room, where Hollenbeck and Longo were standing guard outside.

"They just brought Gary in," said Hollenbeck.

"How's he doing?" asked Harvath. "Has he come around yet?"

"Dr. Trawick's with him. It's pretty serious," replied Longo, stepping aside and holding the door open for Harvath. As Herman and DeWolfe tried to follow, Longo held up his arm. "Too many people inside already. I'm sure you guys can understand."

Harvath looked back and gave his companions a polite nod that indicated he would be okay by himself.

"Sure," replied Herman. "We understand. Scot, if you need anything, we'll be in the waiting area."

Scot smiled his thanks and pushed through a set of double doors where a nurse promptly blocked his path and pointed to a sink where he was required to scrub in.

His hands and forearms scrubbed, Harvath donned a sterile paper "bunny suit," along with a hat, booties, and a mask, and then joined Skip Trawick next to Gary Lawlor's bed.

"How's he doing?" asked Scot as he heard the rhythmic click of a ventilator and saw the tube protruding from Gary's mouth. A myriad of monitors, with brightly colored displays, quietly whirred and beeped around the head of Lawlor's bed as if they had come together to form some sort of protective technological halo.

"Not great," replied Skip. "The bullet just missed his heart, but managed to do some major arterial damage and nicked his aorta. He went into deep hypothermic cardiac arrest. They had to do a cardiopulmonary bypass."

"Jesus," said Harvath. "Is he going to be okay?"

"At this point, nobody's sure. It's not looking very good."

"When do you think he'll be coming around?"

"It was a pretty long surgery. The anesthesiologist told me he used Isoflurane. It's an inhalation agent, so we have to wait for Gary's lungs to excrete it before he comes to."

"How much time are we talking about here? I

have some very important questions to ask him," replied Harvath.

"Twenty to thirty minutes probably, but Scot, you have to be prepared for the fact that he might not be able to answer any of your questions."

"They're going to extubate him when he wakes up, right?"

"Probably not. They'll want to watch him for a while and see how he's doing and then the decision will be made. If they don't think he's strong enough, they'll leave him on the vent."

"Will he be able to write? I'll get him a pen and pad."

"Scot, listen. Gary is not a young man. On top of the bullet wound, he aspirated a lot of blood and they had to insert a chest tube. He also took some very serious blows to the head, which means there is a high probability that he has some acute intracranial injuries as well. His abilities, especially to communicate, could be severely impaired."

"Skip, if I have to sit here and take notes while the man blinks out Morse code, then I'm going to do it. The information he has in his head is critical to our assignment."

"I understand that and believe me, I appreciate what's at stake here. I just want you to be prepared in case he can't be of any help to you."

"If he can't," said Harvath, drawing up a chair to the side of Gary Lawlor's bed and sitting down, "we're all in a lot of trouble."

• • •

It was one of the recovery room nurses who first noticed Gary Lawlor's eyelids fluttering. She slid past a dozing Harvath and began speaking to Gary in English as she checked his vital signs. Trawick, who had been across the room speaking with one of the other nurses, saw the commotion and quickly made his way over to the bed. Harvath, now wide awake, slid his chair back and stood up as he watched the nurse soothe her groggy patient and urge him to resist the urge to pull out the tube.

When Gary had sufficiently awakened and she was confident that he wasn't going to try and pull the trach tube from his throat, she nodded to Dr. Trawick and then proceeded to the foot of the bed to annotate his chart.

Dr. Trawick took a look at Lawlor's vitals and shook his head before turning to Scot and saying, "A couple of minutes at most, Scot. Okay? Take it slow. And whatever you do, don't upset him."

Harvath nodded his head, assuring Skip that he understood and then slid his chair back over next to the bed as Skip and the nurse left them alone. Lawlor's eyes were open, but he didn't seem to be focusing on anything in particular.

"Gary?" said Scot, trying to get his attention. "It's me, Scot. Can you hear me?"

It took a moment, but Lawlor's eyes slowly tracked over until they made contact with Harvath's face. Scot couldn't be sure, but he thought he detected a flicker of recognition. Taking the man's hand he said, "You're going to be okay. You're in Berlin's Charité Hospital. You were shot, but everything is all right now. As soon as you're stable, we're going to move you to Landsthul." Landsthul Regional Medical Center, located five kilometers south of Ramstein Air Base in the German state of Rheinland-Pfalz, was the largest American hospital outside of the United States. There, Lawlor would not only get the continuing medical attention he needed, but also the security, as LRMC was located on a permanent American military installation.

Lawlor released Harvath's hand and weakly pantomimed writing. He wanted to tell him something. *So much for taking things slow*, thought Harvath.

He produced the pen and pad he had borrowed from one of the nurses and, lifting Gary's hand, helped him grip the pen in his fist and placed it on the pad where he could see it.

Each motion of his hand was extremely labored and whatever he was doing seemed to take forever. Finally, he finished and began drawing slow circles around what he had written on the pad. Harvath looked down and saw the letters *HD* followed by a question mark. They made no sense to him and he decided to press harder. "I have spoken with Frank Leighton and—"

Lawlor wasn't listening. He had begun writing again. *H.E.L.M.*

Harvath wondered if Gary even knew he was in the room talking to him.

When he was finished writing, Gary once again

made a circle on the pad. Harvath looked down and saw the name *Helmut* with another question mark next to it. He had to have been referring to Helmut Draegar, but why? Why after all these years would he be thinking about him? Harvath stopped for a moment and realized that there probably wasn't a day that went by that Gary didn't think of him. He'd killed the man's wife after all.

"Helmut's long gone," said Scot. "You killed him yourself." He waited for some response, but all he saw was exhaustion. He decided to press on. "Stay with me, Gary. I need your help. Frank Leighton is testing me and I need—"

Once again, he was interrupted by Lawlor's tortured writing. This was getting him nowhere. Lawlor just wasn't with it. Harvath watched as he began drawing a larger circle around Helmut's name and decided to give it one last shot.

Placing his hand atop Gary's, he stopped him from the incessant circle he was drawing, which was almost tearing through the paper, and looked directly into his friend's eyes. "Gary, this is very important. You have to listen to me. Pay attention to what I'm saying."

Exhausted from trying to get his message across, Lawlor's body slumped. His eyelids appeared to grow heavier and it seemed he was on the verge of falling back asleep.

"Gary," said Scot. "C'mon now. I need to make contact with Frank Leighton via the *emergency contact point*. I need to know how I do that."

Lawlor struggled against his drooping lids and gripping the pen tighter, drew a box and then drew an upside down *U* on top of it. Harvath looked at it for a second and then guessed at what he was seeing.

"Is that a suitcase?"

Lawlor said nothing.

"Gary, I want you to tap the pen once for yes, twice for no."

He tapped his pen once.

"It's a suitcase, good. Is it Frank Leighton's suitcase?"

Two taps—*no.*

"Is it *your* suitcase?"

Yes.

"What about it? Is there something in your suitcase?"

Yes.

Harvath lowered his voice. "Is it the burst transmitter?"

Lawlor was silent for a moment; the only noise between them was the metallic click of the ventilator. Then he tapped his pen once for *yes.*

"Okay. I've got your transmitter," said Harvath.

Lawlor drew a question mark on the pad.

"You and Frank Leighton both had mugs in your houses from the Leydicke pub. I got lucky."

One tap—*yes.*

Harvath smiled at Gary's response. Maybe he was inside there after all. "Do I make contact with Leighton, or will he make contact with me? And what about the encryption code?"

Lawlor was frustrated and slowly tapped his pen over and over again.

"I'm sorry," said Harvath. "One question at a time."

One tap—*yes.*

"Do I call Leighton?"

Two taps—*no.*

"He calls me then?"

One tap—*yes.*

"Okay, where?"

Lawlor motioned to Harvath to flip to a clean page and when he did, Gary began trying to write something then gave up and drew a crown with the letter *G* in the center and beneath it the letters "Mme."

Great, thought Harvath, *more gibberish.*

"Is this a place?" asked Harvath, watching the pen for Gary to tap out his response. Several moments passed. Harvath looked up and saw that Gary's eyes were closed. "C'mon, Gary. I only have a few more questions. Are you with me?"

Harvath heard the pen touch the pad in what he thought was a *yes* response, but as he looked down and saw it fall from Gary's hand, a shrill whistle began to pierce the air of the recovery room.

Trawick ran over, took one look at Gary, and then checked the monitors above his bed. "Shit!" he exclaimed. "He's going into ventricular fibrillation. Nurse! Code Blue. Get me the defibrillator." Turning to Harvath he said, "Outside. Now!"

Harvath reluctantly gathered up the pad Gary had been writing on and backed out of the room.

The last thing he saw was a team of nurses gathered around the bed helping Skip prep Gary as the defibrillator was wheeled over and powered up.

Outside the recovery room, Hollenbeck and Longo were still standing guard. Harvath filled them in on what had happened, and they all stood around in silence until Skip emerged ten minutes later with word that Gary had been taken back into surgery. It didn't look good, and Skip suggested that Harvath make himself comfortable as it was probably going to be a while.

Hollenbeck and Longo followed Trawick up to the operating room while Harvath set off in search of Herman and DeWolfe. He found them watching TV in a small waiting room just off the Intensive Care Unit.

"How is he?" asked Herman as Harvath walked in.

"Not good," replied Scot. "He was only awake in recovery for a few minutes and then he crashed. They just took him back into surgery."

"I'm sorry to hear that," said DeWolfe as he got up and turned down the volume on the TV set. "Were you able to talk with him at all?"

"Not really. He was still intubated, and Skip said he might have suffered some cranial trauma during his ordeal. The best I could do was ask questions while he scribbled on this pad," said Harvath, holding it up. "None of it, though, makes much sense."

Harvath grabbed a chair and placed the pages from the notepad on his lap. "Like I said," he began, "none of this makes much sense. Gary just wanted to know about the man who killed his wife fifteen years ago."

"Why do you think he would do that?" replied DeWolfe.

Harvath took another look and said, "I've got no idea. I think this was what Skip was trying to warn me about. The damage to his head might have impaired his ability to focus and communicate properly."

"Did he know you were talking to him?"

"He seemed to. When I asked him some yes-or-no questions, he would tap the pen on the pad in response. Once for *yes* and twice for *no*."

"What's on the last page there?" asked Herman.

"That one makes even less sense," said Harvath, picking up the piece of paper and peering at it. "He drew it after I asked him where the emergency contact point was. To tell you the truth, it looks like a gang sign to me."

"Maybe it's a place or some sort of location," replied Herman.

"Or a clue to where he hid his cookies as a little boy," answered Harvath. "I can't vouch for the authenticity of any of this."

"Back up a second. What's the drawing look like?" asked DeWolfe.

"It's a crown with a *G* in it with some letters underneath," answered Harvath.

"A crown with a *G* in it?" said Herman. "Let me see that."

Harvath handed the page to Toffle who removed

a pair of glasses from his coat pocket and took a closer look.

"When did you start wearing glasses, Herman?" asked Scot.

"None of your business, and you never saw this," responded Toffle.

"Hey," said Harvath, "wearing glasses is your business. And if that's the way you want it, then I never saw anything."

"Not my glasses, you *Blöde Fotze*. This symbol. You've never seen it before?"

Harvath, who felt sure *Blöde Fotze* wasn't a term of endearment, leaned in closer to Herman to take another look at Lawlor's drawing. "Absolutely not," he said, after a closer inspection. "I've never seen it before. Have you?"

"Maybe. Let me ask you something about your friend Gary Lawlor."

"Herman, if you know what that symbol is," said Harvath, his voice a mix of eagerness and frustration, "let's have it. Don't beat around the bush with me."

"How can I put this delicately?" replied Toffle.

"Herman. Fuck *delicately*. We don't have time for it. What the hell is it?"

Herman paused either for effect, or to figure out the best way to give voice to his discovery. Harvath suspected it was the latter and his suspicion was confirmed when Toffle said, "It's the logo for a bordello called the King George. It's located in the Steglitz district."

"You're sure?" asked Harvath.

"Positive."

Harvath was well aware of his friend's proclivity for loose women; a character trait Herman Toffle claimed he had wholeheartedly sworn off when he had gotten married.

Toffle looked at his friend and then said, "The King George is actually not a bad choice for a contact point. It is open at all hours and it wouldn't look odd for anyone to be seen entering or leaving there. What confuses me are these three letters 'M M E' underneath the logo."

"They must stand for something."

Harvath looked at his Kobold Phantom chronograph. "Well, we've got less than two hours, so I suggest we put our thinking caps on."

"Let me take a look at that," said DeWolfe, as he walked across the room, took the paper from Toffle, and studied it. "Harvath, I can't believe you missed this."

"Missed what?"

"I thought you spoke French," replied the communications expert, handing the drawing to him.

"A little, yes." Harvath looked harder and then it hit him. Smiling, he said, "Now we know who to ask for when we get to the King George."

"How'd you figure that out?" demanded Toffle as he grabbed the page back and looked at it.

"*M-m-e*, Herman," replied Harvath.

"Yeah, so?"

"It's the French abbreviation for *Madame*."

irst a porn production facility and now a brothel. Harvath had always thought that Amsterdam was Europe's most colorful capital, but he was beginning to change his mind.

The King George looked like any other five-story gray stone building in Berlin. With its handsome balconies and decorative fleur-de-lis ironwork covering the mullioned windows of the first three levels, it could have been the headquarters of a successful multinational, or a multifamily dwelling.

After parking their car, the trio walked up a short flight of stone steps that gave onto a large door painted a subdued green and accented with brass fixtures. Herman rang the bell and when a voice came back over the intercom, he announced himself as "Herr Toffle."

"You take me to all the best places," said Harvath as the door unlocked and Herman pushed it open.

"Don't joke," replied Toffle. "This *is* one of the best places in all of Berlin."

The threshold of the marble foyer was covered by a long Persian runner leading right up to an enormous metal detector. Flanking the metal detector were two colossal security guards. Their shaved heads and massive builds stood in stark contrast to their dark Savile Row suits, impeccably knotted silk ties, and handmade, custom-fitted John Lobb shoes.

"Uh-oh," said DeWolfe under his breath to Harvath.

"What? You're just as good-looking as these guys and with ten thousand extra, could be dressed just as nice," replied Scot.

"Very funny, Harvath. I was referring to the metal detector. Something tells me this is not a business that welcomes heavy iron."

"Are you saying you came armed?"

"Right. And you're packing nothing more than that sparkling personality of yours."

"Don't worry," smiled Harvath. "I'm sure Herman has this all taken care of."

At that moment, Toffle limped through the metal detector, and its alarm immediately went off. Harvath and DeWolfe hung back and waited.

The two guards approached Herman and asked him to raise his arms. The big German smiled politely and began to do as they asked. As soon as they were close enough, his hands shot out in a move that seemed to defy the laws of physics itself. The two guards were left in a tangle of rumpled, yet expensive fabric, minus their sidearms, which Herman now had trained on them.

"Oh, shit," said DeWolfe, who quickly pulled his gun to back up Toffle.

Several tense seconds passed. Then, both the security guards and Herman began laughing.

His index fingers in the trigger guards, Toffle released his grip and spun the pistols so he could hand them back, butts first.

"What the hell is this?" asked DeWolfe, not sure of what he was seeing.

Harvath began to laugh. He remembered when he was a SEAL and had first met Herman in a cross-training exercise. Herman loved to sneak up on people and steal their sidearms without them knowing. What's more, he had a particular affinity for it. Harvath, though, was the one person he could never get the better of. "You've still got it, Herman."

"Of course I do. In fact I never lost it."

"What the hell is going on?" asked DeWolfe again.

"Put your gun away," said Harvath, "before you shoot somebody."

DeWolfe did as instructed. "I've never seen anything like that."

"Everybody should have at least one good trick," said Herman. "Now, gentlemen, I'd like you to meet Kiefer and Verner." Herman didn't offer Harvath and DeWolfe's names, and being the professionals that they were, Kiefer and Verner didn't ask for them.

After the men shook hands, the security guards

waved Harvath and DeWolfe around the metal detector.

"You sure you've sworn off these places?" said
Harvath to Herman as they walked down a short
hallway toward a stylish reception area. "The boys
at the door sure seemed to know you very well."

"They're ex-army. Their uncle is an old friend of
mine. I got them their jobs here," said Herman,
showing his two colleagues into a beautifully appointed anteroom.

"Herr Toffle," exclaimed an attractive blonde in
her mid-twenties, who walked out from behind an ornately carved wooden desk to greet her guest. "How
lovely to see you again." She was dressed in a perfectly tailored blazer with just the right hint of hug
around her perfectly shaped breasts. Her skirt, though
it rode a bit above mid-thigh, was still tasteful in its
cut and expertly straddled the tantalizing line between revealing and concealing all at the same time.

"Hello, Nixie," said Herman, grasping the two
hands the young woman presented to him and kissing her on both cheeks. "How are you?"

"I am well, Herr Toffle. Thank you for asking,"
responded Nixie, who turned toward Harvath and
DeWolfe and said, "You are going to spoil the girls
by bringing such handsome colleagues with you.
Maybe we should ask Kiefer and Verner to accompany you this evening for your own protection."

Harvath had to admit, the woman was flaw-
less—both in her outward appearance and how she
handled her customers. She reminded him of the

VIP concierges he had seen in Las Vegas who were charged with looking after a hotel's high rollers. This was very much the same situation. Though they treated you with respect and a healthy dose of attention and flattery, the bottom line was the same. They wanted you to spend as much money as possible and enjoy spending it so you would come back again. Though it was a brothel, Harvath had to admit that by what he had seen of it so far, it was a class act.

"Unfortunately," said Herman "we're not here for pleasure this evening. This is more of a business call."

For a moment, Nixie appeared crestfallen. But in an instant, her professional demeanor returned, with just a hint of a childish pout lingering on her extremely full red lips.

Yup, thought Harvath, *this woman was a pro all right*. If the rest of the women at King George's were like Nixie, he couldn't help wondering how any man ever walked out of there with any money left in his pockets at all.

"Well, when it is settled, maybe you'll agree to stay?" asked Nixie, the consummate saleswoman.

"Maybe next time," said Herman with a smile. "We need to speak with Gerda. Is she in, please?"

It shouldn't have surprised Harvath that Herman knew the madam by her first name, but it did nevertheless. He looked over at DeWolfe, who was standing in front of a flat-panel monitor in a gilded frame showing what looked like runway footage from the Victoria's Secret fashion show, but what Harvath assumed was a promotional piece highlighting the staff of the King George.

"Boy are Carlson and Avigliano going to be sorry that they missed this," said DeWolfe, whose eyes were glued to the screen. "I think I just fell in love. Yup. Oh, wow! It just happened again. These women are incredible."

"Easy, Trigger," said Harvath. "As well funded as you boys are, there's no way tricky Ricky would let you expense something like this. And you could save up a week's per diem and not be able to pay for what you're looking at there. So do yourself a favor and step away from the monitor. That's it, step *away* from the monitor."

DeWolfe did as Harvath suggested and rejoined his colleagues at Nixie's desk.

Hanging up the phone, the attractive blonde said, "I'm sorry, Herr Toffle, but it appears Frau Putzkammer was called away a short time ago and has not yet returned."

"Do you have a cell phone number we could reach her at?"

"I tried her handy already, but there was no answer. I hope it is nothing serious."

Herman looked at Harvath. "How much time do we have?"

"Less than forty-five minutes," replied Harvath, checking his Kobold.

"Actually, Nixie," replied Herman. "This is very serious and we don't have much time."

"Herr Toffle, if there is a way I can be of assistance to you, please say so."

Herman looked again at Harvath, torn as to how much he should share with Nixie. When Harvath raised his watch ever so slightly and tapped it, Herman decided they only had time for the direct approach. "Years ago, Gerda, Frau Putzkammer, worked closely with a group of American military men, and now one of them has been very badly injured here in Berlin. We believe he was a friend of Frau Putzkammer's and that if she knew about his situation, she would want to help him."

"Of course," said Nixie. "She has often spoken of the American military men who were some of her best customers."

"I am sure and that is very kind of her, but these men were very serious, elite soldiers. We're not talking about ordinary American GIs. This group, Frau Putzkammer would definitely remember."

Nixie's façade seemed to soften. "When would these men have been in Berlin?"

"Before the wall came down. They were a small group charged with—"

"*Für die Sicherheit?*" asked Nixie, cutting off Herman's sentence.

"Yes," answered Harvath. "But how could you know that?"

"Let me get someone to take over for me, and we can talk," said Nixie as she pressed one of the many buttons on her phone and spoke in rapid-fire German. Moments later a stunning redhead emerged from a discreet side door to relieve Nixie, who then showed her guests out of the reception area and into a small elevator.

They rode to the fifth floor where the elevator opened up onto a gorgeous, antique-filled penthouse apartment.

This was a part of the King George even Herman had apparently never seen before. "Frau Putzkammer's abode?" he asked.

"Actually, it is *our* home," replied Nixie.

"You mean *you* and Gerda *are?*"

"Mother and daughter," said Nixie, cutting Herman off before he could say what he really thought their relationship was. "My full name is Viveka Nicollet Putzkammer."

"I had no idea," offered Herman, stunned.

"Not many people do. That's the way Mother has always wanted it. After private boarding schools in both France and Switzerland, I received my bachelor's degree at the University of Southern California and my MBA at Kellogg in Chicago, then I returned home to Berlin to help run the family business."

"And from the looks of everything," replied Herman, "you've been doing a very good job."

"But how did you know about *Für die Sicherheit?*" interjected Harvath.

Nixie motioned for her guests to take a seat in the sunken living room, as she crossed a series of beautiful oriental carpets and retrieved a large beer stein from atop one of the many bookshelves lining the far wall. Returning with the mug, she smiled as she handed it to Harvath and said, "One of my mother's most prized possessions."

He didn't need to read the inscription on it to know what it was. Seeing the piece of barbed wire wrapped around the bottom was enough.

"Where'd she get this?" asked Harvath.

"It was a gift," replied Nixie.

Harvath recalled the stein that Hellfried Leydicke had above his bar and half-assumed that Gerda Putzkammer had been another helpful outside supporter of Gary's team. But when he flipped the stein upside down and saw the serial number, he was stunned. 10/12. *Ten of twelve. A real team mug.* A quiet, subconscious ping echoed in Harvath's mind as if his mental radar had bounced back off of something he had been looking for.

"The man who gave that stein to her was named John Parker," said Nixie. "My mother loved him very much. Enough to let him go back home to America when he was recalled after the wall fell."

"Did he know that your mother was pregnant?" asked Herman, taking a guess.

"No. In fact, my mother didn't even know until he had already gone."

"She never tried to make contact?"

"You have to know my mother. She is a very proud woman. The last thing she would want is for people to think that she needed a man to take care of her."

"How about you?" asked DeWolfe. "Don't you want to have a relationship with your father?"

"I do have one. Although not the kind you're thinking of," replied Nixie. "My mother told me that my father had died shortly after I was born, and for many years I believed her. Then, one day, I found the room where she hid her diaries and other personal effects. I spent weeks sneaking into that room. I read everything that I could get my hands on and eventually discovered who my father was. That's why I decided to do my undergrad work at USC.

"I nannied for their family in Thousand Oaks for four wonderful years. He had married his old sweetheart shortly after returning to the States from Berlin. Though I would have preferred he had married my mother, his wife was a wonderful woman and he is a wonderful man. I like to think that had he known my mother had gotten pregnant, he would have done the right thing by her. But it was Mother's decision to keep things quiet and knowing her the way I do, I can respect that. Though my father didn't really know who I was while I was working for him, he nonetheless treated me as if I was one of his very own daughters. We still keep in touch via email."

Harvath hated to do it, but he took a deep breath and said, "Nixie, I'm sorry to tell you this. John Parker is dead."

"No," said Nixie, blanching. "That can't be true."

"I'm afraid it is," replied Scot. "They killed almost all of the people on his Berlin team."

"Who killed him? And what do you mean *almost all* of the people on his Berlin team?"

"At this point, I'm not at liberty to tell you who killed your father, but I can tell you this. Two people on the team are still alive. One of those people was your father's commanding officer. That man has been like a second father to me and the same people who shot and killed your father have shot and tortured him. Right now he is being operated on in a Berlin hospital and no one can say for sure if he is going to make it."

Nixie was doing the best she could to control her emotions. "Who is the other man?" she asked.

"The other man," said Harvath," is another of your father's teammates. The King George was a covert contact point for them a long time ago."

"That comes as no surprise. This entire building is riddled with secret doors and passageways that helped certain people sneak in and out during the Cold War. My mother was very proud of her involvement in foiling the Russians and their East German counterparts."

"And so she should be," said Harvath. "But what we need now is *your* help. We have a chance to stop the men who killed your father, before they can kill anyone else. What do you say?"

Nixie was silent. She strode across the sunken living room to a cocktail cart where she dumped a scoopful of crushed ice into a stainless steel cocktail shaker and filled the balance with vodka. Placing a lid atop, she shook the canister while she retrieved a martini glass from one of the lower shelves and sprayed the rim with a vermouth atomizer.

Filling the glass, she inhaled the martini's deep aroma for a moment as if she were savoring a fine wine, and then took a long drink, draining the glass. Finally, she turned to Harvath and said, "Yes, I will help you, but on one condition."

"What is it?" replied Scot.

"When you find the man that killed my father, I want you to kill him. No trial, no jail time. I want you to promise me that he will die."

Harvath was up against it, and he knew that there was only one answer he could give. After a long silence, he answered, "I promise."

" . . . and the phone on the desk is her private line. It's the most secure place my mother could have provided your friends if they needed to conduct this type of call," said Nixie as she showed the men into the hidden room her mother used as a private office. "I know this is confidential, so I'll wait for you downstairs in the reception area. Good luck."

Harvath thanked Nixie as DeWolfe found the corresponding phone plugs in the small plastic case they had brought with them. DeWolfe attached the burst transmitter to the phone line first from the jack, and then ran another cord from the transmitter to the phone so that Harvath could either talk or burst without having to rearrange any of the equipment.

The transmitter connected, they sat down with a piece of paper and tried to figure out the encryption code Gary would have established with Frank Leighton, while Harvath continued to glance at his watch.

After seeing the stein in the Putzkammers'

living room, Scot had become convinced that the
code somehow involved the serial numbers on the
bottom of the team mugs.

"So what was Leighton's number then?" asked
DeWolfe.

"He was somewhere in the middle. Five or six, I
think," replied Harvath, trying to remember back to
the stein he had seen in the laundry room that doubled for Leighton's home office back in Maryland.
"No, wait. It was seven."

"Are you sure?"

"Yes, I'm sure," replied Harvath.

"That's still only three digits—the seven and the
twelve."

"Not if you put a zero in front of it," said Herman who was looking through some of the boxes of
memorabilia that Gerda Putzkammer had stored in
her office. "That would be the correct way to do it."

"So it would read 07 of 12?" asked Harvath.

DeWolfe wrote it down and said, "That would
work, but what about the rest of it?"

"I've been thinking about that too," said Harvath. "Gary was a Patton fan. Actually he was more
like a Patton freak."

"As in General Patton?" asked DeWolfe.

"Yeah, he had studied the guy up and down. He
knew all of his moves, and just like Gary, Patton
didn't care for the Soviets one single bit. In fact, at
the end of World War II, Patton wanted permission
to go after them. He said if the U.S. would give him
ten days, he'd start a war with them that would make

it look like their fault and the U.S. could be justified in pushing them all the way back to Moscow."

DeWolfe, concerned with their dwindling time-frame, said, "So Gary liked Patton. Patton hated the Communists and wanted to get rid of them. Being Army guys, Gary's men probably also liked Patton. That is a legitimate connection. Now, what can we take numbers-wise from him? It has to be something relatively easy to remember."

"I've been thinking about that," said Harvath. "Patton commanded the Third Army in World War II, and they spent 281 days fighting in Europe."

"Possible," said DeWolfe with a certain degree of skepticism as he wrote it down.

"He invented the 1913 Patton sword."

DeWolfe continued writing. "Okay."

"Don't forget the M-46 and M-47 Patton Tanks," said Herman, picking up another catalog.

"I think we're really reaching on these," replied DeWolfe.

"I can also give you his birth date, death date, and the date he was buried."

"That's a bit better. All right, we'll give these a try, but if we can't crack it, you'll have to wing it with Leighton. The mere fact that you located the proper emergency contact point should win you some credibility with him."

Harvath nodded his head in response, but knew that if he couldn't fulfill the terms of the emergency contact plan, Leighton wasn't going to listen to a thing he had to say.

DeWolfe powered up the burst transmitter and waited as it cycled through the welcome screen and then dropped him into the calendar program. "Okay. We're in the calendar function. As I said before, the key here is to tap into the correct date. What do we want to try first?"

"Birth date," said Harvath. "November 11th, 1885."

"The scheduler doesn't go back that many years. Let's just focus on the actual month and day," replied DeWolfe as he found November 11th and went to the appointment scheduler.

"Anything?" replied Harvath.

"Nope. Just a regular page."

"No prompts for a security code when you try to make an appointment?"

"No. Let's try another date."

They tried the date Patton died, the date of his burial, and even the date of his car accident, without any luck.

"How much time do we have left?" asked DeWolfe.

Harvath checked his tactical chronograph. "Less than fifteen minutes."

"What do you want to do?"

"Try July 22nd."

"What's that correspond to?" asked DeWolfe as he scrolled to the date.

"Patton's capture of Palermo."

Harvath could tell by the look on DeWolfe's face that the date wasn't a winner. "Try August 16th. The capture of Messina."

"Nothing," said DeWolfe.

"Shit. May 8th. Victory Day in Europe."

"Still nothing."

"Well," said Harvath, "does anyone have any other suggestions?"

Herman cleared his throat on the other side of the office and asked, "Did you ever see the movie *Patton* with George C. Scott?"

"Sure," replied Harvath, glancing again at his watch, "I don't know a single red-blooded American military person who hasn't, but what does that have to do with what we're trying—" Suddenly, he had an idea. Turning to DeWolfe, he said, "Try June 5th."

"What's June 5th?"

"The opening scene in the movie is the speech Patton gave the Third Army before the D-Day invasion. I should have thought of that earlier. It's probably the greatest speech Patton ever gave."

"You're welcome," said Herman, who went back to reading his catalog.

"Bingo," exclaimed DeWolfe. "The scheduler is asking us to enter a code. What now?"

"Let's start running through some of the numbers we came up with. Try Leighton's stein number and subtract the amount of days the Third Army was in Europe, plus today's date."

Harvath waited until DeWolfe looked up from the transmitter and said, "Negative."

"Okay, Leighton's number minus the 1913 sword classification, plus today's date."

Once again, DeWolfe responded, "Negative."

"Patton's sidearm was a .45-caliber Colt Peacemaker. How about substituting 45 for 1913?"

DeWolfe ran the equation, but still came up empty. "Zip," he said.

"Damn it," replied Harvath, his frustration mounting as the minutes ticked away. "I know Patton believed in reincarnation and really identified with Hannibal, the Carthaginian general. Hannibal began his march on Rome in 218. Try that."

"Scot, you're reaching way far here."

"Do you have a better idea?"

"No, but—"

DeWolfe was interrupted by a snort from Herman.

"What's so funny?" snapped Harvath. "You got a problem with Hannibal?"

"I wasn't laughing about Hannibal," replied Herman.

"What were you laughing at then?"

"Never mind."

"No. What is it? I want to know."

"In the beginning of the King George, Gerda Putzkammer apparently offered her customers printed *menus*, just like in a restaurant. And no matter what it was, every price ended in sixty-nine *pfennings*. Very kitsch."

Harvath was just about to tell Herman he wasn't helping, when he got that ping in his head again and this time it shook something loose. "Take 68 and subtract Leighton's 0712, plus today's date," he said to DeWolfe.

"But what's 68?" asked the communications expert.

"Just do it.

Harvath was sitting literally on the edge of his seat until DeWolfe looked up with a smile and turning the transmitter toward him said, "We're in."

"We are?" said Herman, setting down the materials he was looking at and walking over to the desk. "Where the hell did the number 68 come from?"

"Don't ask me," said DeWolfe. "Ask Harvath. He finally figured out the code."

With his eyes glued on the burst transmitter, Scot replied, "When we were driving back to the hospital, DeWolfe and I were talking about how burst codes needed to be easy to remember. That made me think about Patton and how he said that when he wanted his men to remember something and really make it stick, he used eloquent profanity. Sometimes, so did Gary. You just reminded me of an old joke of his that I hadn't thought about in a long time. *What's a 68? It's like a 69, except you do me and I owe you one.*"

"Are you sure Gary wasn't a SEAL?" laughed DeWolfe. "How much time do we have left?"

"Three minutes."

"Then you'd better get cracking on your message. Take the stylus and tap the icon for the keyboard. When it comes up, type it out just like we talked about and put it into the *waiting to be sent* folder. When it's time to burst, you just tap the send icon. Okay?"

"Seems easy enough," answered Harvath, who wrote out the message as quickly and as succinctly as he could.

Less than three minutes later, Frau Putzkammer's telephone rang. Herman and DeWolfe were
completely silent as Harvath picked up the receiver
and said, "This is Norseman."

After a second of what could only have been
shocked silence, Leighton said. "So you made it."

"I told you I was for real."

"That may be, but you're not home free yet."

"And neither are you. Are you ready to receive
my transmission?" asked Harvath.

Twelve hundred kilometers away in the Gulf of
Finland, Leighton checked his burst transmitter and
said, "Go ahead."

As the message appeared on his screen,
Leighton was stunned by what he was reading:

Your mission has been compromised.
Entire Dark Night team terminated. Gary
Lawlor seriously wounded. Prognosis un-
clear.

Mission parameters now changed. We
are coming to you. Will explain at your
location. Hold position and exercise extreme caution. You are being watched.

*The entire team has been terminated? They think I'm
being watched?* Though a million other questions
were racing through Frank Leighton's mind, he

knew he would have to wait to get his answers and so typed a concise and professional reply:

```
Message received and understood. Will
continue to hold position. What is your
ETA?
```

Harvath read through Leighton's response and typed:

```
Within next twenty-four hours. Keep
all weapons on safe. We will be making
covert insertion and don't want any
friendly fire. Leave package in place
until our arrival. Be ready to move.
```

As Harvath was about to tap the *send* icon with his stylus, the lights dimmed and then went out, plunging the room into complete darkness.

"What the hell is going on?" asked DeWolfe.

"Maybe too many vibrators recharging at the same time," replied Herman.

"Very funny," said Harvath, retrieving his Sure-Fire flashlight. "Hey, DeWolfe? Does this burst transmitter have a backlight function so I can see it better?"

"It should. Go to the star logo in the upper-left-hand corner and click on it, then select *settings* and there should be a *backlight* function box. Select *yes* and it should fire right up."

Harvath followed DeWolfe's instructions and the screen began to glow a deep red. It was an interesting color for a device masquerading as a civilian product, but made perfect sense for a piece of covert equipment that might be called upon to operate in difficult nighttime conditions where the least visible light spectrum would be required.

"Got it," said Harvath, who, after tapping the screen several more times added, "Shit!"

"What's going on?" asked DeWolfe.

"I'm getting a message that says *no carrier*," replied Harvath as he started saying into the phone's mouthpiece, "Hello? Hello? Can you hear me?"

"No carrier?" continued DeWolfe. "That could only mean that—"

"The phone line's dead," said Herman as he withdrew his twin Beretta Stock 96s from beneath his jacket.

"Jesus Christ," exclaimed DeWolfe when he saw the weapons. "Who walks around with that kind of firepower?"

"Welcome to the Federal Republic of Germany," answered Harvath, disconnecting the burst transmitter and illuminating his way around the desk with his flashlight to reconnect the phone directly to the wall jack. "If you think that's impressive, you oughtta see what his cousins carry."

"Forget about my cousins," said Herman as Harvath picked up the receiver and listened for a dial tone. "What's the situation with the phone?"

"Dead," he replied. "So the problem appears to be on our end."

"Coupled with a convenient loss of electricity. I don't like it."

"Neither do I," said Harvath, removing the H&K from his BlackHawk tactical holster. "Either a car outside happened to ram the local power and telephone poles, or we've got a problem."

"This part of Berlin doesn't have power or telephone poles," replied Herman. "Everything is underground."

"Then we've got a problem," said DeWolfe, the last to draw his own weapon, a "special order only" Beretta Model 93R.

"Talk about firepower," quipped Harvath, eyeballing the extended twenty-round magazine of the handgun cum machine pistol, as DeWolfe flipped down the front grip and then switched the firing selector to three round bursts. "Where'd you get that thing?"

"I've got a good friend at Beretta and a healthy weapons allowance."

"Like I said. When it comes to funding, you CIA guys aren't hurting at all."

Harvath tucked the burst transmitter into the back of his jeans and led the group out of the office. Cutting back through the living room of the penthouse, they found Nixie who showed them to another of the King George's hidden features, a concealed stairwell. With the power out, the elevator was out of the question.

They were halfway to the ground floor when

they heard the shots. Hurriedly, the group took the stairs as fast as they could. As they drew closer to the lobby and the shooting intensified, Harvath began to sense a whole new problem. Toffle, who had taken over the lead despite his bad leg, was picking up a good head of steam and dashed down the stairs two at a time. He seemed hell-bent on charging through the lobby door, but something wasn't right and Harvath yelled for him to stop.

Confused, Herman pulled up short and turned around to look at him as he came running down the last flight of stairs followed by DeWolfe and then Nixie. "Why are we stopping?" asked Toffle.

"Can't you feel it?" replied Harvath.

"Feel what?"

"The air in here. It's grown thinner."

"And hotter," said DeWolfe as he joined his colleagues at the bottom of the landing.

Herman scowled. "We're wasting time."

Nixie sniffed the air a moment and added, "And what's that smell?"

The minute she pointed it out, Harvath knew what it was—*accelerant*. Pushing his way past Toffle, Harvath reached out his hand and gently placed it against the stairwell door.

Immediately, he snatched his hand back away from the heat and said, "There's a fire on the other side of this door."

"Oh my God," replied Nixie. "We have to get everyone out."

"First things first," replied Herman, raising his weapons. "Kiefer and Verner may be in trouble."

"We all might be in trouble. Let's be smart about this," responded Harvath as he tugged the sleeve of his leather jacket over his hand so he could pull the door open. "Everybody back up. When I count to three, I'm going to slowly open the door. Ready?"

DeWolfe and Herman repositioned themselves so they could cover Harvath and then nodded their heads, while Nixie flattened herself as best she could against the near wall of the stairwell.

Harvath indicated his countdown with his fingers and then slowly cracked the door. Instantly, he was blown backward as the roaring conflagration forced its way into the stairwell, desperate to feed on the fresh supply of oxygen.

Instinctively, DeWolfe and Toffle hit the deck, but Nixie stood in abject horror as she watched the roiling fireball come racing for her and engulf her in flames.

Harvath was the first to regain his feet and he ran to Nixie, covering her with his coat and knocking her to the ground. He rolled her from side to side, slapping at her body with his bare hands as he tried to put out the fire. Once he was convinced that he had it out, he began to remove the jacket and right away smelled the sickening scent of burnt hair and flesh coming from her body.

Her once stylish designer suit now hung in charred strips from her blistered torso. Her eyebrows were gone, as was much of her once beautiful mane of blond hair, but she was alive. Harvath did a quick assessment of her injuries and found her to be unresponsive. Most likely, she had gone into shock. "We need to get Nixie to a hospital, fast," said Harvath, but neither DeWolfe nor Toffle was listening. They had exited the stairwell and leapt through the flames into the foyer of the King George.

Harvath yelled to them, but doubted he could be heard over the thunderous roar of the fire. Now that the door was open, his nostrils were filled with the unmistakable tang of the accelerant that someone had used to deliberately set this fire. The sting of the noxious odor was so pungent it was like being slapped in the face. As the acrid smoke began to intensify, Harvath worried about how safe it was to be breathing such rapidly deteriorating air. He called out again and was answered by two three-round bursts of semiautomatic weapons fire, which he assumed were from DeWolfe's Beretta.

Making Nixie as comfortable as he could, he propped her against the railing and crept over toward the door where he aimed his H&K at the sea of blinding orange fire, just in time to see an enormous silhouette making its way toward him. Through the jagged blades of flame, he tried to make out who or what it was, but the scorching intensity of the fire made it impossible. As he stared into the inferno, Harvath's brain tried to make out what he was seeing, but he couldn't categorize it.

The dimensions were all off. Reflexively, he raised his pistol, ready to fire.

Then, he heard a low, guttural roar and made a last-minute decision to roll out of the way, just as Herman Toffle leapt through the wall of flames separating the foyer from the stairwell. He landed with an amazing crash, dropping the body of Kiefer, the security guard, whom he had fireman-carried all the way back through the blaze.

"Verner's dead," said Toffle, gasping for breath as he beat his hands around his body, making sure neither his hair nor his clothing were on fire.

"Where's DeWolfe?" asked Harvath.

"He saw someone in the foyer and chased after him."

"Who?"

"I don't know. I didn't see him."

"What about other people in the building?"

"From what I can see, the whole downstairs is on fire. There's no getting out this way."

"Why haven't the sprinklers kicked in yet?"

"The building is pre–World War II. It probably doesn't have them."

"Okay, then," said Harvath, thinking. "Then the only way we can go is up. Can you make it?"

Herman was coughing and obviously suffering the effects of smoke inhalation, but the resilient former terrorism expert flashed Harvath the thumbs up and tried to force a smile.

With Harvath helping Nixie and Herman carrying Kiefer, they struggled up the stairs to the next level, where the stairwell door was actually a false piece of richly engraved wood open to a long handsomely paneled hallway. Doors were spaced evenly along the corridor and it was readily apparent that this was where a good part of the King George's business was conducted as customers and employees in various states of undress were running screaming up and down the hallway.

Getting his bearings, Harvath found the door to one of the bedrooms he assumed faced the front of the building and kicked it open. Three very attractive young women and one balding, overweight middle-aged man had shattered the window and were frantically trying to pry loose the decorative fleur-de-lis ironwork that stood between them and a one-story drop to freedom.

"Stand back," ordered Harvath as he laid Nixie on the bed and took aim at the grating. He fired five shots in quick succession, sending sparks and chunks of masonry in all directions.

When Harvath lowered his pistol, the middle-aged client quickly moved back to the window and began shaking the ironwork for all he was worth. He was a man possessed, and when the grating failed to give way, he began crying, convinced he was going to die. Spent, the man fell to the floor and continued to sob.

"*Passen Sie auf!*" yelled Herman as he set Kiefer down on the floor and after picking up an antique bureau, ran at the ironwork-covered window with all his might.

There was the sound of splintering wood and groaning metal as the improvised battering ram struck its target head-on and the fleur-de-lis grating tore from its moorings and fell with a crash onto the sidewalk below. Wheezing, Herman withdrew the dresser from the window and shoved it into the corner. Immediately, the sobbing man began scampering out the window.

"Hey," yelled Harvath. "Get back here."

Herman reached through the window, grabbed the man by his trousers, and yanked him back in.

"*Was?*" implored the man.

"First of all, you're welcome," replied Harvath. "Secondly, do you speak English?"

"Yes, of course," answered the man in a heavy German accent.

"Good. We're going to need your help."

"But this is the only way out. We already tried to go down the stairs. There is too much fire. Please, we must hurry."

"We will hurry, but here's what I want you to do. You and my friend," said Scot as he nodded at Herman, "are going to gather up all of the mattresses you can from the rooms on this floor and throw them out the window so people have something to land on. Then I want you to let people in the hallway and the stairwells know they can get out this way. Tie the bedding together and use it to lower the injured."

"What are *you* going to do?" asked Herman.

"I'm going to find DeWolfe."

"Be careful. All of this happening just after we arrived is a little too coincidental and I don't believe in coincidences."

"Neither do I," replied Harvath, who inserted a fresh magazine into his H&K as he turned and left the room. "Neither do I."

CHAPTER 33

The hallway was quickly filling with more smoke and more screaming people as Harvath swung the red dot of his pistol's laser sight into every room looking for DeWolfe. Aside from the fact that the rooms seemed to have unusually low ceilings, there was nothing else very remarkable about them.

As he passed the panicked throngs, he instructed them in his best German possible to stay low to the floor and make their way to the bedroom he had just come from at the right front of the building. With each face he looked into, the realization began to grow in him that any one of them could be the killer who had started the fire, and he would never know it. He had to find DeWolfe.

Harvath fought his way up one of the public stairwells and found that the third floor was laid out much the same as the second. He checked each room, but there was still no sign of DeWolfe.

Back on the stairs, he could hear people below him, but the terrified tide making their way down from above had stopped. Hopefully, they had all gotten the message and had headed for the second floor.

After climbing two more flights of stairs, Harvath carefully pulled open the door and crept into what he expected to be another long hallway similar to those he had searched on the previous two floors. Instead, he found himself in a large chamber with rough-sawn hardwood floors. Harvath quickly swept the filtered red beam of his flashlight around the room and realized he was in a mock-up of some sort of medieval dungeon. Chains hung from the ceiling and there were assorted torture devices scattered around the room.

As Harvath made his way to the lone door on the far side of the chamber, he heard a sudden noise off to his right. Dropping to one knee, he spun and pointed his pistol in the direction from which the sound had come. Raising his flashlight and depressing the thumb switch, Harvath illuminated a long leather couch and, as he tilted it upward, he found the helpless form of DeWolfe, gagged and shackled against the wall but still struggling against his restraints. The man's eyes appeared to be bulging out of their sockets and Harvath had no idea if it was from abject fear or fury.

Whoever had hung DeWolfe up like a trophy probably wasn't too far away. He pulled the suppressor from his pocket and screwed it onto the threaded barrel of his H&K. Taking careful aim, he put two quick rounds into the hinges of the metal restraints that were pinning the communication expert's wrists to the wall. Just as he lowered his weapon, someone punched him incredibly hard right in the small of his back. At least that's what it felt like.

Without even thinking about it, Harvath released the thumb switch of his flashlight, plunging the room back into darkness, and began rolling along the floor in the direction he had come. As he did, he could hear the pop of dry wood as a course of bullets from a silenced weapon tracked his progress, tearing up a straight line across the floorboards right at him.

Without the beam from his flashlight Harvath was completely blind, and he rolled hard into something big and sturdy, smacking his head against what he assumed was some sort of table leg. He scrambled to get out of his attacker's line of fire and knew that the only way the person could be following his movements was with night vision goggles. It made perfect sense. Cut the power and blind your opponent. Bait the trap properly and when he comes to you, killing him will be easier than tipping over drunk Frenchmen at a Beaujolais festival. That plan, though, had one major problem. Scot Harvath was not that easy to kill.

Reaching out to find one of the legs for orientation, Harvath quickly pulled himself beneath the table. Taking a deep breath, he lunged upward in a squat-thrust maneuver flipping the table over and affording himself at least the appearance of better cover. Though his attacker was using a silenced weapon, the word *silenced* did not mean completely devoid of sound and Harvath had developed at least a vague idea of where he was.

He could see only one means of escape. After flipping up the hinged red filter cap from his flashlight, he reached around to the small of his back and pulled the painfully oversized PDA from his jeans. He felt along its smooth surface for the place where the device had deflected the shot and saved his spinal cord from being severed and said a quick word of thanks, then sent the device arcing in the direction of his attacker. When he heard it smash against the far wall, he jumped from behind the table and aimed the 225-lumen power of his Sure-Fire flashlight in the same direction in order to blind his attacker. The white-hot beam sliced through the blackness of the chamber, lighting up the entire far side of the room, but the shooter wasn't there. *The son of a bitch had moved.*

Harvath ducked back down behind the table just as one of the uppermost legs splintered into hundreds of ungainly toothpicks. The shot had come from over his right shoulder. The shooter was right behind him! Harvath turned and opened fire as he raced to get out of the open and find a new place to hide, but where the hell could he go? Without turning his flashlight on, he couldn't see a thing. He needed to formulate another plan, and fast.

Harvath rolled along the ground back over to where he had first seen DeWolfe. *There had to be a way out of this.* When he found him, DeWolfe was lying on his back trying to catch his breath.

"Are you okay?" whispered Harvath.

DeWolfe nodded his head, slowly.

"Can you sit up on your own?" continued Scot as he disconnected the laser sight from beneath the barrel of his gun.

"Yeah."

"All right. I'm going to give you my laser sight so you can draw this guy's fire. Do you think you're up to that?"

DeWolfe held out his hand for the device.

Harvath smiled. "Good. I figure he's at about our two o'clock, so when I say 'go' I want you to raise that thing above the couch and start shining it over there like we're to trying to pick him off, okay?"

"What are you going to do?"

"I'm going to pick him off, what else? Ready?"

DeWolfe nodded his head.

"Go!" said Harvath as he rolled across the floor.

DeWolfe sat up and started pointing the laser sight as if he were aiming a gun of his own. The shooter went for the bait and immediately fired several rounds into the couch DeWolfe was using for cover.

The muffled spits were enough to give Harvath a lock on the shooter's location. Harvath depressed the thumb switch of his SureFire and lit the guy up like an inmate going over the wall at San Quentin.

Just as Harvath suspected, his assailant was

wearing night vision goggles, but what he hadn't expected were the man's superb instincts. Instead of being startled and turning into the beam from Harvath's flashlight, the man shed his goggles, dropped to the ground, and began firing.

Harvath had to roll hard and quick to get out of the line of fire. As he rolled, he got off a series of shots, one of which he was positive had made contact when he heard his opponent groan in pain.

"Gotcha," coughed Harvath as he found shelter behind a long bench covered with short metal spikes, the uses for which he couldn't even begin to fathom.

Smoke was filling the room and it was becoming more difficult to breathe. *The fire was getting closer.* Harvath worried that if he and DeWolfe didn't get back down to the second floor soon, they were going to have to find another way out. And with very little clue as to the layout of the building, Scot wasn't exactly crazy about their chances. *He had to do something, but what?*

Suddenly, there was what sounded like large pieces of furniture being hurriedly dragged across the floor. *Was the shooter creating more cover for himself? Was it some sort of ruse?* Harvath didn't know what to think. The one thing he did know was that his opponent could smell the smoke just as well as he could and was just as aware of how close the fire was getting. At that same moment, something else struck Harvath. If this man had started the fire, he wouldn't have brought DeWolfe all the way up to the fourth floor without some plan for his own escape. *But where would he go?* Something Nixie had said about the King George was suddenly echoing in his mind, "The entire building is riddled with secret doors and passageways to help certain people sneak in and out during the Cold War."

Why not? thought Harvath. If his group had used one of the secret passageways, why couldn't this person use others? It was possible, but it not only begged the question, how did this person know about the passageways, but also who the hell was he and what did he want?

There was no time for that now. Harvath needed to focus on getting himself and DeWolfe out of the building alive. He felt around himself and found a large cardboard box. Reaching inside, he wasn't surprised to find what felt like leather cat-o'-nine-tails, vinyl masks, and other assorted S&M toys, but it was something in the far corner of the box that gave him a new idea. Harvath pulled out a round tin, about the size and weight of a small can of shaving gel. Unscrewing the lid, he knew right away what it was—*Vaseline*.

The contents didn't matter as much as the size, shape, and heft of the container. Not only was it very similar to a small can of shaving gel, it was also very similar to a flashbang grenade. And sometimes, as Harvath had learned in his counterterrorism training a long time ago, throwing a dud could be better than actually throwing a live device.

Flashbangs, more properly referred to in the industry as NFDDs—Noise Flash Distraction Devices, often required the use of surprise in order to be fully effective. That said, there were three major physiological effects that could not be quickly protected against.

Flashbangs produced an incredibly bright light—approximately two million candela, which even with eyes closed would cause a bleaching of the rhodopsin, the visual purple in the eye, creating the spots and temporary blindness most people have experienced and referred to as the *flashbulb effect*.

Then there was the noise, right around 174 decibels, a thunderous roar that was just below the threshold of damage to the eardrum, but which was still likely to produce a startle reflex even in those expecting the concussion.

Finally, there was the pressure wave. The atmospheric pressure inside a room was raised so that it compressed the body, causing a level of severe uneasiness.

For those who were prepared for it, or had trained extensively in their presence, flashbangs were not a big deal, especially as most teams had trained to enter rooms just after the flash, and concurrent with the bang. But that's where Harvath's training and a little trick he had learned was about to pay off.

Harvath made sure the lid on the tin of Vaseline was on tight before calling out, "DeWolfe, flashbang!" and chucking the container toward where he had heard all of the furniture being moved.

If someone was familiar with NFDDs, which Harvath suspected their shooter was, one of the biggest distractions to present them with was an inert device that did not go off. When a flashbang has been loosed anywhere near you, it is nearly impossible not to pay attention to it because you *expect* it to detonate. When it doesn't, it is extremely disconcerting and you end up focusing on it and the direction it came from, wondering what the hell happened. The tactic was something that Special Operations personnel liked to refer to as UW—unconventional warfare—and in this case it worked like a charm.

Harvath counted off the appropriate amount of seconds and then popped up from behind the bench with his flashlight blazing and his pistol ready to fire. This time, he caught his opponent full in the face with the beam from his SureFire. The man was sixty, if he was a day. He had a full head of gray hair and worn, leathery skin—not at all what Harvath was expecting. There was also, at this moment, an expression of arrogant defiance on his face. Though Harvath had never seen him before, there was something familiar about him. It was a gut feeling and he had learned a long time ago that those feelings were seldom wrong.

Whether or not he knew him, the man was still a killer and Harvath wasn't above helping make him a little more aerodynamic, so he took aim and pulled the trigger.

Once again, the man expertly ducked down trying to get out of the line of fire. Scot kept the flashlight on him as he fired, only to see him disappear right through the wall. It was not the first time he had seen that trick and Harvath was beginning to understand why the man might feel so familiar, but there was also something else—something he couldn't explain.

Crawling back under the canopy of smoke to where he had left DeWolfe, Harvath asked, "Can you stand up?"

"Of course I can stand up," replied DeWolfe, angrily. "The guy just got the drop on me. That's all. I'll be fine."

"Where's your gun?"

DeWolfe was silent.

"So he got your gun too?"

"Don't start with me, Harvath."

Harvath held up his hands. "I'm not starting anything. I'm just trying to assess the situation."

"I don't need a gun. His ass is mine. I'm telling you. I'm going to get that motherfucker if it's the last thing I ever do."

Harvath could understand the operative's frustration. Nobody liked being bested. "Alright, alright, but we've got to get the hell out of here."

When they reached the stairway and opened the door, the thick smoke and quickly rising fire made it obvious that they were going to have to find another way out of the building.

"What do we do now?" asked DeWolfe.

"Let's go see if we can get your gun back."

Harvath led DeWolfe to where he had watched their attacker seemingly disappear through the wall.

"What are we looking for?" asked DeWolfe.

"Some sort of false door or panel. I saw the guy vanish, so I know it has to be here."

As the pair searched, the room seemed to get hotter, and the air more difficult to breathe. DeWolfe, who had been rapping every square inch of the wall with his knuckles, said, "Harvath, I'm not seeing anything and we have to get the hell out of here."

"There's got to be something," replied Scot. "Keep looking."

"There isn't anything."

"So you're telling me the man who was shooting at us just disappeared? I don't buy it."

"Well, if we don't get out of here soon, we're both going to *buy* it."

DeWolfe was right. Harvath bent down, with his hands upon his knees, to get a clean breath of oxygen and that's when he saw it. Bathed in the brilliant beam of his flashlight was the almost imperceptible outline of a small trapdoor. Harvath glanced around at the heavy displaced furniture and understood why the shooter had been so frantically moving things around. *He was trying to find this trapdoor.*

Harvath waved DeWolfe over and silently instructed him to lift the door, while he readied his weapon. When the communications expert sprung the hatch, Scot swung his pistol and flashlight back and forth across the small opening, but nothing was there. Carefully, Harvath slid into the crawl space with his H&K ready to take out anything that moved. The entire space looked like some sort of labyrinth in miniature. As Harvath wriggled his way along, he found side passages on the left and right, branching off at regular intervals, just like the bedrooms on the second and third floors.

Following one of the junctures off to his right, Harvath's suspicions about the purpose of the crawl space were confirmed when five feet in, he found a large monocle attached to a braided cable mounted to the floor in front of him. Harvath peered into the monocle and was granted a perfect, albeit relatively dark view of the bedroom beneath. Apparently, Madame Putzkammer was not above spying on her customers.

As Harvath looked around at the relatively outdated, yet still highly effective surveillance equipment, he realized that the King George was not only set up to take still pictures of their customers in action, but audio and video as well. And from the looks of it, Frau Putzkammer had probably been up to it for a very long time.

"Harvath!" yelled DeWolfe from the main passage behind him. "I think I found the Madame."

Harvath crawled back out of his side tunnel and backtracked to DeWolfe. Inside one of the other side tunnels was the body of a woman shot once in the head. It had to be Nixie's mother. The resemblance was unmistakable.

"What do you want to do with her?" asked DeWolfe.

"There's nothing we can do," replied Harvath. "The tunnels are too tight to drag her with us." After turning around, he began leading the way forward again. Thirty feet later, the choking smell of smoke mingled with ripples of something else—*fresh air.*

The main passageway opened up onto a large ventilation shaft that looked to run the full height of the building. Glancing up, Harvath could see the night sky between the blades of the slowly oscillating fan. He climbed into the shaft, followed by De-Wolfe and they carefully made their way up and out onto the roof.

Looking over the intricately molded parapet onto the street below, Harvath could see the pile of mattresses that had been used to evacuate the building's occupants. A crowd of onlookers had formed, and knowing Herman the way he did, Scot expected he had helped the wounded as best he could and then had faded a safe distance away from the scene. No doubt he was somewhere nearby, trying to ascertain his fate as well as DeWolfe's.

By the close proximity of the other buildings, it wasn't hard to figure out the route their attacker had taken in his escape. Harvath couldn't ignore the dull but insistent throbbing deep in the pit of his stomach. It was telling him the name of the person who had attacked them, but he didn't want to believe it. It was all too impossible. Or was it?

CHAPTER 34

hree blocks away, Helmut Draegar stumbled into his newly rented Volkswagen, closed the door, and started the engine so he could get the heat going. *How could I have been so stupid?* he asked himself as he unbuttoned his shirt to look at the wound. Thankfully, the bullet had only nicked the upper part of his left arm, just below the shoulder. It hadn't entered. Yes, the wound was bleeding, but the bleeding would eventually stop. There was always the chance of infection, as with any bullet wound, but that too was easily handled. He would drive until he found one of Berlin's all-night pharmacies where he could purchase some antibiotics. At this point, an infection was the least of his concerns.

The triage of his injuries complete, Draegar fashioned a makeshift bandage around his arm and pulled away from the curb, his mind a tempest of self-loathing over the string of failures he ultimately could blame on no one other than himself.

In the beginning, Überhof had seemed to Draegar

an inspired choice. During the Cold War, Überhof had been based in East Berlin and attached to one of the Soviets' highly secretive Spetsnaz details. The Spetsnaz were Russian Special Forces units charged with wreaking maximum havoc upon the enemy in the days just prior to a war by destroying infrastructure, command and control centers, and weapons systems, as well as assassinating or snatching high-ranking military and diplomatic officials. When the East Berlin team wasn't training, they often took "freelance" jobs working for the KGB, or in Überhof's case, the *Ministerium für Statessicherheit*.

It was while working for the Stasi that Überhof had first come to Helmut Draegar's attention. The man was an exceptional operative, and on assignment after assignment had never let Draegar down. In fact, it was Überhof who had saved Draegar's life.

Even though it was fifteen years ago when one of Draegar's former contacts had popped up, claiming to have "valuable" information for him, it still felt like yesterday. Because Draegar had been suspicious, they chose to meet at the remains of an old monastery on the outskirts of the city. It was raining that night and there were a million other places Draegar would have rather been, but again, his contact had always been reliable and had always been able to get his hands on extremely sensitive material. If nothing else, Draegar at least needed to see what he had.

When the man arrived, he led Draegar deep into the ruined church where he claimed to have hidden a very special package. Draegar was reluctant, but pro-

ceeded nevertheless and followed the man down a set
of worn stone steps into a rotted and moldy crypt.
When Draegar ducked beneath the mortised archway
and entered the decayed undercroft, he knew that his
premonition had been correct. It was an ambush.
Standing in the center of the burial chamber, with his
gun pointed at him, was Gary Lawlor.

Draegar knew why he was there. He had killed
Lawlor's wife, and the man had come for revenge.
There was no use even asking his would-be execu-
tioner how he had uncovered him as the driver in
the hit-and-run. Someone had given him up; who,
though, he had no idea. He turned to look at his
once reliable contact, but the man refused to look
him in the eye. There were no allegiances when it
came to the information trade. Lawlor handed the
man an envelope and after checking its contents,
the man turned and disappeared up the crumbling
crypt stairs.

Draegar did not even attempt to beg for his life.
He may have entered the monastery alone, but he
did so wearing a wire. He chose his words carefully,
deliberately, conveying his exact position and situation in such a way that Lawlor would not take notice, but his team would. Hearing the exchange, it
was only a matter of time before his backup would
arrive.

What Draegar didn't know was that the thick
walls of the underground burial vault were impeding
the signal from his wireless transmitter. That was
precisely why Lawlor had chosen it. He had thought

that Draegar might bring backup, but had given the professional operative credit enough to know that he would keep them out of sight. The only way he would have been able to communicate with them was via radio. By obstructing his transmission, Gary was given enough time to do what he had to do—and he didn't waste a single minute of it.

After instructing Draegar to remove his gun, drop it on the ground, and kick it over to him, Lawlor ordered him to strip. That was when he found the wire. There was no time to go through Draegar's pockets, and Lawlor didn't want to risk frisking him. Almost instantly, Draegar began shaking from the cold.

Gary steered him to the far end of the vault, past door after rusted ancient iron door protecting small burial alcoves that had long since been looted, to a stone wall beneath a large iron ring where he made him sit. Though Lawlor had tested the ring to make sure it absolutely could not be pulled loose, he had underestimated the bulk of his prisoner's thick arms and shoulders. It would be impossible to run the handcuffs through the ring and secure both of the man's wrists. He'd only be able to secure one. With time running out, Gary decided to improvise.

Throwing the handcuffs to Draegar, he instructed the man to attach one of the bracelets to his left wrist and then hold his left arm above his head.

"Fuck you. Just shoot me and get it over with," Draegar had responded.

Lawlor was tempted, but it wasn't the type of ending he had envisioned. Carefully, he approached, and with his pistol cocked and pressed against Draegar's forehead, he shackled the man's left wrist and attached it to the iron ring. Though he would have liked nothing more than to pistol whip his wife's killer, Lawlor restrained himself. He didn't want to risk Draegar losing consciousness. He needed him awake for the revenge he had planned.

With his free hand, Lawlor removed a roll of duct tape from his coat and used his teeth to unravel a long section, which he wrapped several times tightly around the Draegar's mouth, completely gagging him.

His prisoner now secure, Gary set his pistol down on a nearby sarcophagus and picked up a large piece of dislodged masonry. It was about the size of a concrete cinder block and he brought it down in one crushing blow upon Draegar's left ankle. The Stasi agent howled in pain as his bones splintered and popped, but his cries were effectively muffled by the layers of duct tape.

Though he would have loved to have savored the moment further, Lawlor had no time. He quickly picked the block back up and repeated the hobbling treatment on Draegar's right side. There was no way the man could stand at this point, so escape was futile. All he could do was watch the last minutes of his life, quite literally tick away until he died.

"My wife," said Gary, as he emptied the contents of three duffel bags and assembled them in piles just out of Draegar's reach, "had no idea her life was about to end. I guess in that respect, she was fortunate. You, on the other hand, are not going to be granted that sort of mercy."

Draegar stared at the brick-sized parcels wrapped in what looked like brown wax paper and knew exactly what they were—cakes of C4. *Where the fuck is the backup team? Did Lawlor actually manage to take them out?* Draegar began to panic.

Gary was pleased to see the look of fear in the man's eyes. He'd been prepared for his wife's killer to maintain an icy calm all the way to the end and not grant him any added satisfaction. This sudden change in his demeanor was a pleasant bonus.

Lawlor rigged the charges and in front of each neat little stack of plastique placed glass jars of road tacks, essentially overgrown children's jacks with their points filed down into razor-sharp spikes. Though the explosion alone was enough to kill the man, Gary wanted to add a little something extra for Draegar. Hopefully, the thought of the shrapnel tearing through his body would add another layer to the man's fear.

His work complete, Lawlor activated the timer and placed a large, red LED display on top of one of the piles so Draegar could watch the last minutes and seconds of his life melt away.

Gary had run through his mind a million times what he was going to say at this moment, but as he retrieved his gun from the sarcophagus and turned to speak, somehow what he had prepared didn't seem to matter anymore. He could have laughed, he could have simply smiled, but instead he cast one last look at the man who had killed his wife and his eyes said it all—*Now it's your turn*. And with that, he turned and left the burial chamber.

For the first time in his life, despite all his intense training, Helmut Draegar was actually terrified. His restraints wouldn't give, the LED readout was ticking down, and had he not seen the rusted iron hinge on the door of the alcove behind him, he didn't know what he would have done. Knowing that the hinge would not be sharp enough to cut through bone, he first had to break his own wrist. Using a small stone about the size of a baseball, he snapped the radius, then the ulna of his shackled left wrist, and then with a primitive tourniquet in place, began the unthinkable.

Überhof, concerned with the prolonged radio silence, was the first of the backup team to break cover and investigate. He found Draegar, who had dragged himself up from the crypt, missing a hand, bleeding profusely, and very near death on the rain-soaked ground of what was once the monastery's church. He was able to get Draegar away from the ruins just as the piles of plastic explosive detonated in the undercroft and destroyed what remained of the old religious structure.

Fifteen years later, driving the streets of unified Berlin in search of an all-night pharmacy, it was still hard for Draegar to relive that night. The Russians had given him sanctuary in the days and years after the event. They had made sure East German police reported finding a horribly charred body in the rubble and that it was leaked to intelligence services that one of the Stasi's best operatives had met with foul play.

After he had recovered, the Russians had used Draegar and his exceptional skills to train not only their agents, but also the espionage agents of governments they were friendly with. Until recent events had necessitated his evacuation, he had been in Iraq, training Iraqi intelligence officers and helping them to get visas so they could travel to Western countries. He had also been providing despotic leaders in the region with lists of assassins that could facilitate "hits" for them in the West, as well as introductions to Russian companies willing to provide sensitive, banned military equipment such as satellite jamming systems intended to interfere with U.S. weapons.

As far as the world was concerned, Helmut Draegar was dead. And how did he thank his benefactors for giving him a renewed chance at life? He did it by screwing up one of the most important operations they had ever undertaken. Draegar had failed to get the information he needed from Gary Lawlor, which in turn had forced General Stavropol to come to Berlin. Überhof, as good as he once was, was Draegar's choice, but he had not only missed his opportunity to take out the men who had appeared at the Goltzstrasse apartment, he had allowed himself to be followed to the *Geisterbahnhöfe*, compromising all of them, and getting himself killed in the process. Not only did they lose Gary

Lawlor, and Draegar's long-awaited opportunity for revenge, but in the fury of the takedown, Stavropol, who had come to Berlin to aid in the interrogation, had dropped his most prized possession, a specially engraved pistol given to him by the Russian High Command—something he valued above all else.

Stavropol was incredibly angry and blamed Draegar. Berlin was his operation after all, but he had been given a chance to redeem himself and now he had blown that. Fearing the security he assumed had been established at the hospital, Draegar decided to follow Agent Scot Harvath. When the young American operative, whom Stavropol had filled him in on, had driven to the King George, Draegar knew that the Americans had a better handle on the situation than any of them had expected. If you were going to unravel a series of threads, it made sense to begin where the first one started, but the question still remained, *What exactly was Harvath doing there?* How had he discovered the place where their entire plan had been hatched?

A small-time, petty blackmailer, Gerda Putzkammer had no idea that twenty years ago Draegar and his men had not only discovered where she had hidden the information she collected on her customers, but that many nights they were creeping through the crawlspaces themselves collecting as much intelligence as possible from the higher profile clientele that patronized the King George.

The smartest move of all was when one of Draegar's men had suggested bugging Putzkammer's penthouse apartment. For the longest time, they went without uncovering anything of value, but finally, their efforts yielded a particularly precious gem—an American operative by the name of John Parker.

While Parker never discussed anything in outright detail, the things he did say, along with surveillance of other team members proved extremely helpful in putting together the big picture. In fact, it was Heide Lawlor's suspicions of her own husband that were the icing on the cake. Listening in on Heide and her caseworker provided the details the Russians needed. Had the woman not been so insistent to her caseworker that her husband was up to something, there might not have been such a need to kill her. But at the rate she was going, she would eventually blow her husband's operation and the Russians couldn't tolerate that. They had come too far. It was a plum too ripe to let spoil. Heide had to be removed and it had to look like it was done for other reasons. With her out of the picture, the Dark Night operation would be allowed to proceed and they would be able to keep their eye on it.

But why now was this Scot Harvath returning to the King George? What exactly was he looking for? Though Draegar didn't get a chance to interrogate the man himself, hopefully by burning the building, he had prevented Harvath from getting whatever it was he was after.

It would have to be good enough. Berlin wasn't safe for Draegar anymore. He needed to get back to Russia.

CHAPTER 35

SOMEWHERE OFF THE FINNISH COAST
STATE OF THE UNION ADDRESS—5 DAYS

The Advanced SEAL Delivery System, or ASDS, moved silently through the frigid waters of the Baltic Sea. It had been delivered to a secret Swedish naval base on the island of Gotland, via a U.S. Air Force Lockheed Martin C5 Galaxy cargo plane, in what the Swedish government believed was an impromptu, covert NATO training exercise. Harvath and his team flew by private jet to Gotland from Berlin, where they boarded the ASDS with their gear and rendezvoused with the USS *Connecticut*, a Seawolf-class nuclear-powered attack submarine, waiting two miles offshore. The ASDS was able to attach to the larger submarine via a lock in/lock out chamber in its floor and a dry-deck shelter mounted behind the *Connecticut*'s conning tower. This combination of watertight hatches allowed free passage between the *Connecticut* and the Advanced SEAL Delivery System while the *Connecticut* was underwater and approaching their target area.

The enormous nuclear-powered attack subma-

STATE OF THE UNION   355

rine was designed with emphasis on high-speed,
deep-depth operations. Its engine quieting, combat
systems, sensor systems, and payload capacity were
greatly improved over its predecessors, the Los An-
geles-class attack submarines. It was an investment
in technology that kept the U.S. Navy on the cutting edge of maritime warfare and tonight, that investment had more than proven its value.

With an unusual number of vessels from Russia's Baltic Fleet prowling the Gulf of Finland, all of
the *Connecticut*'s extraordinary stealth capabilities
had been called upon to maneuver it undetected
into a position off the Finnish coast where it could
launch the ASDS.

The bone-dry, completely enclosed, sixty-five-foot
long minisub was considered one of the hottest pieces
of equipment the U.S. Special Operations Command
had ever put into service. It could travel at ranges up
to 125 miles with a speed of just over eight knots on a
series of lithium ion polymer batteries. Its integrated
control and display systems, dual-redundant flight
control computers, operational software, forward-
looking sonar for detecting natural and manmade
obstacles, as well as side-looking sonar for mine detection and terrain/bottom mapping, were all state-
of-the-art. In addition to a Navy-certified submarine
pilot and SEAL navigator, the craft could accommodate anywhere from eight to sixteen SEALs, depending on the amount of gear their mission required.
Tonight, though, Harvath, Morrell, DeWolfe, and
Carlson were taking up most of the room.

As they came within range of their objective, the pilot, whom Carlson had referred to incessantly as "Captain Nemo" since they had boarded in Gotland, told his passengers to begin preparing to get wet.

Because of the amount of equipment they had to transport, they were limited to exiting in pairs from the lock in/lock out chamber in the floor of the ASDS.

All four of the men wore brand-new amphibious diving suits developed by the Army's Soldier and Biological Chemical Command lab in Natick, Mass- achusetts. The amphibious diving suits acted and looked like the typical dry suits designed to keep their wearers warm by preventing water from reaching the skin, but in this case, once the wearers climbed out of the water, the polyurethane-based, three-layer polymer membrane was also designed to soften and become more amorphous, so sweat mol- ecules could pass through it and perspiration could escape, preventing wearers from overheating. Gone were the days of having to change into a separate set of clothes for land-based operations. That said, the waters of the Baltic were absolutely freezing at this time of year, and as added insurance, the men wore an additional fleece-lined layer beneath their suits.

Their LAR VII closed-circuit rebreathers were complemented by military full facemasks with unimpeded field of vision, which provided added fa- cial protection from the icy water. Rebreathers were always the system of choice for covert operations.

Regular scuba equipment not only gave off clouds of large visible bubbles, but was also noisy. Closed-circuit oxygen rebreathers, on the other hand, were quiet, gave off no bubbles, and filtered the user's exhaled carbon dioxide, recharging the remaining nitrogen gas, which makes up a large part of the air, with pulsed oxygen. This economical system allows a diver to stay submerged for four hours or more. The main disadvantage, however, is that the diver is limited to operating in shallow water, as pure oxygen begins to become toxic at depths greater than thirty feet.

Waterproof combat bags protected the team's M4 machine guns, a lightweight version of the M16, which possessed a shorter barrel and a collapsible stock.

"Dummy corded" to each man, to prevent it from being dropped while underwater, was a highly classified weapon made by Heckler & Koch that didn't appear in any of their catalogs—the H&K P11.

The P11 was a special pistol, which could fire five 7.62-caliber darts both above and *below* water. But once those five shots have been fired, the P11 takes even longer than an antique black-powder rifle to reload, as it has to be sent all the way back to the H&K factory.

To navigate the strong currents around Aidata Island, each man commanded a Farallon MkX DPV—Diver Propulsion Vehicle. The Farallon MkX model DPV was a result of a joint research project between the U.S. Special Operations community

and Farallon to give American combat divers an extended mission range and greater top speed than
normal commercial DPVs delivered. One of the
greatest benefits of a DPV was that because a diver
didn't have to propel himself to an objective, he
wasn't doing any work, so his air could last up to
fifty percent longer—essentially doubling his dive
time.

The devices looked like minitorpedoes. Because
they incorporated a revolutionary new hydrogen-
based propulsion system, as opposed to the silver
zinc batteries being used by other companies, they
were much faster than anything previously produced.

Once Harvath, Morrell, DeWolfe, and Carlson
were all outside the mini-sub, they activated their
waterproof night-vision monocles, powered up
their DPVs, and followed their GPS displays on pre-
determined courses for Aidata Island.

though he had long since deleted the message, the final transmission Frank Leighton had received from Berlin still floated in the forefront of his mind:

```
Your mission has been compromised.
Entire Dark Night team terminated. Gary
Lawlor seriously wounded. Prognosis un-
clear.


Mission parameters now changed. We
are coming to you. Will explain at your
location. Hold position and exercise ex-
treme caution. You are being watched.
```

Frank Leighton had spent most of the last twenty-two hours wrestling with a multitude of questions. *Who had killed his teammates? Who exactly was watching him? Was it the Russians? What had hap-*

*pened to Gary Lawlor? How had the Dark Night opera-
tion been compromised? Who was this new player, Norseman? And why had his burst transmission been
terminated so abruptly?*

Though Norseman had managed to discover the
emergency contact location and the code for the
burst transmission, Leighton was still not one hundred percent convinced that he was who he said he
was and decided to slant the playing field as much
in his favor as possible.

When Norseman said, "we are coming to you,"
undoubtedly he meant that he would be arriving
with a team of some sort. If they really were concerned about being observed, they would probably
arrive under cover of darkness and most likely via
the water.

The first thing Leighton did was booby-trap the
site where he had secreted his nuke. If worse came
to worse and he was captured, he could at least
march his captors into an ambush and maybe be
able to escape.

Next, he made sure his boat was ready to sail.
He went over the entire craft from stem to stern
and made sure everything was literally shipshape.
After that, there was nothing left to do but wait.

Hidden within a small outcropping of rock on the
side of the inlet where his boat was moored, was a
narrow fissure just big enough for Leighton to wedge
himself into and be concealed. The waiting seemed to
last an eternity, but he was patient. The night was
dark and did not offer much ambient light, which

greatly reduced the effectiveness of the old night vision binoculars now clutched in his hands. When he finally did notice something near the beach, he thought his tired eyes were playing tricks on him. Leighton squeezed his eyes shut for several seconds, trying to dissipate some of the "orange burn" so common with use of night vision optics.

When he looked back through the binoculars again, the shapes appeared not to have moved. *Probably just piles of kelp washed in by the tide,* he thought to himself. The Baltic was famous for the large seaweed forests that populated its sea floor. Then, as he was about to lower the binoculars and give his eyes another rest, he noticed it—*movement*. They were here.

As Leighton extricated himself from his hiding place, it took several minutes for him to get the blood flowing into his legs again. Though the site had provided an exceptional vantage point, he should have stretched more often. His body was not as forgiving as it used to be.

With his Finnish-made JatiMatic PDW drawn, Leighton quietly crept toward the beach. He picked his way along the jagged shoreline, slogging through frigid knee-deep tidal pools, while using the abundance of large rocks for cover as best he could.

When he neared the field of smooth, ocean-tumbled stones that functioned as the inlet's beach, Leighton crouched behind the last large rock that stood between him and the wide-open space. As the waves splashed against the shore and further soaked his already drenched trousers, he once again raised the night vision binoculars and studied the two shapes he had been looking at before. Upon closer inspection, he still couldn't tell if they were piles of kelp or something more. But he had seen movement. He was sure of it.

At that moment, a voice from behind and to the left caught him completely off guard. "Mr. Leighton, I presume?" Leighton stiffened in surprise.

"Please set down your weapon and turn around slowly," continued the voice.

Leighton did as he was told. As he turned around, the man who had addressed him lowered the M4 he had pointing at him, pulled off the strings of camouflaging kelp that were hanging from his dry suit, and stepped the rest of the way out of the water. "I'm Norseman," the man said, holding out a gloved hand.

Leighton was speechless. He hadn't even heard so much as a ripple from the water. Whoever this guy was, he was good. Though he cautiously shook the man's hand, Frank Leighton still wasn't convinced they were on the same side.

Harvath shouldered his weapon and removed his fins, tucking them under his left arm. Taking off his gloves, he slid them underneath his weight belt and then signaled the beach and the rusting trawler with a small, waterproof IR strobe. When his signals were returned, Harvath removed his facemask and said to Leighton, "It looks like a nice night for a boat ride. Let's get going."

On the beach, they rendezvoused with Leighton's

two piles of kelp, operatives Morrell and DeWolfe. Knowing that he had spotted at least part of the team made Leighton feel only slightly better. Though his skills were still good, they weren't near what they used to be.

Forgoing the courtesy of an introduction, Morrell asked, "Where's the device?"

"Let's establish some bona fides first," replied Leighton.

"I thought we already did that."

"We're off to an okay start, but if you think I'm going to hand my responsibilities over to a group of frogmen who show up and just happen to speak English without any accents and claim to be on my side, you're quite mistaken."

"Listen," snapped Morrell. "Don't try my fucking patience. This suit is good for only about ten more minutes and then my body heat, which you are prematurely raising, is going to begin leaching out. I'm sure our friends the Russians out there on the water are using thermal imaging to keep an eye on this place. If they notice more than one warm body on this island, they might think there's a little beach barbecue going on and want to come in for a closer look. We can't let that happen."

Leighton, far from being a pushover, went toe-to-toe with Morrell and said, "Then you'd better keep your cool."

Morrell raised his M4 and pointed it right at Leighton's chest. "No, I think you'd better get with the fucking program."

"This guy always have a mouth like this?" asked Leighton, turning toward Harvath.

"Not usually. He must have lost his thesaurus on the swim in."

"Very funny," said Morrell. "Now we've got nine minutes and counting. Either you're part of the solution, or I'm going to spread you across the beach and you can become part of the landscape."

"He's serious, isn't he?" asked Leighton.

Harvath simply nodded his head.

"I've got some questions I want answered first. And like I said, we'll start by establishing bona fides."

"And like I said," returned Morrell, "we don't have time for that shit. We've already proven ourselves. We're all on the same team here."

"Well, without me on the team, you're going to have a hard time finding what you're looking for, so I suggest you cooperate, take a few minutes, and answer my questions."

Morrell removed a small handheld device. "I've got the GPS coordinates for what I'm looking for, so I don't really need your cooperation, do I?"

Leighton smiled. "Those coordinates might get you there, but that's about all they'll get you."

"Why? What have you done?"

"Let's just say what you're looking for is *very* well protected."

Morrell's eyes widened. "You booby-trapped it, didn't you?"

Leighton remained smiling.

"Carlson," called Morrell over his throat mike as

he turned to face the trawler moored in the inlet. "I need you on the beach, ASAP."

Carlson, who, along with Avigliano, was prepping the *Rebecca* with a special surprise, thought he had a better idea and voiced his opinion.

"No, I'm not sending Harvath to do it," barked Morrell in response to Carlson's voice in his earpiece. "Fuck his SEAL training. You're the demo expert, so get your ass over here now."

Leighton looked at the men on the beach. "Who's Harvath?"

"What the fuck do you care?" growled Morrell.

"You've got a SEAL named Harvath. I want to know who he is."

"You want, you want, you want. You know what? Fuck you."

"Easy, Rick," said Scot, stepping in to separate the two men. "I'm Harvath."

The binoculars had fried Leighton's eyes worse than he had thought. After squinting a moment, he said, "Of course you are. You look just like him. You sound like him too. I can't believe I didn't see it right off the bat."

"What the hell are you talking about?" asked Morrell.

Leighton ignored him. "You're Mike Harvath's son."

"You knew him?" asked Scot.

"Yeah, back in Vietnam when I was with Army Intelligence. Gary introduced us. We did a couple of joint ops together. He was a good man."

"Yes he was."

There was silence on the beach. Morrell raised his eyebrows and looked back and forth several times from Harvath to Leighton. "Have we established our bona fides now?"

Though he didn't care much for Morrell, the resemblance Harvath bore to his father was enough to satisfy Leighton that these men were who they said they were. "We're good. Follow me."

"Fabulous," sneered Morrell, who activated his throat mike and addressing Carlson said, "Scratch that last order. You and Avigliano finish prepping the boat. We're going to get the package. Be ready to move."

arvath gave everything on the *Rebecca* a final check before raising anchor and sailing the old trawler through the island's narrow channel and out into the open sea.

The noxious blue smoke of the coughing diesels couldn't mask the smell of the salt-laden air. The scent stirred up a flood of memories in Harvath. Despite the amount of time he had spent in and around the ocean as an adult, its smell always reminded him of time he had spent with his father as a young boy. As far back as Harvath could remember, the ocean had been part of their life. They lived near it, swam in it, fished in it, and sailed upon it. While some fathers and sons talked and bonded over baseball or other sporting pursuits, Scot's father, who was not a very communicative man to begin with, was always able to talk about the ocean. He spent hours teaching his son about navigation by stars and currents, sextant and compass. The younger Harvath had incredible recall and could name any type of Navy vessel in San

Diego Harbor after only seeing it one time. The same went for battleships, frigates, and the like, which his father would point out in books. By the time he was twelve, Harvath had read all of the Hornblower novels, courtesy of his father's vast maritime library. In fact, Scot had long suspected that had it not been for the Navy, his father would have very likely selected some other seafaring profession that would have kept him connected to the mistress he loved so dearly.

And there was no doubt in Scot's mind that the sea was his father's mistress. Many times in his young life, Scot felt that the sea mattered more to the man than his own family, but then, Scot himself had joined the Navy and began his own affair with it. Though Scot had very much enjoyed his career as a competitive skier, if he was honest with himself, he would have to admit that there had always been something missing.

The U.S. Ski Team, as much as he had cared for his teammates, was really no team at all. It was every man and woman for themselves. All that mattered was you and the judges. There might not have been any "I" in team, but there was "me." Harvath had been hungry to be part of something more than just his own selfish pursuits and the SEALs had given him that opportunity.

For the first time in his life, he had discovered the true meaning of the word *team* and what it meant to be part of something greater than yourself. It didn't take long for him to realize what the

SEALs had meant to his father. In a way, Scot's time on the teams had given him a sense of something he had never before experienced, a sense of belonging—belonging to something that really mattered and really made a difference in the world. With the SEALs, character, honor, integrity, loyalty, and duty meant something. They weren't just empty words. And though he often liked working on his own, being able to still do that as part of a team, where everyone had a shared objective and where every participant's performance mattered, was one of the most fulfilling undertakings he had ever pursued.

As he thought about it now, he wondered if maybe his decision to follow in his father's footsteps was less about searching for something from his father and more about searching for something in himself.

Harvath's concern over his mission drew his mind back to more relevant issues. As he glanced out the back of the wheelhouse to check on his Diver Propulsion Vehicle, which had been tied to the rear of the trawler, he hoped the rest of the team had made it to their objective safely.

After Frank Leighton's nuke was retrieved and brought down to the beach, it was placed in a long, streamlined tube, which Carlson and Avigliano gently slid into the water and connected via towropes to their DPVs. Once Leighton was outfitted in his own dry suit, flippers, facemask, and rebreather, the men submersed themselves beneath the water and headed for the Advanced Swimmer

Delivery System waiting a few miles offshore. From there, it was a short cruise to the Finnish mainland, where a group of three cars would be waiting for them with money and instructions on how they were to cross into Russia, as well as what Leighton's new mission parameters were.

As Harvath headed farther into the Eastern Gulf of Finland, he monitored the trawler's antiquated radar system and tried to assess the proximity of the Russian patrol boats he knew were shadowing him. The *Rebecca*'s equipment was useless. Random islands, fishing boats, patrol boats . . . they all looked the same on the cracked, green display screen. It was only a matter of time before the Russians would be on top of him.

Almost as if rushing to meet the challenge head-on, Harvath shoved the trawler's twin throttles farther forward, trying to coax as much speed as he could from the struggling old engines.

Three hours and twenty-seven minutes later, after a short stop to change the trawler's registration markings from Finnish to Russian and substitute one country's flag for another, Harvath found himself less than three kilometers inside Russian territorial waters when the trap was sprung. A lone Federal Border Guard Service high-speed Sokzhoi-class patrol boat had appeared virtually out of nowhere and was bearing down on him off the starboard bow. Harvath, per the plan outlined by Rick Morrell, quickly turned the *Rebecca* around and attempted to head back into Finnish waters. Even though he knew he'd never outrun them, it made him look guilty as hell and that's exactly what was supposed to happen.

A second Sokzhoi joined in the chase and fired a warning shot from its 30mm cannon across the *Rebecca*'s bow. Though the plan had called for Harvath to throttle back to neutral at this point, he decided to push his luck a little further. The Baltic water was freezing and the shorter he could make his impending swim, the better. Besides, the prevailing assumption was that the Russians wanted to take Frank Leighton alive. If they blew up the boat they thought he was on, not only would that put a serious dent in their plans, but it might also detonate the device they believed he was carrying. Harvath glanced out at the Sokzhois and hoped he was right.

Pressing the throttles as far forward as they would go, Harvath heard the engines groan in protest. Just then, another 30mm round was loosed, landing much closer to the bow than the one before, throwing up a large sheet of spray that covered the wheelhouse. Harvath began to realize that dead or alive, the Russians had no intention of letting him leave.

With the high-speed crafts staring him right in the face, Harvath's decision to get back into the cold water was made a lot easier. He doused all of the *Rebecca*'s lighting and then "lit the candles," as Carlson had put it, on the special "cake" he had baked for the Russians. Blocks of C4 had been placed strategically throughout the vessel, with special attention focused on the engine room and its remaining stores of diesel fuel. As Harvath grabbed the boat's flare gun and exited the wheelhouse, he activated a waterproof timer strapped to his wrist. It was synced to Carlson's digital fuse aboard the *Rebecca*, which had already begun its own deadly countdown.

Arriving at the rear of the trawler, Harvath was suddenly illuminated by one of the most powerful spotlights he had ever seen. A voice over a loudspeaker commanded him first in Russian and then English to stop where he was and prepare to be boarded. *Fat chance of that*, Harvath said to himself as he readied the flare gun. Aiming it over the top of the patrol boats, he pulled the trigger.

The bright red signal flare soared high into the night sky and hopefully carried with it the eyes of the Federal Border Guard agents so intent on capturing him. Placing the regulator in his mouth and flipping over the side, Harvath was far beneath the surface when the crews of the Sokzhois began strafing the water with rounds from their 14.5mm machine guns.

As he was no longer carrying his M4, the bulk of Harvath's gear was now contained in a medium-sized buoyancy bag, which could be partially inflated via a small, attached bottle of air, thus rendering the bag weightless underwater. Harvath inflated it to the proper buoyancy and, using carabiners, secured the bag to two eye-hook-style receivers mounted beneath his DPV. Cutting the cord that connected the Farallon Diver Propulsion Vehicle to the *Rebecca*, he let himself drift downward for several meters while he got his bearings before firing up the DPV.

His rendezvous point was off another island, just inside the Russian maritime border, about five kilometers away. It was a tiny, insignificant port where fisherman stocked up on fuel and supplies, as well as waited out storms or repairs to their boats before putting back to sea. The vessel Harvath was meeting, complete with the SEAL team that had commandeered it, would fit in perfectly.

As Harvath fixed his location with the DPV's Global Positioning System, he wasn't surprised to hear the low grumble of Zevzda high-speed diesels coming from one of the Sokzhoi patrol boats on the surface. It had made a beeline straight for the *Rebecca* the minute he had abandoned ship. It was exactly what he had been counting on.

Depressing the trigger switches of his DPV, Harvath began to move as quickly as he could away from the *Rebecca* and the Russian boarding party that was probably already clambering over her gunwales.

Despite his dry suit and all the other precautions he had taken, the water was still freezing. Not only was the suit not keeping him as warm as he would have liked, but along with the buoyancy bag suspended from the bottom of the DPV, it was also creating a lot of drag. Had he been more streamlined, he might have been able to get away a lot faster from what was about to happen.

Illuminating the timer strapped to his wrist, Harvath counted down the final seconds before the *Rebecca* exploded. When the timer reached zero, he said to himself, "*do svidaniya*, motherfuckers," but was unprepared for the incredible concussion wave that followed.

Had it not been for the MkX's locking forearm cuffs, Harvath would have lost the DPV for sure. His ears were ringing and he was completely disoriented. He fought to hold on to consciousness as the change in pressure slammed his body into a deadly spin. It was like being caught beneath the biggest wave he had ever imagined. Over and over he turned as the force of the blast threatened to squeeze the life out of him. The regulator was knocked from his mouth and he had no idea which way was up.

There was a tightness in his chest and as he struggled against the blackness overtaking his head, he realized he was holding the triggers of the DPV in a viselike death grip and that it was pulling him straight down. Harvath let go and the machine's propeller came to a halt. Unlocking one of his arms, he located his regulator and placed it back into his mouth. For several seconds, all he did was breathe, but the air tasted funny and was searing his lungs. He looked at the depth gauge strapped to his other wrist and saw that it read forty-three feet. He had transcended the thirty-foot threshold and his oxygen was becoming toxic. He needed to climb.

As the DPV pulled him on a gradual ascent toward the surface, Harvath felt the pressure on his body lessen and his mind began to clear. There was no way the blast he had felt was from the *Rebecca*, he was too far away when it had gone up. It had to have been something else.

Approaching the surface, Harvath could once again hear the low diesel grumble of one of the Sokzhoi patrol boats. This one was very close. Though he was tempted to take a look, he decided against it. Pointing the DPV in the opposite direction, he depressed the triggers and set about putting as much distance between himself and the Russians as possible.

Surprisingly, the sound of the engines didn't fade. In fact, they grew louder. Harvath changed course again and so did the patrol boat. It was as if they had some sort of lock on him, but how? Then he realized—*sonar.*

The Sokzhoi was one of the most efficient, best-equipped patrol boats the Russians had. There was no doubt that it would have been outfitted with all the bells and whistles and with his DPV, Harvath was unquestionably giving off a small, but distinct sonar signature. Though a small, moving target was hard to hit, if the Federal Border Guard agents were using grenades to force him to the surface, they wouldn't have to be dead-on accurate, just being in the general neighborhood would be enough. Harvath had to act fast.

Diving, Harvath pushed the limits of toxicity for his rebreather as far as he dared. At just below thirty-two feet, he hovered and braced for impact. Moments later, the explosions came. The first two were far enough away, but the third rattled him so hard, he almost blacked out.

Using the sound of the high-speed diesel engines as his guide, Harvath slowly made his way toward the surface. As the patrol boat's bright searchlight swept the water looking for him, Harvath located the dark shadow cast by the vessel's hull. Now, it was all just a matter of timing.

Harvath dove back down and unlocked himself from the DPV's arm cuffs. The patrol boat was right above him and had come to a dead stop as its searchlight continued to carve through the water. Goosing the Diver Propulsion Vehicle just to the edge of the Sokzhoi's shadow, Harvath then opened the attached buoyancy bag's air bottle as far as it would go and released it.

The carabiners snapped tight and the buoyancy bag began to pull the DPV upward as Harvath swam toward the bow of the boat and began his ascent.

When the DPV broke the surface, it was immediately spotted by several heavily armed Federal Border Guard agents crowding the ship's railing. With their attention diverted, the first thing Harvath did was take aim at the Sokzhoi's searchlight.

The silent dart raced from the H&K P11 underwater pistol and hit its mark dead on. The searchlight exploded in a shower of sparks that rained down upon the forward deck of the patrol boat. For the moment, Harvath had the advantage, but it wouldn't last long.

Just beneath the surface of the water, he activated his night vision monocle, and took aim at the men along the railing. The first three were felled with shots to the chest while the fourth, who was seating another 40mm round into his grenade launcher, caught his in the stomach.

Harvath watched the man double over and lurch against the patrol boat's cable railing. His forward momentum carried him over the side and into the water where he landed with a loud splash. Alarms were ringing and men were rushing out onto the decks, but there was nothing they could do to save their fallen comrades, especially the man in the water.

After relieving the dying man of his weapon, which he slung over his back, Harvath retrieved the DPV and started purging the air from the buoyancy bag. Powerful handheld floodlights were being distributed to the patrol boat's remaining crew, but by the time they began lighting up the surrounding water, Harvath was nowhere to be found.

Bobbing just out of view, he watched as the floodlight beams went from a disorganized free-for-all to a defined focus in his general direction. The patrol boat's engines growled back to life and Harvath realized that their sonar must have picked up his signal again. Any second, the heavy 30mm guns and 14.5mm machine guns would start and the chase would be on once again.

Unshouldering the grenade launcher, Harvath took aim and waited. He had only one shot. Less than half a mile away, the fiery remains of the *Rebecca* and the other patrol boat burned in tandem, painting the night sky with an eerie orange glow.

As the remaining Sokzhoi barreled down on him, Harvath sighted his weapon, took a deep breath, and squeezed the trigger.

With an effective range of 350 meters, he worried that maybe he had overshot, but then he saw the Sokzhoi's bridge explode in a colossal ball of fire, sending a hail of fiery debris in all directions.

By the time the first flaming piece of wreckage hit the water, Harvath was already back below the surface, making his way to his rendezvous point.

CHAPTER 38

President Jack Rutledge was beyond exhausted. While most of his senior staff had begged him to get some rest, Rutledge had rolled up his sleeves and spent every single moment in the Situation Room beneath the White House with the vast array of experts who came and went around the clock to put in their two cents' worth on how the crisis with Russia could best be dealt with.

Finally, Rutledge had had enough. Politely thanking the visiting experts, he had them shown out and then immediately restricted any further access to the Situation Room to representatives of the Joint Chiefs and his National Security Council. There were less than five days now until the State of the Union address and they still had no solid plan.

After a couple of hours of catch-up sleep, Rutledge convened his "war council" and wasted no time getting down to business. "Ladies and gentlemen, you represent the best and the brightest this country has to offer and the future of this country might very well rest upon what you are able to come up with in this very room. For the next half hour I want to hear what our possible options are. Anything goes. If we have to tear the tail off the Devil himself, I'll consider it, let's just throw it all out there and see what we can come up with. This is a worst-case scenario and I want to hear anything you can come up with."

The clock ran well past the half-hour mark with ideas being floated on everything from introducing a forward-engineered strain of the Ebola virus into Russia and then quarantining the entire country with an unprecedented land and naval blockade, to launching an all-out bombing attack with airplanes and nuclear weapons from the World War II era that many believed would be unaffected by the Russians' new air defense system, which seemed to affect modern electronic guidance systems.

After Rutledge had had his fill of talk about killer satellites, commandos suspended from jet-propelled parachutes, and even plague-infested rats with plague-dispersing backpacks, he retired to the residence for a quiet meal with his daughter, Amanda, whom he had pulled out of school and was keeping under close guard at the White House around the clock—not an easy thing to do with a young woman who had just passed her seventeenth birthday.

"Dad," she said, after the steward set down their salads and then quietly left the room, "has America been fucked with a capital F?"

While the president had been known to privately extend a certain amount of latitude to his staff in their vocabular selections, that policy most certainly did not extend to his daughter. "First of all," he began, "I don't care how close USC and college life may appear to you, I don't ever want to hear that language again. Am I clear?"

The rebuke was extremely embarrassing for Amanda Rutledge. It had been one of her first forays into an adult conversation with her father and it had failed miserably. Having overheard two of the agents on her Secret Service detail speaking, she had thought she might engage the president on a gritty, adult level, but the attempt had crashed and burned. Instead of relating to her as a knowledgeable young adult, her father had immediately shut her down as a child whose opinion didn't matter. Nevertheless, Amanda Rutledge wasn't one to be deterred. "I may not have used the best language, Dad, but I'm only repeating what I already heard. Is America in trouble?"

"Of course not," said the president, making sure he smiled as he reached for the salad dressing.

"Then why'd you pull me out of school? I'm not stupid, you know."

Rutledge dribbled the salad dressing onto his plate for as long as he could and wished for the millionth time that breast cancer had never taken his wife. She was so much better at handling these things than he was. Tackling the truth head-on was his forte, but breaking it down in such a way so as to not completely shatter the world of a seventeen-year-old, was almost totally beyond his realm of expertise.

No matter how much he wished things were different, though, his wife wasn't with them anymore. He had no choice but to explain things to his daughter. "Amanda, I'm not going to lie to you. America is facing a potentially serious threat right now, but no matter what happens you're going to be okay. I promise you."

"What about you?" she asked.

"I'll be okay too. We'll both be together. So don't worry. Okay?"

"Dad?" Amanda continued as she stabbed her fork into her salad. "What about the rest of the people in America? Are they going to be okay too?"

"I'm doing everything I can to make sure that they are," responded the president.

"I know you are," she said, before turning her attention back to her salad.

After several minutes of strained silence between them, Amanda asked, "Dad, are we going to die?"

CHAPTER 39

T he first thing Harvath noticed upon exiting St. Petersburg's dingy train station, known as the *Finlandsky Vokzal*, was the bronze statue of Vladimir Ilyich Lenin standing atop an armored car. Harvath followed the statue's finger to where it ironically pointed across the frozen Neva River to a large orange building with a tall antenna—the *Bolshoi Dom*, literally *The Big House*, home of the Interior Ministry and local headquarters of the FSB. For a country that had supposedly sworn off Communism, it had always seemed strange to Harvath how many prominent statues and monuments from that era they still displayed. For their part, the Russians claimed that having been defined by Communism for so long, it was impossible to erase every vestige of it. After all, it was Communism that had brought them prominence, notorious though it was, in the modern world and, like it or not, the experience of living under Communism had become part of the Russian soul.

Well, Harvath didn't like it. What had seemed

up to now like an idiosyncratic clinging to a failed
political experiment had taken on a new and graver
significance for him over the past several days. The
idea that the Soviets could have faked capitulation,
only to now hold his own country hostage from
within, made him sick to his stomach.

Passing the statue, Harvath noticed a small stray
dog pick up its leg and urinate against old Vlad.
"Good boy," he whispered, as he threw the dog the
last cookie from the pack he had purchased from one
of the countless vendors on the rickety train known
by locals as the *elektrichka*. It felt good to find a kin-
dred spirit so soon upon his arrival in Russia. He
only hoped that Viktor Ivanov's daughter would turn
out to be one as well. The Defense Intelligence
Agency had an asset who had worked with her before, and it was through that asset that she had
agreed to meet with him. Harvath was counting on
her willingness to help him with whatever she knew.
At this point she was his only lead, and time was
quickly running out. The State of the Union address
was only four days away.

Though he could have taken the St. Petersburg
Metro, Harvath wanted to get the lay of the land
before his meeting. Following the cheap tourist
map he had picked up in the station, he headed
south and crossed the Neva River via the Liteynyi
Bridge. The air was cold and damp, much damper
than it had been in Berlin. Heavy, snow-laden gray
clouds crowded the sky, while a thin layer of silvery
flakes covered the streets and sidewalks.

As he walked, Harvath reflected on everything that had happened over the last four days, culminating in his misadventures on the Baltic with the two Russian Federal Border Guard Service patrol boats. After a long time in the water, he had finally rendezvoused with the Navy SEAL Team assigned to bringing him the rest of the way into Russia. They were operating a commandeered smuggler's boat, which thankfully had a fully equipped galley. After changing out of his dry suit, Harvath downed about a gallon of water, then ate a meal of fried eggs accompanied by a cup of black coffee and a hunk of rye bread.

They dropped him off just up the coast from a town called Zelenogorsk, where he caught the *elektrichka* to St. Petersburg. He wore a fisherman's turtleneck sweater, jeans, boots, and his black leather jacket. He also wore a superlightweight KIVA technical backpack, which contained a hydration system, a change of clothes, and some other goodies the SEALs had provided him with.

As he cut through the Mikhailovsky Gardens, Harvath saw his third group of Russian schoolchildren and decided that Fridays in St. Petersburg must be field-trip day. Beyond the gardens, stood his destination—the majestic Hermitage Museum.

The museum was one of largest in the world, second only to the Louvre in Paris, and it occupied six buildings along the Neva. The most impressive of those buildings was known as the Winter Palace, former home of the Russian czars. Entering the

green-and-white Winter Palace along the *Dvortso-
vaya* Embankment, Harvath bought a ticket for 300
rubles and made his way through the Russian
Baroque Rastrelli Gallery, with its massive columns
and intricately vaulted ceiling, until he came to the
Hermitage Café.

He ordered a small, open-faced sandwich and a
bottle of mineral water at the counter and then
chose one of the few remaining empty tables. He
slid his chair around so that he could sit with his
back to the wall and after marking where all the
exits were, pulled the Friday edition of the *St. Petersburg Times* out of his backpack and set it to the
left of his tray as he'd been instructed. It was now
time to wait.

As he ate his sandwich, Harvath alternated between gazing out of the large windows that looked
out onto the central courtyard of the Winter Palace
and studying the faces of the other patrons in the
café. The museum was packed today and the selection of the café, with its high ceilings, stone floor,
and attendant ambient noise, was an inspired
choice for a rendezvous. Even if someone had
wanted to listen in on a surreptitious conversation,
it would have been extremely difficult, if not impossible.

Harvath kept watching the faces of people as
they entered and exited the café. When Alexandra
Ivanova finally arrived, it was nearly impossible not
to notice her. She was even more stunning than her
photograph.

As she moved across the room, one of the first things Harvath noticed was her height. He put her at around five-foot-eight, maybe taller, but with the boots she had on it was hard to tell. They came to just about mid-calf and were only the beginning of her outfit. She wore winter leggings and a short skirt, which did little to disguise her very attractive, long legs. A tight, ribbed sweater was partially exposed beneath a heavy shearling coat, and to finish it all off, she had on a pair of funky frameless purple sunglasses and a tan crocheted cap that looked like it had come from an ABBA revival concert, beneath which her blond hair hung in two long braids.

Not exactly subtle, thought Harvath as she came up to the table, but there was no way a woman this good-looking could disguise how attractive she was.

"It appears as if you are alone," said Ivanova. "May I join you?"

"With over three million works of art in this museum, I would hardly consider myself alone, but you are welcome to sit down," replied Harvath, using the phrase he'd been given to establish his bona fides with Ivanova.

"Unfortunately, only a small percentage of it is ever on display at one time," she returned, setting her tray next to Harvath's and taking a seat. "This is a museum you need to come back to over and over again to really appreciate."

"I'll keep that in mind," said Harvath, their bona fides now established. "You're late."

"I was busy."

"Busy with what?"

"That's none of your concern," answered Alexandra. "I don't have all day, so let's, as you Americans say, *get to the point*."

There are very few things in the world as pleasing to the ear as English spoken by a Russian woman. The experience is made doubly enjoyable if the woman in question is as attractive as Alexandra Ivanova.

Because of her very appealing accent, Harvath could almost forgive her for being so rude. Almost.

"I'm sorry if I'm keeping you from something," replied Scot, the condescension apparent in his voice. "I'll do my best to keep this short."

Ivanova simply nodded her head with disinterest and began to blow on her tea.

"I need your help. There's information your father may have had that could—"

"After all these years, the Americans have decided he is once again a viable source," she responded, glaring over the top of her teacup. "I'll be happy to give you the address where you can find him, though he's not much of a conversationalist anymore."

Harvath could tell where this was going and did his best to diffuse the situation. "Listen, I can see that you're upset—"

"No, you listen to me. You have no idea how I feel or what my father went through because of you people."

"Maybe I don't, but that was the world your father was living in. Double-dealing in intelligence is a tricky business."

Alexandra set her teacup down. "You make it sound as if somehow he was disloyal. Every single thing he did was for the good of his country. You people sold him out."

"*Sold him out?* What are you talking about?"

"You know what I'm talking about. Your intelligence services cut him loose and then leaked to the KGB that he had been cooperating with them."

"That's ridiculous. We never would have done that. That's not our style. We don't reward people that way," said Harvath.

"The KGB could never officially prove it, but somehow they knew what he had done and they punished him for it anyway. You say the leak didn't come from your side. Why should I believe you?"

"Because I told you, that's *not* how we do business."

"You're a liar."

God, the woman was an ice princess. "Hey, I'm not the guy you've got an ax to grind with. You don't even know me."

"Oh, no?"

"No," replied Scot.

"Scot Harvath. Former internationally ranked U.S. Freestyle Ski Team member who quit the circuit shortly after his father's death. You left to study political science and military history at the University of Southern California, where you graduated cum laude before joining the Navy and passing

selection to become a SEAL. After postings to both
Teams Two and Six, also known as Dev Group, you
were recruited to the Secret Service to help improve
White House operations and presidential security.
Your current posting is unknown."

Harvath was floored. "How the hell do you
know all that?"

"I keep very good track of people who have
crossed me, Agent Harvath."

"*Crossed you*? I haven't crossed you. I don't even
know you."

"You don't?" asked Ivanova, fluttering her eye-
lashes. The move was not at all flirtatious. It was
inappropriate and meant to be insulting.

"Believe me," replied Scot, trying to remain
calm and not rise to the bait, "if our paths had
crossed, I would have remembered it."

"Do you remember Istanbul?" she asked. "Five
years ago. A prominent American businessman and
his family taken hostage?"

Of course he remembered, *but how could she know
about it?*

The scenes came rushing back. Harvath was
with SEAL Team Six at the time and had been put
in charge of the ransom exchange. He showed up
with what the kidnappers assumed was the money,
but in reality was an H&K MP5K submachine gun
covertly mounted inside a briefcase with the firing
mechanism incorporated into the handle.

The expressions of shock and surprise on the
kidnappers' faces had barely had a chance to regis-

ter before Harvath took out every last one of them. They had never seen it coming. When the rest of Harvath's team stormed the building, there was nothing left for them to do but help escort the businessman and his family safely back to the U.S. Embassy.

"What's this all about?" Harvath asked the woman.

"I was stationed in Istanbul."

As well as London and Hong Kong, Harvath remembered from Rick Morrell's briefing. "So?"

"So the kidnappers you took out were part of an arms ring we were investigating, who were responsible for smuggling heavy weaponry to several rebel groups in the Caucasus."

"So?"

"They were the middle men. They were going to put us next to the ones running the organization, but you killed them."

"Sorry," said Harvath, turning his palms upward.

"I was in charge of that investigation."

"Sorry, again," replied Scot.

"We had an agent on the inside and you killed him."

Harvath had had no idea. His recent disaffection with the Russians notwithstanding, the fact that he had killed an innocent man did not sit well with him. "I didn't know. I'm sorry. But by the same token, what the hell was he doing mixed up with a kidnapping? He should have known better. He shouldn't have been there when the exchange went down."

"He wasn't," said Alexandra.

"What?"

"He wasn't there. He was working on putting together our meeting with the organization's top members."

"So, I couldn't have possibly killed him then."

"Not directly, but because he was new, the organization was already suspicious of him. His conspicuous absence from the bloodbath that was your ransom exchange was enough to tip their paranoia, and they shot him."

"The key word here being *they*," interjected Harvath. "*They* shot him."

Alexandra asked, "Do you know how long it took us to get inside that group?"

"Probably longer than for us to take them out."

"That is not amusing, Agent Harvath."

"I think it is. You want to blame me for things I had absolutely no control over. While you're at it, why don't you talk about the 1980 Winter Olympics and how I blew it for the Soviet hockey team and handed the Americans the *Miracle on Ice*."

"I think we're done here," said Alexandra, pushing her chair back.

Things were quickly falling apart. "Wait a second," offered Harvath, getting himself back under control. "I apologize. You lost an operative and had a serious investigation compromised. That's not something to make jokes about."

"You're right, it's not," replied Ivanova.

"Then why don't we get back to the matter at hand?"

"The information my father may have had."

"Exactly, although it's not a question of whether he may have had it or not. We know he did."

"You mean, *now* you know he did."

Harvath understood the anger she felt on behalf of her father for having been rebuked and subsequently disavowed, but that didn't mean that her obstinacy wasn't getting under his skin. He reminded himself of why he was there and what he was after—what hung in the balance. "Your father had information about a plot by five Russian generals to take the United States hostage."

"Is that how your country is viewing it? As a *hostage* situation? How very American."

"What is that supposed to mean?" asked Scot.

"I always understood that a hostage situation involved the potential for bargaining. From what I understand, the goal was the complete and total surrender of the United States."

"So your father did take you into his confidence."

Not until he had died, thought Alexandra, *but that was none of Harvath's business.* "Your code name is Norseman, is it not?" she asked.

"What does my code name have to do with anything?"

"Are you familiar with the Russian word, *Varangians*?" she continued.

"My knowledge of Russian is somewhat limited."

"*Varangians* is our name for the Norse princes invited in to restore order to Russia in the Middle Ages. We don't need any more Norsemen here. We can solve our own problems."

Harvath had finally had it with her. "This isn't just your problem, it's *our* problem. If we don't do something, these men are going to start World War III."

"Who says I'm not doing something?" asked Alexandra.

"I don't know. I have no idea what you're doing because you haven't told me anything. Do you mean you and the FSB are aware of what the generals are up to and are working to put a stop to it?"

"I'm not certain if the FSB is aware of what is going on or not. I am sure that at some level there is knowledge of the plan. After all, our esteemed Russian president was once the head of the FSB's predecessor."

"You're saying the Russian president is a part of all of this?"

"Of course he is, but there are layers of what in America you call *plausible deniability* to keep him isolated."

Harvath was shocked. "And you approve of what they're doing?"

Ivanova pulled her chair back up to the table and got right in Scot's face. "No, I do not approve," she snapped. "It is unquestionably the worst thing my country could ever undertake. It is an insane plan hatched by insane old men from an entirely different era. They might as well be from another planet for all the sense this makes, but the plan has already been put into action and there's nothing you can do about that."

"The hell there isn't," replied Harvath.

"Oh, really? What are you going to do?"

"Whatever it takes to stop them."

"Good luck," responded Alexandra, sliding her chair away from the table again.

"Wait a second. You said you thought this was the worst thing Russia could ever undertake."

"And I meant it."

"So why aren't you doing something?"

"I am. On my own."

She wasn't making any sense. "Then what did you mean by now that the plan has been put into action, there's nothing we can do about it?"

"I said there's nothing *you* can do about it."

"Okay, hold on a second. We keep losing focus here."

"I'm losing nothing, Agent Harvath, except my patience with having my time wasted."

"I understand," replied Scot. "I can see, after what happened to your father, regardless of who was responsible for the leak, why you would be reluctant to tell me what you know."

"Can you?"

"Yes, I can, but we need to work together on this."

"Why is that? Do you have some sort of information that may prove helpful to me?"

"Maybe," replied Harvath.

"I think you're lying. I don't think you have anything at all to offer. If you did, you wouldn't be here."

She was right. She had him. She was his only lead. He needed to get her to cooperate. "No matter what you think, you can't do this alone. I can help you."

"There's one small problem, though," said Ivanova.

"What's that?"

"I don't trust you."

"But you don't even know me."

"You're an American, and that's enough for me."

"Then why even agree to meet with me?" asked Harvath.

"Because I wanted to see the look on your face when I told you *no*."

"What? Because of Istanbul?"

"No. When I said yes to the meeting, I had no idea they were sending you."

"Then what was it?"

"I'll tell you what it was. I wanted to look into the eyes of an American, a representative of the *great* United States and see that the only reason his country had sent him to me was because it had been humbled and had nowhere else to turn. I wanted to see your government finally admit that they had made a mistake with my father."

"So this is about revenge?"

"No, it is about satisfaction."

"*Satisfaction?* How much satisfaction are you going to feel if millions of innocent people, both in America and Russia, end up getting killed because your petty resentment prevented you from doing the right thing?"

"I'm not going to let that happen."

"And neither am I. As strange as it sounds, you and I are playing for different teams, but we're both on the same side. We can accomplish more by working together than we can apart."

"We have a saying in Russian," said Alexandra, as she stood up from her chair. "Having been burnt by milk, one blows on vodka."

"Once burned, twice shy," responded Scot.

"Exactly. I plan to continue blowing on my vodka. Goodbye, Agent Harvath, and good luck."

Alexandra Ivanova turned and exited the Hermitage Café, leaving Harvath with only one option.

ecause of St. Petersburg's northern latitude, the sun set very early in winter. Often, the arrival of evening was accompanied by brutally cold winds and this evening was no exception.

The sky was completely dark when Harvath collected his pack and followed Alexandra Ivanova out of the Hermitage. She appeared to be wandering aimlessly, which, considering the weather, made no sense. After strolling the famous Nevsky Prospekt and browsing in several shops, she backtracked and made her way toward the beautiful onion-domed Church of the Resurrection of Christ. Harvath waited several moments and then entered, staying hidden in the back where he could continue to observe her. Though it wasn't as warm as the Hermitage had been, he was happy to at least be out of the cold.

After lighting a candle, Ivanova sat down by herself on one of the long pews in the center and closed her eyes. At first, Harvath thought maybe she had come to pray, but as she repeatedly stole furtive glances at her watch, he realized what she was really doing was killing time. Either someone was coming to meet her, or something else was going on.

Harvath watched as a stream of worshippers and tourists moved through the church, each guided by their own calling, but none of them tried to make contact with Ivanova. After an hour had passed, she glanced at her watch one final time and then stood up and walked slowly to the exit.

By the time she emerged, Harvath was already secreted on the edge of the small esplanade waiting for her. When she hailed a nearby cab, Harvath quickly followed suit, telling the driver in his somewhat passable Russian, *"Sleduytyeh za toy zhenshchinoy."* *Follow that woman.*

They came to a stop in a neighborhood of rundown factories lying cheek by jowl. Up ahead, Harvath could see a line of people standing in the cold beneath a brushed-aluminum sign that read BREATHE.

Harvath watched as Ivanova walked to the front of the line, said something to the bouncer, and was granted admittance to the club. Once she was inside, Harvath paid the fare and climbed out of the cab. He waited until the cabbie had driven away before casing the perimeter of the building and finding a place to hide his backpack. Bypassing the line just as Ivanova had done, Harvath approached the bouncer, slipped him a hundred-dollar bill, and asked if it was possible to get a table.

The bouncer showed Harvath inside, where a

scantily clad hostess led him to a table, presented him with a menu, and wished him a pleasant evening.

Glancing around the crowded nightclub, Harvath could see that it had once been a foundry or a factory of some sort. The focal point was an enormous riveted vat with large portholes, around which the bar had been built. Harvath could see patrons with masks clasped to their faces indulging in the latest trend to sweep Russia—scented oxygen.

When the waitress arrived to take his order, Harvath was tempted to ask for a martini, but thought better of it when he realized the ice would be made from St. Petersburg's foul-smelling, foul-tasting, pollutant-laden, giardia-infested water. Russian vodka could kill a hell of a lot, but Harvath doubted it could conquer what crawled out of local spigots. He opted for a beer instead.

By the time his Vena Porter arrived, Harvath had politely chased off three hookers. Obviously, word had quickly spread that there was a wealthy American at table number one. Knowing that it was much more difficult to hit a moving target, he left some money for his drink and got up to check out the rest of the club.

The clientele were all New Russians, sporting the latest in trendy designer fashions. While Ivanova's outfit had seemed a bit much at the Hermitage Café, now it made complete sense. Though she was a tall gorgeous blonde, there were a lot of tall gorgeous blondes here and she was proving very hard to locate. Harvath tried to put himself in her shoes. If he was going to conduct a clandestine meeting in a crowded, noisy nightclub, he'd want to position himself somewhere on the fringes of the action, someplace with the best view possible, yet concealed enough so that the meeting wouldn't draw any undue attention.

Harvath approached the large dance floor and kept his attention on the clusters of seating areas on the other side. The DJ had just begun spinning "One Nation Under a Groove" by George Clinton and the Funkadelics when the crowd parted and Harvath caught a glimpse of Ivanova. She was sitting in a somewhat secluded booth and had just been joined by a middle-aged man in a bad suit with an even worse comb-over. He looked like he'd be more at home at a bookbinding convention than at a hip Russian nightclub, but whoever he was, Ivanova had gone to a lot of trouble to meet him and therefore Harvath wanted to meet him too.

He worked his way around the edge of the dance floor, trying to move through the thick crowd, but as he got about halfway to the booth, something was wrong. Ivanova had disappeared.

Moments later a voice from behind said, "Why am I not surprised?" as Harvath felt something hard jabbed into his back.

"Of all the oxygen bars in all the towns in all the world—" he mumbled as he looked over his shoulder and saw Alexandra using her coat to hide the gun she was holding.

"Quiet," she replied, turning him around. "I had a feeling I was being followed."

"Guilty," replied Harvath as he tried to put on his most charming smile, "but now that I'm here, how about introducing me to your friend in the booth?"

"I don't have much choice, do I?" said Ivanova as she scanned the crowded dance floor. "If I let you go, you'll hang around and wait for him, won't you?"

"Probably," replied Harvath as he watched Alexandra scan the dance floor yet again. She seemed nervous and very tightly wound. "Are you expecting somebody else?"

"I don't know."

Bad events seemed to radiate a certain electricity that Harvath was often able to pick up on. The hair on the back of his neck began to rise and seconds later he heard someone scream.

Alexandra wasted no time. She pulled the silenced Walther P4 from beneath her coat and ran for the booth.

When she finally fought her way through the crowd, she found the man in the bad suit laying slumped in the booth and bleeding profusely from several stab wounds to his neck and chest. It was soon complete pandemonium, with patrons screaming and running toward the front of the club. Not knowing how close the attacker was, Alexandra turned and swept her weapon back and forth, looking for any face in the crowd that didn't look right.

Harvath was only two steps behind her. He arrived at the booth with his H&K drawn. He and Ivanova both saw the attacker at the same time, but it was too late. Expertly using the stampeding crowd as cover, the man smiled before disappearing into the sea of rushing people. Harvath had seen the man's face before. It was the same man who had pulled off the attack at the King George, but how could he have followed Harvath all the way to St. Petersburg? *It was impossible.*

Harvath glanced at the man slumped in the booth and leaned in to feel for his pulse. It was very weak, and Scot was taken by surprise when the man suddenly reached out and beseechingly grabbed for his arm. He told him to stay calm, that help would be there soon, but the man just shook his head. He withdrew something from his pocket and pressed it into Harvath's hand. He opened his mouth to speak but collapsed before he could get the words out. Harvath once again felt for the man's pulse, but there was none. He was dead.

"Cover Nesterov!" Ivanova said as she kept her weapon trained on the quickly dissipating pack of fleeing customers.

"There's nothing to cover," replied Harvath as he stepped away from the booth. "He's dead."

"Damn it," swore Ivanova.

"Who was he?"

"A scientist."

"What was he working on?"

"It's not important now."

"Not important? Obviously somebody thought it was important enough to kill him over. Do you have any idea who was shooting at us?"

Ivanova stood and said, "Russian military."

"Well that makes sense," responded Harvath.

"If you knew the depth of what was going on here, it *would* make sense," snapped Ivanova.

"I think I understand well enough. The man who killed your scientist, I've seen him before. He tried to kill me two nights ago in Berlin."

"Helmut Draegar was in Berlin? What was he doing there?"

Harvath was floored. Gary Lawlor hadn't been ranting. He had been trying to warn him. "That doesn't make any sense," continued Harvath. "Helmut Draegar was killed fifteen years ago."

"You don't know very much, do you?"

"Why don't you fill me in?"

"There's no time," replied Ivanova as she nervously scanned the room.

Harvath could hear what sounded like several men in heavy boots making their way toward them. *Probably the club's bouncers coming to investigate.* "We need to get out of here."

"We can't. Not yet," replied Ivanova, turning back to the booth. "I need to check his pockets. He was supposed to have something for me."

"Like this?" said Harvath, holding up the folded piece of paper Nesterov had given him.

Alexandra couldn't believe her eyes.

"It looks like we're going to be working together after all," said Harvath as he grabbed her arm. "Now let's move."

CHAPTER 41

A fter leaving the oxygen bar and retrieving Harvath's backpack, Scot and Alexandra looked for a place to rest and decide what their next move would be. The Hotel Oktyabrskaya was situated in a busy neighborhood just across from St. Petersburg's Moskovsky railway station and was a perfect place for them to hole up while they waited for morning.

Harvath grabbed a pen and a small pad of paper from next to the telephone in the bedroom and began to reexamine Nesterov's note. After several minutes replacing the Cyrillic letters with corresponding characters from the English alphabet and rearranging bits and pieces in the lines of text, Harvath could finally read it. "Universal Transverse Mercator."

"*Mercator?* As in latitude and longitude?"

"Exactly. Hours, minutes, and seconds both north and east. What we're looking at is a Geo coordinate."

"A Geo coordinate for where? What does it point to?"

"According to his note," replied Harvath, "somebody named Albert."

"Ring any bells?"

"None at all," said Alexandra.

Harvath set the note aside. "Then the first thing we need to do is to pinpoint those coordinates."

"There's a twenty-four-hour internet café in St. Petersburg called Quo Vadis. All we'd have to do is get online with one of their computers and find a website where we can enter in the coordinates."

"I don't like it. With those networked systems it's too hard to erase your tracks. We'd be leaving a trail of electronic bread crumbs. Isn't there a bookshop on the Nevsky Prospekt across from the Kazan Cathedral?"

"Yes, it's called the Dom Knigi."

"Good," said Harvath. "We'll wait until a half hour after they've opened and then go in separately. I'm going to buy a couple of books, one of which will be an atlas, and you are going to go to their stationary section and buy some pencils, a notebook, and, most importantly, a ruler."

Alexandra now understood what Harvath was up to. "We're going to plot the coordinates the old-fashioned way."

"Exactly. I just wish we had a way to get around. There's too much potential downside in renting a car right now."

"We don't have to," replied Alexandra. "I already have a car. I parked it in one of the long-term lots near the airport. It's easier to move around St. Petersburg without it."

"We can't do it. It's too dangerous. If they're on to you, they'll be looking for your car too."

"Technically, it's not my car. It's a nice Grand Cherokee that belonged to someone who tried to kill me a couple of days ago. It's a long story."

"Well, we've got several hours until the store opens," said Harvath, who grabbed a nearby chair and sat down. He put his feet up on the bed and then reached over and opened the minibar where he grabbed an ice-cold beer for himself and a minivodka for Alexandra, which he threw to her and said, "Feel free to blow on yours before you start."

Whether or not it was her belief that she would be able to dump Harvath as soon as she got what she needed she didn't know, but for some reason she felt it was okay to talk to him. After all, with no idea of who she could trust in the SVR, Harvath's willingness to listen to what she had been through was more of a relief than she would have expected.

Alexandra told Scot about her father's dossier and how he had kept it a secret from her until his death. She explained the meeting at the hunting lodge outside of Moscow where she had seen Stavropol dragging three bodies outside along with the help of another man whose face she couldn't see very well, but thought might have been Draegar. She told how she had helped save General

Karganov's life only to have Milesch Popov come along with his gaudy Pit Bull pistol and its armor-piercing rounds and end it. As she withdrew the gun from inside her coat and showed it to him, she detailed how she had salvaged the SIM card from Popov's cell phone and that her would-be killer had been dumb enough to store Stavropol's number under the general's real name. By scanning the call log, it was easy to ascertain to whom Popov had been talking when she had captured him. He had been negotiating the price for her murder, as well as Karganov's, and the man on the other end of the line was none other than Sergei Oleg Stavropol.

Though she was sure that Stavropol originally had no idea of her involvement when he had sent Popov hunting for General Karganov, there was no question that he knew about it now.

Alexandra quietly reflected on the fact that not only was being seen with Nesterov enough to cement her guilt, but if Draegar recognized Harvath, which Alexandra was fairly confident he had, then Stavropol would automatically assume she was working with the Americans. It was only a matter of time before he had every law enforcement officer and military person in the country looking for her. In the blink of an eye, she had lost the anonymity she had worked so hard to preserve and had become Russia's equivalent of public enemy number one.

Things could never go back to the way they were. There was no middle ground, not now that they knew she was on to them. They wouldn't rest until she was dead and she had to be just as tireless in her efforts to stop them. Like it or not, it was beginning to look not only like she might have to work with Agent Scot Harvath, but that she actually might need him. Either she succeeded in her undertaking or she died.

"Tell me about the scientist, Nesterov," said Harvath, filling the void as Alexandra had stopped talking and her mind seemed to have traveled elsewhere.

"*Nesterov?*" she repeated, bringing her focus back to the present. "I thought he might be helpful."

"So you tracked him down and he agreed to meet with you, just like that?" asked Harvath. "You must have said something to him to make him risk so much."

Alexandra was quiet and for several moments and once again seemed very far away. "Nesterov was one of two scientists working on this project whom my father had thought might be cooperative with his investigation; scientists who viewed their duty as being to their country and countrymen first and not necessarily their government."

"Well, whoever this Albert is," said Harvath as he laid his H&K across his chest and closed his eyes, "let's hope he feels the same way when we track him down tomorrow."

CHAPTER 42

Leaving St. Petersburg's Dom Knigi bookstore with two fly-fishing books and a thick Russian atlas, Harvath stopped at a local sporting goods shop and then met up with Alexandra at the Moskavskya metro station, where they caught the shuttle for Pulkovo Airport.

Popov's forest-green Jeep Grand Cherokee wasn't as bad as Harvath had thought it was going to be. In fact, the vehicle was relatively unremarkable in a country where conspicuous consumption ran rampant.

It took them a little more than four-and-a-half hours driving north-northeast to reach their destination. The tiny, Byzantine domed chapel sat alone in the heavily wooded countryside on the outskirts of the city of Petrozavodsk. Petrozavodsk, located on the western shore of Lake Onega—the second largest lake in Europe, was the administrative center of Karelia, an autonomous republic in the Russian Federation. The city was not only the site of Petrozavodsk State University but also a branch of the Russian Academy of Sciences. In his dossier, Alexandra's father had identified Petrozavodsk as the location where the Russian scientists were working on the secret air defense system.

As Alexandra pulled the Cherokee to the side of the road, Harvath gave his map and coordinates a final check.

"This is it?" she asked, staring out the windshield at the little church. "This is where we're supposed to find Nesterov's Albert?"

"It looks like it," replied Harvath as he placed one of his fly-fishing books onto the dash and carelessly threw the other into the backseat. Coupled with the rods, reels, waders, and other gear he had purchased and left in the cargo area, to anyone who might come upon them, he and Alexandra would look like two New Russians pursuing the hottest sporting craze to sweep the country since golf. Even in winter, fly-fishing was still a very popular pastime, especially in the Karelia region where the winters were much milder than the rest of Russia. If anyone should happen to ask what business they had at the church, they would simply state they were taking a break on their way to fish one of the many popular rivers that fed the nearby lake.

As it was, they didn't have to worry about feeding anyone their cover story because the church was completely empty. In fact, were it not for the supply of fresh candles, Harvath would have sworn it had been abandoned altogether.

Alexandra left a coin and lit one of the candles. She closed her eyes for several moments and when she opened them, she saw that Harvath was looking at her. "For my parents," she said.

Harvath nodded his head and began walking around the small church, which was formed in a perfect circle. It smelled of earth and cold stone, solid, as if it had been there since the beginning of time and would continue to stand until the very end of it. The whitewashed walls were decorated with painted panels depicting the lives of saints and various religious events. "Who uses this place?" asked Harvath as he continued studying the copious artwork. "There aren't any houses for miles around."

"Country people most likely, though sometimes people from a nearby town or city will adopt a small church and help with its upkeep and maintenance, as well as buying or donating other things that it might need," answered Alexandra from the other side of the room.

"This would go a lot faster if we knew what this Albert guy's connection with this church is," said Harvath as he abandoned his review of the paintings. "Why do you think Nesterov picked this place?"

"Who knows? It's close enough to Petrozavodsk and the Academy of Sciences to have been convenient for him, yet remote enough to keep whatever he was doing well hidden. Maybe Albert is the priest," replied Alexandra as she continued around the edge of the room, examining the paint-ings and artifacts.

Alexandra was making her second pass of the artwork, this time paying less attention to the im-ages and more attention to their titles. When she arrived at a rather unimpressive iconostasis and read the neatly written placard proclaiming that she was looking at "*St. Albert in Agony* by Andrey Rublyov," something didn't seem right. She stood back to examine the faded triptych that greatly re-sembled Da Vinci's *Madonna of the Rocks* and after several moments said, "I think I've got something."

"What is it?" asked Harvath as he came over to join her.

"According to the title plate, this work of art is by Andrey Rublyov and is called *St. Albert in Agony*."

Bingo, thought Harvath, but there was also something else about the title that rang a bell with him. It was as if he'd heard the saint's name before, sometime long ago in his past. "What about it?"

"Well, first of all, I don't believe the Russian Or-thodox Church has a St. Albert."

"Are you sure?"

"I'm pretty sure."

Harvath was pretty sure, too. Pretty sure he knew that name and that Alexandra was right. It didn't belong in this church. Then it came to him. "The patron saint of scientists."

"The what?" said Alexandra.

"St. Albert. He's the patron saint of scientists. I knew I knew that name. I went to a Catholic grade school, and St. Albert's picture hung in our science lab. The teacher would look up and literally refer to him on a daily basis."

"Then this must be Nesterov's Albert," said Alexandra. "What else would a Catholic saint be doing in a Russian Orthodox church?"

"Keeping an eye on the competition?" offered Harvath as she ripped the screen away from the wall.

Alexandra didn't answer. Ignoring the adjacent plaque recognizing the Nworbski family for its generous donation, Ivaona unceremoniously tore the hinged painting from the wall and dropped it onto the floor.

"Not much of an art lover, are you? I guess you didn't see the hinges?" said Harvath as he bent down and easily flipped over one of the sidepieces, revealing a manila envelope taped to the back of it.

"So maybe I'm a little overzealous," replied Alexandra, ripping open the envelope and shaking its contents onto the floor.

Harvath didn't bother arguing. Instead, he helped her sift through the documents, which comprised pages of schematics, printed pages, and a sheaf of handwritten notes.

"I speak Russian a lot better than I read it, which isn't saying much," he offered as he handed the notes to Alexandra and returned to the schematics. "Let me know if there's anything interesting in there."

Alexandra skimmed the pages and read Nesterov's account of how he progressively became aware of the true purpose of the project he was working on. After his last meticulous, laser-printed entry were a series of handwritten notes. "Scot?" she said, drawing his attention. "You need to take a look at this."

Harvath set down the schematics he was looking at and turned his attention to Alexandra. "What is it?" he asked.

"The notes on the bottom of this page. They've got yesterday's date. Nesterov must have stopped here on the way to St. Petersburg to—" she paused.

"To what?"

"To update his memoirs in case something happened to him."

"Let me see those," said Harvath as he stuck out his hand.

Alexandra handed over the page, and Harvath looked down at the hastily inscribed entry. The notes obviously referred to his meeting with Ivanova, but there was also a reference to the final deployment of the technology that he and his follow scientists had been working on.

It appeared to be a command and control system capable of feeding commands up to a series of Russian military satellites. When Harvath read that the system was designed to be mobile, the blood in his veins ran cold. If it was mobile, it could be anywhere.

At the bottom of the page, Nesterov had written two words and placed a question mark next to each—*Arkhangel? Gagarin?*

"Do you know the significance of these words?" asked Harvath.

"*Arkhangel*. It means the same in English, *archangel*. Maybe it's the name of the program."

"But why would Nesterov have placed a question mark next to it? Wouldn't he have known the program's name?"

"Not necessarily. Maybe the scientists weren't told. Maybe they called it Project 243 or something like that."

"True," said Harvath. "What about *Gagarin*?"

"The first thing that comes to mind is Yuri Gagarin."

"The Soviet cosmonaut?"

"Yes. He was the very first human being to fly in space and became a national hero for all of Russia."

"And the air defense system incorporates satellites, so maybe there's a connection."

"Or—" Alexandra said, trailing off.

"Or what?"

"Or it's a place. Maybe it has something to do with where the mobile command center is. There's a city named after Gagarin southwest of Moscow in Smolensk," she said, her enthusiasm quickly fading, "but there's also the Gagarin Cosmonaut Training Center in Star City just outside of Moscow and I think there's even a Gagarin Seamount somewhere in the Pacific Ocean."

"Wonderful," responded Harvath. "Another needle in the proverbial haystack."

"That's not all. Arkhangel is also a place. In fact,

it's the next region just east of here. Its capital city, also called Arkhangel, is a major port on the White Sea."

"*The White Sea?*" he repeated, sitting up straighter. "That would make sense."

"What would?"

"Look," he said, spreading out the drawings in front of her, "I can't believe that equipment of this magnitude is even considered mobile in the first place. Whatever they're using to transport it has to be very big. The satellite dishes alone that it requires are the size of a house."

"So, what? You think it is on some sort of cargo ship?"

"Maybe. Do you still have the information from Popov's SIM card?"

"Yes," answered Alexandra, fishing the folded piece of paper from her pocket. "But what's that going to tell you?"

"I don't know, yet. Which of these numbers is Stavropol's?"

As she pointed to it, Harvath made a few notes on the back of one of the schematics and then picked up his backpack.

"Where are you going?" she asked as he headed toward the stairs that led up into the church's dome.

"To make a phone call. I think I might know where our mobile system is."

CHAPTER 43

I've been reviewing FEMA's worst-case scenarios," said the president to Harvath over an encrypted satellite link, "and not only is there no safe way we can evacuate the cities we think the Russians may be targeting, but if they hit more than four of our major metropolitan areas, our emergency response capabilities are going to be stretched to the max. Even if they only detonate a fraction of the devices they have, this is going to be the worst disaster the world has ever seen. Not only will the loss of life and injuries be terrible, but can you imagine UN planes and helicopters being shown on TV bringing in food and medicine because America's infrastructure has been so badly decimated we can't take care of our own citizens?

"We absolutely can't let that happen. Do you understand me? We *cannot* let that happen."

After agreeing, Harvath listened as the president continued to speak and then handed him off to various experts and analysts from the CIA and Department of Defense who briefed him that Rick Morrell and his team were wrapping up their operation and were being sent to rendezvous with him for his next assignment.

It was three hours later when Harvath was finally able to close the dome's wooden hatch and replace the collapsible field antenna and satellite radio into his backpack.

Climbing down the stairs, Harvath rejoined Alexandra in the church.

"That was a very long phone call," she said.

"You know how it is when you haven't talked to people in a while," replied Harvath.

"You said you might know where the mobile command system is. Did you find it?"

"I did better than that. I also found Stavropol."

"How?"

"The location of the mobile system was more of a hunch than anything else. During the Cold War, the Soviet Union's spyships were on the cutting edge of signals intelligence, but in the modern era, the way intelligence was being gathered rendered most of them obsolete and they were reassigned to other duties. That got me wondering if maybe one of these spyships was being used to transport the mobile command system. I learned a fair amount about them in the Navy. There was the *Bal'zam* class, the *Primor'ye* class, and then I remembered another class—the *Gagarin* class.

"Only one ship was ever made in the *Gagarin* class—*The Cosmonat Yuri Gagarin*. It was adapted from the unfinished hull of a tanker to control Soviet spacecraft and satellites from the open ocean. And best of all, it sports four huge dish antennae each the—"

"Size of a house?" interrupted Alexandra.

"And then some."

"But how can you be sure the *Gagarin* is what we're after?"

"Because our National Reconnaissance Office has satellite imagery of it along with three nuclear icebreakers leaving port in Arkhangel two days ago."

"That still doesn't mean—"

Now it was Harvath's turn to interrupt. "Did you know that Stavropol was using a satellite phone?"

"No. I assumed he was using a cell."

"Cell phones will operate sometimes up to a couple of miles out to sea, but it depends on how built-out the network is back on dry land. A satellite phone is much more reliable in this case and Stavropol knew that. What he didn't know was that you were going to be able to get a hold of his number."

"Why? Were you able to trace it?"

"Yup."

"But I thought those phones were encrypted," said Alexandra.

"They are," replied Harvath, "128-bit digital encryption standard, but he's using one of the same models that embedded reporters used during the war in Iraq. The U.S. Military had to tell them to turn them off in many situations because they could broadcast their position via GPS."

"And that's how you found him?"

"That's how we found him. The NSA was able to use his mobile ID number and pinpoint his whereabouts."

"So where is he?"

"In the White Sea, just off the Kola Peninsula."

"Most of which lies north of the Arctic Circle and it's almost the end of January," responded Alexandra. "What are we supposed to do?"

"We're supposed to stop him, of course," said Harvath.

"Of course. And how are we supposed to do that? Wait, one thing at a time. Why don't you start by telling me how we're supposed to get out to a ship floating in the middle of an ice-encrusted sea. Is one of your American submarines going to take us there?"

"Not as long as the Kola Peninsula is still home to Russia's Northern Fleet."

"Then how?"

"Stavropol is going to help us."

"How nice of him," said Alexandra, her voice laden with sarcasm. "Why would he do that?"

"Because you have something I'm sure he'll want."

"And what's that?"

Harvath smiled before responding. "Me."

Alexandra was silent. *Had he lost his mind? He*

wanted to give himself up to Stavropol? The man would kill him in an instant.

"Oh," continued Harvath, "and just to sweeten the deal, we're going to throw in a nice little man-portable nuclear weapon. Does that sound fair? Do you think he'll go for it?"

Now she knew he was crazy. "What are you talking about? You don't have any man-portable nuclear weapons."

"Not yet. You and I are going to pick one up."

"Just like that?"

"Just like that."

"And where is this pickup supposed to happen?"

Harvath began walking toward the front door of the church. "We're not exactly picking one up. It's being delivered. Have you ever been to Arkhangel City before? I'll buy you dinner on the way and explain the rest of the plan."

Alexandra followed him out the door and into the snow. The sun had set and the air had grown bitterly cold. She couldn't help wondering if the three hours Harvath had spent in the dome of the church hadn't somehow affected his brain.

CHAPTER 44

SOMEWHERE OFF THE KOLA PENINSULA,
WHITE SEA, RUSSIA
STATE OF THE UNION ADDRESS—2 DAYS

The next day, when Milesch Popov's name came up on Stavropol's Caller ID, he thought it must be some kind of a joke. Not only was Popov dead, but the police had found his bullet-riddled cell phone near the crime scene. There was no way it could be him calling. Immediately, Stavropol was on guard. Somehow, someone had connected him with that contemptible street thug. This was a distraction he did not need at the moment, as he was already preoccupied with pinning the murders of Generals Primovich, Karganov, and Varensky on Popov and a "wayward" accomplice. At this point, all they needed to do was locate the accomplice. Draegar had assured them that he had the situation well in hand, but just as in Berlin, he had once again disappointed them.

Stavropol had come to the conclusion that Draegar might no longer be a reliable asset and he would have to do the job himself, as he activated his Sat phone and tentatively took the call. *"Da?"*

"Comrade General, I hope I am not catching you at an inopportune time," said the voice on the other end.

Stavropol didn't need to ask who was calling. He could guess to whom the voice belonged the minute he heard the first words. He couldn't believe his good fortune. It was better than he could have hoped. She was the perfect person to frame as the wayward accomplice who had assisted Popov in killing Primovich, Karganov, and Varensky. "Agent Ivanova. It is a pleasure to hear from you, but how did you get my telephone number?"

Alexandra knew he was toying with her, but had been counseled to play along with him, to an extent. "I removed the SIM card from Milesch Popov's phone right after he tried to kill me."

"An unfortunate misunderstanding," said Stavropol, who had not even thought about the SIM card. When he had gotten a hold of the police report detailing the evidence from the murder scene, including the damaged phone, he had assumed that Popov had taken the secret of their relationship with him to the grave. Obviously, he had been wrong.

"I think the misunderstanding here," continued Alexandra, "is in your failing to recognize what a useful asset I could prove to be."

Stavropol smiled. "Now it is you who must forgive me for disbelieving. I am well aware of what your father most likely told you."

"Indeed. My father told me everything, and as

far as I am concerned, he was a fool to try and get in your way. He let his misguided feelings overrule his duty and obligation to his country."

"Very convincing, Agent Ivanova. The SVR has taught you well, though you cannot believe that I would fall under your spell so easily. I know what you are doing."

"What am I doing?"

"You were seen with Dr. Nesterov, as well as the American, Scot Harvath. You have been colluding with them in order to achieve your father's reckless pursuits."

"And I told you my father was a fool. I was using Nesterov for bait."

Stavropol was momentarily taken aback. *"Bait? How so?"*

"I used him to lure the American."

"But why? Why get involved at all?"

"Because I was interested in clearing my father's name. Up until his death, I had only heard rumors and innuendos about his sedition. When I asked him, he would always deny it. Then on his deathbed, he made me aware of a dossier he had compiled."

Stavropol had suspected as much, but his clean teams had never been able to find anything. There was nothing in Viktor Ivanov's office or in his residence. "What dossier?"

"My family rented a garden plot outside the city. He buried the dossier there."

Stavropol was fuming. There *was* a dossier, and

his men had missed it. Viktor Ivanov had indeed been a cunning operative. Stavropol had wanted to kill him a long time ago when they had the chance, regardless of what information he might have compiled, but he knew that the man's untimely demise, no matter how accidental it might have looked, would have caused more trouble than it was worth. Instead, they silently drummed him out of the KGB. As it stood, when the Americans turned their backs on Ivanov, and Stavropol was able to leak the story, a cloud of treason hung over Viktor Ivanov until his dying day and was enough to guarantee that no one ever trusted, much less listened to him ever again.

"And that dossier is what led you to General Karganov?" asked Stavropol, trying to put the pieces together.

"As well as Dr. Nesterov."

"Where is the dossier now?"

"I've hidden it somewhere for safekeeping."

For the most part, the bulk of the dossier's contents would soon be immaterial, but there were still ways in which they could be very damaging. The file needed to be buried for good and Alexandra Ivanova along with it, but until she was, Stavropol had no choice but to deal with her. "Why are we talking?" he asked.

It was time for Alexandra to make her case. "We each have something the other wants."

Stavropol laughed. "What could you possibly have that I would want?"

She wasted no time in getting to the point. "An American operative on Russian soil with a tactical nuclear weapon. Surely, you would like to have this man and his weapon in your custody."

There were several moments of strained silence as Stavropol thought it over. Though he was loath to negotiate with her, it seemed that she alone had the power to deliver to him the prize that had eluded them on the Baltic and caused the loss of two of their patrol boats—an American agent who had smuggled a nuclear weapon into their country. He didn't trust Alexandra Ivanova one bit, but she was dangling a very attractive carrot that was hard to resist.

Ever the tactician, Stavropol kept talking as his mind worked to develop a plan to gain the upper hand. "You said we each had something the other wanted. What is it you desire from me?"

Alexandra stuck to the script, just as Harvath had laid it out for her. "First, forgiveness. Though my father's actions were wrong, his motivations were correct. He placed his country above all else and for that I want his name cleared. He is to get a proper burial with full recognition for his loyalty and years of service to Mother Russia."

"What else?"

"Next, I want your personal guarantee, in writing, that I will be publicly recognized for my cooperation and loyalty."

"That's all?" asked Stavropol.

"No, that's not all. In addition, I want a promotion within the SVR, to at least deputy director, complete with commensurate pay grade, a new apartment, and a new automobile."

"Capitalism rears its ugly head at last."

"No, it has not," replied Alexandra. "While I support our country's long-overdue return to Communism, I also believe that outstanding service to the State should be rewarded. But if you do not agree with me, I'd be happy to release Agent Harvath and his nuclear weapon and let you try to retake him before the Americans have executed whatever it is they are planning."

This time Stavropol didn't hesitate. "Absolutely not," he replied. If Ivanova really was prepared to deliver on her offer, Stavropol couldn't afford to let her go. "Where are you?"

"Arkhangel City," she replied.

Stavropol told her to hold, while he cupped the mouthpiece and consulted one of the men standing next to him. There was no time for him to go to her. She would have to come to him. He gave her a time and directions to a location just outside the seaside village of Tova, about 150 kilometers up the coast from Arkhangel City, and then unceremoniously terminated the connection.

Before Alexandra could power down her cell phone and change out Popov's SIM card, Harvath already had his atlas out and was speeding the Jeep Cherokee toward their destination. They would have to hurry. The last thing he wanted to do was to give Stavropol enough time to set up an ambush.

CHAPTER 45

A winter storm, accompanied by a brutal cold front, was in full effect when Scot and Alexandra dropped the rest of the team and then pulled into a desolate farmer's field bordered on all sides by trees on the outskirts of Tova.

As the Jeep's wipers fought to keep up with the heavily falling snow, Harvath alternated between staring at the temperature reading, which was now down to minus fifteen degrees Celsius, and staring out the windshield toward the far edge of the field.

When the appointed time arrived, he heard the staccato *whump, whump, whump* of helicopter rotor blades cleaving the frigid air. The low cloud cover and inclement weather made it impossible to see the craft as it circled above them and then moved off to the far edge of the field where it hovered still out of view.

Harvath assumed the helicopter was equipped with forward-looking infrared, also known as FLIR, and was right now scanning the perimeter of the landing zone. He hoped that they were only using

first-generation technology because if it was anything better than that, they were quite literally
going to be dead.

With first-generation FLIR capability, it wasn't impossible to blend in with trees and avoid detection. To
be successful, though, several factors needed to be
taken into consideration, such as how long a person
had been in the cold, what they were wearing, how
much activity they had undergone just prior to the engagement, and if they were carrying anything hot, like
a recently fired weapon. Though second-generation
FLIR could even spot the heat signature of a recently
deposited handprint and engage an automatic detection and targeting system, fooling a low-hovering,
first-generation FLIR-enhanced helicopter was by no
means a walk in the park. It was still one of the hardest pieces of technology on the battlefield to beat.

Alexandra held up a pair of plastic flexi-cuffs
and asked, "Are you ready?"

"Not really, but we don't have much choice, do
we?" replied Scot as he placed his hands behind his
back.

"Don't forget whose idea this was," she said as
she loosely secured his wrists.

"Don't remind me," responded Harvath.

Exiting the Cherokee, Alexandra swung Harvath's pack over her shoulder and urged her "prisoner" forward. They walked toward the middle of
the clearing as a biting wind tore at their clothing.
With his arms behind his back, the best Harvath
could do to avoid the weather was hunch his shoul-

ders and tuck his chin into his chest. Alexandra kept her silenced Walther trained on him the entire way.

Suddenly, the sound of the rotors grew louder, and Harvath looked up through the snow to see the underside of a Russian-made Mi-17–1V Assault Helicopter as two long lines were kicked out the doors and a pair of commandos fast-roped to the ground on each side.

"Spetsnaz," mouthed Alexandra, who then cemented upon her face a look of austere professionalism.

Harvath turned his eyes away from her and watched as the men, intimidating in dark uniforms and black balaclavas, fanned out with their silenced nine-millimeter AS assault rifles up and at the ready. Approaching Alexandra, they called for her to lower her weapon. She did as they commanded and watched as one of the men frisked Harvath, while another kept him squarely in his sights.

"I already checked him," she shouted in Russian, holding up his backpack. "His weapon is in here, along with several other pieces of equipment provided by his government."

"Orders," snapped the Spetsnaz operative, who then made his way over to her. Waving his gloved hand, he indicated in a very condescending manner that she surrender her weapon. "Also orders."

Alexandra made a show of being very displeased at her treatment. After which, the Spetsnaz operative began to frisk her in a very inappropriate manner. Having brushed against her breasts no less than three times, and satisfied that she was clean, he withdrew a walkie-talkie and radioed the helicopter to land. Next, he turned to Alexandra and said, "I assume the nuclear device is in the car?"

Alexandra nodded her head.

"And the keys?"

"Also in the car," she responded.

"You couldn't have parked any closer?"

"And if someone had come along while we were waiting and asked us why we had driven off the road into the field? What should we have told them?"

"Good point," said the soldier who got back on his walkie-talkie. He instructed the second team of Spetsnaz troops, who had secured the landing zone, to go get the Cherokee and drive it over to the helicopter so they could load the nuclear device on board. As he finished his communication, he unshouldered his rifle and directed Harvath and Alexandra toward the helicopter, which was just touching down.

"He's my prisoner!" insisted Alexandra as they approached the bird and she pushed Harvath ahead of the soldier, "I will see to him." As soon as they stepped on board, all hell broke loose behind them.

Seeing Harvath and Alexandra climb into the helicopter, Morrell gave the go command over his throat mike. "The playground is ours. I repeat the playground is ours."

Avigliano, who was hidden in the woods next to Morrell, dropped both of the Spetsnaz troops nearest the helicopter with perfect head shots from his silenced M4, while Carlson and DeWolfe, who were hidden on the other side of the field, did the same to the other two soldiers approaching the Cherokee.

Back in the helicopter, Harvath wasted no time in slipping out of his flexi-cuffs and charging the cockpit. When the pilot peered into the cargo bay and saw Harvath racing up the aisle, he immediately went for the nine-millimeter Gyurza pistol strapped to his flight suit, but it was too late. Harvath was already on top of him.

Harvath landed a vicious punch to the man's jaw and wrestled the pistol away from him just as the copilot grabbed the microphone of his helmet to radio for help. What happened next was more reflex than anything else. There was no time to think. Harvath pulled the Gyurza's trigger and sent two rounds into the copilot's head, killing him instantly. Turning the pistol back on the pilot, Harvath disconnected the comlink from the man's helmet and said to him, "There's been a slight change of plans."

After Morrell and the rest of the team had stripped the Spetsnaz soldiers of their uniforms and deposited their naked bodies in the woods, they pulled the SUV alongside the helicopter, off-loaded their improvised tactical nuclear weapon and then ditched the car.

When everyone was on board, Alexandra climbed into the copilot's seat and with her silenced Walther P4 pointed right at the pilot's privates, ordered him to take off.

CHAPTER 46

T he flight was not only long, but extremely uncomfortable. The winter storm had created a lot of rough air and many of the helicopter's passengers wanted to puke from the bumpy ride, but were all too macho to do so, including Alexandra. When they neared their destination upon the White Sea, the pilot was instructed to fly in a large circle around *The Cosmonat Yuri Gagarin*.

It was an incredible vessel. With a displacement of more than 45,000 tons, the *Gagarin* was 774 feet long and had a beam of just over 101 feet. The ship was outfitted with two eighty-eight-and-half foot in diameter Ship Shell and two forty-one foot in diameter Ship Bowl stabilized communications and tracking dish antennae, as well as two Vee Tube HF communications systems and four Quad Ring yagi arrays. As they passed the enormous devices, DeWolfe narrated based upon experience and the recent intelligence he had been sent from Washington. Harvath, on the other hand, was less concerned with what was on the ship than what was around it.

Though he stole occasional glances at the vessel itself, his eyes were predominantly focused on the assault helicopter's tracking and display systems. From what he could tell as they made their pass, the *Gagarin* was being watched over not only by the three nuclear icebreakers, but by no fewer than three Russian submarines as well. Getting out was going to prove a lot harder than getting in.

As the helicopter banked and approached the *Gagarin*'s landing pad, they went over their plan one more time. Speed, surprise, and overwhelming force of action were the keys to a successful outcome, though every one of them had silent reservations as to whether this was really going to work.

When the Mi-17–1V touched down on the *Gagarin*'s aft deck, Carlson quickly unbuckled the pilot and yanked him into the cargo area. He removed the man's helmet and then knocked him out with a quick punch to the head. "You've got to be the worst pilot I've ever flown with," said Carlson, who then looked up at the rest of the team staring at him. "What? He gave us that shitty ride on purpose. Fuck him."

No one disagreed. Avigliano and Morrell quickly gagged the man, tied him up, and stashed him in the back of the copter. A pistol was placed in the hand of the dead copilot and he was positioned in such a way that if anyone should happen to look in through one of the windows, it would appear as if he was diligently posting guard over a large plastic suitcase.

When they were good to go, Morrell and his men rolled down their own black balaclavas, readied their Russian assault rifles, and opened one of the helicopter's side doors. Carlson and Avigliano jumped out first and were joined by Alexandra. Next came DeWolfe, who shoved Harvath out onto the deck and kept his weapon on him as Morrell slid the door shut behind him.

As two of the *Gagarin's* crew members rushed up to attend to the helicopter, Alexandra barked at them to back off. She told them that the pilot and copilot had been instructed to guard their cargo with their lives and to shoot anyone but herself or General Stavropol who came too close. She asked where she could find the general, and one of the men gave her instructions on how to find the control center. Then he and his shipmate immediately backed away. *So far, so good.*

The control center was located just beneath the bridge near the bow of the ship. As the imposing party of would-be Spetsnaz troops, a beautiful blond woman, and their prisoner entered on the main deck level and purposely made their way forward, every soul they came across jumped to get out of their way.

The whole team—Harvath, Ivanova, Morrell, Carlson, DeWolfe, and Avigliano—mentally recorded security measures, evacuation points, crew makeup, and force strength as they marched toward the bow. From what they could see, a good portion of the ship had been retrofitted, though some Soviet-era trappings were evident from time to time. From the state-of-the-art infirmary and movie theater to the restaurant, health club, and indoor swimming pool, the *Gagarin* had been designed to remain on station and completely self-sufficient for very extended periods of time.

Turning a corner, they arrived at the elevator for the control center, and Carlson and DeWolfe immediately disappeared down an adjacent stairwell into the bowels of the ship, while Morrell and Avigliano accompanied Alexandra and Harvath to their rendezvous with General Stavropol.

The elevator doors opened onto an enormous, dimly lit room filled with technicians seated in high-backed, ergonomically designed chairs at wraparound workstations with everything within arm's reach. The seats reminded Harvath of those in the Navy's Mark V Special Operations Craft, which were designed to keep SEALs stable and comfortable during prolonged insertions, extractions, and patrols on even the roughest seas.

As Alexandra pushed him out of the elevator, Morrell and Avigliano followed right behind. They stepped up onto a raised floor that was designed to accommodate the massive tangle of computer cables and wires running beneath. Though it was absolutely freezing outside, an air-conditioning system was running at full strength to prevent the massive amount of equipment in the room from overheating.

While Harvath had expected to see something that resembled NASA's Mission Control in Houston, Texas, what he found was something completely different. Instead of tiered sections grouped in order of importance and facing a common set of screens at the front of the room, there were semi-circled networks of workstations grouped around what could only be referred to as viewing screens. They were concave pieces of Plexiglas that were not only full-color, two-sided monitors, with different images playing on both sides, but were also completely transparent depending upon what angle you were looking at them from. Technicians manipulated data not by plugging away at traditional keyboards, but via keyless entry systems, the likes of which Harvath had never seen before. In fact, the more he looked around the room, the more he realized the technology he was seeing would be more at home aboard the *Starship Enterprise* than a Soviet-era research vessel. The sophistication of it all was literally beyond his imagination, and Harvath had a pretty good imagination.

The last thing he noticed was the utter lack of security. Whoever was in charge of this operation was feeling pretty confident.

"Agent Ivanova," said a man with a salt-and-pepper-colored crew cut, who spun his chair around and stood up from one of the workstations. He was at least six-foot-three inches tall and a good 275 pounds. Looking past the malformed nose, which had obviously been broken on several occasions, and the pockmarked skin, Harvath took in the general's dark, penetrating eyes and understood why the enormous man had been nicknamed Rasputin. He had an extremely intimidating presence.

"General Stavropol," replied Alexandra politely. "Here I am, as promised."

"Excellent," he smiled.

"What about my reward?"

"What about it?" he asked, the smile never leaving his face.

"I have brought you the American as you asked, and his nuclear device is in the helicopter. The pilots have been instructed not to let anyone but you or me near it."

"Very neat and tidy, but wouldn't you agree that it is somewhat unusual to demand a reward after having betrayed your country?"

"I have done no such thing," she replied, maintaining her composure. "We have a deal and I expect you to honor your end of the bargain."

"That's funny considering the fact that your father—"

"Do not mistake me for my father," interrupted Alexandra as her icy stare bore into Stavropol's own. "Not only have I delivered the American and his weapon to you as promised, but I risked everything coming here."

"Really?" replied Stavropol. "What did you risk?"

"My life. My career. *Everything*."

"Or so you would lead us to believe."

"If you don't believe me, believe Helmut Draegar. He was one of the men who tried to kill me."

"He already has told us."

"And you still question my loyalty?" asked Alexandra.

"That depends," Stavropol responded. "What did Nesterov tell you?"

"*Nesterov?* He didn't tell me anything. I barely got the chance to talk to him before Draegar killed him. This is ridiculous. Where is Draegar? I want to talk with him myself. I will not have my loyalty questioned like this."

"He's in America at the moment. Unfortunately, one of our operatives seems to have gotten cold feet, but it's none of your concern. Draegar will see to it," smiled Stavropol.

That was all Harvath needed to hear. His plan had been to pinpoint Draegar's whereabouts on board the ship so they could take him out as well, but now with him gone, there was no reason to delay the rest of their mission.

"Okay, time's up," said Harvath as he drew his H&K from the small of his back and pointed it at Stavropol's forehead. "I want names, descriptions, everything on all of your sleepers. I want to know where they are, how you contact them, and where their nuclear devices are being hidden."

"You're very brave, Agent Harvath, but also very stupid," replied Stavropol. "Do you actually think my men are going to let you just take over?"

Now it was Harvath's turn to smile. "These

aren't your men," he answered with a jerk of his head toward Morrell and Avigliano, who then removed their balaclavas and trained their weapons on him.

Stavropol's smile never faltered. "Those aren't the men I'm talking about." With a snap of his fingers, scores of soldiers wearing plain clothes, who had been mixed in with the technicians, stood and pointed their guns at Harvath and his party. They were overwhelmingly outgunned and knew they were beaten.

Stavropol raised a walkie-talkie to his mouth and barked a series of orders before turning back to Harvath and saying, "We received the pictures your government sent of several man-portable nuclear devices placed around our country. I can only assume you were part of that effort?"

Harvath didn't respond.

"I had heard that you were a highly skilled operative, but frankly I am disappointed."

"I wouldn't get too bent out of shape over it. I still might prove you wrong."

"We'll see about that," said Stavropol as the elevator doors opened and two technicians wheeled out a dolly carrying Harvath's supposed man-portable nuke. It had been dismantled and lay in pieces.

"You Americans still underestimate us. Did you think our pilot wouldn't find some way to get a message to us?"

"Shit," said Morrell.

"But I heard everything he said," countered Alexandra. "There was nothing that—"

"It wasn't what he said," interrupted Stavropol. "It was what he didn't. When he failed to give the proper approach codes, we knew something was wrong. For a moment, I briefly debated just shooting your helicopter right out of the sky, but now I'm glad that I didn't.

"As far as the device itself is concerned, the Americans seem to have forgotten that we already have all but one of them from their Dark Night program. It does take a certain amount of care to dismantle them, but it soon became obvious that care was not necessary with this one. It's a fake. Until we were sure that this was not going to turn into some suicide mission and that your nuclear device had been placed in a fail-safe mode, there was little else we could do but play along.

"I am going to assume then that the devices in the photos are also fakes, which means that only Frank Leighton and his device are still at large. Our teams will soon find him. In the meantime, I understand from our deck crew that there were two other men with you who came aboard with you and are still at large. I'm confident that they will be joining you shortly."

"None of this going to work," said Harvath. "America isn't going to just roll over for you."

The general smiled once again. "I never expected them to. In fact, had they not resisted I would have been most disappointed."

With that, Stavropol waved over a group of soldiers to take control of the prisoners and transport them below decks for safekeeping. As he did, Harvath saw beneath the general's jacket the finely engraved butt of a Tokarev TT-30, a weapon chambered to fire the 7.62mm Soviet M30 round.

Something told Harvath he was looking at the weapon that had helped put Gary Lawlor into the hospital, clinging to life itself.

CHAPTER 47

A s Carlson and DeWolfe were tossed into the narrow holding cell along with Harvath, Morrell, and Avigliano, the first thing they noticed was the absence of Alexandra.

It was the question all of them were asking themselves, but which none of them really wanted to know the answer to. "She's being held someplace else," offered Harvath.

"She's a big girl and can handle herself. Right now we've got other things to worry about," said Morrell, focusing the team's attention on the matter at hand. Though he doubted the makeshift brig was wired for sound, there was no sense in taking any chances. Stavropol and his team were proving to be very accomplished adversaries, and so he lowered his voice as he turned to Carlson and asked, "Did they get the detonator?"

"The charges were already placed, but they got everything else that was left in my bag," responded the demolitions expert, "including the detonator."

"Fuck," responded Morrell, who then turned to

DeWolfe. "How about you? Were you able to sabotage the air defense system?"

DeWolfe crossed his fingers and held them up for Morrell to see.

"That's it then," said Harvath. "Now we wait."

"Screw that," whispered Carlson as he began scanning the room. It looked like it had been some kind of refrigeration unit at one point. "We're going to find a way out of here."

"We've already looked. That door is it," replied Avigliano.

"So, what? We just give up?"

"No," said Morrell. "We continue to try and find a way out of here."

Carlson looked at his watch. "Well, whatever we do, we've got six minutes to get it together. I targeted their main power supply, as well as their auxiliary. I had no idea we'd end up in a room that depended on a mechanical ventilation system for its air."

"Okay," said Morrell, taking control of the situation, "so we've got six minutes and counting. We can do this. Everybody put your thinking caps on and I don't want to hear a single word unless it has to do with how we can get ourselves out of here."

The room was completely silent as the men went over it again inch by inch. The ventilation system itself was too small for any of them to squeeze through so they spent their time probing for loose ceiling panels or a way to trigger the locking mechanism from their side of the door. Their efforts, though, were all in vain.

Carlson's eyes were glued to his watch as the final seconds of electricity ticked away before the main power shut down. The backup system momentarily came to life, and then it too went down. DeWolfe tried to comfort his colleagues by explaining that from what he had been able to gather, the air defense system, like the fire alarm system, had a battery backup and so his part of the operation would still be successful. The response to his revelation was lackluster at best, as the men took pains to conserve their oxygen.

The first thing they noticed was the suffocating heat. The amount of warmth that could be generated by five men in such a small, enclosed space was amazing. Condensation amassed upon the ceiling and either slowly dripped on top of them or trickled down the walls in thin rivulets.

As they began breathing in short gasps, DeWolfe wondered if maybe their captors had no idea that they were running out of oxygen. He pounded on the steel door until he lost the feeling in both of hands and then he kicked at it until he was so dizzy from hypoxia that he had to sit back down.

As time wore on, Harvath developed a pounding headache accompanied by severe dizziness, but what frightened him most was the sense of euphoria beginning to overtake him. He heard a voice somewhere within the recesses of his mind warn him that after euphoria came the fourth and final stage of hypoxia, wherein victims lost consciousness and quickly succumbed to death. He tried to fight his fatigue and rally against another voice that was quickly gathering strength in his mind. It told him that there was nothing he could do and that he should relax and let it happen. He had nothing to fear.

Harvath knew the message was a lie; that he should not listen to it. He closed his mind against the darkness and tried to focus on his breathing. He needed to slow his heart rate and respiration. The ship's crew was probably already working on restoring power and they would have breathable air again soon. *Breathable air.* He kept repeating the words to himself until the darkness of hypoxia finally overtook him.

here were strange, unintelligible words followed by a burst of heat in his lungs. Then silence. Soon, another burst followed, accompanied by more words and a heaviness on his chest. A bright light drifted on the edges of his field of vision.

The hot burst came again, but there was also another sensation, something soft, something moist. It reminded Harvath of water and he suddenly remembered that he was thirsty. He went to lick his lips but the moistness quickly receded.

He drew another breath and realized what was happening. *He was breathing.* As Harvath greedily gasped for air, consciousness slowly returned. He heard voices, women's voices. The words that had been so unintelligible only moments before now found their place in his mind—Russian. The light he had seen was a flashlight held by one of the women as her compatriot attended to the other men in the room. Slowly, he sat up as he continued to suck in great gasps of air.

"Are you okay?" said a voice in English as a beam of light shone in his face. Harvath recognized the voice as Alexandra's.

"I think so," replied Harvath as he tried to stand up. "How did you find us?"

"I didn't," replied Alexandra, handing him a bottle of water she had found in one of the adjacent storage rooms. "Raisa did. She knows the ship inside and out."

"Is she one of the scientists?"

"Yes. She was also Nesterov's mistress, but they kept it an absolute secret."

"Is she . . ." panted Harvath, who paused to take another long draught of water.

"The second scientist my father mentioned?" said Alexandra, finishing the thought for him. "No question. She told me about periodic communications she had with him."

Harvath lowered the bottle and as he wiped his mouth along his sleeve, glanced around the room and took in the rest of the team in their various states of recovery. "What about Stavropol?"

"Everyone is going crazy upstairs over the half-empty demolitions bag Carlson was found with. All of the lower decks near where they found him are being searched for bombs he may have planted. We have to get out of here."

"What about in the control room?"

"Something has gotten into the system," offered Raisa. "They can't figure it out. They think it might be a worm."

"Not a worm," coughed DeWolfe as Harvath handed him the bottle of water, "a logic bomb."

"A *logic bomb*? How did you get in?"

"The schematics Dr. Nesterov had hidden in the church showed the location of a remote-access terminal. Your system is completely self-contained, so it had to be hacked from within. Dr. Nesterov knew this and programmed a code into the operating system that would provide access whether or not the user had an established account. All it took was the password."

Raisa couldn't believe what she was hearing. Nesterov had never discussed this with her. "But we have safeguards. We constantly do cleanups of the system to remove any such back doors."

"By removing the source code for the compiler and then recompiling it, right?"

"Exactly."

"That was the genius of what Dr. Nesterov did. He set it up so that each time a cleanup happened, the compiler surreptitiously plugged the code right back in. It just kept perpetuating itself. If you knew where to look, the back door was wide open. If you didn't, you wouldn't be able to find any trace of it in the source codes. It's totally invisible. Quite a moby hack if I do say so myself."

"What's the purpose of your logic bomb?"

"I downloaded something onto your system that the geeks at Fort Meade like to call the Hungry Hungry Hippo. Right now it is grazing through your entire system, gobbling up everything it comes across."

"But," said Raisa, "after they isolate your bomb, they'll just shut the system down and reboot."

"By that time," rasped Morrell, "there won't be anything left to reboot. But right now, I agree with Alexandra, we need to get the hell out of here."

Raisa led them down a long corridor and through a series of steel bulkheads. "What happened to you?" Harvath asked Alexandra as they continued to move.

"I don't want to talk about it," she replied.

"Did Stavropol do anything to you?"

"I said I don't want to talk about it."

Before Harvath could press the point any further, they arrived at a steep metal staircase. Raisa fished underneath it and pulled out Scot's technical pack and Carlson's demo sack. "I believe these are yours," she said as she handed them over.

"Where did you find this?" asked Harvath.

"The head of the security team left them in his office for safekeeping."

"And in the rush, he just left his door wide open?"

"Nobody trusts anyone aboard this ship. All of the doors are always locked."

"Then how'd you get in?"

"The same way I got into Stavropol's cabin to free Alexandra," smiled Raisa as she held up a ring of keys. "You'd be surprised how careless the ship's engineers can be with their property."

Harvath removed the silenced Walther, the Pit Bull, and the silenced H&K from his backpack.

"This is the extent of our firepower at the moment. Now all we need to do is to come up with some sort of diversion that will allow us to get out of here."

"I'll bet I could figure out a way to get a nice warm fire going," replied Carlson as he pulled a roll of det cord from his sack.

CHAPTER 49

As Carlson prepared to ignite their diversion, Alexandra said to Harvath, "Scot, you need to see this."

"Later," he replied.

"Fifteen seconds," called out Carlson.

"No, you need to see it now."

Harvath glanced at the notebooks she was examining, which she had taken from Stavropol's stateroom. Wedged in between the pages was a picture of him with his head circled in red with crosshairs through it. There was no question of where it had been taken.

"From what I can tell," said Alexandra, "Draegar was given a copy of this photo along with your home address."

"Now that I know he's coming, I'll have to rush back and bake a cake for him," replied Harvath.

"Time to move," commanded Carlson, cutting off any further conversations as he popped the sparks at the bottom of his time fuse coils.

Harvath grabbed the photo and shoved it into

his pocket as Alexandra gathered up the journals and everyone headed for the gangway. Outside, they formed a conga line with Morrell and Carlson on point, and Avigliano covering their six. The goal now was to reach the helicopter, which Morrell was qualified enough to pilot. They had only needed the Russian pilot to fly the chopper from Arkhangel City and handle any radio traffic on the way in, but now that they were on their way out, Alexandra could handle any radio inquiries and hopefully weave enough bullshit to protect them until they got to the border with Norway and were safely out of Russian airspace.

They weren't even halfway amidships when they ran into their first problem. Carlson, wearing the night vision goggles that had been in Harvath's pack, spotted movement up ahead and held up his fist, indicating that the column should stop. "Contact," he whispered as he raised Alexandra's silenced Walther P4 and pointed it down the corridor.

Morrell leaned in close and said, "Don't pull that trigger unless you're sure you sighted a hostile. We don't want any casualties among any of the crew or technicians."

"These two are definitely hostile," replied Carlson. "Both look like they're carrying assault weapons."

"You're sure?"

"Positive."

"All right, take them."

Carlson's weapon bucked twice in his large

hands accompanied by two muffled coughs. "Tangos one and two down," he said.

"Let's strip 'em," said Morrell as he waved the team forward.

The Spetsnaz soldiers were indeed carrying assault weapons, two nine-millimeter PP-90M submachine guns. Harvath took one, and Avigliano traded Alexandra the Pit Bull for the other. The soldiers were also carrying several fragmentation as well as flashbang grenades, which Morrell divvied up amongst the team. Though it would have helped their cover if they could have gotten Harvath and Alexandra into the Spetsnaz uniforms with their black balaclavas and pretend that Raisa was helping guide them around the ship, there was no time for that. They needed to keep pressing on toward the helicopter parked on the aft deck.

Eventually, one of the engineers was able to restore the emergency lighting and the hallways took on an eerie red hue. Raisa watched with a great deal of apprehension as they passed by four lifeboats outlined in reflective tape just outside the windows. She was beginning to doubt whether Alexandra Ivanova and her colleagues were going to live up to their end of the bargain or if they were more concerned with saving their own skins and sneaking away without a trace. "We need to raise the alarm," she said. "The people on this ship need time to evacuate. There's some light now, that will help, but they need to get started. Your fire is going to spread very quickly."

"Once we have the helicopter in sight," said

Morrell, "we'll sound the alarm, but not until then." Seeing the look of concern on her face he added, "Don't worry. Your colleagues are going to have plenty of time to abandon ship."

"And once they do? Then what? It's below freezing outside."

"There are three nuclear icebreakers and two submarines waiting out there. Trust me, this is one group of people that Russia will not want to lose."

Raisa reluctantly accepted Morrell's answer and settled back into line, trying to ignore the remaining lifeboats that they passed.

They were less than fifty meters from the aft deck when Gordon Avigliano dropped to one knee and yelled, "We've got company," as he opened up with his weapon on full auto.

Harvath turned and saw at least five Spetsnaz soldiers as they dove through open doorways on either side of the corridor behind them. "Let's get some cover quick," he yelled.

Morrell immediately responded, "There's no place to go but aft."

Harvath was about to say something, when two of the Russian troops pointed their weapons into the hall and pulled the triggers.

The corridor acted like a giant funnel, channeling the deadly fire right toward them. Thankfully, the Spetsnaz rounds went high and missed the team as they dove to the floor.

"Go," yelled Avigliano to his colleagues. "I'll hold them."

"No way," replied Harvath. "We all go together."

"We can't. Somebody needs to keep them pinned down. I'm not going to argue about this."

"Gordy, listen," began Harvath, who then stopped as he felt a hand reaching into his coat pocket. Before he could stop her, Alexandra had removed the two fragmentation grenades Morrell had given him and pulled both pins.

"Men," she snorted as she pitched the devices down the hallway toward where the Spestnaz troops were hiding.

Harvath yelled "Grenade," but it was hardly necessary. Not only had the rest of the team seen what Alexandra had done, but they were already on their feet running for the helicopter.

Seconds later, the fragmentation grenades exploded, neutralizing the Spetsnaz troops behind them and starting yet another fire. This time, Raisa didn't wait for Rick Morrell's permission. At the next fire alarm they passed, she pulled it and ran.

Before they even burst outside onto the aft deck, they could already hear the heavy chopping of the assault helicopter's rotors. "Sounds like somebody else is trying to leave without us," said Carlson.

"Damn it," snapped Morrell, turning to the demolitions expert. "Hit the hull charges and send this fucker to the bottom of the ocean right now."

Carlson reached into his demo sack and removed a lightweight transmitter, about the size of a portable MP3 player, which was part of an improved Remote Activation Munition System, or RAMS. Developed by the Army Research Lab in Adelphi, Maryland, RAMS allowed Special Operations teams to remotely detonate munitions from ranges of over two kilometers away. In this case, it wasn't the distance that mattered, but rather the amount of metal the signal had to penetrate to successfully activate the blasting caps on Carlson's charges.

He depressed the buttons in quick succession. A series of resounding *thuds* began at the bow and came racing toward them. The entire vessel shuddered as the muted blasts signaled one gaping hole after another being torn in the enormous ship's hull. Even if the crew raced to seal off the bulkheads of the compartments now filling with icy water, they wouldn't be able to prevent the *Gagarin* from meeting its fate.

Charging out onto the deck, the team found that during their time inside, the storm had grown much worse. Thick snow was being driven in heavy sheets by a sharp arctic wind. Visibility had been severely impaired, but not to such an extent that they couldn't see General Stavropol as he reached the door to the helicopter. Harvath raised his weapon, but before he could fire, the team was under attack from above.

More Spetsnaz troops, this time armed with AK-105s, were shooting at them from the upper deck. While Morrell and the rest of the team maneuvered to return fire, Harvath, along with Alexandra, held their positions.

The ferocious wind was incessant and, combined

with the thick snow, made it all but impossible to find an opportunity to take a shot as they heard the helicopter lift off. As it did, the blowing snow receded and through the glass Alexandra not only saw General Stavropol safe and sound on board, but also the lopsided smile stretched across his pockmarked face.

Ignoring the fact that the hull of the *Gagarin* had steadily been filling with freezing water, Alexandra took aim, but just as she applied the final pressure to the trigger, there was a deafening groan and the ship listed steeply to starboard. The Pit Bull discharged, but the round completely missed its target as Alexandra came crashing down hard onto the perilously inclined deck and dropped one of the notebooks. As she did, the chopper's rotor wash swept the other completely overboard.

Alexandra lunged for the remaining notebook and felt herself sliding down the deck toward the *Gagarin*'s iron railing. She threw her arms out and fought to find any kind of handhold she could, but it was no use. There was nothing between her and the fast-approaching railing to stop or even slow her ever-increasing speed.

She felt herself slip beneath the railing and as if she were a cloud, become perfectly weightless. Her stomach leapt, the same way it did when she took an abrupt hill too fast in her car, and then suddenly she felt a great pain in her arm. *But that was impossible.* She knew she had slipped beneath the railing. Then she heard the voice and realized how wrong she was.

"Alexandra, help me! I can't hold on to you."

It was Harvath.

Alexandra opened her eyes and looked up. Harvath was leaning over the edge of the ship. He was holding on to her wrist with his left hand.

The pain of suspending her in subzero temperatures several stories above the White Sea was emblazoned like bright red neon across his features. "Alexandra!" he yelled again. "Reach up with your other hand!"

Alexandra tried, but she couldn't. She opened her mouth to speak, but try as she might, no sound would come out. She could feel Harvath's grip slipping and was paralyzed with fear.

"I'm losing my grip," groaned Harvath, his arms feeling as if they were going to tear away from his body at any moment. Summoning every last ounce of strength he had, Harvath roared and gave one final tug, which succeeded in hauling Alexandra the rest of the way back onto the icy deck, where he lay in a heap next to her, totally spent.

Harvath never noticed the two Spetsnaz soldiers until they were standing right over him and by then, it was too late. Harvath went to grab for his gun, but one of the men put his boot down on his hand.

"Easy," said Morrell. "It's us."

Morrell helped Harvath up while Avigliano assisted Alexandra.

Rejoining DeWolfe and Carlson, Morrell gave Harvath and Alexandra the pick of Spetsnaz bodies and told them to get out of their clothes and into the Spetsnaz uniforms as quickly as possible, before more of the troops showed up. As it turned out, more soldiers were not what they had to worry about, as the Mi-17–1V helicopter, which had been hovering off the aft deck, turned and came back in with its 23mm gun pods blazing.

"Incoming!" yelled Morrell as the team dove for cover.

The helicopter peppered not only the aft deck, but also half of its housing, showering them with broken glass, splintered wood, and twisted metal.

As the helicopter swung out and prepared to make another run, Harvath reached for his gun, but something else caught his eye. Leaning against a pile of coiled rope was Alexandra's Pit Bull.

The helicopter was fifty meters out and closing fast when Morrell and the rest of the team took aim and began firing. The Mi-17–1V answered with its own deadly barrage of fire, but when it got within spitting distance and Harvath could see it as well as he could through the blinding curtains of snow, he began firing.

One, then two, followed by a third of the armor-piercing rounds found their mark and the assault helicopter exploded in an enormous ball of fire.

"That was for Gary, asshole," said Harvath as he watched the burning chopper crash into the sea.

As the team regrouped, Carlson commented on how their primary means of escape was now charred and sinking to the bottom of the ocean.

Ever the tactician, Morrell quickly sifted through the possibilities for escape and said, "We've got options," he said, "We'll figure something out."

"Whatever it is," said Carlson, "we'd better do it fast."

Alexandra cleared her throat and suggested, "How about the *Vyesna*?"

"What's the *Vyesna*?" asked Avigliano.

"It's one of the nuclear icebreakers," she said, pointing over the side of the *Gagarin* through the snow. "The large red one off the port bow."

"You think the Russian Navy is just going to let us sail right out of here with it?" asked DeWolfe.

"First of all, they don't have to know we're on it," replied Alexandra, "and secondly, the Russian Navy doesn't have much to say about it. Especially if they believe that the *Vyesna* is having a problem with its reactor."

DeWolfe was starting to see what she had in mind. "But they'll want to put one of their people on it to check it out."

"I doubt it. The icebreakers aren't part of the Russian Navy. They're all privately owned by a Russian conglomerate called the Murmansk Shipping Company. The *Vyesna* is one of the oldest in their fleet. It should have been retired a long time ago. My guess is that if there's an accident on board, complete with the threat of a radiation leak, the Russian Navy won't want to get anywhere near that boat. They'll want it out of the area right away."

"They'll expect it to return to port though," said Carlson.

"That's what I'm counting on. The service base for the Murmansk Shipping Company is on the Kola Peninsula only a hundred kilometers south of the Norwegian border. Once we are on land, we can find a car, a truck, or whatever is available and go. Up there, it is still the two months of constant darkness known as Polar night, so we'll have added cover."

With the fire alarm still blaring and Morrell expecting more soldiers to show up at any moment, he looked at Harvath, then studied the team and said, "I vote we grab the nearest lifeboat and get the hell out of here. If anyone's got any better ideas, now's the time." When no one offered an alternative, he shouldered one of the AK-105s and instructed the team to watch their backs as they moved out.

Fifteen minutes later, once they were a safe distance away in one of the *Gagarin*'s lifeboats, Harvath and the rest of the team looked back together and watched as the giant ship rolled completely onto its starboard side and began to slide beneath the icy water.

While his teammates congratulated one another on sinking the air defense system that the Soviet Union had created to blackmail the United States and pointed the lifeboat toward the nuclear ice-breaker known as the *Vyesna*, Harvath was uncharacteristically quiet. Something, he didn't know what, told him that America wasn't out of the woods yet. Not by a long shot.

CHAPTER 50

With its nineteen-inch-thick armor-plated steel hull and twin steam turbine engines, the nuclear icebreaker *Vyesna* made the four hundred and fifty kilometer trip to Murmansk in just under seventeen hours. The dummy charges Carlson rigged in the reactor room and at other strategic points throughout the vessel, which he threatened to detonate via remote if there was any trouble, were enough to ensure the crew's complete cooperation. The men were professional sailors, not soldiers, and had no desire to die.

Via encrypted messages transmitted back and forth to Washington, Harvath learned that the threat of a pending Russian attack was already beginning to leak out. People in America were hoarding food, water, and medical supplies, while millions were fleeing major metropolitan areas, unsure if they had been targeted.

Now that Harvath had succeeded in disabling Russia's previously envisioned impregnable air defense system, hawks in Rutledge's cabinet were calling for a full-on first strike to neutralize the Russians and calm fears at home. The president, though, was still concerned about the Soviet nukes secreted on American soil and urged Harvath to get back to DC as quickly as possible. There were less than two days until the State of the Union address.

By the time the *Vyesna* crashed its way into the Kola Inlet, General Paul Venrick of the American Joint Special Operations Command had established a rendezvous point just across the border with a Norwegian Special Forces Team.

After DeWolfe had disabled the ship's communication equipment and Carlson, with Alexandra translating, warned that he could still detonate his explosives from up to twenty kilometers away if the crew did anything stupid, the team lowered one of the icebreaker's rigid inflatable boats over the side and headed for land.

They beached just down from a small town called Platonovka, where Avigliano located an old UAZ-brand cross-country vehicle and, seeing no one around, promptly "commandeered" it. Stopping at two gas stations, Alexandra and Harvath went inside where they allowed the attendants to hear them speaking English. Alexandra then asked for directions in Russian to a village on the Finnish border about two hundred kilometers to the southwest. At no time did they allow the attendants to see the car they were driving.

With enough of a false trail in place to occupy the police and the military until they could make it out of

the country, they headed for the Russian border with
Norway, using back roads whenever possible.

Two hours later, they ran out of road and had no
choice but to abandon the UAZ and hike the rest of
the way in on foot. When they made it to the rendezvous point, the Norwegian Special Forces unit
allowed them a few minutes to catch their breath
before making their presence known. Harvath, having been tasked to SEAL Team Two—the Navy's
cold weather experts, also known as the Polar
SEALs—was well versed in winter warfare and noticed the soldiers before anyone else. The rest of
the team was taken somewhat by surprise, as the
men appeared virtually out of nowhere.

Once identities had been established, the unit
commander called in a Royal Norwegian Air Force
Bell 412 helicopter for their extraction. They were
transported to Kirkenes Airport about forty kilometers away where the CIA Air Branch Cessna Citation X, which Harvath had flown over to Berlin on
six days ago, was deiced and waiting.

The Mach .92 Citation X traveled nearly at the
speed of sound. With a range of three thousand
nautical miles it was necessary that they put down
in Greenland to refuel. They stopped at Sondre
Stromfjord airport and were on the ground for less
than fifteen minutes before being airborne again.
Harvath and Alexandra hardly noticed the minor in-
terruption and declined to exit the craft to stretch
their legs and instead remained on board and continued to pour over Stavropol's journal.

The man might have kept extensive notes, but he was no fool. Sensitive information was encoded somehow and it was only now, after almost three-and-a-half hours and two thousand miles of flight that Alexandra was beginning to get a handle on it. The fact that the man wrote in cursive Cyrillic and had terrible handwriting to boot, relegated Harvath to the backseat while Alexandra twisted her hair in knots, broke pencil point after pencil point, and wore down several erasers trying to crack Stavropol's code. The code itself wouldn't have been such a problem had they not lost the first journal. Much of the encrypted information seemed to directly relate to earlier entries in the other notebook.

Leaving Greenland's airspace, Harvath had received an intelligence update. He was told that Gary Lawlor's condition had stabilized and that he'd been transported to the Landstuhl Medical Center in southwestern Germany, near Ramstein Airbase. That was the good news. Then came the bad. Not only had none of the Russian nuclear devices been discovered, but until they were verifiably locked down, president Rutledge wasn't taking any chances. With less than twenty-four hours left until the State of the Union address, his aides were preparing two separate speeches. Though giving the speech the Russians wanted would create world-wide financial chaos and do immeasurable harm to America's economy, he was not willing to risk the greater damage to American lives and infrastructure that would be created by the detonation of nuclear weapons on American soil.

Being cooped up in a plane more than two thousand miles from home, Harvath had never felt so impotent in his life. Sitting on his hands was driving him insane.

They were over Newfoundland when Alexandra began excitedly rifling through her stack of notes, pulling out several pages in particular and laying them in front of her. Next, she tore four pages out of Stavropol's journal and placed those to her side. Without even looking up from what she was doing, she told Harvath to go find her more paper.

When he returned, she grabbed a sheet off the top of the small stack he held in his hands and told him to sit down. He slid into the seat across the table from her and said, "What is it?"

"I finally figured it out," she said as she placed one of the pages from the journal side by side with a blank piece of paper and began writing. "It's a combination of something we call *Poluslovitsa*, or half-word, where certain letters are purposely left missing, and an old form of Russian fast-written characters."

Harvath watched as she filled in the missing Russian words and then translated the text into English. As its meaning became clear, Harvath scrawled down a message and rushed it to DeWolfe, who encrypted his words and sped them ahead of the plane to Washington.

CHAPTER 51

When the Cessna Citation X landed just a few miles southeast of Washington, DC, at Andrews Air Force Base, it was met by a contingent of agents from the FBI's Critical Incident Response Group.

Established in 1994, the CIRG represented the FBI's highest-end tactical and investigative resources. CIRG teams could be deployed anywhere in the country to handle critical incidents requiring an immediate law enforcement response such as hostage takings, child abductions, prison riots, and terrorist attacks. One of the CIRG's best-known units was the FBI's famed Hostage Rescue Team, which had a helicopter standing by to transport Harvath and the rest of the team to FBI Headquarters at 935 Pennsylvania Avenue.

As the Bell 412 helicopter raced across the dark Metro DC sky, agents of the Behavioral Analysis Unit pumped Harvath and Alexandra for anything they knew about Helmut Draegar that might give them the edge in stopping him before he could carry out his assignment.

The questions continued as they rode the elevator down from the improvised landing pad on the roof and made their way into the FBI's Strategic Information and Operations Center, or SIOC.

The main operations area was pulsing with activity as harried operatives simultaneously worked the phones and computer terminals. Large, flat-panel monitors surrounded the room and tracked everything from street traffic to air traffic. Utility and public works departments were being monitored, as was the main 911 Emergency Call Center. Representatives from the Capitol Police Containment & Emergency Response Team were present, as well as representatives from the US Park Police SWAT team, the Federal Marshal Service's Special Operations Group, the Washington, DC, Metropolitan Police Department Emergency Response Team, the Secret Service's Counter Assault, Uniform Division Emergency Response, and Counter Sniper Teams, the Department of Energy's Nuclear Emergency Support Team, the Joint Chiefs of Staff, the National Security Council, and a host of other agencies.

Security was always extremely tight leading up to a State of the Union address, but with a confirmed nuclear terrorist threat in the works, the CIRG had been operating at an exhausting, almost overloaded capacity for the last week.

Harvath and Alexandra were shown to a conference room above the frenetic main floor, while Morrell and the rest of his team were taken to another part of the center to be debriefed by both CIA and Defense Department officials.

As the door to the crowded conference room opened the first voice Harvath heard belonged to Homeland Security Director Driehaus. "*If* it's found in time."

"If it's not, then the president is reluctantly prepared to evacuate the Congress and give his address from the White House," replied the chief of staff, Charles Anderson.

"Taped, of course." said CIA Director Vaile. "Your people can record it now and then feed it out tonight while he's safe and sound aboard *Air Force One.*"

"The president's not very happy about that option," answered Anderson. "It's not his style. He doesn't like the idea of hiding out while millions of American lives are at risk."

"But like it or not, it's his duty to remain alive," interjected Driehaus. "If this thing does come down, the American people will want to turn to him for his guidance and leadership in the aftermath."

"You've got no argument with me," said Anderson. "Anyway, unless we're one hundred percent certain that the threat has been neutralized, he's giving the Russians what they want and going with the alternate speech. The international and economic pieces will just have to fall where they may."

"Hold on a second," said Driehaus as he suddenly noticed Alexandra standing next to Harvath in the doorway. "Who the hell cleared them to be in here?"

"I did," replied FBI Director Sorce, who instructed the two newcomers to take a seat.

"She's a Russian SVR agent, for Christ's sake!"

"Who has given us one of our biggest breaks in this case."

Driehaus was incensed. "What if she's a plant? What if everything she's given us is disinformation? I want to go on record that I object to her being here and believe that her presence at this meeting puts our national security in serious jeopardy."

"Duly noted," replied Sorce.

"What for?" rebutted Driehaus. "She's already decoded and provided us with the list of sleepers and their locations before she and Agent Harvath even landed in DC."

"True," replied Sorce, "but we still do not have the *means* by which to contact them and therefore we believe she may still be useful. There's no telling how much of a head start Draegar already has on us in activating them."

"What about the sleepers here in DC?" asked Harvath, anxious to avoid a protracted pissing match between Sorce and Driehaus. "What have you been able to find out about them?"

The FBI director took a deep breath before responding. "I'm afraid I'm going to have to agree with Secretary Driehaus at this point. We're going to need to talk about those two privately." Looking at Alexandra he said, "We have a team here in the main operations area coordinating the pickups of the sleeper agents across the country. As we pop them, our field agents will be feeding back live video of their interrogations and the searches of their cars, residences, and so on. On each field team is an agent who can speak Russian, just in case Draegar tries to make contact. That being said, you've been a very big help to us so far, and if we can impress upon you to assist us further we could really use your help down on the floor."

Alexandra agreed, and Sorce had one of his assistants show her to the area the sleeper pickup teams were being managed from. Once she was out of the conference room and the door had closed behind her, the FBI director looked at Harvath and said, "Out of the names you gave us, one is dead and one is missing."

"Who are they?" asked Harvath.

"The dead guy owned a very successful antique store on Wisconsin Avenue in upper Georgetown. His client list reads like a who's who of Washington insiders. No priors, never bothered his neighbors, regular churchgoer, no outstanding debts, you know the profile."

"Was he Russian by birth or did someone turn him here?"

"That's something we're still working on."

As Sorce handed him the file, Harvath looked it over and said, "Draegar's cleaning house. Why?"

"The Russians are tying up their loose ends," offered Driehaus.

"My guess is that the antiques guy changed his mind," said Sorce. "That's always the risk you run with a long-term sleeper. When it came to the point that he was actually called into action, he didn't want to do it. His ideology had changed. He liked what he had going on here and didn't want to give it up, so Draegar broke into his apartment and killed him."

"Where did he live?" asked Harvath as he continued to scan the file.

"In some apartment building near Dupont Circle."

"What about the other guy?"

"That's the one that really stings," said the FBI director as he handed over the other file. "His name is David Patrick. He's an aide to the National Security Council's deputy executive secretary. Apparently, he went to Moscow on a goddamn Fulbright Scholarship."

"Our American tax dollars at work," replied Harvath.

"His job at the NSC put him in a perfect position to slip that ransom note into the president's briefing papers."

Harvath closed the file and slid it back over to the FBI director, "So where's our man now?"

"At this point, it's anybody's guess. We've cast a very intense net for him. If he's out there, we'll get him."

"I assume you've got a team at Patrick's apartment," said Harvath, "just in case he comes back."

"We do. I reassigned the guys I had on Gary's place. Why? Are you thinking about going over there?"

"I'd like Agent Ivanova to see it, and the antiques dealer's home and office as well. She's got good instincts and might pick up on something we missed."

"Now that she's in the building," interrupted the homeland security secretary, "I don't know if I like the idea of her leaving it."

Sorce had no choice but to agree, it was too dangerous.

Harvath, though, disagreed. "I know the idea of an SVR agent running around loose while we're dealing with a major threat from the Russians is a little unorthodox, but I'm telling you she has a very good eye. It's precisely because she's Russian that she can be of help to us. She can approach this from a completely different angle."

"And if she tries to rabbit?" asked Sorce, playing Devil's advocate.

"She won't."

"But if she does?" prodded Driehaus.

"Then I'll put a bullet in her," replied Harvath. "As sure as I'm sitting here, if Agent Alexandra Ivanova tries to run, I give you my word that I'll kill her myself."

hey ended up spending half of the day in the SIOC. With Alexandra's knowledge of Helmut Draegar, Russian Intelligence, and the events that had transpired, she was suddenly deemed an asset too valuable to let go.

As Harvath watched, she fielded question after question and gave her opinion to the agents taking down sleepers on everything from interrogation tactics to potential hiding spots for Russian nukes. Soon, no one made a move without consulting her first. Though the shift in operational control unsettled some of the FBI's higher-ups, one look at what Alexandra was doing was enough to convince them that the trust their agents were putting in her was well founded. Her advice was solid.

The good news was that the pickup teams had gotten to the sleepers before Draegar did. The bad news was that they were proving extremely resolute. Across the country, once captured, they gave up little to no information whatsoever.

Finally, Harvath had seen enough. His country

needed him. If Alexandra Ivanova wanted to continue to play oracle at Delphi, that was fine with him, but he needed to check out their other leads. Standing around doing nothing was more than he could stand.

It took Harvath another hour to track down the FBI's director, but once he did, the man pledged to him any support he needed.

The first thing Harvath needed was a helicopter that could get in and out of tight spaces—one that could land on a building without a helipad or in the middle of a narrow DC side street, and the HRT Bell 412 sitting on the roof of FBI Headquarters just didn't fit the bill. What's more, HRT's other birds were already in use. It only took one call to Andrews Air Force Base to track down an MH-6 Little Bird and a Nightstalker pilot from the Army's 160th Special Operations Aviation Regiment who was ready to see some action.

Harvath also needed a support team he could trust, and Rick Morrell and Company, still in the building on reserve, were more than happy to help him out. A quartermaster and armorer from Quantico were sent up to see to all the team's needs. The team was outfitted in black, fire-retardant Nomex fatigues, HellStorm tactical assault gloves, and First Choice body armor. Included with the cache laid out by the armorer were several newly arrived futuristic .40-caliber Beretta CX4 Storm carbines, as well as Model 96 Beretta Vertec pistols, also in .40 caliber. There was something about being able to interchange their magazines that Harvath found very comforting.

A Picatinny rail system allowed him to outfit the CX4 Storm with an under-mounted laser sight and an above-mounted Leupold scope. He shoved as much extra ammunition as he could get his hands on into his empty pockets and after grabbing a pair of night vision goggles, headed up to the roof with the rest of the team.

When they were all on board, the improved MH-6 Little Bird with its new six-bladed rotor and upgraded, silenced engine lifted off and headed northwest to upper Georgetown and the antique shop.

The pilot found a relatively empty parking lot where he could set the Little Bird down and as soon as the skids were within two feet of the ground the team was out and running. The State of the Union address was less than eight hours away.

They were met at the shop by an FBI forensics detail that respectfully stood back as both Harvath and Alexandra searched for anything out of the ordinary. When they had questions about phone records, the contents of the computer hard drive in the shop's office, or who the antiques dealer's predominantly high-end customers had been, one of the forensic agents would pick up one of the detail's many clipboards, sift through the pages, and once she had found it, deliver the information as quickly and succinctly as possible. The message had come down loud and clear: Harvath and Alexandra were in a hurry and there was no time to waste.

The antiques shop was a bust, as was David Patrick's nearby apartment. Their last stop was an upscale high-rise called the Park Connecticut where the antiques dealer had lived right up until he had been murdered. It was located in a DC area known as Northwest and occupied a prime piece of real estate just above Dupont Circle along Rock Creek Park. The Nightstalker pilot landed the Little Bird on the Park Connecticut's rooftop terrace and the team took the fire stairs down to the ninth floor.

Another forensics detail met Harvath and his colleagues at the door and led them through the grand foyer, past the gourmet kitchen with its granite countertops, and into the spacious living room, which had been crammed full of beautiful hand-carved antique hardwood furniture. Framed thank-you notes from diplomats, boutique hotels, private collections, and individual customers recognizing the dealer's prowess and eye for rare pieces lined one entire wall. Though this FBI detail was confident that they would find something to tie the killer to the crime scene, they had no idea what the bigger picture was. They knew who had killed the antiques dealer. It was Draegar. What they didn't know was where Draegar was now and what he was planning to do next. That was the type of clue they needed to find.

The apartment included a gas fireplace and French doors that opened out onto the balcony. In addition to its lavish master bedroom, there was also a den and two marble bathrooms. Harvath and Alexandra quickly began picking the place apart piece by piece.

They went through closets, drawers, and bookcases while they fired off questions at the forensics agents to try and get a better picture of the antiques dealer.

They studied the blood-stained tub where the man's body had been found, shot twice in the face. Looking at his Kobold, Harvath noticed it was closing in on five o'clock p.m.—right around the approximate time yesterday that the forensics people claimed the antiques dealer had been killed.

After completely tossing the bathroom, Harvath headed back into the living room and asked one of the forensics agents, "We've got a copy of the building's surveillance tape from yesterday, right?"

"Of course we do," the man answered, rummaging through an evidence box and pulling it out for Harvath to see. "We already went through it and there's nobody on there that matches Helmut Draegar's description."

"How far back did you go?"

"Hours, just on the off chance that he had snuck in here early and had laid in wait for the victim."

Harvath fired up the antique dealer's television and VCR. The tape showed pictures from four different cameras placed throughout the building, including the front and back doors, as well as the garage.

"I'm telling you," said the forensics agent, "we went back and forth over that tape and there was no sign of your man on it at all. If there was, we would have caught it."

"Not if he didn't want you to," replied Harvath as he began shuttling the tape forward.

"You just passed at least five guys on there," said Avigliano, wondering how Harvath could make sense of any of the images at this speed.

But somehow, Morrell knew what Harvath was doing and stated, "You're not looking for guys, are you?"

"Not looking for *guys*? What are you talking about?" asked DeWolfe.

"It would be just like Draegar," said Alexandra. "Perfect tradecraft. He'd befriend somebody, probably another tenant, and then use them."

Finally, Harvath found what he was looking for and paused the tape. Yesterday afternoon at 4:07 p.m. a couple entered the building through the garage. The man's face was totally obscured from view by the woman who appeared to be helping him carry several packages.

"Jesus," said DeWolfe, "Do you think that's him?"

Harvath advanced the video frame by frame. Draegar was a pro. With the woman shielding him and his face turned away from the camera, there was absolutely no record of him ever having been in the building. "I know it's him."

"So he was here, in the building. We know that much," offered Morrell. "That's good."

"We also now know something else," offered Harvath as his eyes remained locked on the TV screen.

"What's that?" asked Carlson.

Picking up his CX4 Storm as he headed for the door, Harvath stated, "Where he's hiding."

CHAPTER 53

With less than three hours before the State of the Union address, president Jack Rutledge had cleared the Oval Office so he could be alone and he now stared at two different folders sitting on the desk in front of him, which contained two very different versions of his State of the Union address.

One gave the Russians what they wanted—a message from a humbled American president pulling his country out of the sphere of world politics, while the other was a spit in the eye and a hearty *fuck you* to any individual, terrorist organization, rogue state, or internationally recognized nation who thought they could blackmail the United States.

The irony that one speech lay in a red folder and the other sat in one of presidential blue—all the while separated by a white desk blotter—was not lost on Jack Rutledge.

Meanwhile, outside the Oval Office, Rutledge knew that his aides were pulling their hair out, wondering what his next move would be. Most of them, along with Congress, save for the absolute diehards, had either been evacuated to a secure location outside the Metropolitan DC area, or had been sent home to be with their families while the tangled web of events played out.

All that anyone knew at this point was that President Rutledge had taped two State of the Union addresses from the Oval Office and no one was certain which one was going to air.

If the truth be told, Rutledge himself didn't even know. His daughter, Amanda, had already been evacuated to Andrews Air Force Base and was awaiting him aboard *Air Force One* while he sat within the deceptive calm of what could only be described as the eye of the most deadly hurricane to ever descend upon the Oval Office.

With his personal helicopter, designated as *Marine Corps One*, sitting hot and ready to move just outside the West Wing, Jack Rutledge tried to put the pleadings of his staff and Secret Service detail out of his mind. Like president George Washington over two hundred years before him, he was bound and determined to deliver his State of the Union address live, not via tape, while he and Congress cowered either in a plane 35,000 feet above the United States or deep inside some secret underground complex. What's more, President Jack Rutledge was going to be damned if his stewardship of the United States of America was going to be undermined by the Union of Soviet Socialist Republics or whatever name the fucking red horde was calling itself these days.

Rutledge glanced at his watch and, though he knew time was very tight, decided he would wait just a little bit longer. After all, the Americans had something going for them that the Russians didn't.

CHAPTER 54

A *Mulland* Jacket," repeated Harvath into his microphone, louder this time so Morrell could hear him over the roar of wind pouring through the Little Bird's open doors. "It's a very exclusive tweed coat made for hunting by a company called Holland and Holland. The president gave it to Gary a couple of years back as a gift on one of their pheasant trips and Draegar had one on in that surveillance tape."

"And that's what makes you think he's been using Gary's house as his home base?"

"Why not? It makes perfect sense. The FBI has pulled off their surveillance and it's safer than checking in to a hotel or motel. Draegar's not stupid. All we'd need to do is circulate his photo and sooner or later we'd have him."

"Why not shack up with one of the sleepers?"

"I don't think he trusts them. Would you? I agree with Sorce that the reason the antiques dealer bought it was because he was probably trying to back out. If you were having second thoughts, the

best thing you could do would be to kill Draegar."
Harvath paused a moment before continuing. "No,
he couldn't risk counting on the sleepers to put him
up. It could jeopardize the entire mission if they
were caught together. He'd want somewhere he
knew he could be completely safe. Besides, what
better way to rub it in Gary's face than to use his
own place as a safe house?"

"You could burn it," replied Morrell as an uneasy silence settled over them.

They watched as the helicopter cut through the
cold air, west, toward Fairfax. There were less than
three hours to go until the State of the Union.

The Little Bird touched down in a field half a mile
from Gary Lawlor's home and rendezvoused with another helicopter transporting two HRT assault teams.
In conjunction with Fairfax law enforcement, Harvath
helped sketch a picture of Gary's neighborhood, his
property, and then the house itself. He detailed all of
the windows and doors and then discussed what he
felt were the best entry points for the HRT teams,
which had been labeled Red Team and Blue Team.
Harvath and Alexandra, along with Morrell and his
men, were labeled Gold Team. Though Director Sorce
had been dead set against Alexandra carrying a gun,
Harvath gave her his Beretta pistol anyway. In his
mind, if they were all taking the same risks, they all
deserved to be afforded the same protections.

Once the fine points of the takedown had been

established and agreed to, the Fairfax officers transported the three assault teams in as far as they could. A perimeter had been established by uniformed officers for four blocks in every direction around Gary Lawlor's home. Until Harvath said so, no one was getting in or out of that part of the neighborhood.

Both the MH-6 Little Bird and the HRT chopper were equipped with second-generation Forward Looking Infrared and having them keep an eye on things from above made Harvath feel a lot better as he and the rest of his Gold Team crept through the woods bordering the rear of Gary's property.

It was an eerie sensation, not only because he was right back where he had started from a week ago, but because whoever took the picture of him at Gary's barbecue that he had found on board the *Gagarin* had come this exact same way.

When they reached the edge of the tree line, Harvath used his night vision goggles to scan the property. It didn't come as much of a surprise that he wasn't seeing anything. The other teams radioed in from their positions. Besides a car parked in the driveway in front, there were no other signs that anyone was home. The helicopters weren't picking up anything from inside the house either. They all knew, though, that that didn't mean there wasn't a surprise waiting for them. After all, had the same helicopters been there a week ago, when he was wearing his IR camouflage suit they would have had no idea Harvath was inside.

Everyone listened over their earpieces as the

Red Team leader counted down the seconds before giving the *Go* command. Assaulters had positioned themselves under windows and alongside the house with ladders as Harvath and his team crept through the backyard and got ready to breach via the back door. To everyone who was there that night, the next several seconds seemed to last a lifetime.

When the command came, Red Team tossed flashbang grenades through the front windows and used shock rounds to blow the hinges off the front door. Blue Team used long poles to break the upper windows and pitch in their flashbangs, while the rest of their team scrambled up ladders or tossed more flashbangs through the lower windows and prepared to dive in.

Harvath swung an enormous sledgehammer that one of the Fairfax police had given him and shattered the lock assembly on the mudroom door. He and Morrell were first in, followed by Alexandra and then the rest of the team.

The mudroom was littered with coats and other assorted items that had been knocked off of the pegs and shelves. A bucket of OxiClean had spilled onto the floor and in the greenish glow of his night vision goggles Harvath thought he could make out a footprint.

Opening the door to the kitchen, Harvath yelled out, "Banger!" as Morrell pitched in an under-handed flashbang. The members of Gold Team turned their heads away from the blast and once the device had detonated, rushed into the room unopposed. None of them noticed the trip wires until it was too late.

Alexandra was the only one to hear the slight twang, like a piece of piano wire being plucked, followed by a barely audible pop as the explosive was engaged.

"We've got a body here," began one of the members of Blue Team, who had come in through one of the house's second-story windows. He was quickly cut off by Alexandra's frantic cries of, "Get out! Get out! It's a trap!"

"Gold Team," said Red Team's leader with the calm and presence of mind that came with being a seasoned operative, "give us a Sit Rep. What are you looking at?"

Harvath's eyes swept from side to side and then down to the ground, trying to see what Alexandra was yelling about. Morrell did the same, but soon they were both being yanked by their collars as Alexandra pulled them backward.

"The house is booby trapped! It's going to explode," she yelled as the rest of Gold Team cleared the way behind her. "All teams pull your men back now!"

Gold Team barely made it out the back door before the house erupted in an incredible pillar of fire. Harvath had seen an explosion like that only once before in his life, and it was in an ATF video of a moonshiner who had convinced himself that with the case against him he had nothing left to live for and had decided to take every government agent into the af-

terlife with him that he could. The man had rigged
his home with explosives, but had kept gallons upon
gallons of accelerant contained in perforated gas cans
so there'd be no real smell until it was already too
late. The bizarre parallels between the explosions
aside, Draegar either had known that someone would
be on his trail eventually, or had left a little present
for Gary on his eventual return home.

Gold Team was showered with broken glass and
smoldering debris as they rolled across the backyard and tried to extinguish the burning embers
that clung like red-hot coals to their Nomex suits.
Had it not been for Alexandra, most of Gold Team
would no longer be alive.

The explosives had been concentrated in the
center of the house and the trip wires rigged so that
entire assault teams would have time to make it inside before the fireworks started. Whoever Draegar
was preparing for, he had made sure that there was
very little possibility of them getting out alive.

That night, the FBI's Hostage Rescue Team suffered more fatalities than during any other assignment in the two-plus decades they had been in
existence. Eleven men were dead.

While Gold Team wrapped a wrist here and
pulled glass out of a laceration there, they each
found time to privately thank Alexandra for saving
their lives. Harvath, though, stood off to the side
alone and wondered if there was any limit to what
Helmut Draegar would do to complete his assignment. It was an exercise in futility. He knew that

there was not only no limit to what Draegar would do to succeed in his mission, but that the man also approached his personal animosities with the same, if not a greater passion.

The fire had torched a good portion of the house, a testament to Draegar's knowledge of explosives and the amount of accelerant he had sloshed around the interior of the structure.

Harvath knew that Gary would be heartbroken. He and Heide had built this home together, and it was one of the precious few tangible reminders he still had of their life together.

As multiple fire engine companies arrived to help extinguish the blaze, Harvath became fixated upon the body that the Blue Team operative had seen upstairs, as well as the car, which had been parked in the driveway, and was now nothing more than a flaming hulk.

The wondering was killing him and he stuck to the Fairfax County Arson Investigator like glue as the man, along with hastily summoned ATF agents, probed further into the wreckage of Gary Lawlor's home and the firefighters got the blaze under control.

One of the firefighters eventually brought out a badly charred wallet and, using a pair of forceps provided by one of the Fairfax EMTs, Harvath pulled out several damaged pieces of identification. Laying them side by side it was easy to see who they had originally belonged to—David Patrick, aide to the deputy secretary of the National Security Council.

The firefighters continued to battle the blaze as Harvath regrouped with the rest of his team. "So what the hell do we do now?" asked Avigliano as he flexed his hand and tested the bandage that had been wrapped around his left wrist. "I'll be fucked if I'm going to stand here and roast marshmallows," he said and then quickly added for Harvath's benefit, "No offense."

Harvath understood his sentiment completely. When men you know die, not only are the stakes considerably raised, but so is your desire to finish what you and those men had started together. Draegar had made this assignment even more personal for them.

With the house in flames, Harvath turned his attention to the car smoldering in Gary Lawlor's driveway. He assumed that it belonged to David Patrick, but at the same time, something inside told him that when it came to anything having to do with Helmut Draegar, nothing should be accepted prima facie.

He instructed a team of firefighters to get as much water on the car as possible. If the license plates couldn't be salvaged, he wanted the VIN number, and he wanted it within the next five minutes.

The firefighters had the VIN number for him in three. They were glad that's all he wanted. Everything else was burned beyond recognition.

Harvath asked the Fairfax police chief to run it. In the meantime, SIOC called Harvath with the latest update on the sleeper arrests. The evidence techs had been instructed to make lists of everything, no matter how insignificant, and to run those lists against what the other field agents were finding.

They had come up with two commonalities, neither of which made very much sense. The first was that each of the sleepers was carrying two portable hydraulic jacks with jack stands in the trunk of his car and the second was that in the last twenty-four hours each sleeper had purchased flowers. Harvath put the controllers at SIOC on hold while he explained the latest development to Alexandra, only to find she was just as confused as he was. The jacks might have something to do with how heavy the devices were, but why would you need two of them, and what the hell could flowers possibly have to do with what they were up to?

Harvath told SIOC they would get back to them and ended the call. He and Alexandra were still wondering aloud what the flower connection might be when the Fairfax police chief returned with a positive ID on the car sitting smoking in the driveway. He thanked the chief and then turned toward the backyard and yelled for DeWolfe.

The communications expert came limping up on his damaged ankle and asked, "What's up?"

"We've got a positive ID on the car in the driveway. It's a Dollar Rent-A-Car out of Dulles from two days ago."

"You want to know who rented it?"

"No," said Harvath. "I've got a pretty good idea who rented it. I want to know where it's been."

DeWolfe was wiped out. He looked from Alexandra to Scot and in all sincerity said, "How the fuck am I supposed to do that?"

Harvath could read not only the pain from his injury, but also the stress that was written across the man's face and replied, "When I was training with the Secret Service before I moved to the White House, I worked a counterfeiting case where some Colombian was bringing bogus fifties and hundreds into the country. The bills were almost perfect. He'd even run them through his clothes dryer at home along with a couple of hundred poker chips to give them just the right look. We were going crazy trying to nail him. He wasn't considered a very big fish by the higher-ups, and therefore the amount of resources allocated to the case were less than what we would have liked to have seen."

"But you found a way to pop him anyway, didn't you?" said DeWolfe.

Harvath smiled and replied, "There's something about flying into Miami International that automatically makes people forget about everything else. I don't know if it's the sea breeze, the palm trees, the beautiful women, or what, but this guy cleared passport control, then customs, and went outside and boarded one of the Thrifty buses to go get his big fancy four-door rental car."

"So? What does any of that have to do with this car here?"

Harvath was still smiling as he responded, "Thrifty and Dollar both use the same company for fleet management."

"What the hell is fleet management?"

"Something so innocuous sounding that they've been able to post it on top of their rental agreements for the last several years without anybody asking any questions."

"I still have no idea what it is."

"A Canadian company called Air IQ has contracts with rental car companies to install transmitters, like LoJacks, that allows all the movements of all the cars in their fleets to be tracked via satellite."

Suddenly, DeWolfe was with the program. "Are you telling me that Dollar knows where this car has been?"

"Not Dollar," responded Harvath, "but Air IQ. I need you to get a hold of them, give them the VIN number, and find out everything you can about where this car has been in the last two days."

CHAPTER 55

A graveyard?" said Harvath.

DeWolfe scanned through the printout that had been faxed to one of the Fairfax patrol cars. "That's what it says here. Two visits to Congressional Cemetery over the past two nights."

"How'd he get a car in there at night? Don't they close the gates?"

"I asked one of the SIOC guys about that and he told me that the place is open around the clock."

"What about security?"

"Nonexistent."

"And dead men tell no tales," said Harvath as the pieces began to come together. Congressional Cemetery was only about three miles from the White House and half that distance from the Capitol. In fact, every major city the Russians had put sleepers in probably had some sort of cemetery close to its most populated area. Suddenly, the sleepers buying flowers didn't seem so strange anymore. "I want the exact coordinates of where that car was parked. Have the NEST team ready to move and get SIOC to pull some real-time thermal imaging of the cemetery from the National Reconnaissance Office."

"The *NRO*? Why not use the HRT bird?" asked DeWolfe. "It has second generation FLIR and can be over the target area in less than fifteen minutes."

"No. No helicopters. Tell SIOC it has to be satellite. If Draegar's there, I don't want him to have any clue that we're coming. He's switched cars now, which means he's being even more careful. Find out the make, model, color—everything about the car Patrick drove—and put out an APB. If anyone sees it, they call it into SIOC, but under no circumstances are they to try to stop it. Got it?"

"Got it. What are you going to do?"

"I've got a score to settle for an old friend."

As the MH-6 Little Bird helicopter raced them due east for the Anacostia Naval Station, Harvath explained that Congressional Cemetery got its name not because one necessarily had to be a member of Congress to be buried there, but rather because of its proximity to the Capitol and the government's frequent use of it over the last two hundred years.

Alexandra was not completely unfamiliar with the Congressional Cemetery and made mention of the fact that the grave site of former FBI Director J. Edgar Hoover had been a favorite clandestine meeting spot for KGB operatives throughout the

seventies and eighties. As interesting as that fact
was, Harvath had a feeling they weren't going to
find Draegar just leaning against Hoover's tomb-
stone.

Landing at Anacostia, Harvath received word
that the NRO satellite had failed to locate any
human heat signatures in the cemetery. They did,
though, pick up a warm car engine not too far from
where Air IQ had placed Draegar's rental over the
last two nights.

When Harvath asked if the engine was running,
he was told that it wasn't. In fact, it was in the
process of cooling down. That could only mean one
of two things. Either Draegar had ditched this car
as well and was nowhere near the cemetery, or he
had settled in and it was just a matter of finding
him. But where could he be hiding? Short of joining
the permanent residents, there weren't that many
places in a graveyard where the NRO's sophisticated, high-tech equipment wouldn't be able to pick
up his heat signature.

The Anacostia Naval Station was three miles
downriver from the Congressional Cemetery, and
Harvath had been serious about keeping any unnec-
essary helicopters away from the area. Of course,
with the State of the Union address less than two
hours away, the skies were being heavily patrolled,
but buzzing the graveyard would only have served
to tip their hand. The best way in was by water.

Because of his bad ankle, DeWolfe was forced to
sit this one out. Everybody else, though, was on

board, their minor injuries all but forgotten as they focused on what lay ahead.

The fifteen-foot black Zodiac combat rubber raiding craft was ready and waiting for them as they made their way down to the river. Harvath and the rest of the team checked their weapons and their communications gear one last time before pushing off. If anything needed fixing or replacing, now was the time to do it. Once they were underway, there was no turning back, not for anything.

The silenced outboard drove the heavily reinforced inflatable craft quickly up the Anacostia. They beached the boat just under the Pennsylvania Avenue Bridge, and covered the rest of the distance on foot.

Based on maps of the cemetery, it had been decided that the best entry point would be over the south wall. Harvath radioed SIOC for a final Sit Rep off the satellite before they went in. "Negative," came back the voice from SIOC. "The graveyard is still cold."

No kidding, thought Harvath as he took a deep breath before scaling the wall.

Once on the other side, the team fanned out behind the sea of headstones and Harvath pulled out his map of the cemetery. It was based on a grid system corresponding to range values and site numbers. Though he would have preferred GPS coordinates, it was nevertheless a fairly decent map. The tiny thoroughfares were well indicated and it wasn't difficult to place their current position in relation to their objective—a series of family vaults on what the cemetery referred to as "Mausoleum Row."

It had been decided that Harvath and Alexandra would check out Mausoleum Row, while Morrell, Avigliano, and Carlson went to investigate the nearby car, which was parked unusually close to the grave of J. Edgar Hoover.

The team split up and Harvath and Alexandra cut across a wide, grassy expanse. As they passed, the headstones glowed a ghostly greenish-white through their night-vision goggles. They hugged the side of a small road until they reached the first intersection, and Mausoleum Row.

The vaults were built into a small hill with regular graves just above and behind them. Harvath was about to try the first iron door when he noticed the second mausoleum's door was slightly ajar. He traded Alexandra the Beretta carbine for the pistol, which was much more suited for going into such a tight space, and had her stand guard outside.

He listened at the door for several seconds until all he could hear was the pounding of his own heart as the blood rushed in and out of his ears. Harvath grabbed hold of the door with his free hand, and slowly pulled it back, praying there wouldn't be any loud squeal of metal on metal that would give them away.

The old door cooperated and didn't make a sound. It effortlessly swung back as if on freshly oiled hinges. As Harvath stepped inside, he suddenly realized what the jacks in the trunks of the

sleepers' cars had been for. Still secured upon their
stands, two hydraulic jacks balanced a marble faceplate easily weighing three or four hundred pounds.
Harvath maneuvered around the heavy piece of
marble and found a stone bench behind it, which he
stood upon to look into the open crypt halfway up
the wall.

Instead of a coffin, the crypt contained a sophisticated communications array. It appeared he had discovered how Draegar planned on communicating
with the sleepers. By now he would know they had
been picked up, and he would be one desperate man.

Harvath wanted Alexandra to see what he was
seeing and engaged his throat mike, but there was
no response. He was about to try one more time
when he heard what he knew in the marrow of his
bones was a grenade being rolled into the vault.
Without thinking twice, he dropped onto the stone
bench behind the faceplate, opened his mouth,
closed his eyes, pushed his fingers as far as he
could into his ears, and curled into the tightest fetal
position a man had ever attempted.

Harvath had worked with demolitions before,
but never in his life had he been so close to such an
overwhelming explosion. Despite his desire to keep
his mouth open to help equalize the pressure, he
bit down so hard he thought for sure he had
cracked all of his teeth. The pain of the blast was so
intense it felt as if a hand had reached up inside
him and was flattening all of his organs. And as for
deadening the sound by plugging his ears, he was

confident that even Quasimodo himself had never experienced the ringing he was now host to.

As the initial shock of sharing a broom closet with a hand grenade began to recede, Harvath assessed the rest of his situation. The marble faceplate had absorbed most of the grenade's blast and it now lay on the floor in several pieces. The walls of the mausoleum hadn't fared much better and were charred and pitted by shrapnel.

The ringing in his ears from the grenade was slowly replaced by the ringing of the words of the FBI's director who asked Harvath what he was prepared to do if Alexandra Ivanova tried to run. How could he have been so wrong about her? Though his reply to the director had been simple and to the point, right now putting a bullet in Alexandra Ivanova was a somewhat distant second to what he had been sent here to do.

The mausoleum door had been closed, but not locked, and Harvath quietly pushed it open. Knowing that Alexandra still had her radio, he ignored Rick Morrell's repeated hailings demanding to know what his situation was, and maintained complete radio silence.

He knew that Morrell, Avigliano, and Carlson would eventually come and investigate the source of the explosion they had heard, and as Harvath pressed himself up against the cold stone façade of the mausoleum, he started off in the most likely direction they would be coming from.

Suddenly, he heard what sounded like the sharp

clap of small-arms fire, followed by the broken voice of Rick Morrell crackling through his earpiece, ". . . under fire . . . been hit and have two men down. I repeat, we are under fire and I have two men down."

Harvath began running toward them. He wished like hell that he could have called in for a Sit Rep to see where the shooter was, but it was out of the question. The greatest advantage he had going for him was that Draegar and Alexandra thought he was dead.

As he passed the last mausoleum, an incandescent glow from inside caused Harvath to stop dead in his tracks. With his Beretta pistol clasped in both hands, he crept closer to the entryway and used his left elbow to pry open the iron door. The entire mausoleum appeared to be lined with lead and it was now clear why they had failed to pick up any heat signatures in the cemetery. He used his night vision goggles to scan the interior and what he saw scared the hell out of him. The marble faceplates of all six crypts had been removed and each one contained a Russian tactical nuke, their display panels flashing, indicating the weapons had been activated.

It was now apparent how the Russians had been so successful in hiding their nukes all of these years. Harvath had been right on the money when he had said, "Dead men tell no tales." It was also apparent that the previously unaccounted-for nukes were not in the cities of U.S. allies after all, but were right here in Washington.

There was enough in this crypt to blow the entire capital off the face of the map and Harvath had a feeling that no matter what speech the president gave, the Russians fully intended to send an overpowering message that times had changed and that they were now in control.

The Russians had made one fatal mistake—they hadn't cleared their message through Scot Harvath, and he was going to be damned if those lying communist bastards caused the collective head of the United States of America to bow even a fraction of an inch in deference to the new world order they planned to unleash. He'd been to Russia, and he'd seen what a shitty country it was. As far as he was concerned, they'd gained too much prominence on the world stage, and it wasn't time for the United States to step back, it was time for someone to shove the Russians the hell off.

When a shadow fell across Harvath's shoulder, he knew he was in trouble.

"Don't bother turning around," said a voice from behind that he was sure belonged to Helmut Draeger. "Just put your hands up in the air where I can see them."

Harvath did as he was told.

"Good. Now drop your weapon and kick it away from you, please."

Once again, Harvath complied.

"I didn't know if I would be seeing you again," Draeger continued in English so perfect, there wasn't even the hint of an accent, "but I'm glad you're here. I'm going to slide a pair of handcuffs across the floor to you and I want you to clip one end to your left wrist."

"Why bother?" asked Harvath. "The whole graveyard is surrounded. You'll never make it out of here alive."

"Neither will you I'm afraid," said Draegar as he laid a pair of cuffs on the ground and kicked them over to Harvath. "Now, do as I say."

"Why don't you just shoot me?"

"Your friend Gary Lawlor left me to die in much the same fashion and now I intend to return the favor."

"By what? Handcuffing me to one of these nukes? I hate to tell you, but when this thing blows—" said Harvath as he started to turn around to face Draegar.

"No moving!" yelled Draegar. "I told you to stay still. And keep your hands up where I can see them."

"They're up and I'm not moving anymore, okay? Let's just all stay calm here."

"Mr. Harvath," said Draegar as he regained his composure, "Naturally, once the bomb detonates, there will be nothing of you left behind to identify. I realize this. If my goal is to cause Mr. Lawlor an excessive amount of grief, he must be fully aware of how you suffered. Thankfully, I have a cell phone with a built-in camera, which I borrowed from a young government aide who won't be needing it anymore."

"So that's your plan? You're going to strap me to one of these devices and leave me to die?"

"Like I said, it's exactly what Gary Lawlor did to me. I'm sure the symbolism of my returning the favor won't be lost on him. Of course, you're free to try and chew through your wrist or arm to get free. Trapped animals in the wild, especially wolves, have been known to choose that option. I assure you it's not a very pleasant alternative, but you do have that choice. You'll need to make up your mind very quickly though, as the timers are set to give me just enough of a head start to outrun the blast."

"So regardless of what the president says in his State of the Union address tonight," replied Harvath, "you're still going to detonate these nukes."

"You took all of our sleepers off-line. All of them! What choice have you left me? My superiors might disagree with my actions at first, but in time I think they'll come around. Especially with what's to be gained."

"What could you possible gain from this?" asked Harvath as he lowered his hand toward his leg pouch where he'd placed his flashlight.

"*What's to gain?* The gains are boundless," sneered Draegar. "September 11th might have drawn your country together, but an attack of this magnitude coupled with the loss of your entire national leadership will absolutely decimate you. It's the blow America has needed for decades. Worldwide opinion of the United States is the lowest it has ever been. Though the attack will be seen as a tragedy, not many tears will be shed for your country. Like it or not, America will be forced to turn inward and focus on its own rebuilding, and with America's understandable withdrawal from world affairs, Russia will step in and claim its rightful role as *the* world superpower."

The man's unflappable confidence and dedication to his task were chilling. "You forget one thing," said Harvath. "Every single blast crater will have Russia's name written all over it. The residue will be irrefutable proof that the nukes came from your country."

Draegar's sneer turned into a smile. "Actually, every blast crater will have *your* name written all over it. The fissile material in each of these weapons was taken from one of your Dark Night nuclear devices. The facts will speak for themselves."

Harvath just shook his head, his hand closing in on his flashlight. He had pulled the same stunt in Berlin without success, but prayed that at much closer range, and in such an enclosed space, this time it would work.

"You don't think so?" chided Draegar, consumed with the hubris of his plan. "Let me ask you. Which story do you think the international community will be more prepared to accept? That Russia carried out an unprovoked attack against America or that the arrogant, warmongering United States suffered another catastrophic terrorist attack because of its insidious desire to force its will on the rest of the world? People have suspected for years that many of our suitcase nukes have gone missing. They just didn't know that we were the ones who took them."

"You'll never get away with it," said Harvath.

Draegar laughed and raised his prosthetic hand in salute. "Somehow I knew you were going to say that. But no more games now. I hope you brought your appetite. The sooner you get started, the sooner you may actually get out of here. Chew, chew, chew."

As Draegar stepped forward to make sure his prisoner properly cuffed himself, Harvath pulled out his flashlight, flipped up the filter, and said, "Chew on this, asshole," as he depressed the thumb switch on the tail cap.

While the former Spetsnaz soldier and East German Stasi operative had been able to dodge the overwhelming 225-lumen beam in Berlin, this time he wasn't so lucky. The man was instantly blinded.

Harvath dove to the ground and struggled to get to his Beretta before Draegar could raise his own weapon and fire. But all at once, he knew his efforts were in vain. The figure of Alexandra Ivanova had appeared in the doorway and the room was instantly filled with brilliant muzzle flashes accompanied by the sharp reports of the CX4 Storm carbine Harvath had given her.

CHAPTER 56

Harvath avoided the hustle and bustle of Pennsylvania Avenue and entered the White House via the southwest gate. Unlike previous visits, he was asked to wait in the guardhouse until his escort arrived. It seemed an odd request, as Harvath was a former member of the president's protective detail and had never been asked to wait before. When Secret Service Agents Tom Hollenbeck, Chris Longo, and Kate Palmer arrived to walk him up West Executive Avenue, he had a feeling something was up.

As they walked, his friends made small talk. Palmer told him how good he looked, while Hollenbeck and Longo regaled him with stories about the two nurses they had met at the hospital in Berlin.

Though the trio refused to tell him why he needed an escort, Harvath decided not to press it and instead took the good-natured, albeit incessant, ribbing in stride. He allowed himself a few minutes to get lost in the unseasonably warm February day and the relaxed fellowship of his former Secret Service coworkers—each of whom mattered more to him than they would ever know.

After holding the door open as they arrived at the West Wing, Hollenbeck jumped ahead of the party and steered them toward the White House Mess.

"Tom," said Harvath. "What's going on?"

"They're not ready for you yet in the Situation Room, so I thought we might get a cup of coffee together in the Mess," replied Hollenbeck.

Though Harvath was wary, he went along with the request and the minute he turned into the cafeteria he was greeted by an overwhelming wave of applause. In addition to all of his former Secret Service colleagues, it appeared as if every White House staffer was in attendance.

Uncomfortable with such fulsome praise, Harvath thought things couldn't get any worse until Dr. Skip Trawick popped up in the back of the room with a pint glass in hand and began singing in his mock Scottish accent, "For He's a Jolly Good Fellow." The rest of the assembled guests joined in and Harvath had to suffer through it until they finished and a glass of punch was shoved into his hand. He was then led over to a cake decorated with an American flag and the words *Forever May She Wave*, where he cut the first piece and then handed the knife over to Longo and placed him in charge.

A call came over Tom Hollenbeck's earpiece and he waded through the crowd of grateful well-wishers to extricate Harvath and accompany him to the Situation Room.

"They don't really have any idea of what we did, do they?" asked Harvath as they exited the Mess.

"Not really," answered Hollenbeck. "Technically, the entire event with the Russians never happened."

"Then what was that all about?"

"The White House needed a reason to explain why Congress had been put into hiding and the president had conducted his State of the Union address from the White House. As far as the press and everyone else is concerned, there was a credible terrorist threat against the capitol, and you and Gary Lawlor, along with several federal law enforcement agencies and the DC Metro Police, helped to neutralize that threat. The folks at the White House just wanted to show their appreciation."

"Folks at the White House," asked Harvath, "or you, Longo, and Palmer?"

Hollenbeck stopped and turned to face Harvath. "So what if they don't know what really happened? The gratitude you witnessed and hopefully felt back there was genuine. For once in your life, take a moment and enjoy some of the praise that you so rightfully deserve. You're damn good at your job, Scot, and your country is lucky to have you."

Hollenbeck didn't wait for Harvath to respond. In fact, he didn't want any response from Harvath; that's not why he said what he had said. He said it because he meant it. When he took his little boy to

ball games and sang "The Star Spangled Banner,"
when they got to the part about America being the
land of the free and the home of the brave, there
was a handful of guys he thought about and Harvath was one of them.

They arrived at the security checkpoint before
Harvath could come up with anything to say. Hollenbeck briefly put a hand on his shoulder and then
turned and walked away as the two Marine guards
looked over Harvath's ID and waved him through.

There was the familiar hiss as the airlock released and the Situation Room door swung open.
As Harvath entered, he expected to see a mass of
agency heads seated at the long cherrywood table,
but there were only three people present—the president, Defense Secretary Hilliman, and General Paul
Venrick, commander of the Joint Special Operations
Command. Though Harvath had no idea how they
had gotten hold of it so fast, each of them had a
small piece of his cake sitting in front of them.

Harvath took a seat where the president indicated and waited for the commander in chief to
start the meeting.

"For once, I find myself in a meeting with no
idea of how to begin," said the president, with
more than his customary economy of sentiment.

Harvath was at a loss by the show of emotion on
the face of the normally rock-steady man. The uncomfortable silence that descended upon the Situation Room was broken when General Venrick took
the lead, stood up from his chair, and saluted Scot

Harvath. The general was quickly joined by Secretary Hilliman, and even the president himself. The men held their salute until Harvath rose from his chair and returned their expression of esteem.

No matter what followed, this moment was the greatest honor Scot Harvath had ever experienced in his life.

"Okay," said the president, sitting down and stabbing at a piece of cake, "let's bring Scot up to speed."

Defense Secretary Hilliman was the first to speak. He described how the FBI, in conjunction with NEST teams from the Department of Energy, had been able to locate all of the sleepers' nukes in each city and successfully deactivate them. Each had been hidden in a mausoleum with the same family name as the one Scot and Alexandra had uncovered in the Congressional Cemetery—Lenin.

While on the subject of Alexandra, Hilliman explained the high points of her debriefing. While waiting for Harvath outside the first mausoleum, she had heard something and thought it might be Draegar. She went to investigate, but it had been a ruse. Draegar drew her away from the mausoleum, and the next thing she heard was the explosion. By the time she saw Draegar again, he had already attacked Morrell and his men and was making his way back to the mausoleum where he was holding Harvath captive.

Hilliman went on to explain that Alexandra had been offered asylum, but had asked instead that

General Stavropol's journal be entrusted to her care. Other than that, all she wanted was a flight home. As those were her only requests, the United States had willingly granted them to her, after, of course, photocopies had been made and she had fully explained how to decipher the coded entries.

Once the report that Gary Lawlor was doing much better and would be transported Stateside soon was delivered, Secretary Hilliman turned over the meeting to General Venrick.

"The president," began Venrick, "has asked me here to bring you up to speed on the operations end of things."

"What's our position with the Russians after all of this?"

"They still claim that the nukes we uncovered here had been stolen from them."

"After everything that's happened, they're still denying it?" asked Harvath. "The Russians aren't going to pay any price?"

"No, that's not what I'm saying. They've definitely paid a price. Not only did you sink two of their Sokzhoi patrol boats, but thanks to you and the rest of the team, you were also able to sink the *Gagarin*. That was a major tactical coup.

"In the meantime, we've got our people working around the clock on the notes and schematics that Dr. Nesterov left behind. The NSA already thinks they've found a way to subvert the Russian air defense system if they ever bring it back on-line."

"What do you think the chances of that happening are?" asked Harvath.

"At this point, not so good. We've already quietly gotten word to the World Bank and the International Monetary Fund about what the Russians have been doing with their aid money, and they are not very happy."

"So what's next?"

Defense Secretary Hilliman leaned forward and, taking a handkerchief from his pocket, took off his glasses and began cleaning them. "Things are going to get pretty frosty for Moscow. They were a pain in the ass for us during the whole Iraq situation, and we've now seen that we can't trust them at all as an ally. While it would be foolish for us to completely break off ties with them altogether, they are going to be relegated to a very low rung on our ladder of diplomatic and international priorities."

The president stood and walked around the table. Upon reaching Scot he extended his hand and said, "You are one of the most valuable assets the United States has. Your patriotism, loyalty, and service to your country is something that we will always be grateful for. Don't ever forget that."

"Thank you, sir," replied Harvath. "I won't."

"Good. There's something else. Until Gary Lawlor is back on his feet, I need you to handle things at the OIIA. Do you think you can do that?"

"Those are some pretty big shoes to fill," answered Harvath.

The president smiled. "I've already talked it over

with Gary, and he agrees with me that there's no-body better suited to do it. Just don't get too comfortable. He'll be back to work before you know it."

"I'm looking forward to that. Thank you, Mr. President. I'll do my best." Sensing that the meeting was over, Harvath added, "Is there anything else, Mr. President?"

The president looked at his watch and indicated that Harvath should remain seated. Fifteen seconds later, the voice of Charles Anderson, the president's chief of staff came over the speaker phone and said, "Mr. President, I have President Nevkin of Russia on the line."

"Good," responded Rutledge. "Put him through."

"President Rutledge. Jack," came the voice of the Russian president over the speaker phone. "You certainly have taken your time in getting back to me."

"As you are well aware, we've been a little busy here."

"So I have seen on the news, but so busy that you were not able to return my phone calls?"

"President Nevkin," said Rutledge, "Let's not waste each other's time. Tomorrow afternoon at approximately 1300 GMT, an American C-130 is going to land on the Valhalla Ice Shelf three miles below the North Pole. On board will be the man-portable nuclear devices you planted in our country."

"But, Jack, I told you they were stolen by the—" began Nevkin.

"Chechens, I remember. We also have eighteen

sleeper agents from your country in custody complete with enough evidence to bury you for the next two hundred years."

"These aren't Russian agents. Whomever you have caught are terrorists," replied the Russian president. "Plain and simple."

"*Terrorists*," laughed Rutledge, "If that's what you're calling your disavowed agents, that's fine by me. But you and I both know who they are, why they were here, and who sent them."

"This comes as a complete shock," said Nevkin. "If it does turn out that these 'sleepers,' as you call them, were indeed sent by someone in Russia, I can guarantee you that I had no idea that—"

Rutledge was sick of listening to the Russian president's BS and said, "No more lies, Dmitri. You made your move and you lost. There is going to be a very heavy price to pay for what your country has done. And believe me, Russia is going to pay it, whether you like it or not. In the days ahead, against my better judgment, I am going to exhibit tremendous restraint. That said, I suggest you get out of Moscow for a bit. I'll give you my personal guarantee that your villa on the Black Sea won't be targeted."

The Russian president was aghast. "Certainly," he implored, "you are not going to conduct a nuclear strike against the Russian Federation."

"No," replied Rutledge, "but we are going to respond. And whatever we do, you are going to absorb it without retaliation."

"Jack how can you expect—"

"That's *Mr. President* to you," said Rutledge. "You thought you could hold the United States of America hostage and you were wrong, dead wrong. Now it's time to pay the piper. I'll extend you the courtesy of telling you that we are only targeting military and governmental assets. You have twelve hours to get your people out. You brought this upon yourself and if you even think of engaging any of our fighter aircraft or attempt to shoot down any of our missiles I will not only double, but treble our retaliation. Is this clear?"

There was a long moment of silence before the Russian president responded, "Yes, it is clear."

Rutledge disconnected the call and turned to Harvath. "So? How'd I do?"

"Perfect. I couldn't have handled it better myself."

"I'm glad you agree," responded Rutledge. "Now get upstairs and enjoy yourself. No disappearing out the back door."

Scot stood from his chair. "Is that an order, sir?"

"You'd better believe it."

"Then I'm on my way."

EPILOGUE

Though it was two months overdue, it was finally the fitting memorial service Maureen Harvath had envisioned to mark the ten years since the passing of her husband, Michael.

The day had been long and emotional. After dropping Mrs. Harvath back at home, Scot, Meg, and Gary returned to the Hotel Del Coronado. While Gary had been given permission by his doctors to travel, he still wasn't back to full speed and declined joining Scot and Meg for a drink in the bar.

Scot ordered a margarita for himself and a glass of wine for Meg, and when their drinks arrived, they took them outside. The sun was just beginning to set as they took off their shoes and walked down to the Hotel Del's white sand beach.

As they strolled, Harvath reminisced about his grueling SEAL training, most of which had taken place not very far from where they were right now. Meg put her feet in the surf and got a laugh out of Scot when she commented on how cold the water

was. Those had been some of the toughest days of
his life, and he remembered at times envying the
families and casual tourists strolling along the
beach while he and his fellow classmates endured
frigid swims, never-ending runs, and being forced
to help hold a combat rubber raiding craft above his
head until he thought for sure his arms were going
to fall off. Looking back on it now he realized that
while he was competing against his classmates and
most definitely against the elements, more than
anything else he had been competing against himself.

He had also come to another realization. Scot
Harvath was comfortable with who he was and
what he did for a living. Though his father might
have had some influence on his becoming a SEAL,
it was Scot who had mustered the strength, sta-
mina, and integrity to stay one. Yes, he loved his father very much and he missed him too, but who his
father had been had nothing to do with who he was
now. The career changes from SEAL to Secret Service and now OIIA had nothing to do with trying to
please his deceased father. It was about finding new
challenges for himself and being there when his
country needed him most. The fact that the highest
point in his life had come when he had been saluted
by General Venrick, Defense Secretary Hilliman,
and President Rutledge two months prior in the
White House Situation Room told him everything
he needed to know about himself.

Harvath didn't require accolades or parties in

his honor; that wasn't why he did what he did. Scot
Harvath did what he did out of honor. An honor instilled in him by his father, but an honor that he
had come to know, understand, and deserve as an
adult. While he couldn't go back and fix the way
things had been between them before his father had
died, he could appreciate the man for who he was.
Scot also came to peace with the fact that he was
proud of himself and what he had been able to accomplish and in life that was all that mattered.

As Meg walked beside him, she slipped a reas-
suring arm around his waist and leaned her head on
his shoulder. They had done a lot of talking over the
last two months and had both come to the conclusion that slowing down didn't have to be a bad
thing. Scot had the brand-new OIIA to help organize, and Meg decided that it would be best for her
to develop a client base in DC first, before possibly
relocating her office there. For the time being they
would coordinate their schedules so they could see
each other whenever they could and decided that if
things between them were really meant to be, then
everything would work out—long-distance relationship and all.

Scot put his arm around Meg, and they watched
as the sun slid beneath the horizon and was swal-
lowed up by the deep Pacific Ocean. Neither of
them was in a hurry to get back to the hotel. It was
their last night together and in the morning they'd
be taking two different planes to two different
cities.

They dragged their feet in the sand, each silently asking time to slow down, but eventually arrived back where they started. Part of Harvath was tempted to hold on to Meg, keep walking and never look back, but when he saw Gary Lawlor standing on the steps of the Babcock & Story bar, his curiosity got the better of him and he steered Meg away from the beach and toward the hotel.

"I thought Gary turned in early," said Meg upon seeing Lawlor perched at the top of the stairs.

"Me too," replied Harvath.

"Maybe he's changed his mind about having a drink with us."

"Maybe," said Scot, though by the look on Gary's face, he doubted it.

As they approached, Gary put on a smile for Meg's benefit and asked, "It looked like a beautiful sunset. Did you have a nice walk?"

"We did," replied Meg, who then asked, "Did you change your mind about having a drink?"

Gary's smile faded. "Actually, no. I need to talk to Scot."

Harvath knew it. "What about?"

"I just received a call from DC. We've got a situation."

"What kind of situation?"

"There was a shooting in Paris at the Montparnasse train station. You'll be briefed en route with all the details. Your plane leaves at midnight."

Harvath began to probe for more details but was interrupted by Meg as she slipped her arm through his and said to Gary, "I'll have him packed and downstairs by ten-thirty."

"The car's going to be here for him at ten," replied Lawlor. Catching the look on Meg's face, he smiled and said, "but ten-thirty will be just fine."

Scores of Russian KGB and Russian military intelligence officials who have defected to the United States over the last fifteen years claim that the Soviet Union hid numerous man-portable, suitcase-sized nuclear weapons in caches across the United States. Both the FBI and CIA have expended vast amounts of money and manpower to locate these caches (which they also believe contain cash, radios, pistols, and other items necessary to support Russian sleeper agents positioned throughout America), but have come up empty. Though the matter has never been resolved, many in the Department of Defense and the intelligence community still believe these weapons caches exist.

ACKNOWLEDGMENTS

As I have mentioned in previous acknowledgement sections of my novels, no author is an island unto himself. There is no way I could do what I do without the generous help of others, and I owe the following a deep debt:

First and foremost, I want to thank my beautiful wife, **Trish**. Not only did she support me all the way through the writing of this book, she also gave birth to our first child. Marrying her was the smartest thing I ever did. Honey, thank you for our beautiful baby and for your unwavering support of my career.

Chad Norberg: Once again, your insight into geopolitics, wide sweeping knowledge of the way the real world works, and your grating sense of humor have all come together to help see me through another odyssey. Thanks for everything.

Chuck Fretwell: His keen eye for detail and unfailing commitment to the right way of getting things done have proven a godsend to me on more than one occasion. Nothing gets by Chuck and I'm honored to have had so much of his help throughout the writing of this book, both within the Special Operations community and without. Many thanks.

Steven Hoffa: Hoffa's help on this book, especially in the area of tradecraft, went beyond measure, and he has my deepest gratitude. Steve, I mean it when I say that I couldn't have done this without your incredibly generous assistance.

Mike Noell, US Navy SEAL (retired): In addition to being an invaluable resource for me when it comes to SEAL culture, tactics, etc., I have a tremendous amount of respect for Mike, who has seen more than his fair share of action around the world and now helps to make sure that the good guys have every advantage.

William Kinane, FBI (retired): Bill served with great distinction as legal attaché at the American embassy in Moscow, establishing the official liaison with the MBD (Ministry of Interior), the national police force of Russia, the FSB, the Prosecutor's Office, and the Tax Police regarding Organized Crime, Terrorism, Movement of Nuclear Materials, and Fraud-Corruption investigation. When it came to Russia, its culture, and the inner workings of its intelligence and military organizations, Bill's help was invaluable.

Scott Hill, Ph.D.: Scott, as always, I appreciate not only your friendship, but your willingness to brainstorm both character development and plot points with me. You are one of my key sharpshooters and your aim never faltered.

Gary Penrith, FBI (retired): Once again, thanks for helping answer all of my questions and of course, thanks to you and Lynne for the ongoing learning process at our annual in Sun Valley.

Colonel Robert Birmingham, US Army (retired): As former head of the Army's Comanche Helicopter Program, Bob helped out in several key areas and his assistance was very much appreciated.

Frank Gallagher, FBI (retired): Several FBI elements, including the SIOC and related scenes at headquarters, would not have come together in this book if it weren't for Frank, who is still a gentleman of the highest order.

Gabriel DePlano, Beretta USA: A great guy who was always there for me when I wanted to know more about Beretta products. Thanks not only for the technical assistance, but also for offering to read relevant sections of the book.

Patrick Doak and David Vennett: My two Washington insiders who are both serving their country with distinction in two different areas of the government. I owe you both more than a couple of drinks the next time we get together.

Mike McCarey: Ballistics, body armor, tactical gear, Mike's knowledge of what the good guys carry and how they use it is bottomless. Thanks for all of your help and the in-depth education.

Richard Levy, American Airlines: My very good friend whose knowledge of aviation and all things German was once again right on point. The next time I'm in Dallas, *I'm* picking up the tab.

Dan Brown and Kyle Mills: I couldn't be happier for your respective successes. Thanks for being there to talk about the process. Your wit and wisdom went further than you can imagine.

I would also like to thank:

"Crazy" Kenny Murray for his help in the flash-bang department. **John Chaffee, Ph.D.,** for plugging me in with the portable nuke info. **Charlie Connolly** for his international economic info. **Richard R. Greene,** LD, for his O.R. assistance. **Phil Redman** for his communications wisdom. **Tom Gosse** for the interment lesson, as well as **Bill Fecke,** who went the extra mile for me at Congressional Cemetery. **Bob Boettcher** for his help with the Citation X. And finally, **Rudi Asseer** at Farallon for all the DPV help.

In addition to those mentioned above, there are a handful of very key people I couldn't live without:

Emily Bestler, Atria Books, who is my superb editor. It hardly seems fair to call what we do together work. Thanks for keeping me on the straight and narrow, and for becoming such a wonderful friend in the process.

Heide Lange, Sanford J. Greenburger Associates, who is my agent extraordinaire. Thanks not only for feeding me dinner the night the lights went out in NYC, but for every other thing, both great and small, you do for me on a daily basis.

Judith Curr and Louise Burke, Atria/Pocket Books, who are my publishers both in hardcover and paperback. In addition to having a fabulous agent and editor, as a writer you also need to have terrific publishers who believe in your work and want to do whatever it takes to help you succeed. I am fortunate enough to have that in both Judith and Louise.

Esther Sung and Sarah Branham, who put in loads of work day in and day out, yet still found time to make some major contributions to the novel. As always, I am deeply appreciative.

Scott Schwimer, who is equal parts brains and brawn. I sleep a lot sounder at night knowing he is on my side of the table. Thanks for being my guide through the maze of Hollywood.

The Atria/Pocket Sales Force—Simply put, nobody does it better. Thank you for everything you have done and continue to do for me.

The Atria/Pocket Art Department—Paolo, et al., thanks once again for the fabulous artwork.

The Atria/Pocket Books Publicity Department—
Radio, TV, print . . . you always have a million balls
in the air and you handle every single one of them
masterfully. Many, many thanks.

Finally, I couldn't close without thanking you, the
readers. In the end, all of the hard work is for you.
Thank you for your continued support and all of the
wonderful letters and emails.

Sincerely,
Brad Thor

ATRIA BOOKS
PROUDLY PRESENTS

THE FIRST COMMANDMENT

**The next thrilling novel
by Brad Thor**

**Turn the page for a preview
of *The First Commandment*. . . .**

De inimico non loquaris sed cogites —
Do not wish ill for your enemy . . .
plan it

U.S. NAVAL STATION
GUANTANAMO BAY, CUBA

When hot and humid, Cuba hovered somewhere between absolute misery and "the bath is ready, does anyone have any razor blades?" But when it was cold and raining, Cuba was downright unbearable. Tonight was one of those nights.

When the guards arrived at X-ray block they

were in a bad mood—worse than usual. And it wasn't because of the weather. Something was wrong. It was written all over their faces as they pulled five of the camp's most dangerous prisoners from their isolation cells and ordered them at gunpoint to strip.

Philipe Roussard hadn't been at Guantanamo the longest, but he had definitely been interrogated the hardest. A European of Arab descent, he was a sniper of extraordinary ability whose exploits were legendary. Videos of his kills played on continuous loops on jihadist websites across the Internet. To his Muslim brothers he was nothing short of a superhero in the radical Islamist pantheon. To the United States, he was a horrific killing machine responsible for the deaths of over one hundred U.S. soldiers.

As Roussard looked into the eyes of his jailers he saw more than the pure hatred they normally viewed him and his fellow captives with. Tonight it was coupled with absolute disgust. Whatever middle-of-the-night interrogation tactic the Task Force Guantanamo soldiers had in store for Roussard and his four colleagues, something told him it wasn't going to be like anything they had seen before. The guards appeared on the verge of losing control.

Had an attack been successfully executed against the United States? What else could have put the soldiers in such a state?

If so, Roussard felt certain that the Americans would make the prisoners pay. That was how life was at Guantanamo. The guards were petty and never missed an opportunity to lord their power over them. Undoubtedly, they had devised yet another humiliating exercise designed to insult their Muslim sensibilities. Privately, Roussard hoped it involved the attractive blond soldier who would disrobe down to her underwear and rub herself against him. Unlike the other prisoners, Philipe was not exactly a devout Muslim. His sensibilities were more along the lines of his captors, and his fantasies of what he wanted to do to that woman more than kept him occupied through many of the long, lonely hours of isolation he withstood on a daily basis.

He was still speculating about their fate when he heard the door at the far end of the cell block shut. Roussard looked up, hoping it was the blond, but it wasn't. Another soldier had entered carrying five paper shopping bags. As he passed, he threw each of the prisoners a bag.

"Get dressed!" he ordered in awkward Arabic.

Confused, all of the prisoners, including Philipe, removed the civilian clothing from their bags and began to get dressed. Not accustomed to seeing anyone other than their guards, the prisoners looked at each other as they tried to figure out what was happening. Roussard was reminded of stories he'd heard about Jewish Concentration Camp prisoners who were told they were being taken for showers when they were actually on their way to the gas chambers.

He doubted the Americans were dressing them in new clothes only to take execute them, but nevertheless the uncertainty of what they were about to face filled him with more than a little trepidation.

"Why don't they try to make a run for it," one of the guards whispered to his comrade as he stroked the trigger guard of his M16. "I just want one of these fuckers to rabbit on us."

"This isn't right," replied the other. "What the hell are we doing?"

"You two, shut up!" barked their commander who then called in a series of commands over his radio.

Something definitely wasn't right.

Once they were completely clothed, shackles

were placed around their wrists and ankles and they were lined up against the far wall.

This is it, thought Roussard as he held the stare of the soldier who was hoping for one of the prisoners to rabbit.

The soldier's finger went from his weapon's trigger guard to its actual trigger, and he seemed about to say something when a series of vehicles ground to a halt just outside.

"That's us," shouted the Task Force commander. "Let's mount up."

As the prisoners were shoved toward the door and maybe when they got outside and he could see where they were going things would make more sense.

That plan was dashed as one-by-one, hoods were placed over each man's head before they were taken outside to a waiting column of tan Humvees.

Ten minutes later, the convoy came to a stop. Before Roussard's heavy hood was removed, he could make out the distinct, high-pitched whine of idling jet engines.

On the rain-soaked tarmac, the prisoners stared up at an enormous Boeing 737 as their shackles were removed. A metal staircase had been rolled up against the side of the aircraft, and its door stood wide open.

No one said a word, but based on the demeanor of the soldiers, Roussard came to a stunning conclusion. Without being directed to do so, he took a step forward. When none of the soldiers tried to stop him, he took another, and another until his feet touched the first metal step, and he began climbing upwards two at a time. His salvation was at hand. Just as he had known it eventually would be.

With the sound of the other prisoner's pounding up the gangway behind him, Roussard burst into the cabin. Five rows of seats had been completely removed and replaced with five surgical beds. Bolted to the floor next to each were large medical contraptions which looked like dialysis machines and next to those coolers marked *Human Blood*.

Roussard raced past the medical personnel toward the back of the plane searching each of the faces he saw for the one that would convince him this all wasn't just some dream born of prolonged and tortuous isolation. That face never materialized.

Instead, Philipe Roussard felt a heavy hand on his shoulder. When he turned the plane's first officer addressed him in Arabic. "We were told to give you this," he said as he handed him a heavy black envelope.

Without even opening it, Roussard knew who it was from.

"If you wouldn't mind taking a seat," continued the first officer. "The captain is eager to be underway."

Roussard found an empty place near the window and buckled himself in.

He then opened the envelope and read its contents. A slow smile began to spread across his face. Not only was he free, but it looked as if he would have his revenge—and much sooner than even he would have thought.

Opening his window shade, Roussard could see the soldiers climbing back into their Humvees and driving away from the airstrip, several with their hands out the windows, their middle fingers raised in mock salute.

As the aircraft's engines roared to life and the heavy beast began to roll forward, cheers of "Allah Akbar," *God is great*, erupted from the front of the plane.

Allah was indeed great, but Roussard knew it wasn't Allah who had arranged for their release. As he caressed the black envelope, he knew their gratitude was owed to someone much more powerful.

Turning his attention back to the window and with the soldiers quickly disappearing from view, Roussard cocked his thumb and forefinger took aim, and pulled his imaginary trigger.

Now that he was free, he knew it was only a matter of time before his handler turned him loose inside America to enact their revenge.

UNFORGETTABLE
BESTSELLERS
FROM POCKET BOOKS

Blue Valor
Illona Haus
To solve a crime that defies the imagination,
a Baltimore cop must take a twisted journey into
the dark recesses of a killer's mind.

Saving Cascadia
John J. Nance
Washington state's Cascadia Island is a tranquil
Northwest paradise—until a disaster only one
man can predict threatens the lives of thousands.

The Pandora Key
Lynne Heitman
She's a tough, sexy private investigator—and
she's unlocking explosive secrets form the past.

Live Wire
Jay MacLarty
A high-stakes delivery and a high-risk courier
make for an explosive combination.

The Greater Good
Casey Moreton
Even in the top-secret world of Washington
politics, some crimes can't be justified.